Saturday's Child

SCEPTRE

Saturday's Child

VALERIE BLUMENTHAL

SCEPTRE

Copyright ©1998 Valerie Blumenthal

First published in Great Britain in 1998 by Hodder and Stoughton
A division of Hodder Headline PLC
A Sceptre book

The right of Valerie Blumenthal to be identified as the Author of
the Work has been asserted by her in accordance with the
Copyright, Designs and Patents Act 1988.

10 9 8 7 6 5 4 3 2 1

All characters in this publication are fictitious and any
resemblance to real persons, living or dead, is purely coincidental.

A CIP catalogue record for this book is
available from the British Library

ISBN 0 340 67494 6

Typeset by Palimpsest Book Production Limited,
Polmont, Stirlingshire

Printed and bound in Great Britain by
Mackays of Chatham PLC, Chatham, Kent

Hodder and Stoughton
A division of Hodder Headline PLC
338 Euston Road
London NW1 3BH

Dedicated to all the misplaced children,
casualties of a species called homo sapiens
(from the Latin, *sapere*, meaning 'wise').

Acknowledgements)

Nigel R. Merrett, D.Sc.
Graham Irons, Listing Officer, Truro Crown Court
Detective Constable Andy Matthews, Truro Police Station
Jo Jamieson, HMP Bullingdon
Irving D. Stone, Solicitor
Medina Marks, Barrister
Gareth Gwenlan, Director/Producer, BBC Television

∫

Lies. Flies. Breeding like.

'So why did you do it?' he asks her.

'I did it because . . . Do you know the French word *éclat?'*

'I'm not sure. I'm not much of a linguist.'

'*Éclat de: éclat de soleil.* A burst of sun. That's what her face did. And inside me I . . . it singed me. I can't explain it. It wasn't something I can just explain.'

'But it was out of character.'

'I suppose so. Until then I'd never done anything out of the norm. My life was very structured.'

But leading up to it were pointers, had she chosen to tweeze them from her subconscious and examine them. A random collection of influencing factors accumulated over the years, which a psychologist would have latched on to with a satisfied snap of the fingers.

'And you regret it.' Spoken with the rhetoric of assurance.

She wraps her arms around herself. Looks tiredly up at him. At her peeling nails. At the window with no view and her silver reflection in it.

'Isabella? Surely—'

She turns back to him, and he is struck anew by how her face can switch from plain to beautiful with a flicker of expression in her eyes; she shakes her head as she thrusts out her palm in a typically eloquent gesture: 'What can I say? How can I possibly regret it?'

The night before she did it. And there she is, in her flat, on her bed with its antique silk Chinese cover, having frenetic sex with her lover of one and a half years. Peter, soon to be twenty-seven, is thirteen years younger than her. They share a birthday. Earlier that evening he told her she had put on weight. Since she has known him he has become more assertive. Perhaps she has contributed to his confidence; and now, having assisted him in worldly ways, he can fend for himself. Also earlier that evening she discovered for herself a pair of corresponding new-moon crescents either side of her mouth and the tiniest pouch of skin at the right corner. Even as they make love that night and Isabella is intent on reminding him that never again will he find anyone to match her, she is conscious of how her face must look looming over his and of the flesh falling forwards (gravity, she grimly refers to it); of the spread of her thighs as they flatten over his taut young belly. He is an actor. When she first met him he was hopeful and shy. He used to be needy of her common sense, her attention. He had the ability – still does – to make her laugh with his talent for mimicry. But nowadays his own attention span has a low threshold. So – this is not love. It never is, and she does not expect it. And whatever this is and was is about to have run its course. Which, as an intelligent woman, Isabella knows is to be anticipated.

'See you when I get back from Nottingham.' And when is that? He hasn't said. And an affectionate slap on her backside at six o'clock in the morning as he departs. A teasing 'Oh dear, oh dear, what have we here?' Grabbing at her naked bottom. Herself tossing a pillow after him. Which last night she had propped beneath her buttocks.

She rolls over and lies on her tummy amidst the devastation of the bed. Combined odours of sex and garlic souring the air. Diffused greyish light sieved through the muslin curtains. Her limbs are heavy and aching. Emptiness washes over her. Of late this sensation – hard to pinpoint in its ambiguity – is something she has been experiencing more and more, and it is disturbing for a woman who believes herself to be so purposeful, level-headed and certain of what she does and does not want.

It is Saturday, and it unfolds. Saturday, 31 August. Isabella will have reason to remember the date. She goes about her usual routine: puts the kettle on, grinds coffee beans, opens the curtains to bright sun after all – and the geraniums in their terracotta pots outside on the patio shedding night's moisture. Herself dry-mouthed, early-morning-dry-skinned. Invasive middle age drying her out. Not everywhere yet, thank God. Picks up Garibaldi and fusses him.

'Yes, you're getting middle-aged spread too.' As he clambers up her chest towards her neck and thrusts his striped head under her jaw. She can feel his purrs reverberating against her throat. 'No, don't do it,' as he massages his claws into the silk of her dressing gown.

Talking to the cat, to herself, to her car, to her furniture, which she is forever moving around. 'No, I think you'd look better here,' she will say, shifting a chair or table from one position to another. An old maid. That is how people will one day look at her. Maybe they do now. In fact she was married once: a youthful attempt to put wronged childhood behind her with this most grown-up of declarations: I do.

She has her coffee; and an orange because it is slimming – it acts as a diuretic – whilst listening to *Today* on Radio 4 and simultaneously reading a manufacturer's promotional report on its latest HGV, which she has to translate into both Italian and French. Washes up, baths, gets dressed, waters the plants, packs a few things into an overnight bag, puts enough food and milk into Garibaldi's bowls for twenty-four hours, and leaves her flat. Isabella is a woman like thousands of others as she locks the door behind her and walks towards her car: she has several close friends, is independent, attractive, successful, social, capable, vivacious, childless by choice. There is nothing irrational or obsessive about her.

But this morning she is rather tired, a little deflated. She does not analyse these feelings as she climbs into her seventeen-year-old MGB GT; is more concerned with getting the thing to start – 'Come on. I'll sell you if you're not careful. Good money after bad and all that' – and when after several turns of the engine it does, she is jaunty with relief. 'A new battery for you,' she says, pushing in a tape. Her car is her single eccentricity; it has an insouciant style, she says when people tell her she should change it for something more reliable. And Isabella has great style.

Off she heads, up Hampstead High Street – coming to life at ten o'clock – towards the North Circular. The sun's brightness piercing the windscreen and her eyes; and she reaches for her sunglasses by the gear-stick. Domingo as Pagliaccio singing of his anguish. And how much shelf-life does her relationship have left? They could stagger on until their mutual birthday in a couple of months' time; but she can't stand hypocrisy. It would be better to slide out now. I think you need your space, she'll say; she has said before. No. I think *we* need our *respective* space. Cli-ché, chants her head.

Dissatisfaction swilling about in her. And she does not care to examine this. Isabella has evolved into the woman she is without self-questioning; past, present or future.

The traffic is light. Halfway down the North Circular she realises she has not bought her friend anything, and when she comes to a shopping parade she pulls in there and parks. Wanders past various shops: a greengrocer's, launderette, chemist's, newsagent's, Indian restaurant, off-licence, twenty-four-hour Spar, butcher's, hairdresser's – with a line of old-fashioned hairdryers like wilting tulips visible through the window. Outside the newsagent's is a child strapped into a stroller. She decides to buy a bottle of something and perhaps a box of chocolates as well. Goes into the wine shop, where she declines the offer of help from the young male assistant, preferring to browse on her own. She has plenty of time – had not expected to sail down the North Circular so freely. She does not have to be in the Cotswolds for a couple of hours. There are no other customers in the shop. In fact the precinct is a fairly dead sort of place altogether. A pass-through zone without soul, where 'To let' boards jostle for space above several buildings.

She takes her time and settles on a Chilean Chardonnay.

'Do you sell chocolates – you know, praline types?' she asks the assistant as he rolls the bottle in green tissue and tapes the ends.

'No. The newsagent's or Spar might.'

She thanks him, leaves the shop, bag in one hand, wine in the other, and makes for the newsagent's a couple of doors away. The child in the buggy is still there.

'Hello,' Isabella says to her as she pushes open the door.

The toddler gazes back. She has grave, shadowed eyes, a frail pixie face. It strikes Isabella that the child has been left alone for a long time: she was at least ten minutes in the off-licence, and who knows how long it was there before that? She is a further ten minutes in the newsagent's by the time she has bought a box of chocolates, *Vogue* for herself, and filled in a lottery card on an impulse. And when she comes out, there is the child, silent in her buggy, playing with a knitted toy of some sort.

This can't be right – to leave it so long by itself. There is no sign of the mother amongst the disinterested passers-by. She hovers uncertainly, thinking that perhaps she should enquire in one of the shops. The mother might be in the hairdresser's, it occurs to her. And in she goes – hit by warm moisture and the drone of hairdryers and cheerful female voices.

'Is anyone the mother of a little girl outside the news-agent's?' she asks a stylist in the middle of winding a woman's hair round tiny perming rollers.

'Well, I'd had it up to here—' The stylist breaks off and looks at Isabella. 'No, love. They're all grandmas in here. So I said, "If ever you speak to me like that again—"'

The other possibility is the launderette. Music blasting within. The thudding, whirring and spinning of machines, slopping of water and soap; flashes of swirling colour through portholes. Sitting around are three men, a teen-age girl, a weary-looking faded blonde, and an elderly woman. And a platinum-haired assistant folding sheets mechanically.

'Excuse me,' Isabella shouts above the hubbub, 'has anyone left a little girl outside the newsagent's?'

Blank eyes stare at her. One of the men leers. 'No, but I'll take you home, darlin'.'

She makes a quick exit – what a depressing place – and returns to the child; crouches beside her.

'Where's your mummy, then, eh?'

At that moment the girl drops her toy. Isabella picks it up and gives it back to her.

'Here's your rabbit.'

It happens then. The *éclat*. The child's smile is like a brilliant flash. It illuminates her face in a burst of light as she curls her fingers round the knitted toy, and Isabella is rooted to the spot, frozen in her crouching position like a victim of Pompeii as she is seared by an extraordinary rush of emotion. Slowly she straightens up and rests her elbow lightly on the stroller's handle. Within those few seconds the transition has taken place. Isabella has gone from being one woman to being another. And inside her is this incomprehensible yearning that is almost painful in its intensity.

She waits another couple of minutes. The child is silent, solemn, clutching her rabbit. Several people go by, then comes a lull. Isabella is conscious of the acceleration of her heart, and at one point she realises she has been holding her breath as though she is under water. Another couple of minutes elapse as she prevaricates, and does battle with the overwhelming urge that has seized her. And then the child drops the toy again; deliberately, it seems. Again, Isabella retrieves it.

'Poor rabbit.'

She strokes the child's hand. Its dimpled smallness, its softness, make her throat snag. The child doesn't smile this time. She stares at Isabella with an unfathomable expression. And suddenly it is as if someone is prodding her back, galvanising her forward, and this woman who is Isabella but not is walking briskly away, pushing the child in the buggy past the chemist's, the launderette, and the greengrocer's, in the direction of her car, expecting at any moment to feel a tap on her shoulder: Excuse me, madam, what do you think you're . . . She's got my child. She's stolen my little girl, a woman is shrieking . . .

This isn't me. I'm not doing this. She increases her pace.

She arrives at her car and unlocks it. Her fingers are trembling to such an extent that twice she misaligns the key with the lock. She realises that she no longer has the bottle of wine, or the chocolates and the *Vogue*, that in her urgency she has mislaid them. There is no question of going back to find them. She unstraps the infant and is about to lift her inside when it dawns on her there is no special seat. The next immediate problem is that try as she might she cannot make the buggy collapse. While keeping a firm grip of the passive, unresisting child with her left hand, with her right she pushes and pulls various levers, to no avail.

'Are you having a problem?' a voice behind her says, making her leap. And she wheels round.

'Sorry, I didn't mean to startle you. I just wondered if you wanted any help.' A young man is grinning at her.

'It seems to be jammed.' Shaking her hair forward; hiding her face, her blushing cheeks.

'You've obviously not mastered it yet. We've got one of these. They're very nifty when you get used to them. May I?'

She nods, watching intently as he raises the buggy's lower bar with his toe, presses down on the handles, and lifts the safety lock behind the seat. The buggy collapses, folding up like an umbrella.

'Madre,' Isabella says. 'That's brilliant.' Corrects herself quickly. 'I mean you are. I just couldn't get it to work.' Gives one of her expressive hand gestures.

'No problem.'

'Well, thanks anyway.' The man is still grinning at her, just standing there. What's he hanging around for? And she is worried he will notice there is no child seat in the car.

'Love the old MG. It's a Jubilee edition, isn't it? Want to sell it?'

'No. Excuse me, I'm rather late for—'

'Sorry, I didn't mean—'

'No, no. Thanks so much. You've been awfully kind.' Gushing to compensate for her brusqueness.

She watches him disappear into the Spar and lifts the child into the car. In the back, on top of her luggage, is her cardigan-jacket and she rolls this up and pads the girl with it; then she fastens the seat belt snugly round her. Shuts the door and double-checks it.

'That'll do. That'll have to do. Oh, madre.'

Her armpits are sticky with perspiration. She reeks with it. Pungent, unfeminine. She can smell herself. And the day is stifling. Day after day of heat wave. Her car windscreen is smeared with the remains of kamikaze insects. Isabella's heart battering her chest.

She climbs in her side – the MG starts first time – and drives off, back towards Hampstead. Imagines strobic blue lights in her mirror, baying sirens closing in on her. Every traffic light, every hold-up, tests her nerves. She dreads that someone alongside will notice the improvised arrangement with the seat belt and the child.

. . . She had long red hair and was wearing a white dress – Isabella can hear the young man describing her at this very minute – racing green, Jubilee-edition MG. She seemed tense . . .

At regular intervals Isabella takes her eyes off the road to glance at her small passenger – so strangely quiet, gazing about her, the knitted rabbit on her lap.

'Almost home,' she says, and stretches out to touch the froth of light hair. 'Don't you talk? How old are you? Two? Three?'

She parks a few yards away from the red-brick Victorian building where she has her garden flat, and sits on for a moment slumped over the steering wheel, her forehead pressed against it. Here, in the leafy familiarity of her surroundings, rationality claims her once more and she knows that she must take the child to the police. She feels a sense of loss as though she has just miscarried.

'We'll go indoors for a bit. I need to unwind first.'

The child seems to like her chattering. A spark of curiosity comes into her languid eyes. There is a square Elastoplast on her forehead which Isabella only notices now that her fringe has been blown back.

'Have you been in the wars, then?'

Oh madre, and she must phone and cancel Sally. She

cannot possibly drive there now. She lifts the child from the car, leaving the stroller inside it, and, holding her by the hand – what a strange and enchanting sensation it gives her: like a small bun in hers – walks the short distance to her gate.

Four steps lead from it down to her front door. And suddenly the girl becomes rigid and starts screaming.

'What is it? Hey – shush – what is it?'

Isabella is shocked, doesn't know what to do. She is afraid the neighbours will hear . . . My sister's little girl . . . The words are already on her lips.

The child is beside herself, her face red and contorted. Isabella scoops her up. 'Hey – *cara* – what is it? Nothing's going to hurt you.' She has a soft voice. It draws people to her, her low soft voice, as much as her red hair and Latin dark eyes. The mixed dominant genes of her Scottish mother and Italian father.

The sobbing subsides. The child's body relaxes against her, after its initial resistance. But she has wee'd. Her jeans are drenched.

'You see, you're all right now, aren't you? Look, we'll carry you down, and then you'll be fine. Did the steps frighten you? Look – one, two, three, four – here we are. Safe and sound. This is my home.' Isabella sets her down carefully and unlocks the door.

Garibaldi greets them, tail upright, its white tip quivering.

'Ca',' the child cries out, pointing. 'Ca'.'

'You can talk!' Isabella bends to hug her, laughing. 'Yes, he's a cat. His name's Garibaldi.' She pronounces it with an Italian accent. She strokes the cat, who rubs himself against them both and winds his tail round the child's legs.

The child giggling with pleasure, dancing from foot to foot, repeating, 'Ca', ca'.'

Isabella leaves her there in the sitting room to make

her phone call from the kitchen. Her friend answers after interminable ringing.

'Sally, it's Isabella.'

'Oh, hi. I was in the garden picking tomatoes to shove in the salad.'

'Cara, I can't come.'

'You're kidding. Why?'

'I—' Sally is her oldest friend. They were at Bristol together. They founded an all-female rock band. Isabella had been going to tell her the truth as it now is: she has picked up an apparently abandoned child and is about to take it to the police.

'I think I've got flu,' she, who never lies, says instead.

'Oh, no. I'm really sorry.'

'I am too.'

'I was really looking forward to seeing you. We all were. It's been ages. Oh, shut up, Geoff—' Her husband. 'He's yelling something. Hang on . . . What? Oh, he says he was going to slaughter you at ping-pong . . . What? . . . Oh, and he says to give you a love bite on your delicious bum.'

'Tell him don't be too sure to the first; and that I value our deep friendship too much for the second. I'm sorry to let you down.'

'No, it can't be helped. Get better soon. Dose yourself up.'

'Shall do.'

She rings off. Her first lie.

In the sitting room the child is on all fours by the armchair, behind which Garibaldi has taken refuge.

'So what are we going to do with you, then, eh?' Isabella says from the doorway. At the sound of her voice the child looks up. 'Ca',' she states.

'Can you say anything else? Would you like a drink? Do you know the word drink?' Isabella does not use a 'baby' tone; would feel foolish doing so. She speaks gently, but as she would to an adult. She holds out an arm. The child looks at her blankly. Isabella goes towards her and picks her up. Feels her flinch.

How strange: Isabella knows not the first thing about children; has always been outspoken in the past about not wanting them, about how they upset the order, the balance of one's life, are demanding, self-centred; and one has only to venture into a supermarket to be deterred for good. Yet this seems completely natural. Instinctively she knows what to do. And Isabella, who has attained the age of nearly forty and has never held anyone special nor been held dear in return, finds that she now craves both. She is captivated by this small, mysterious person. A warmth of pleasure is seeping into her, filling some hitherto unrealised vacancy within her.

In the kitchen she gives the child some utensils to play with while she pours orange juice into a mug. The child sits on the floor, without attempting to play. Isabella is conscious of her eyes on her, watching her every movement.

'Don't you want to play, then? Here's your drink, anyway.' She joins the child on the floor. 'I'll help you, shall I?' Holds the mug while the child sips – frowning up at her slightly, her fingers curled on top of Isabella's. And Isabella, who scarcely ever cries, who cannot remember the last time she cried – not when her mother died, and never since – finds her vision blurring.

Halfway through drinking, the child loses interest and pushes the mug away. The orange juice spills down her clothes and on the tiled floor. She stares at the pool as though in terror, then her features crumple and darken, and the hysterical screaming starts again.

Isabella immediately enfolds her in her arms. The child's legs flail against her. Frightened, Isabella clings on to her.

'Hey, what is it? Cara – what's the matter? It's only a bit of spilled juice. Shush, there. It's OK. Cara, it's OK. Hey –

tell you what—' She carries her into the living room, where her Spanish guitar leans against the wall by her desk; sits down, perching the child on her knee, and begins to play and sing.

'Puff the magic dragon lived by the sea, and frolicked in the autumn mist . . .'

Hot cheeks against her own. Small juddering chest against her breasts. The sweet scent of her hair. And once more the child is soothed and the sobbing dies away. But she has wee'd again. Even her shoes are wet. Isabella decides to wash her clothes and stick them in the tumble dryer before going to the police station. Another half-hour or so will make no difference.

'Let's get you cleaned up a bit, shall we?'

She has never undressed a child. Has a sudden recollection of herself alone, playing with a doll in the flat above the restaurant. Her parents hollering at each other from the kitchen below. 'Be quiet,' she shrieked through the floorboards, stamping her foot. 'Be quiet, be quiet, be quiet.' Nobody heard her, and systematically Isabella pulled the doll apart, limb by limb, before wrenching out the hair. She must have been about seven.

The child stands up obligingly. She is tiny, skinny, like a little worm. Isabella tackles the jeans first. They have an elasticated waistband and slide easily over her hips, falling about her ankles.

Isabella, kneeling, stares, appalled. Her legs are smothered in bruises.

'Madre mia. Madre mia,' she repeats against her hand clapped to her mouth. She feels quite, quite sickened. She draws the child to her – compliant now – and rocks her against herself without saying anything further. Then she resumes undressing her, bracing herself. She peels down the saturated knickers with great care – there are more bruises to her cup-sized buttocks – next takes off the wet shoes and socks. Oh madre, she is so fragile, her legs whisker-thin; and she is so quiet, steadily regarding Isabella, with that expression Isabella now recognises as wariness. It is shattering to see it in so young a child's eyes. Her head is throbbing in a six-eight rhythm; she can feel both temples pulsating as though the skin would rupture. Gently she unbuttons the cardigan. Her upper arms are in the same state as her legs and buttocks.

'Poor cara. Poor, poor little carina.'

And Isabella cannot help herself. With one arm encircled round the child, she brings the other across her own face to shield it, and she starts to cry. Except for a slight sound that escapes her throat, the crying is contained within her, and her chest aches with the effort of keeping it locked within.

She takes control of herself once more.

'Well, this won't do, will it?' she says to the child.

It is then that she sees the note attached by a safety pin to her T-shirt. She unfastens it. The paper is lined and grubby. The message, written in blunt pencil in an ill-formed hand, says, 'To huever. I cudn help misel. im skert wot il do. her nem is hana. don luk fo me.'

This time, when she comes to the decision to keep the child, it is not with the unreasoned rashness of earlier, but with a sober sense of inevitability. Even as she makes it she is afraid. Isabella is perfectly sane. She knows that what she is contemplating is legally wrong; that it defies logical explanation. That by her actions her life is about to be disrupted. And by her decision she has just wielded a mallet to her future peace of mind. That from now on she will be living a lie. All this is quite apart from the fact that she has on her hands a child who is obviously traumatised. How strange, it strikes her, that the words *rash* and *rational* should sound so similar and have almost the opposite meanings.

And she is rational, a few minutes later, as she snaps

away with the Polaroid camera, capturing on film the child's naked body, closing in on the bruises; weeping within herself, raging within herself: How could anyone? How could *anyone* . . . ?

That evening, when the child is asleep in the double bed, which the night before had been a sexual trampoline, Isabella sits at her desk in the neutrality of her living room. Garibaldi a sleek whorl on her lap. In a hardback notebook she writes, 'Today something extraordinary happened. I am going to keep a record of events, both for my own purposes and for possible future evidence.

'At approximately 10.00 o'clock this morning, Saturday, 31 August, I stopped to do some shopping in a parade off the North Circular Road (heading south, towards the A40). Outside a newsagent's . . .'

She is truthful about her initial impulse; the child's sunburst smile, her own atypical covetous yearning (This is not a shoplifting offence we're talking about – a bewigged prosecutor springing, lifelike, into her head – this is stealing someone else's child). It is important to mention this first instinct in order to show her subsequent change of mind and intention of going to the police.

'I have reached my revised decision to keep the child for a number of reasons . . .'

And what are they? The shock of seeing the pathetic body? The fact the police might think she herself has inflicted the injuries? The powerfully protective emotion the child has evoked in her? An inexplicable rapport? A sense of fate? Most of all, fear for the child: that at best she will be put into care, shunted from foster home to foster home, at worst returned to an abusive parent, another casualty of red tape. At all costs, Isabella is resolved to avoid both these possibilities.

And the child has a name now. Hana. Hannah.

Do not look for me, the mother requested.

Isabella, whom fate conspired to have stop at a shopping parade that particular morning, has been granted the mother's permission.

2

'Isabella, cara Isabella,' her father murmured through the shadows in a dove-throaty voice, when she was nearly thirteen.

'*Che cosa fa*, Papa? What are you *doing*. Don't do that.'

'*Scusi. Mi scusi . . . Sono spiacente, cara . . .*' Stumbling back away from her with a half-sob. '*Facevo niente.*' I wasn't doing anything.

She was saved from facing him the following morning. He was gone.

Her mother, her sharp-tempered, sharp-featured mother, was left to run the restaurant. Her mother, with her excoriating Scottish tongue, who drove herself and her daughter to the brink, pushed and pushed – Show me what you did at school . . . No, I said you can't go out . . . The lights of Sutton in a string piercing the unlined curtains of the flat while she did her homework. Her mother's sewing machine on the same table; and the globe on its stand. Hated. Enforced geography. Her mother would test her, covering place names with the end of a pencil.

'Do you want to end up with the same life as me?' her mother said, when Isabella protested. 'Don't think I haven't seen it: generation after generation of repetition.'

From the restaurant below old Neapolitan melodies drifted upwards, selling impossible dreams. For the next year, evenings after homework, weekends, holidays would find Isabella in the tiled and stainless-steel kitchen, peeling onions and potatoes, slicing zucchini into matchsticks, filling aubergine shells with stuffing, opening giant cans of plum tomatoes, scrubbing cauldron-sized saucepans stained orange with bolognese. She could hear the diners' laughter and the indistinct hum of conversation, see blurred heads – the women's back-combed hair – through the glass in the upper part of the dividing door.

Who was this woman who was her mother? Why had she borne Isabella, when plainly motherhood was another encumbrance? Why had she married Isabella's father? Or he her? Presbyterianism at odds with Catholicism. And did her father huddle in the confessional box and admit to that night's aberration?

'The sod,' her mother said the morning he went. 'Well, don't think we can't do without him.' And as if to prove it she was wearing lipstick for the first time in years.

A brief hug for her daughter about to set off for school as usual; a quick but thorough check of the correctness of her uniform (the cerise blazer clashed with her hair); a small adjustment to the tie, jerking it so that it was more central.

'You OK, then, hon?'

'Yes.'

'We'll be fine, you'll see.'

There is no indication the child misses her mother. Isabella tries to visualise her. A stereotype composite is all she can muster to her imagination: a young – maybe under twenty – weary woman whose man has done a runner; no money; a damp room in one of those god-forsaken streets off the North Circular, in a building where half the windows are boarded up. Or perhaps she lives high up in one of those graffiti-daubed tower blocks in the same area.

Not a bad girl, judging from the note – there was love apparent in it – just desperate. That anyone can batter such a tiny creature, whether the victim be human or animal, is beyond Isabella's comprehension; yet she feels sympathy for this woman, who had been unable to escape repetition. Perhaps she is suffering from depression. Perhaps she has an ungovernable temper that takes hold of her. Perhaps she is of below-average intelligence. Certainly she is ill-educated. There is no doubt she needs help.

Isabella envisages her with long straggling hair and eyes hewn so deep from the sculpted boniness of her face that they appear almost gouged out. The child has turquoise eyes in certain lights, grey in others. Troubled eyes. With the wisdom of hindsight, does the mother regret abandoning her daughter? There must be some ambivalence. Such an act could not be undertaken without a measure of grief. Hannah, the sacrificial lamb. And at this moment, whilst Isabella is wondering, is the mother wondering: where is my child, who has my child?

Isabella communicates silently with the benefactor of her magic gift, as she refers to Hannah: 'My cara, my little magic gift.' Telepathy does not work. And if the mother is aware of the outrageousness of what she has done, then equally so is Isabella of what she has done. For both, the deed is irrevocable.

There has been nothing on the news, to which for the last day and a half Isabella has listened every hour on the hour. No anguished, pleading, repentant mother (and what would Isabella do if there were?). No police message. No 'missing child' report in the papers.

Monday. And the scales this morning revealed she has lost just over three pounds. Anxiety has always suited her body. But her eczema has flared up on the underside of her arm – the crook of her elbow and inside her wrist. *Breakfast Extra* on the television carries loud and clear through the flat. They have spent the weekend getting to know one another. Everything, but everything, is new to Isabella, yet she has slipped naturally into this alien role: feeding the child, dressing her, holding her on the toilet, wiping her little bottom, massaging arnica cream into her bruises, which are changing colour, becoming a dull cadmium and merging into each other. She talks to her constantly, in her soft, low voice; and all Hannah can say is 'Ca'', when she catches sight of Garibaldi. She responds to Isabella with a tilt of the head, a light in the eye, or wary mistrust. Twice Isabella has elicited from her that brilliant burst of a smile which drew them together in the first instance. She is discovering in herself reserves of patience she did not know she had. The peculiar empathy she feels towards the child makes her sensitive to her needs, moods and terrors. Her pallor, her shadowed eyes, her discoloured flesh, are constant reminders of what she has been through, which Isabella cannot conceive of. Isabella is instinctive in her handling of situations and in her reactions. She is fairly phlegmatic by nature – quick to become irritated, slow to anger. She has a wry humour, sees humour where others might not. Some people find her too self-contained, dauntingly independent; but she exudes down-to-earth calm, and this seems to communicate to the child, who no longer flinches at Isabella's touch.

But – at nights she whimpers, and sometimes wakes, sobbing. And bathing her poses a problem. Hannah is petrified of the bath and shower. She cowered when Isabella led her into the bathroom and ran the water. The frightful wailing started up and she shot naked into the hallway, where she stood flinging her arms about.

And yes, Isabella has received a visit from a concerned neighbour. 'I'm looking after my sister's little girl,' she explained. 'She's homesick.' And could this be true, she wonders?

The child screams when she wets herself. She screams when she drops or spills anything. And Isabella realises that these were crimes that had resulted in punitive treatment. From her horror of the outside steps Isabella can guess at the form one punishment took. There are other things that trigger a hysteria attack: the hairdryer, any sudden loud noise, a raised voice on the television or radio, the dark, cigarettes – until now Isabella smoked moderately, between five and ten a day; no longer. All these are clues that enable her to build a picture, and which she assiduously records in her report.

'All I have done,' she wrote last night, in conclusion of yesterday's events, 'is circumvent bureaucracy.' Mitigating herself on paper for the future.

'. . . This woman had no conscience,' sneered the bewigged, robed figure pointing an indicting finger, in Isabella's sleep. Or was it sleep? 'No sense of right or wrong. There *were* no mitigating circumstances. She twisted the situation to her advantage, to satisfy a whim, because – to coin an expression – her biological clock was running down.'

And following this: a dream; in it she had legitimately fostered a child; but it was not Hannah. This was a Down's syndrome boy in his teens. A year later the boy was returned to the mother, who had meanwhile received therapy and was now living in a mansion surrounded by a moat and drawbridge, which was in fact Bristol University campus. Isabella and the boy were dragged apart, weeping.

And in reality that is how it could be. Could have been. Had she gone through the appropriate channels.

Isabella sitting up in bed, hugging herself, arms in an X around her chest and shoulders, deliberately slowing her breathing. Beside her, the child's regular and deep breathing; honey-smelling moth-wing exhalations from her slightly parted mouth. The hall lamp was on and the door ajar, and the bedroom was partially illuminated by a prism of light. It allowed Isabella to decipher the outline of Hannah's face on the other pillow, the fluffy hair, and her hand curled and lost in it, the knoll of her body – clad beneath the duvet in a white blouse of Isabella's. So sweet. So sweet. And Isabella was like the she-wolf in *The Jungle Book*, filled with protective tenderness – and that had been the name of her rock band at university: the She-Wolves; Isabella had been lead guitarist – and she lay back again, positioning her own body in a sickle shape around the child, not quite touching; inhaling her skin.

And now the sun glints through the kitchen window on to the wheaten head of the child and the copper one of Isabella, on whose lap Hannah sits, being spoon-fed muesli with warm milk and brown sugar. She is too small, too low down on the chair to sit by herself, and anyway has a tendency to wriggle. With more than one cushion beneath her she could slip and fall. Isabella is almost zealously concerned for her safety.

The telephone has rung several times during the course of the last couple of days and she has not taken any of the calls. Has stood by the answering machine, pen poised to write down the messages: a couple of friends – one of them Sally, enquiring if she is better; a man she has met a couple of times out hacking on Hampstead Heath. He is a banker or something. Last time she told him her phone number. Useful to have him in reserve; although he is rather British and pink-looking. Neither of them had anything to write with on them at the time. 'No matter,' he'd said, and repeated the number several times. She is amazed he remembered it. The mother of the boy to whom she gives private French coaching has got chickenpox, which suits Isabella fine. The final call was her agent, just a few minutes ago, reading out a fax he will be sending to a firm of French publishers, with whom he is trying to negotiate a deal. If it comes off she will be a few thousand pounds better off, and will be kept occupied for several months. The book concerned is a six-hundred-page tome on the influence and development of rural France through the ages. It could, her agent says, have an impact on her future.

The trouble with Isabella's work is that it can be lonely, isolated at times, and at times boring. A writer of other people's scripts. A writer without the glory, whose name is rarely recalled by the reader. But sometimes there are challenges, sometimes the material itself is interesting. There is always plenty of work to be had. Good, faithful-to-the-original trilingual translators who do not seek self-glory are not that easy to find. And the work itself can be fitted into her own hours; if she is busy during the day, she can work through the night. Then there are the business, political or press conferences – perhaps half a dozen a year – where she will accompany a personage and be on hand at all times, ready to interpret speeches, questions and responses. These can be fun, and are well paid. And you never know who you might meet. Over the years she has had quite a few dates this way. Or less euphemistically, one-night stands, one or two of which have led to brief but intense relationships.

On the mantelpiece above the fireplace the testimony of her independent and busy life is displayed: invitations to parties, book launches, a first night, private viewings, previews, an embassy dinner. Isabella is the provider for herself; provider for her own social life, her career, her wellbeing. A strong woman. A survivor by necessity. In her wardrobe hang several designer-label outfits. In her wallet are advance tickets for the theatre and the opera – the Coliseum. And she is about to turn her back on it all. She has no plans, no formulated thoughts other than she must get away.

There are things to do first.

It is a ten-minute walk to the motor accessory shop in

Haverstock Hill, and on the way there they meet a woman with a Labrador on a lead.

'God,' the child says from the buggy, stretching out her arm to it, and Isabella bends to hug her. Then realises she knows the woman. She goes to the same Latin American dancing class on a Monday evening. There is no avoiding conversation. Her first real test.

'Hello. I didn't recognise you out of context for a minute.'

She tries not to sound as flustered as she feels, but she has just recalled that the woman is a child psychologist and is acutely self-conscious; is aware of her eyes resting on Hannah.

'Well, you're recognisable anywhere. That hair,' the woman responds.

The words play in her head for a few seconds: recognise her anywhere. Instantly recognisable.

'Lovely dog,' she says, stooping to pat it.

'Yes, she's very good.'

'God,' says Hannah.

'I didn't know you had a child.' The woman smiles at Hannah, who is leaning sideways across the buggy, fingers outstretched towards the Labrador's nose.

'She's my goddaughter.' It comes to Isabella easily, so easily. And now, with the adrenalin of confidence, she is inclined to embellish. 'I've got her staying with me for a bit. So I shan't be coming to class tonight.' Has only just remembered it is tonight. The days have lost their sense.

'That's a shame. Well, have fun with your goddaughter. See you soon, then.'

And they part. No problems there. No difficult questions or protracted small talk. Her goddaughter. And in a way is she not? Her magic little gift from God. Except Isabella does not believe in God. She walks with a renewed spring in her step, the explanation ready on her lips for whomever she might encounter.

Dave, in the motor accessory shop, knows her well. She is always popping in for things.

'Wish I was that bloody car, the way you cosset it,' he said to her once. ˙ ⹁

Isabella is not a woman to take umbrage at a bit of innocent leching. She acknowledges that fundamentally men and women are different. She herself enjoys flirting. Far from finding it demeaning, she sees it as empowering. And men like Dave have always existed, will always exist, will never change, and cannot fairly be expected to change. They are almost invariably faithful to their wives, are predictable, work hard, and read the *Sun*. She cannot see where the harm is; it is all meant in a light-hearted way. She has had arguments with other women over this. They believe such behaviour to be derogatory, sexist and insulting. She accuses them of taking themselves too seriously. There are always heated quarrels in the Women of the World Awareness group to which she belongs, and whose meetings are held fortnightly in different homes. It amuses her how the evening always degenerates. Everyone becomes so het-up. Last time someone had attacked her for pandering to the male ego.

'Why don't you reserve your venom for important things?' she said, exasperated. 'Real exploitation, discrimination, harassment, subjugation, abuse, physical mutilation in Third World countries. These are what women's rights are about in the nineties, the issues to be tackled. Whether or not some of us flap our eyelashes at men rates zero on the Richter scale of importance.'

Remembers being coquettish to her father to get what she wanted. Never imagining.

'Mornin', all.' Dave grinning his broken-toothed grin at her as she enters, struggling with the door and the stroller.

'Blimey, that was quick.' Gestures to Hannah. 'Didn't know they came out so big nowadays.'

Hannah stares at him impassively.

'She's my goddaughter,' says Isabella. 'Dave, I need a child seat for the car. Oh, and a new battery.' As she spots one on the shelf.

'You goin' to fix it yourself, then?'

'I thought you—'

'Yeah, yeah. You women. Make mickeys out of us. Suckers. That's what we are. Aren't we?' he says to the child. 'Pretty little thing. Got a funny way of looking at you, though, hasn't she? Like she's seen it all. What about this child seat, then? You need it now?'

'Yes.'

'Your MG got seat belts that cross diagonally and over the lap, or just the lap?'

'The diagonal-and-lap one.'

'That's fine, then. You could have one of them Euroseats. They fit on anything. Basically, they sit on your car seat, front or back – front in your case – and you just shove the car seat belt round it. It's got its own locking device for safety.'

'You don't have one now?'

'Cor, you don't expect much, do you? My son will be coming in a bit later. I dare say I might just be able to get hold of one and nip up lunch-time, say. Install it for you. Fit the new battery for you too. If you're nice to me.' A suggestive wiggle of the eyebrows.

'You're brilliant.'

'Yeah. And look where it gets me.' Gives an exaggerated grimace, and pretends to slit his throat.

Isabella, Alice-like, wandering up and down the colourful aisles of Mothercare, pushing the trolley with Hannah tucked inside, legs threaded through. And no one so much as glancing at them. No one assuming anything but this is her own child, as she merges with a brigade of other mothers. Well, who would have guessed she would ever find herself doing this? Into the trolley goes a fold-up toddler chair, and a potty seat; a collapsible bed-rail – she marvels at so many devices – boxed sets of plates and mugs. She is carried away by the novelty of it; transfers Hannah to another trolley and fills this one with clothes, books and toys, things that did not exist in her day, and even had they done would not have come her way. She adds a Postman Pat toothbrush holder and *101 Dalmatians* bubble bath to her collection, some Wallace and Gromit wash-mittens and a small boat, in the hope that they might make bathing the child easier. She cannot stop buying, cannot recollect the last time she had such fun, is flushed-cheeked as this second trolley, too, heaps up.

'You've had quite a spree, haven't you?' comments the woman on the till.

'She's from Bosnia. I've just adopted her,' Isabella says without a second's hesitation. 'We're starting from scratch.'

Her own ability to lie astounds her. She had never thought of herself as given to fantasy.

'Well I never. Poor little mite. I bet she's witnessed a few things.'

At that moment there comes a loud crashing as another assistant drops a large box, sending a pyramid of other boxes toppling. On cue, Hannah starts screaming. Everyone turns to stare.

'Bombs,' says Isabella, plucking her from the trolley and cuddling her, trying to still her thrashing limbs. 'She can remember bombs.'

In the chemist's a few doors along she enlists the saleswoman's help in choosing a hair colourant.

'And I'd have sworn you was a natural redhead,' the woman remarks, peering at her.

'Just to cover the grey, you know.' Isabella waves her hand ruefully around her hairline.

'Happens to the best of us, luv,' says the woman, patting her platinum fringe and sighing.

'Shall we go north or shall we go south?' she says to the child – rocking on the corduroy horse and cooing to herself, something Isabella has not heard her do before. A contented, heartwarming sound. At first she had not seemed to know what to do with the toys and had sat on the durrie, surrounded by plastic animals and people with their own playhouse, showing only a mild curiosity. With Isabella's encouragement she had begun to pick up the little figures and place them in an order. But it was the unveiling of the horse which did it, which drew from her a spontaneous cry of delight, her illuminating smile, followed by laughter; real, chuckling laughter like bubbles chasing one another.

'A job in Italy's cropped up. I'll be gone at least a month,' she tells several friends on the phone.

'Drop me a line,' says the banker, who turns out to be a lawyer.

'Cornwall,' she says to her agent. And gives him her mobile number.

'It looks hopeful,' he says, and reads her the fax he has received from the French publishers.

South-west.

'". . . And maids come forth sprig-muslin drest,/ And citizens dream of the South and West,/ And so do I,"' she recited at school.

Thomas Hardy's 'Weathers'. She used to devour Hardy. Like so many teenagers of her generation, she *was* Tess.

'"I want to go south, where there is no autumn, where the cold doesn't crouch over one like a snow-leopard waiting to pounce . . ."' Tom read to her from the collected letters of D.H. Lawrence. He also introduced her to Keats's 'Isabella, or the Pot of Basil', which she had not previously known. The poem, taken from Boccaccio's *Decameron*, told of a woman whose lover had been murdered by her brothers and who kept his severed head hidden in a pot of basil, which the brothers then stole.

'"*And so she pined, and so she died forlorn*
Imploring for her basil to the last.
No heart was there in Florence but did mourn
In pity of her love, so overcast.
And a sad ditty of this story born
From mouth to mouth through all the country
Still is the burthen sung – 'Oh Cruelty,
To steal my basil-pot away from me!'"'

read Tom in his drawn-out upper-class accent which, when she'd first met him, she thought he was putting on as an affectation. Later she learned that his parents were in fact upper-class liberal intellectuals. His father was an Oxford don; his mother a Jewess distantly related to the Rothschilds, a writer and researcher on Russian history.

'I don't like it. It's gruesome,' she said. 'I don't even think it's that well written.'

'You try writing sixty-three verses in ottava rima.'

'I don't care. I think it's simplistic. And gruesome,' she repeated.

'Actually, you're in good company. Keats himself was pretty scathing about it. But I don't see that its being gruesome is relevant. One can't be fed on a diet of pleasant things the whole time.'

'I can.'

'You have particularly smooth feet. Speaking of which . . .' he said.

So young. Lying together smoking a joint, on the iron-framed bed with the cover pulled up to their chins, that cold winter before he went out to the newly proclaimed Socialist Republic of Vietnam.

She remembers a week in Cornwall – their honeymoon, actually – in a tiny fishing village on the Roseland peninsula. Tom taking endless photos in the rain. What was its name? She could find it on the map. Also remembers a half-term spent in Falmouth with her mother. Has more memories of Scotland. And is her Scottish grandmother still alive? If she is, then no doubt she is still vituperative, exercising the eroding power of her vocal cords on the other inmates of the old people's home where she ekes out her days. Or perhaps she has been silenced by senility. Isabella wastes no pity on her. She owes her nothing. Her grandmother made her own choice once, when she marked the card of her granddaughter's fate. Isabella's father's parents died when she was a girl. She dimly recollects a wide-lapped, black-clad woman with a hairy wart on her cheek, passionate eyes, and love in her voice. And what of this woman's son, Isabella's father? She prefers not to think of him. If inadvertently a memory, a happy memory, should steal its way into her mind, she sweeps it away.

Isabella coaxing Hannah into the bath. She herself lying in there surrounded by bobbing toys, clapping her hands enthusiastically. And finally the child ventures to peep over the edge, with a half-smile on her lips, hand clasping the rim. Isabella flicks water at her, which makes her giggle.

'It's fun. You're really missing out, you know, Hannah,' Isabella says to her. Lies back with an 'A-a-h'.

The child jumping up and down excitedly. It obviously strikes her as very funny to see Isabella in the water. In one hand is the Gromit wash-mitten. For some reason she took an aversion to Wallace as soon as she saw him. Isabella thought it might be the big teeth . . . And now the child is stretching out her arms to be lifted inside the bath. Isabella has won. It has taken nearly an hour; she is victorious. Later it will all be faithfully recounted in her report. But meanwhile, she opens the bottle that is on the side and lathers the contents over Hannah's head, making a turnip of her fine hair. Thirty minutes later it is the same mid-auburn as Isabella's.

A while later, when the child is asleep, she begins preparing for the morning, puts clothes and toys directly into a couple of newly purchased holdalls; pores over the road atlas to plan her route – the estuaries, creeks, coves and points make the heel of Cornwall's foot appear as though a rat has gnawed relentlessly at it, she thinks; does an hour or so's work: a company profile from Italian into English – peppered with idiomatic phrases, just to make things awkward; sorts out the contents of her desk. Then, finally, worn out, she pours herself a glass of red wine and switches on the television. She is too tired to eat. Has she taken on too much? How will she fit in her work? The child is a full-time job. A commitment. Once she is settled; once she is settled . . .

So many emotions and thoughts sparring in her head. *Moto perpetuo*. It will take a while to adjust from one life to another; from having no responsibilities to being weighed down with them – she who had deliberately cultivated a trouble-free existence.

At times she has the sense she has strolled into someone else's home, or perhaps into a play in which she sees herself in the third person. And with the burst of applause all will revert. At other times she is wrenched into awareness of the surrogate role she has thrust upon herself, and the outlandishness of what she has done slashes across her.

She watches the news again. And following this, on Channel 4, a gentle documentary about the close bond between a cerebral palsy victim and his carer. The film so moves her that instead of turning off the television she waits for the credits.

It was written, produced and directed by Tom.

3

'"Boast not thyself of tomorrow; for thou knowest not what a day may bring forth,"' her mother used to quote from the Proverbs.

And who could have guessed at the surprise that Saturday was to bring? Who can guess at all her tomorrows? But Isabella subscribes to the theory that tomorrow will look after itself.

It takes her almost an hour to load up the MG, squeezing things into every possible niche. And then she realises she has forgotten to make a space for Garibaldi and his basket. A further twenty minutes is spent rejuggling. The child watching with apparent interest from the buggy. Isabella keeping up a muttered running commentary: 'It could fit in this way. No, maybe it's better like . . . Madre, I wish I had a bigger car – I didn't mean it, I didn't mean it' – patting the side of the MG. 'Oh, my guitar. Hannah, you forgot to remind me about my guitar.'

One of her neighbours – a prissy, shabby, beige man who makes her flesh creep – is coming towards her.

'Hello there. Are you going away?' Eyeing the child.

'To my sister's. This is her daughter. Hannah, say hello.'

Hannah says nothing.

'Her father was violent. She's afraid of men.'

'Goodness me.'

He looks as though he might be a flasher, or even a paedophile. He has small, shifty eyes. Nervous shoulders.

'Oh, it's all right. He's no longer around.'

She is thankful it isn't the same neighbour who investigated them a couple of days back when the child's hair was its natural blond. Had forgotten about that. Slams the hatch door, says a hurried goodbye to the man and whisks the child indoors just as she starts screaming at the shock of the loud bang.

Isabella is a private sort of person; likes to remain anonymous except with people of her choice, and although she has lived at the same address for many years she still barely knows her neighbours. Wishes now that she did, so that she could entrust someone with a key, to keep vigil, ensure squatters don't move in; switch on lights or music to deter burglars; forward her mail. As it is, she will have to return on a fortnightly basis. And what will she do with the child if she has to go to a conference?

Just as she is about to lift Garibaldi into his basket, he pins back his ears, leaps out of her arms, shoots through the cat flap from the kitchen on to the patio, and streaks up the fence. Where he sits glaring and swishing his tail. She unbolts the door and approaches him gingerly. He contemplates her slyly until the second her fingers are within a millimetre's reach of him, then down the fence he springs, into the next garden.

'*Bloody* cat.' She swings her fist against her hip.

'Grabla,' states the child, peering up at the fence.

'Say that again, cara.'

'Grabla, Grabla.' Pointing to where the cat had been.

'You clever girl! Yes, carina. Grabla. Ga-ri-bal-di. And he's a bad cat as he's run away.'

The child frowns, as though trying to comprehend.

For the next couple of hours her inane cries of 'Dinnies' do not entice him, since he has already eaten his fill. And next door's bird table provides limitless entertainment. In the end it is the neighbour's terrier which drives him back on to his own patch. This time he zooms through the flap from the other direction, as though through a hoop of flames, straight past Isabella and into her room, where he entrenches himself under her bed. Eventually she manages to disengage his claws from the carpet and pluck him out, hissing, his claws transferring to her bare arm.

'Horrible creature.' She fastens the straps of the basket. Pinheads of blood appear on her skin.

'Grabla,' coos the child, about to poke her finger through the mesh.

'He's not a happy Grabla.' Isabella stops her before the cat's paw lashes out. Cat litter. She has forgotten the cat litter and tray. Will they never get going?

Almost lunch-time when they set off, taking the North Circular; passing the very precinct. She grips the steering wheel. A young man running along the pavement: That's her. I recognise her. That red hair. And the car . . . And in a room somewhere, does a mother mourn? Only when they hit the M4 does she begin to relax. Distancing herself from the scene of her crime. She is a criminal. She, Isabella, is a criminal in the eyes of the law. Switches on Domingo and sings along with him, drowning out Garibaldi's plaintive mewing from the back of the car. Beside her, the child giggling. The car creaking and squeaking with its load. A new suspension system. That will be the next expense.

A couple of hours later they stop just before Exeter at a Granada service station off the M5.

The noise of machines blasts at them as they enter the building: gunfire, zinging, rattling, sirens howling. Groups of youths and girls gathered round, cheering each other on. She can feel the child's whole body tensing, shrinking against her.

'It's OK, cara. Hannah, carina, nothing's going to hurt

you, I promise. Shall I carry you?' Braces herself for the screaming as she picks her up. But although the child's arms tighten round Isabella's neck, she makes no sound. Isabella does not hurry through the hall. Knows that to do so would be a mistake, as though she herself were afraid.

'They're playing with big toys. Look at the cars on that screen.'

The child's legs wrap themselves round her waist. Her hair is silky beneath Isabella's chin. Her glance darts about, as they head first for the ladies' then the restaurant. So many new experiences within a few days. What must she be thinking? What must she be feeling? Does she wonder where she is? Where her mother is?

'You can make something of yourself. Not like me,' Isabella's mother said, not long before she died. 'Don't chuck it over some man.' Coughing. Doubled up with it. Clutching the kitchen table.

And later, when she was in hospital, anger in her eyes because there had only been hard work and disappointments. She went out with another kind of light in her eyes, whispering from St Luke. A nurse laid her hand on Isabella's shoulder.

'Do you want to kiss her goodbye?'

Obediently Isabella did so. It was winter, and there was a lovely cool silence in the room. And what would happen to her? she wondered, standing composed over the deathbed which held no shocks. A tall, large-breasted fourteen-year-old with her red hair pulled back in a ponytail; dark eyes like lacquered stones.

What must it be like, Isabella often thinks, to have such implicit faith? Not a flicker of doubt. One is going to a better life, and that is that. Sometimes, when she is overtired, she has images of herself, dead, her body decomposing under the ground. The images fill her with horror and a dread of her own death. They occur at the oddest times.

Her mother: dutiful, if not loving. And perhaps she loved in her own way. How old, when she died of lung cancer? No more than forty. But old as far as Isabella was concerned. Vanora. Such a beautiful, lyrical name for a woman without a wisp of poetry in her soul. But certainly she'd had hopes once.

'Don't come to me. I can't have her,' said her grandmother.

They have entered the county of Cornwall, land of lore and legends and soft burred voices. Bodmin Moor spreads bleakly either side of the road, the skeletons of disused mines adding to the sense of isolation. Most of the traffic – and that is not much – is heading in the opposite direction. Holidays over for another year. She follows signs for St Austell. Passes china-clay quarries and white pyramids of waste mica and quartz sand. The countryside becomes more undulating and her spirits lift. The sun lowering and evening setting in. The child asleep, head lolling on to her chest. Garibaldi has long given up miaowing, is apparently reconciled to being in a basket for ever. Isabella is completely alone. She turns off, towards St Mawes.

So, says the prosecutor in her head, if she did not regard her actions as criminal, why then did she feel the need to run away?

Because of others, she says. Others would not see it her way.

Does this woman have no conscience, he persists, that she continually justifies herself?

It is growing dark. On her right is a lane, narrow as an artery, and she takes this turning. The lane descends steeply in a series of wishbone bends. High banks either side of her obscure the countryside. Overhead the trees arch to form dense-leaved tunnels. The banks become hedges, and through gaps she catches glimpses of dusk-gentle pastureland and grazing animals. Suddenly her head-lights pick out a fox, and she stops, thrilled. It turns its head leisurely, to stare for a few seconds directly into the beam, blinking, the richness of its coat gleaming in the light, then it saunters in front of her car across the lane. She watches it disappear into the undergrowth and does not move off immediately, wanting to savour the moment.

A mile or so on, she passes an illuminated mill selling antiques, and shortly after it comes to the village of Zerion. On the corner of a small junction of lanes is an inn: the Fox's Retreat. And now tiredness consumes her. It is virtually dark, and she doesn't feel like driving a mile further.

The lights cast a tangerine glow through the windows. She half enters. Above the fireplace, in a glass box, is a fox that didn't retreat fast enough. Also a badger and an owl. The fox upsets her, under the circumstances. The place is fairly busy, and the low hum of voices, the laughter, are curtailed as everyone turns to look at her standing there in the shadows of the doorway.

'I've left my little girl asleep in the car,' she calls across to the man behind the bar. 'I can't really come in. Could we have a room for a few nights?'

'Sure. Hang on a tick.' Smiles at her, finishes pulling a pint, hands it to his customer, wipes his palms on the sides of his thighs, and comes across the room to her. Accompanies her to the car. He is genial; visceral-complexioned.

'Nice old motor . . . You've a fair bit of stuff,' he adds mildly, when he sees everything.

'Oh, it's not all for now. We'll only need a few things for now.'

'I wouldn't leave anything valuable overnight. Your guitar. You should bring that in. And is that a laptop computer?'

'Yes.'

'I'd bring that in. Folks are pretty honest round here, but you never know.' He has a warm, glutinous Cornish accent.

'A cat,' she says, unstrapping the child, and gesturing with her chin to the basket at the back. 'I forgot to tell you I've got a cat.'

And he has two Dobermans, at whom Garibaldi vents all the day's pent-up frustrations through the mesh of his basket as Isabella carries it inside.

The landlord banishes them into a lobby and shuts the door on them. 'They're only boisterous. They're big softies actually.'

'I believe you.'

'No, really.'

'Gods,' says the child sleepily, hanging on to Isabella's other hand.

'Gods?' The publican looks askance.

'Dogs,' Isabella says in a mother's proud tone.

The staircase is steep and uncarpeted. She can see the child's face puckering in readiness; sets down the cat basket and whisks up Hannah.

'My daughter's afraid of stairs,' she says.

'I'll take the cat,' he offers.

They follow him upstairs to a broad landing.

'We were full up till a couple of nights ago. Big exodus Sunday. You timed it well. Hardly a room to be had round these parts.'

He puffs a bit as he talks. Unfit. A beer gut hanging over his belt. Faint sheen of perspiration on his forehead and in the hollow above his upper lip.

'It's just as well we didn't come earlier,' she says.

He unlocks a door and opens it, and goes inside. He puts the cat basket on the floor and parts his arms in an expansive gesture. 'Here you go, then. Not grand, but plenty of room for the three of you for as long as you want. The basin's got hot and cold, but the bathroom's only next door.'

'This is perfect.' She flops down on to one of the twin beds with its flowered nylon cover.

He leaves her, and returns twice more with her other items.

'You might need this' – holding up the bag of cat litter. 'And I also brought you up an old newspaper to put under the tray.'

'Thanks. You're very kind.' She pours litter into the tray and releases Garibaldi from the basket.

He emerges cautiously, stiff from his confinement, gazing suspiciously all around him and shaking each leg in turn.

'Grabla,' cries the child, running towards him.

The cat glares at her and dashes under the bed.

'He's been cooped up for hours,' Isabella says.

'Poor thing. Well, I'd best be getting on downstairs. The name's Dick, by the way.'

'I'm Isabella. This is Hannah.'

'Hello, Hannah. How old are you, then?' He crouches down to the child's level. She stares blankly back at him.

'She's very shy, I'm afraid.'

He straightens up – she hears his knees cracking. 'No problem. So, what about food? Do you want to eat something?'

'Well, I am a bit peckish, and all Hannah's had since lunch is chocolates. So she should eat really. But I don't think your other guests would appreciate—'

'Hows about I bring it up to you on a tray?'

'I feel so guilty. Your waiting on us like this.' Turns the force of her eyes upon him.

'Rubbish . . .' Locks into them for a couple of seconds. 'It's no trouble.'

'Do you have any soup?'

'Cream of carrot. The wife made it today. Ever so good it

is.' Pats the globe of his belly, then draws up his chest. The stripes of his shirt wriggle upwards. The child's eyes never leave him.

'I'd love some soup. For both of us. And maybe toasted sandwiches. Cheese?' Hannah, she has discovered, loves cheese. '. . . And a glass of red wine?

They eat in front of the television. The child sits on her potty, tugging at the toast with her fingers and teeth and cramming pieces into her mouth. Strings of melted cheese hang like fangs from the corners. Garibaldi slithers from under the bed and heads for the litter, squats, gazing ahead of him with fixed concentration, then covers his traces, scattering the granules. His good temper gradually recovers and he begins to investigate the room. A large, high-ceilinged room with a sash window facing the road. Pink vinyl walls, pink fabric light shade, and a matching one for the lamp – which has a brown burn mark on its underside. Ubiquitous red-and-gold carpet. Floral curtains. Avocado basin with lime stains round the plug-hole.

'Hannah wee-wee,' she announces, tottering up from the potty.

'Clever girl.' Isabella hugs her. The child is progressing daily, hourly; witnessing it fills her with pleasure.

She washes her in the room then tucks her in bed. It is their first night in separate beds. She reads to her and shows her the pictures. Kisses her. Turns off the main light, leaving only the lamp. The child follows her every move.

Barely nine o'clock, and she herself is ready for bed, exhausted. She cleans her teeth, washes, tiptoes to the loo next door and returns to the room. The child is still half awake, eyes in watchful slits, but does not seem perturbed by Isabella's short absence. There have been other examples that would indicate she is used to being left on her own.

'There is so much I will never know,' she writes in her report, in bed.

What have I done? flits through her thoughts again. Surrealism. Garibaldi lies across her legs. And she glances over to the child's peaceful form. The three of them safe in this ugly pink room. They have all found each other by chance. Even the cat just turned up outside her door one day.

From downstairs, now the television is switched off in the room, she can clearly hear the conversation from the bar directly below. Some people are discussing her.

'I reckon she's a businesswoman. She had a mobile phone with her. And a computer. Did you see? One of them yuppies from the city.'

'Not with a kid that age.'

'Well, I reckon she's an actress. I'm sure I recognise her.'

This is nothing new. She is always being told she looks like someone. Susan Sarandon or Sigourney Weaver; once some actress from *EastEnders*. Most interestingly, by a smitten man, an art historian with a passion for the Pre-Raphaelites, that she looked like Holman Hunt's girlfriend, Annie Miller, in *The Awakening Conscience*. This man took up where Tom had left off and drove her to the Laing Art Gallery in Newcastle to see Hunt's painting, *Isabella and the Pot of Basil*. But he was fifteen years older than her. Isabella has never been attracted to older men.

'Good-looking woman and all,' says another man's voice downstairs.

'Oh, I don't think so.' A woman's sharp tones.

Isabella smiles. Such a predictable response. She finds it sad that some women can't acknowledge others' attractiveness without bitching.

And then comes another man's voice. 'Well, if you ask me, she's running from something. You don't drive all that way with a kid and a cat and all that luggage on spec.'

And feels a chill run through her.

His observation has briefly silenced the others. Then she hears the woman again:

'A husband, you mean?'

'Well, it makes sense, doesn't it?'

And she breathes again.

4 ∫

Isabella seems so self-assured and poised. There is no bitterness apparent in her features. Her eyes are mink-soft. There is determination in the set of her jaw but not aggression. She is a woman of inherent good taste and style, yet she had no yardstick. What happened to the child who stamped her foot unheard, and dismembered her doll as her parents hollered out their mutual frustrations at each other?

Perhaps that act of destruction was partly responsible: she had lost her most treasured possession and thus only punished herself. Tantrums were replaced by sulks. But sulking was only of use when there was someone at whom to aim it. When her mother died, different rules applied. She had to endear herself. Isabella the chameleon. And yet the guise she assumed was never conscious. She was never deliberately one person or another. And so she watched and learned, picking up a bit here, a bit there; and each place she went brought out another aspect of her character and she became the woman she is today. Whoever that is.

The screeching of an owl from the churchyard opposite pierces her sleep and wakens her. A wind has struck up and the window rattles like mouse teeth. For a moment she cannot think where she is, and then, in the aureole of the night lamp on the table beside the child's bed, the pink room comes into focus and her pupils adjust accordingly, and she remembers.

She had a pink bedroom once. And she went into it after school one day to discover a dress – a skimpy thing she had seen and hankered after and bought with money earned at the hairdresser's on Saturdays – cut into pieces. She said nothing. Determined to be no trouble. And when she would be trying to work in the small pink bedroom – it was perhaps eight foot by six foot, and she hung her clothes on hangers on the door, or folded them into the drawer that formed the base of the bed – on would go the pop music in the room next to hers. Louder and louder it became, drowning ink and print and inspiration and the Roman Empire through the cardboard-thin dividing wall. Nobody to tell.

'Everything all right?' The woman, kind, hearty-bright-voiced, harassed eyebrows, mottled bare legs, would come in with bulging string shopping bags and dump them with a 'phew' and a puffing out of the cheeks on the table.

'Any volunteers to unload?'

And Isabella would oblige.

'Thank you, dear.'

The woman's troubled glance shifted towards the other girl, her daughter, the same age as Isabella, who would slam upstairs to her younger brother's room. Giggling from within.

'Well, you know,' the woman used to say, with nothing prefacing or following it. Just 'Well, you know.' Explicit enough.

A year, Isabella lasted there. Making her fifteen.

Zerion sprawls, with its anachronistic amalgam of architectural styles, in a brook-bound cobweb of lanes within the bowl of three hills. There is that end-of-season feel about it this Wednesday morning, like an empty bag of sweets in which one rummages amongst the sugary deposits for a piece worth eating. The weather has broken. The wind that whisked up in the night blows through zeppelin clouds which hint at rain to come, forces leaves from trees and tosses up summer dust from roads and pavements.

It gives the locals something to talk about, the change in the weather. And in the newsagent's-cum-post office stores, in the lane that runs along the base of the neatly mown triangular green, the proprietor is telling another woman that she welcomes the breeze and the cooler temperature, that her legs have been playing up in the heat and her veins have been like bundles of dates, when Isabella enters with the child, and she breaks off. Both women swivel and assess her openly. News of the visitor has already reached their ears via one of the men from the pub last night, who has just been in for his *Mirror* and a packet of tobacco. And Isabella, who is used to London, where one can go anywhere, do anything without attracting attention, knows that in a small parochial community like this she is likely to find herself the butt of gossip. And so she flashes a smile at the two women and injects a friendly liveliness into her tone when she wishes them good morning and comments on the weather, before asking for the local paper.

'It'll be the *West Briton* you want. There's a Truro edition for round here. It comes out tomorrow, Thursday.'

The proprietor, a mealy-faced woman, takes off her bottle-glass spectacles and rubs them on her lilac crochet pullover, considers Isabella through watery eyes for a couple of seconds and resites the glasses.

'I've got one from last week at the back of the shop' – she has obviously decided in Isabella's favour – 'I could let you have it if you like.'

'Oh, but I'll pay for it.'

'That's not necessary. I was only going to chuck it. It's out again tomorrow.' Disappears through a doorway behind the counter to fetch it.

She is left alone with the other woman, whose right arm is in a sling. A good conversation-opener.

'What have you done to your arm?'

'I fell down the stairs,' the woman says, staring at the floor. She has a small, timid voice inside a big, shapeless body, and Isabella immediately regrets the question; knows that her husband is violent. She pretends to sift through the postcards. Is relieved when the other woman returns, limping slightly on her squat legs. She must buy something, she thinks, and grabs a couple of cards and a toy bucket and spade in a net bag.

'And I'd be grateful if you'd reserve me a copy of the paper tomorrow.'

'There's always plenty, don't worry,' the proprietor says, ringing up on the till. 'So how old's your little girl?'

'Two and three-quarters.'

Perhaps the woman will say Hannah looks older. Or younger.

'She seems very placid.'

'She's a late talker,' Isabella says. 'I was too. I didn't talk until I was nearly four.'

'Now it's funny you should say that. My granddaughter . . .'

And she launches into a lengthy story.

Isabella tries to seem interested; murmurs appropriate comments.

'I'm hoping to rent a cottage in the area,' she says. 'That's why I wanted the paper.'

'Are you now?' The proprietor regards Isabella keenly. 'For a holiday, you mean?'

'No. Longer than that. Maybe a few months.'

'Ah.'

The women nod wisely at each other, then at her. And

she can see them thinking: It's true, then. She's run off. Sympathy clear in their faces. She gives the tiniest of nods herself, as acknowledgment. One of them.

The woman with the sling says, 'There's nothing in Zerion that I know of.'

'Actually, I really wanted to be in Pengarris Cove.'

The child butting her face against Isabella's legs, tugging at the edge of her pullover for attention. Incredible to think that just a couple of days ago she would flinch, almost as a reflex, whenever Isabella touched her. She hoists her into her arms.

'Pengarris Cove's just a couple of miles from here,' the post office woman says. 'There're only holiday places to rent there. A few weeks at a time type thing. And it's the end of the season now.'

The other woman swirls her lips round contemplatively. 'What about old Timothy Abell's place? That's been standing empty.'

'Oh, that'd never suit the likes of her.' The post office woman shakes her head slowly at Isabella. 'That's not for you. For a start it's only got an outside toilet.'

'Who's Timothy Abell?'

'Was. He died a month back. He had the filling station between Pengarris and Port Tregurran before he retired. And Lord knows what state the place must be in. He was more'n ninety when he died. And looked after himself till the day he went. Bad-tempered old goat he was. Hadn't spoken to his daughter since she got pregnant by that . . . what was his name?'

'Collett. Will Collett, you mean, from Penzance way,' the woman with the sling obliges.

'Yes, that was him. A married man. But for goodness sake, a woman has to take what she can get sometimes. And she gave all her best years to her father. Any rate, he kicked her out. And Will Collett wouldn't have nothing to do with her. She lives in Truro with the kid. He's funny in the head. Backward, I mean.'

The three of them mull over the unfairness of it all.

'How do I find out about the cottage?' she asks.

'Babs Carrick at Pengarris post office is bound to know. It's down the hill on the right, next to the Sun Inn.'

Isabella thanks her and leaves. Guesses she has given them plenty to talk about. As she steps out of the shop, her hair blows across her face and she pulls it back and tucks it into the neck of her pullover. Does up the top button of the child's collar. 'There, is that better? You mustn't catch cold.' Pulls forward the stroller's transparent hood. Next to the post office is a garage which, according to the metal sign swinging and creaking musically from the corrugated roof, does servicing, repairs and MOTs, and she rummages in her bag for a pen and paper to jot down the phone number. In the middle of writing she becomes aware of someone's eyes on her.

In the yard a young man is tinkering with a battered white van. He is simultaneously staring at her, and she has the impression he has been doing so for some while. She is both self-conscious and disquieted. She mouths a hello, but he does not respond and continues to drill her with his gaze. She lowers her head and walks on.

'Creepy guy, creepy guy,' she says to the child.

She follows the left diagonal of the green, past the terrace of thatched cottages whose front doors are approached via miniature bridges traversing the brook; the butcher's, with its cheerful cardboard pig alongside a suspended carcass (this always strikes her as rather sick); the art gallery in a converted chapel; past the Zerion Church of England primary school – ghostly, without children for another week – and a row of bungalows with manicured gardens and Dracaenas and gnomes . . .

'Blustery day,' one or two people remark to her.

And an elderly woman on a cylindrical cob plods by, waving to everyone in general.

They arrive at the duck pond, to the side of the church, whose tower can just be glimpsed through the lychgate. And somewhere amongst the pines and the yew in the little graveyard is the screech owl that woke her in the night.

'Some folks round here are superstitious of it,' Dick, the publican, told her at breakfast this morning. 'They're supposed to be a death portent.' And he went on to tell her about the pair of thatched round houses built on the hill on the edge of the village.

'Devil's Ridge, the hill's known as,' he said, pouring her coffee and taking a seat for a few minutes at her table. 'On account of its "horns" either side. Well, this hill was the only site the local vicar – I forget his name – could find to build homes for both his daughters. So he had them made round so that there were no corners for the Devil to hide in. Full of old wives' tales this place is.'

He told her another, amusing, anecdote: about an American tourist to whom he was explaining the history of the church.

'So I says to him' – Dick was laughing as he recounted it – ' "By the way," I says, "It's Norman." "And I'm Jack," says the American. "Good to meet ya." '

'I don't believe that's true.' Isabella joined in his laughter.

'It is. God's honour. I don't know how I kept a straight face.'

And here she is, back at the pub, and her car, parked outside.

She unlocks it and lifts the child inside, fastens the seat straps around her and passes her the knitted rabbit and the new bear, whose ear Hannah has taken to sucking. Folds up the buggy with the expertise of an old hand and puts it in the back. The garage mechanic's glowering eyes remain with her and disturb her.

The lane to Pengarris Cove is winding and narrow, and several times she has to pull in for an oncoming vehicle. Once she hears the scraping of branches against the car's wing. Then, ahead, she has her first glimpse of the sea, turbulent and mossy green. She has a passion for the sea, is always thrilled by that first sighting of it – jokes that it is because she is a Scorpio.

The descent into the village becomes steeper, and as her foot grips the brake the MG clunks metallically. Either side, pastel cottages cling to the lane. Subtropical plants blaze out from gardens. Flower baskets hanging from lime-washed walls swing in the wind. She slows when she comes to the Sun, and notices the post office immediately after it. But there is nowhere to park, and presently the lane splits into two, one fork veering sharply to the left and climbing, the other carrying on for a few yards before shelving in a cobbled slipway on to the cove. At the apex of the lanes, the Ship Inn leans forward from its Tudor gables. Outside, a group of people are sitting in the courtyard.

She deliberates about taking the left fork; the incline seems almost perpendicular and she imagines her car stalling, hurtling backwards down the hill. Resolutely, she puts her foot down on the accelerator, and the MG crawls upward. She grits her teeth all the while during its painful progress. Laughs with relief when they reach the top.

As she stands outside the car, the wind lashes at her hair and cheeks. Seagulls squeal and career overhead. She feels exhilarated; has the urge to cry out and mingle her voice with the gulls'.

'Buds,' the child says from the buggy, pointing upward.

The rocky western headland rises in gorse- and bracken-clad cliffs and sweeps out to sea. There it divides, one prong jutting out in a long tusk, the other embracing the cove like a protective lover. She can see a row of cottages and behind them a bleak-looking chapel. Perched like a phallus on the end of the 'tusk' is a lighthouse. The opposite promontory is softer, cultivated on the upper slopes, and curves to meet the western headland in a ragged lobster's claw.

Up here, along this stretch of road, the houses are hidden from view at the end of long driveways, their names attached to gates or discreetly placed amongst rhododendron hedges; and she instantly latches on to the name 'Rhododendron Drive'. Here there is a sense of prosperity. Here, she guesses, live the professionals, the retired, the councillors, the local chairmen of companies. The lawns are emerald from sprinklers. No doubt croquet is played. Here are held Sunday drinks parties – and maybe she will find herself invited to one.

And what do you do? she asks a silver-haired man in a blazer.

Well, I'm retired now; but I'm a magistrate. And his eyes bore into her . . .

For a few minutes the wind dies down, and in the brief lull she catches the sound of a lawn mower; then of something much closer. It is coming from the scrubby bank somewhere near her feet – tiny, until one isolates it; and then it seems to increase both in intensity and persistence, defiant against approaching autumn and gales and ephemeral existence: crickets. How rarely she has heard crickets in England. Their tintinnabular whirring fires her senses and triggers a keening in her towards something indefinable yet somehow important.

The wind whips up again and the crickets are lost.

Slowly, she walks down the hill with the child in the stroller. Old buildings cascade on top of each other, their rooftops forming staggered layers. Alleys splay from the lane and terminate in courtyards or in steps leading through shadowy arches on to the cove. Salt and seaweed in her nose. A distantly recalled excitement.

At the Ship Inn she unstraps the child, who automatically reaches for her hand. The spontaneous gesture of trust plucks at her emotions. The child is so diminutive – she barely comes up to thigh level – and Isabella is filled with a fierce protectiveness; wonders again how anyone could inflict harm on so small a being. Remembers reading once how certain birds protect their young when they are threatened by predators by feigning injury and deflecting attention away. She had marvelled at that.

The entrance to the harbour is marked by the small weatherboarded coastguard's office and the old granite boathouse with a ramshackle hut tacked on to it. Peering into the dim interior, she can make out a large winch. A lifebelt is roped to the window outside, and below it is a Ministry warning not to bring animals into Great Britain. She stops to read it, curious; also the list of harbour dues. The notice looks as though it has been there for ever. The wording is old-fashioned, and she finds herself smiling as she reads; feels as though she has stepped back into a safer place that has about it an immutable quality. More than anything, this notice brings home to her the utterly different life she is about to lead. Here she is: the original London girl, having wandered into an isolated village at whose very core lie the sea and fishing, and whose people have been bound up with both for generations.

A lichen-covered wall runs round the building and a boy and girl sit astride it back to back, swigging from cans and turning to kiss in between. So young. Fourteen at most. Smoking.

Never smoke, her mother said as she lay dying.

Fishing boats are hauled up on a concrete hard-standing, and beside one, on a square of canvas sheeting, a tangle of cuttlefish writhe balletically. The child stares with huge, transfixed eyes. A couple of other fishing vessels rest on the shingle, and a man repainting the registration number on the hull of his touches his denim cap in greeting as they pass. In the other a young fisherman with sun-bleached hair and a tattoo of an anchor on his cheek is dismantling the outboard engine.

They pick their way between heavy chains and mooring blocks, lobster pots, nets and seaweed deposits towards the sea, their feet crunching and sinking amongst the stones and coarse sand. The child lifts each leg uncertainly, high at the knee, comically – like a hackney pony – before setting it down and letting her foot test the yielding ground beneath it.

The tide is out, leaving a glistening tongue; and they stop just short of where the lip of wet sand begins. The child frowns, as though puzzling at the expanse of water before her; turns to Isabella as if for explanation.

'It's called the sea,' she says, gesticulating with her arm. Repeats the word several times.

'Sea.'

'That's it! Yes, that's it, carina!' Whirls her around in a circle. Their laughter. The child's laughter. High peals. Such a beautiful sound. For Isabella it validates everything she has done over the last few days.

One or two people are watching them, smiling; and yes, they probably present an attractive picture. Fleetingly she sees themselves as others might: a mother and daughter playing together. Alike with their red hair.

She puts her lips to the child's ear and points to herself. 'Mummy.'

The child does not react. Engrossed by the serrated rim of the sea rolling in and out.

'Shall we go? Would you like to walk or go in the stroller?'

When the child makes no response, Isabella stoops to lift her into the buggy.

'No.' Hannah shakes her head firmly.

Isabella tests her: 'You don't want to go in the stroller, cara?'

But it is all she can get out of her; the single 'no'.

It is enough. Her report tonight will be like a fat chicken.

The village's main street has few shops: a chandler's, a barber's, a tea room, a chemist's that also sells knitwear, and the post office stores, wedged between a pair of disused lime kilns and the Sun. She remembers from years ago that it was less spoiled than other villages – too small, maybe, or too remote. And there is no bathing beach. She guesses the bulk of the tourists would head for St Mawes or Mevagissey, or further afield to St Austell or Falmouth.

Displayed outside the post office is a basket of sea urchins on an elm stool. Round like ogen melons, purple, and speckled with raised white freckles, they look as if they have been crafted from porcelain. 'Help yourself. £1.50 each. Put in box,' is written trustingly on the card threaded on to a long stick like a flag in their midst. Another basket is piled with free-range eggs, and beside it is a stack of egg-boxes. Alloy buckets are filled with both fresh and dried flowers, and wooden crates are piled with fruit and vegetables. It is an enticing place.

Babs Carrick is in her late forties or early fifties. She is well groomed and has an American accent.

'Canadian actually,' she says, when Isabella comments on it. 'And I thought I sounded thoroughly Cornish.'

She has an easy smile; striking, Nordic features.

Isabella explains she is looking for a cottage to rent.

'Somebody mentioned Timothy Abell's cottage,' she says.

'You kidding? That place is a dump.'

'Well, is there anywhere else you know of? I'd like to stay here in Pengarris.'

'Wee-wee,' says the child.

Isabella is caught by astonishment. Tries not to let it show in her expression.

'I'm so sorry. Do you have a loo she could use?'

'Of course . . . And that's another thing,' Babs Carrick says, leading the way. 'Timothy Abell's cottage only has an outside one.'

But there is nothing else in the village, and she digs out the estranged daughter's number for Isabella. Writes down her own also.

'You can always come and have a civilised bath in my place,' she says. Adds, 'I do hope you rent somewhere near here. It would be nice to have someone to . . . well, you know what I mean.'

'Yes.'

Instinctively knows she has a friend.

The cottage is a five-minute walk from the centre of the village and is one of the row she noticed earlier on the western headland; the last of a whitewashed terrace of four. It is reached from the lane by a concreted cutting which continues to the lighthouse. Steps hewn into the rock lead to a timber jetty below and to the cove; but only when the tide is out.

Standing in the shelter of the porch, out of the buffeting wind, and with her arm about the child, Isabella can hear the sea slapping against the rocks; can look out on to the entire harbour, part of the village – seen from here as a warren of cottages and roofs – and the opposite headland. Behind the terrace the hill forms a steep escarpment with clumps of purple heather between yellow gorse and bracken. A short paved path ascends to the bleak little chapel, which would not inspire her to religion. Behind it the coastal path climbs and winds out of sight.

The cottage's windows are sixties replacements carved into walls that must be at least two foot six thick. When she leans her elbows on the sill, scabs of cobalt paint and desiccated wood come away beneath the pressure. Through the filthy glass she can just make out a small square room with khaki walls, and an armchair on rockers. She wanders round with the child, squinting through other foggy windows. Discovers the outside toilet. It is a stinking cubby-hole of leaves, mud, cobwebs and old urine. But it could be cleaned up, and it is only a stone's throw from what appears to be the kitchen – she can see a big earthenware sink when she stands on tiptoe. She tries to imagine them living here; visualises: white paint over the Anaglypta, rugs, plants, a few pieces of decent, inexpensive furniture. It needn't cost a lot.

That evening she rings Timothy Abell's daughter. Her voice is curiously monotone. Reminds Isabella of a sloth who has recently awoken from a long sleep. There is no indication of surprise at her call. A meeting is set up for the following morning. Afterwards, she accesses her answerphone.

'Hi, it's me,' says Peter. He sounds like the hesitant boy she first met. 'Where are you? I've tried you twice.' Pause, as though considering what to say next. 'Everything's going really well . . . Listen—' Another pause. 'I need to speak to you. Could you ring me?' Articulates the number clearly.

She does not write it down. There is no need to phone back. It is only to tell her he wants to break it off. And what does she feel? Nothing. Another woman knew him.

A member of the Women's Awareness group, asking if she can host the next meeting, as the woman whose home it should be at has been rushed into hospital.

Her agent: 'I'm sorry, I lost your mobile number. Let's hope you access this. We've got the deal. Phone me ASAP.'

She does so. He sounds ebullient. He is young, enthusiastic, only recently set up on his own; looks like a tubby undergraduate and wears bow ties.

'Well, congratulations,' he says when he hears her voice.

Tells her a contract is being drawn up. 'Five thousand,' he says; and she can almost hear him rubbing his hands. 'I got them up from four and a half. Good, wasn't it?'

'Brilliant.'

'Split the usual way: signature, delivery, publication. Six months to do it. I thought that pretty fair.'

She works it out: ten pages a day, six hundred pages in sixty days – leaving her time for other work. But there is the child to look after, and the cottage to make habitable. Calculates: at least ten days before they sign. She can organise the cottage in that time. Another week settling in. And then she can get down to work.

'OK.'

'You don't seem very excited.' He sounds nettled.

'No, no, it's great, really.'

'So how's Cornwall?'

'Lovely.'

She gives him her mobile number again, and tells him she'll let him know her address for the contract.

She eats downstairs by herself. The child took longer than usual to go to sleep – overexcited, spinning about with that artificial energy that stems from tiredness and culminates in tears. Every ten minutes Isabella slips upstairs to check on her. Only one other table is occupied, by an elderly couple who do not speak to each other except for the briefest of exchanges.

'Nice piece of beef, this.'

'Yes.'

Without glancing up from their plates. She used to see this with her own parents. There was either silence or yelling; rarely anything in between. But her father looked at her, Isabella, with love. Was her mother jealous of their closeness? And with that one fleeting error he demolished it.

She finishes her own meal – chicken in a mustard sauce

– and goes over to the bar to get a second glass of red wine. Several men are drinking there. Dick is chatting to an immense, bearded man wearing jeans tucked into hiker's boots. Lizzie, Dick's wife, appears, pink-faced from the heat of the kitchen, bearing a plate in either hand, and two men move away from the bar, to a table.

'Chicken all right?' she throws over her shoulder to Isabella.

'Delicious.'

'That'll please her.' Dick breaks off from his conversation with the tall man. 'It's the first time she's made it. She was fretting. Here, have this one on me.' Refilling her glass.

'So you've got the MG,' the man with the beard says.

'Yes.' She can't believe his height. He must be at least six foot six or seven.

'I used to have one. An earlier model, though. Chrome bumper. The Roadster, not the GT.'

He is as softly spoken as he is immense. A rolling accent like treacle falling off a spoon. Open, honest features.

'Did you sell it?'

'Yeah. It was years ago now.'

'Go on, Aidan.' Dick leans over and stabs his shoulder with a finger. 'Tell her what you've got now.'

'No, it's not impor—'

'He's got an old Aston, and an XK150.'

'Leave off, Dick . . . I'm doing up the old Jag,' he says to Isabella; looks apologetic and embarrassed, as though afraid he might appear to be showing off. And she warms to him.

'Aidan owns the garage on the corner of the green,' Dick informs her.

'Oh, how funny. I made a note of the phone number from your board outside, as my car's always going wrong.' As she says it she can clearly see the mechanic on the forecourt, his gaze lancing her. Banishes the image. 'In fact I think the suspension's collapsed.'

'More'n like. Car's so low on the ground. And these lanes won't help none.'

'I'm beginning to realise that.'

'There's a concealed dip in the road 'tween here and Pengarris that'll do the trick, if nothing else does.'

'I found it.' Twice. There and back. Her car seemed momentarily to take flight, before banging down with a sickening thud. He laughs when she recounts it. His laugh is a deep rumble like a mild earth tremor.

She has her red wine, buys one for Dick, and another for herself. Offers to buy one for Aidan.

He declines. 'I'm old-fashioned like that,' he says. 'It feels wrong having a woman pay. I'll do the next round.' Assertively.

It transpires he has a blues group, and plays at local gigs or pubs.

'I used to have a group at university. The She-Wolves, we called it. I was lead guitarist.'

'You never!'

They smile at one another. She is aware of feeling slightly tipsy: relaxed, warm, vivacious. And of fancying Aidan. Five days since that last time with Peter, and she can feel the tiny pulses ticking away between her labia; a tingling of the surrounding muscles.

'If ever you need a female guitarist,' she says.

'Well, I might just take you up on that.'

'You two should do a deal,' says another man next to him, rather drunk and slurring.

'What's that, then?' Aidan asks. His black moustache and luxuriant beard are speckled with foam from his beer; he surely cannot feel it, but must know that there is a tendency for this to happen, as he wipes it away with the side of his hand. She wonders what the beard would feel like between her legs.

'She plays in your group and you fix her suspension.' The

man cackles raucously. Pulls his features into an insinuating leer.

'That's enough, Ed.' The humour gone from Aidan's voice.

'I have some work to do,' Isabella says abruptly.

'There, now you've offended the lady, Ed,' Dick chides him.

'Nah, she ain't offended, are you?'

'I really do have some work.'

And she does. Although this is not the reason for her sudden urgent need to leave. Nor is the drunk man's remarks, which don't bother her. Nor even her concern for the child upstairs, which is her next excuse. Framed in the doorway is the intense-eyed figure of the mechanic, just staring at her. How long has he been standing there, unnoticed?

And in echo of her thoughts, Aidan calls out, 'How long have you been standing there, Luke? Come and join us.'

The young man sidles over. He has a curious, silent, crablike gait. His head is shaven to a stubble.

'This is Isa . . . Mrs . . . What's your surname?' Aidan asks her.

'Mercogliano.' She can barely force her own name from her lips.

'Mrs Mercogliano's got an MGB. Suspension needs seeing to.'

On the bar stool beside him, Ed guffaws. The newcomer – now standing just to her left – mumbles something unintelligible and will not now meet her eyes.

'Is that an Italian name, then?' Aidan asks.

'Yes. Excuse me. I really—' Flings her hand out apologetically and hurries upstairs without finishing her drink. She feels quite unreasonably unnerved.

The child is whimpering in her sleep. Stops when Isabella strokes her forehead and hair.

She switches on the lamp by her own bed and sits down at her laptop computer on the extra table Dick has put in the room. Downstairs she can hear someone saying, 'Well, that were all a bit sudden.'

'Bit of a mystery woman, then.'

'I hear she's interested in old Timothy Abell's cottage.'

Wednesday evening, 4 September. What is she doing here? And on the mantelpiece of her kitchen in Hampstead is an embossed invitation for tonight for the opening of a new play at the Royal Court. Another world. And later there will be a party: a lot of air-kissing and performance post-mortems, and canapés and champagne.

She finishes the company profile. Will post it in the morning. At least that is out of the way. Writes up her report on the child. Gets ready for bed. The long-delayed rain rapping like a typist's fingers against the window.

She lies beneath the duvet, corpse-stiff, remembering: the second place she was sent. The boy, the son, had the same look in his eyes as the mechanic. The same obsessive, almost deranged look that drew and mesmerised and repelled. She had blocked it, along with other things.

Dreams. In it a man's arm encircles her tenderly and protectively. She doesn't know his name or who he is, but this is not as important as the feeling of safety and the sense of secure love transmitted to her soul. There is no great passion; but tenderness, knowledge of deep-rooted love and tolerance are present. A very great contentment spreads through her from the arches of her feet. She is sexually stirred, but it is incidental to the serenity within her. His body is Everest. She looks into his face to smile at him, and although gentleness exudes from his eyes she could not say what he looks like. She knows she wants to stay with him for ever.

In her dream she cries softly with happiness, for the beauty of it. Wakes from it, hankering like a widow.

5

Day six. Thursday.

The wide-panning countryside, the fecund hills, remind her. She was about four, and it is her earliest recollection of an outing to the countryside. Prior to that her memories are tiny distorted capsules: part of a room, a snatch of music, her mother laying the tables in the restaurant, the lamplit stretch of the street beneath her bedroom, strung out like a topaz necklace, a parade of shops not unlike the one where she first encountered the child. And inevitably these capsules with their selected contents are bound up with the perpetuity of the places. But that other day can be singled out, egregious in the repetitious pattern of her life: a first recorded glimpse beyond it, a consciousness of seemingly endless space, and of wanting to shout out with the joy of it.

Can such a young child as she was then appreciate that something is beautiful? Since then she has seen countryside that is more impressive by far than Box Hill; nevertheless it is that first long-ago taste of life on a bigger scale from her hitherto assumed parameters which has remained with her.

Her father took her. She went alone with him. He drove them in his newly acquired second-hand red Singer Gazelle. From time to time he pressed her hand as he drove. Innocent contact. She remembers him saying, 'Isn't it nice to be just the two of us, eh?' He always spoke in his native tongue to her. His English never seemed to progress much. Her mother had had to learn Italian. She remembers him singing on the journey (which seemed so long; endless). And herself giggling happily. Glad to be without the shouting. He had a fine singing voice. Her love of opera stems from him. He had a repertoire of all the more usual arias. *'La donna è mobile,'* his baritone would let rip. And he would swing his head in time from side to side and glance at her for her reaction, grinning.

'Te amo, cara.'

He was stout and on the tall side of average, with a large head crowned with wavy metallic hair of which he was overtly vain – she would often catch him combing it, grunting in satisfaction – and her black eyes. A bulbous nose sprang like a turnip from coarse, pitted skin – the result of boyhood acne. His mouth was an uncompromising line between a prominent jaw and prominent cheekbones. He could be morose one moment, jovial the next, with a boisterous humour and a delight in pranks. That same boisterous streak could quickly escalate into rage or tumble into sorrow. She saw similar traits years later in Tom.

That day at Box Hill they had cool drinks and lunch at a table outside a hotel; it was summer and she can even remember her dress, pale blue with smocking and puffed sleeves. Children dressed up in their best for outings in those day, she muses. Remembers dirtying it when she rolled jubilantly down a tempting bank, and the grass smears on the cotton and on her short white socks. The scuff marks on her new red shoes. Remembers lamenting the scuffs – she had been so thrilled with the shoes – and fearing her mother's wrath over them and over the grass stains.

'I'll tell her you fell,' said her father, the conspirator, who had encouraged her to roll down the hill.

Remembers something else, an incident that had nearly

put a blight on the magical day, but not entirely. There was a tennis court a few yards from their table and she was watching a couple playing when, before her eyes, a bird flew into the wire netting that fenced off the area. It seemed to fling itself straight at it. For a minute it struggled and fluttered, its head caught in the mesh, one wing at an unnatural angle, then the beads of its eyes closed and its small body dangled. She began screaming, standing there at the net – just like the child screams – and her father and several other people came chasing over: What's wrong? What's happened? And all she could do was scream and sob and point. And into her father's loving, protective arms she was hoisted up and cuddled and crooned over. Nothing untoward. Nothing except paternal concern and devotion.

Does not wish to think of him.

They drive past the sleeping primary school. It serves as a launching pad for further memories. When she was in the lower fifth they used to take turns helping dry up the dishes and cutlery – there was no machine; she can clearly picture the foul-mouthed cook with her salami arms. Relives the revulsion she experienced as she had to dry plates that had been hauled out of dung-tinted water with pieces of meat and vegetables and fatty bits floating about in it. Minestrone, they all used to call it. Whose turn for minestrone? And the cutlery smelt of stale breath. Remembers herself in a line-up of girls and boys, the matron going through their hair with a nit comb they nicknamed 'bug-rake'. Her mother would have been outraged had she been alive, would have taken it as a personal insult; she with her obsession for cleanliness.

'Lice *like* clean hair,' the matron would recite cheerfully, scraping at their follicles to loud 'ows' and protests.

One of the last images of her mother before she went into hospital: of her buffing the restaurant kitchen floor with dusters tied to her feet. And in a rare moment of fun, doing the twist at the same time. 'When I was a girl we were all taught to dance properly,' she said. 'Whatever class you were, you all had to be able to do the quickstep.' And a glimpse into her, of her, of how she had been before she was worn out.

They come to Aidan's garage. He is alone outside, changing the wheel of a car. On his head is a baseball cap pulled down against the drizzle. His overalls are stained. She toots and slows down, and he comes towards her smiling, wiping his hands on his thighs. He approaches the driver's side of the MG and bends to window level, almost filling it with his face and beard. Dark smears on his cheeks, and rain glistening on his beard. She unwinds the window and leans out. Unreasonably glad to see him. Has the urge to wipe the rain from his beard, the smears off his cheeks.

'I was thinking of you earlier,' he says, with complete naturalness. 'So how's you both, then?'

'Fine. We're fine. We're on our way to Timothy Abell's cottage. I'm hoping to rent it.'

'It could be made nice,' he says thoughtfully, nodding his head; the first person not to be negative.

She is heartened. There is a dependable quality about him, an old-fashioned, rather pedantic pragmatism: if he states something then one knows it is so.

'That's what I think. Look, I'm sorry if I seemed abrupt last night. I realise I dashed off rather quickly.'

'Well, you did a bit,' he agrees. 'I don't blame you, though. It was getting a bit . . . how'll I put it? Heavy?'

For a second she is tempted to tell him the truth: it wasn't that; it was . . . but the mechanic is his employee. In the ensuing pause they just grin at one another.

His huge bulk as he crouches down; the ghastly baseball cap which doesn't look bad on him; his honest, gentle eyes: she notes all these.

'Well, I'd better—'

'I was thinking,' he interrupts. 'I mean, it's probably a bit presumptuous' – rubbing his beard then his thick eyebrows – 'but I was wondering if you'd like to come to one of our gigs some time.'

'That would be nice. Oh, madre—' Remembers the child suddenly. 'I can't. There's Hannah.' Who, at the mention of her name, looks up sharply from playing with her bear.

So, she *does* know her name.

'I dare say Lizzie could keep an eye on her, though she might be a bit busy. Otherwise there's Sophia. You remember Luke, the chap who works for me? You met him last night. Sophia's his wife. She does childminding and cleaning. She's Italian too, or half, or something. I was going to say that but you didn't give me a chance. You were off, like someone'd put a live rod against you. Anyway, she'd help you out.'

'Oh, I'm not sure.' She wants nothing to do with the mechanic.

'You've nothing to worry about. She's ever such a nice girl. I know Luke can be a bit . . . well, between you and me, he's a bit of an oddball, but he's great with engines. She's not like him. I don't know what she sees in him, to be frank. She's rather shy. Loves kids. I could arrange for her to come to the inn.'

'I'd love to, then. Thank you.'

Gives him her mobile number, which he writes in blue Biro on his hand.

'Saturday? How would Saturday be?'

'Fine. Yes, fine.'

How extraordinary: she is shy. Isabella, with all her worldliness, is struck with shyness. Out of her own environment; strayed from her little sophisticated patch.

'Seven fifteen? I'll tell Sophia to be with you a bit before that. You'll want her to get to know your daughter.'

'That's a good idea.' Unused to a man who takes charge,

or to one who is considerate. Unaccustomed to not being
at the helm.

He straightens up slowly. 'See you, then.' Taps the window edge.

'Yes.'

A date. Is this a date?

'Remember the dip in the road,' he calls out as she
drives off.

She forgets. Grits her teeth.

'Wh-ee-ee,' the child squeals joyfully as the MG takes off
then bumps down.

'Bad car,' says Isabella.

'Bad car,' echoes the child.

A tea-coloured sky. The twin headlands enshrouded in
mist. The village huddled beneath a cloak of fine rain. A
sludge-grey sea.

Janet Abell is waiting at the cottage. She is probably about
fifty, although it is hard to tell. The moon of her face is
broken-veined but unlined. She has a rosebud mouth which
reminds Isabella of a knot in a balloon, and lachrymose
blue eyes. A scarf covers her hair, but a few lank beige
strands have escaped. Her voice is the same as it was on
the phone, like a well-rehearsed automaton, as though she
has only learnt with effort what to say in what context;
fed with the appropriate words. Her conversation itself is
normal enough, but the flat monotones convey no emotion.
Her mannerisms are gauche and ill co-ordinated, and her
features, as she speaks, immobile. Isabella wonders whether
she is slightly autistic.

Her son is with her; an overweight Down's syndrome boy
of about eight or nine who stands like a heavy, truncated
tree in the entrance, his hand slack in his mother's, thick
pink tongue lolling like a salmon steak out of his gaping,
drooling mouth. His foot kicks and scrapes at the ground,
which he gazes at steadily. Hannah does not take her eyes

off him. Isabella senses her tensing and picks her up. She suddenly recollects her dream of several nights ago, back in her flat: that she had adopted a Down's syndrome boy. How curious.

'You'll be – wanting – to look – around,' Janet Abell says in her robot tone.

'If that's OK with you.'

'Of course. I'm – afraid it's – a – mess. I haven't set – foot – in here for – years. I didn't know it – would be – like this. I'm – very sorry.'

'Please don't be. It's not your fault.'

The whole place is shambolic; but from the glimpse she had yesterday she had not expected otherwise. The sitting room has obviously not been touched since Timothy Abell's death. The carpet is like a dog with mange. The ceiling is tobacco-stained. In the grate the charred remains of logs poke out from a bed of ash. The low plastic-topped table still has bottles, mugs and glasses upon it, and an ashtray heaped with cigarette butts. She can see him, the old man, eagle-nosed, wizened-faced, in the brown vinyl chair, rocking to and fro in his carpet slippers. There is a beer glass in his hand, silver stubble frosts his face and his eyes are pinned to the television in the corner of the room. She can smell the staleness, the dank, the tobacco; his breath and irritability and loneliness. A man who shunned visitors. But there is a phone, she is glad to note.

The kitchen is poky and greasy, separated from the scullery – where the sink is – by a door; she would remove it to create a sense of space. Off there is a bathroom of sorts. It has a half-bath with a ledge to sit on. There is no space for anything bigger. Upstairs. And the curtains in the two dark bedrooms are still pulled closed. The bed in the larger room is unmade. Imprinted with the old man's hollow. And did he die in it? The wooden floor is swayed like an old horse, and his clothes are strewn about: underpants, grey trousers, a beige cardigan-jacket, navy flock dressing gown. The odours of age and sweat and cigarette smoke. She finds this evidence of his most personal life terribly poignant.

'I'd clean – it – up for you – first – of course,' Janet says, after Isabella tells her she would want to paint the inside. 'It's – disgusting,' she adds. And for the first time there is the faintest inflection in her voice.

When Isabella asks about the furniture, a note of vehemence creeps into her tone: 'I'll get the – lot – burned. I'll be – glad to – burn it. His – clothes – too. He were – cruel, he were. This – weekend. I'll – do it – all – this weekend. You can – have it from – Monday.'

'How will you shift the furniture?'

'I know – someone.'

The 'someone' hangs mysteriously in the air.

They discuss a fair rental.

'Oh no – that's – too much,' Janet protests when Isabella suggests four hundred a month for a period of six months. 'Specially as – you'll be – prettying it up, like.'

She has a point. They settle on two hundred for the first couple of months, and four hundred thereafter. In the kitchen Isabella writes a cheque out in advance, for the first instalment, after establishing that the woman has a bank account.

'Oh no, that's – not – necessary.'

'Please take it.' Thrusts it towards her across the Formica worktop upon which is a plate with the congealed remains of a meal. On it rest a knife and fork neatly together. Beside the plate is an open bottle of tomato ketchup, the contents green with mould. Timothy Abell's last supper. She is suddenly filled with pity for him, cantankerous though he obviously was. His loneliness lingers tangibly, thick as the grime. Sorrier, by far, for this woman with her hard life and its lack of chances; her lost love, her strange, gauche mannerisms, and her son – now mumbling incomprehensibly whilst plugging his nostrils with two fingers of his left hand. His other hand is crushing a pastie his mother has given him. But the 'someone'. She remembers the 'someone'. It must be a man. A married one? Not at weekends. She hopes he is significant. Can well imagine men taking advantage of Janet Abell, and that she would succumb easily, out of gratitude.

'You're very – kind.' Janet folds the cheque carefully and puts it in her purse. Fastens the press stud slowly and firmly.

'No I'm not. You've done me a great favour.'

And does Isabella truly believe she will be here six months hence? Who is to say what will have happened by then? She can only be thankful when another uneventful day has passed.

'Fears for the safety of a two-and-a-half-year-old girl, missing since the weekend, are growing,' says the solemn-voiced, serious-faced newsreader.

Isabella, at her computer, sits upright. She is rigid with shock. Her heart seems to stop beating completely. Then slowly it starts again, accelerating as though there is a machinegun in her breast.

'The mother, Mrs Winnie Edwards, today made an impassioned plea for the return of her child.'

And there she is, the mother: 'If anyone has got my little daughter . . .' Too overcome to talk, tears pouring down her cheeks.

And tears down Isabella's. Swallowing down hysterical laughter. Sagging into her chair.

The woman is black. Afro-black. The child is called Louise.

But how is it that until now she has heard nothing, read nothing, about this missing girl? Could Hannah's absence, too, have been reported without her being aware? And the mother's anguish haunts her.

'Oh Hannah, Hannah.'

Gathers the child to her. Tries, but fails, to draw reassurance.

She was one of the youngest in her year at university: a month away from her eighteenth birthday. Teamed up with Sally straight away: a winsome fair-haired girl with lashings of black mascara, and a humour at gutter-odds with her convent school background. In their second term they formed the She-Wolves. In the third she met Tom. Married him in the summer vacation after a night of incredible sex. He was seven years older than her, and was a reporter for the *Western Daily Press* when she met him; but he had higher ambitions. He was restless, passionate, intense, scathing, fearsomely knowledgeable on numerous topics, self-centred; spoke – in his upper-class accent – at the rate of a runaway hare, or when bored would sit in hooded-eyed, excluding silence. He was pro-devolution, anti-monarchy, anti-Establishment – he would raze the House of Lords – and was a doppelganger for Steve McQueen. He was witty, sardonic, seductive, possessive and irresistible. Like her he loved both opera and rock music. The night before they married they were each wearing headphones while they made love to *Der Rosenkavalier*. After the wedding they headed south-west on his Harley Davidson. She recalls roaring away on the bike after saying, 'I do'. Laughing with a sense of unreality. The only other time she has ever done anything impulsive.

Tom drained her emotionally at times and buoyed her at others. He was not always rational, and there were occasions when she was not sure he wasn't a bit mad. Once, they were taking a short cut through a cemetery and he lay down on a gravestone and closed his eyes. She was appalled. People were staring.

'Get up, for God's sake, get up,' she begged.

'I'm tired,' he said, not budging. 'Go back by yourself if you're embarrassed. You care too much what other people think.'

And yes, that might have been true. It was a proven way of getting by.

Everything about him was so extreme: his obsessions, his generosity, his opinions, his impetuousness – so opposite to her steadiness. And just when she would be thinking, What have I done? I'm going to leave him, I can't take any more of this, he would become the gentlest, kindest, most tender man in the world. His 'sweetest Isabella-Bella', he called her.

She moved into his studio flat, an American-style loft in the old docks area, where many of the warehouses that fringed the wharf were being transformed into trendy housing. You had to climb a wooden ladder to the galleried bed. She loved living by the dark river: the way a mist often hung over it and lent it an ethereal bleakness, especially first thing in the morning; the odd plaintive hoot from a small tanker or tug; the mingled odours of the city and of oil, and salt blown from the sea; the greedy, quarrelsome ducks and swans. And just a minute away was the Mermaid Theatre, where she would attend rehearsals; her autograph book contained dozens of well-known names ('How very bourgeois,' Tom commented when he discovered she collected autographs). She could walk to the university from the flat. Lewis's was convenient. And the BBC. She and Sally were interviewed one evening to talk about the She-Wolves.

'And I gather you met your journalist husband when your band was playing at a private party,' said the interviewer.

'Well—' Isabella knew Tom would be writhing if he were listening.

'He was a guest, wasn't he? Very romantic.'

'That was excruciating,' he told her when she got back, and went into one of his sulks.

'I'm going freelance,' he announced one day in March 1977, when they had been married a year and a half.

'I'm going to Vietnam,' he said a week later, after three days of barely speaking. 'They need reporters out there.'

And returned more than a year later when she had graduated and taken a job. She read his articles meanwhile, heard him over the airwaves, saw him with a microphone in hand, vocalising in his crisp, incisive tones about the problems of the new republic. So strange seeing him, the stranger she'd married, on television, in his khaki shorts, with his tousled bleached hair and charming smile. He was unconnected to her. They had never met, never married, never made love. Yet she was in his flat. After the initial flurry of letters and a couple of hopeless attempts on the telephone, the correspondence dwindled. There were perhaps two or three perfunctory letters over nine months, written by someone who could have been anyone, to someone who could have been anyone. She was married, but not. She longed to be angry with him. He returned an alcoholic and a womaniser, unable to settle to anything. His favourite scornful put-down aimed at her was: 'You haven't a clue. You're so smug.' He was vitriolic towards everyone.

'This country stinks. People are so petty. Petty, prurient, pusillanimous.'

'So why did you come back?'

'Sometimes I wonder.' Looking through her with loveless, lonely, icy eyes which made her shrivel.

'Because,' he said another time, 'Vietnam is in chaos. Because the involvement with Kampuchea is going to escalate. Because the north and south are still irreconcilable. Because I don't owe them anything, and I don't want to grow old there. Because it wipes you out in the end. And you love it and you hate it.'

And that summed it up. Him up. He was forever searching. A searcher. It struck her he would never be satisfied for more than a few months at a time.

'You're drinking too much.'

'Don't nag.'

'Madre, this is hopeless.'

'Yes, it is.'

Divorced before she was twenty-five. She recuperated in Paris for three years.

Day seven.

I've adopted a child from Bosnia, she has decided to tell her friends eventually, when she can no longer keep them at bay. Imagines their astonishment.

It takes ages to drive the few miles to King Harry Passage, as she has to keep pulling over to make way for cars coming in the opposite direction. Once she is forced to reverse about a hundred yards along the lane. Gives a 'V' sign to the tractor who just keeps coming at her. Then she is stuck behind another tractor with a trailer-load of manure behind it. Bits flying up and splattering the windscreen. Straw raining.

'Phooee.' Turning to the child, snorting and wrinkling her nose.

The child laughs. 'Ph,' she says, then imitates the snorting sound.

There is a familiarity about the lanes. She can remember a particularly pretty thatched cottage, and a whitewashed pub she and Tom ate in. Themselves streaking through the countryside. Greenery flashing by. Leaning over so close to the ground as they negotiated bends that she could almost have laid her shoulder against the tarmac.

'Slow down.'

'Why?' laughing.

'I'm frightened.'

'Don't be feeble.'

But when she said, 'You might run over an animal,' he slowed instantly.

They park in a line of other cars and wait for the ferry to clunk across the Fal from the opposite side. Stand outside the car. Isabella's arms tight around the child, holding her flat against her. The air bracing. The seagulls and kittiwakes screeching and circling and diving. A fine veil of rain falling on the expanse of grey water that is dotted with craft: dinghies, fishing boats, small freighters, yachts. And the ferry making its noisy, lumbering passage like a giant steel crate, its twin prows like camel humps, distancing itself from the wooded bank behind it as it draws towards their side on its chains.

She counts the cars as they are driven off, enunciating clearly for the benefit of the child.

'Twenty-three,' she says as the last vehicle disembarks.

Then it is their turn. They are guided on to the boat by a brown-faced young ferryman.

'Handbrake on,' he reminds her. 'Return?'

She nods, hands him two pounds seventy-five; feels a childish sense of anticipation: the boat looks such a bizarre Heath Robinson contraption. When all the cars have been packed on the other ferryman hops up a stepladder and into the driving cabin, perched above one of the prows. From the belly of the boat there comes a metallic grating, a resounding hammering from the engine, grinding of the chains, as gradually the ferry slides forward, then gathers pace, and they are conveyed across.

The child gazes, bird-curious, all about her, her face undergoing a rapid sequence of expressions. She seems to hesitate, then her features concertina into each other and her skin darkens. Isabella hauls her on to her lap just as she begins to bellow. She cradles the child's head; lays her cheek against Hannah's wet one.

'Carina, everything's fine. We're on a boat. Look, we're crossing the water to the other side.'

She quietens. Nowadays it does not take a lot to calm her. She trusts Isabella. It is as though she screams as much from habit as anything else, as though she is thinking: I should be afraid, and behaves accordingly. One day maybe she will not be scared of the unknown. Isabella hopes upon hope that she will be there for that day. Certainly she will have contributed to it. Will anyone believe that?

They stand by the barrier. She points out different types of boats, a couple of massive oil tankers, the reflections on the water, swans.

'And it's stopped raining.' Hugs the child to her: pretty, so pretty, in her yellow bomber jacket, and with her wind-swept curls.

They are fourth in line to disembark. She feels light-headed, as though she has stepped off a fairground ride.

They pass the Trelissick Gardens; and suddenly an image flashes before her of the yard at the back of the restaurant, the spilling dustbins, and a cat her mother was forever shooing off; the cracked concrete with weeds sprouting through (the canary ate the groundsel); and a single valiant small purple flower that gave her hope.

The sign for a village called Come-To-Good makes her smile, and she puzzles over how it might have derived its name.

Beside her, Hannah sleeps. It occurs to her that so long as she has the child she will never again be alone. And her obsessive dread of her own death which sometimes has kept her awake at night, the almost paranoid terror at the prospect of never being part of life again – of nothingness – has for the moment been quiesced. Is this one reason, she wonders, why people want children? To enable them to confront their own mortality?

In Truro she parks in Lemon Quay, by the Pannier

Market. The buildings are an odd amalgam of Georgian, Victorian and Art Deco. The cathedral's spires loom over the city. A zeppelin balloon floats overhead.

'Wake up, Hannah, cara.' She covers the child's slack hand with her own.

The child stirs. Eyes opening – befuddled, then clearing. Her dazzling smile.

'Mummy.'

Joy lancing through her. It floods her head. She can barely contain it. But she knows it is important not to make an issue out of every new word, whatever its magnitude to herself.

'We're going for a walk round the town.'

'Walk?'

'Yes. With the buggy.'

It seems that each minute brings a new surprise; and each to her is a reward that she wishes could be stored so that it could be recaptured at will, as one can look upon a photograph. In the past she has seldom bothered to take them. Now she has a reason: And this was my daughter when she was two and three-quarters . . .

Who is she fooling?

But already she cannot conceive of life without Hannah. In a short space of time Hannah's presence, Hannah's welfare, Hannah's progress, Hannah's pleasure, have become more meaningful than anything she has known. Her own happiness has become inextricably linked to this small person's. And the front page of today's *Guardian* reported that the foster father of a six-year-old girl had just been arrested for her murder. He had sexually assaulted her first. He was a schoolteacher with his own kids. Oh madre, she cannot stand hearing about these cases. Incidents like these confirm that she did the right thing.

They turn into Lower Lemon Street, a cobbled lane lined with shops. Midday, and the city is bustling. Isabella weaves the stroller between the legs of shoppers, the leftover tourists, businessmen, office lunchers; past an old-fashioned perfumery, a jeweller's, a coffee shop – and the smoky aroma from within drifts in a tantalising cloud.

A commemorative statue in Boscawen Street draws her attention and she stops to read the plaque on the plinth. It is dedicated to a soldier killed in the Falklands in 1982. Madre, how long ago that seems. And yet not. She can remember all the controversy at the time. And the shock of seeing Tom on television – referring to an idiotic war perpetrated by a batty English female führer for her personal vanity. For a couple of minutes he raged uninterrupted, watched by millions of astonished viewers, herself included, until a hand yanked the microphone from him, severing his invective midstream. The papers were full of it the next day: he was being sent home in disgrace. Unrepentant. Remembers being amazed – dismayed – to find she still had feelings for him. And until a few nights ago she saw or heard nothing more about him. So now he is making documentary films.

Through the web of streets she and the child wander. In the tourist information office she helps herself to a score of assorted leaflets, maps and guides. In Smith's she buys a book on child psychology. Browses in Monsoon. Shares chicken nuggets and chips out of a paper bag with Hannah. Through the open door of a fish restaurant with Mediterranean-style awnings waft the tobacco odours of char-grilling, along with 'Nessun Dorma'. I might eat here some time, she thinks. Take Aidan? Knows he would never permit that. *Her* taking him. And what of romance, with him or anyone? Now there is the child, what time, what chance for romance; or lust? Down an alley she espies a fortune-teller's. Ten pounds for laying a rosy future before her. A billboard on the wall of a shop selling fishing tackle advertises the films showing at the four-screen Plaza.

At the City Hall tonight is a concert in celebration of Schubert's bicentenary . . . Isabella familiarising herself, casting to memory the names of streets and shops. Treading down roots.

. . . And, Isabella Mercogliano, This Is Your Life!

A policeman directs her to a furniture store. She finds it behind wrought-iron gates: three floors of rattan, pine, rugs and terracotta in a Victorian warehouse. She can order everything she needs from this one shop. Tells the salesman she wants it delivered in a week's time. Assumes he must be on commission, to judge by his ear-splitting grin as he writes down the address with painful care.

They head for the cathedral; and even as they stand by one of the great arched doorways she can feel that desolation pressing down on her, that familiar darkness taking hold.

'*Ny agas Dyn Ergh*,' a notice says; and underneath, the Celtic is translated: 'Welcome to Truro Cathedral'.

She reads it aloud to the child. 'This is a big church where people pray to God,' she says. Feels hypocritical. Just inside the entrance she falters. Yet it is her very reluctance which impels her to go in. Wherever she is. Facing her phobia.

'May I show you round?' A woman guide smiling beatifically at her.

'Thank you, but there's not really time—'

But the woman persists, and she asks a few polite questions; follows the flapping skirt down the nave. Can feel her heart beginning to fill her chest.

'It's the first Anglican cathedral since St Paul's . . .'

The woman's voice, echoing like tin, merging with other echoes and whispers and footsteps. The flashbulbs of cameras.

'Work started on it in 1880, but it wasn't completed until 1910 . . .'

It is always the same: the apocryphal, sinister atmosphere

wrapping round her like a carapace. It is as though her own death is rearing before her, mocking at her atheism and the residue of guilt, the sense of blasphemy she still feels and which occasionally induces her to pray; in case. Her mother so peaceful as she died. Knows she will not be peaceful.

'Hannah go. Hannah go.' The child beginning to sob loudly, raising her arms to be picked up. The sobs becoming wails that rebound off the stone and are hurled from wall to wall, ricocheting in piercing shock waves across the vaulted ceiling.

'I'm sorry. My daughter—'

Fumbles for two pound coins in her wallet as a donation. Grabs Hannah, grabs the buggy.

'And the organ is a Father Willis,' the woman calls desperately after them.

The glorious fresh air. Fresh drizzle on their faces, and the moist leaves of the trees in the square. Strutting pigeons. The reality of the shops: Marks and Spencer's; Lunn Poly travel agency promoting far-off dreams. The post office – and a queue visible inside. Secular, selfish, capitalistic relief.

The child is tranquil again.

'Poor Hannah. Poor little cara. Were you scared?'

And one day will it befall Isabella to tell her about God?

. . . Well, this being may or may not exist. Some people believe . . . whilst others believe . . . There again . . . And whilst I don't wish to influence you, I myself . . .

When she was a girl the Trinity had been laid before her, irrefutable, along with her blue puffed-sleeved dress on the bed and fish on Fridays. No other possibilities had been mooted. Religion was a fact, as much a part of her life as the restaurant and the rows. The computer age, but a decade away, was a mere hint, like the wash on watercolour paper before the tint is applied. PC meant police constable, and he usually rode about on a bike. Women did not sue for sexual harassment. Feminism was a rumble when she was ten; and the Female Eunuch was four years away. Stephen Hawking was only just going up to Cambridge, and God still had the edge over the Big Bang. Madre, what does she know about bringing up a child in today's world? Where are the guidelines for her?

I'll be honest with her. The main thing is to be honest.

Honest? How can she be honest when she has acquired the child by deception in the first place?

Mummy, why do you dye my hair? Mummy, who's my father?

I adopted you. There was this frightful war and . . .

'Bruises almost gone,' she writes in her report that evening. 'Hannah has strung words together for the first time, and has expressed her needs. Her progress is staggering. Doesn't this prove that what I did was correct, if unorthodox? She called me "Mummy".'

Up springs the prosecutor in her head. Retributive Jack-in-the-box: This woman is obviously suffering from delusion. She does not know the meaning of honesty. She has been living a lie through the child, even going so far as to encourage the little girl to call her 'Mummy'. Exploiting her for her own dubious aims. Ladies and gentlemen of the jury . . .

Isabella extinguishes the prosecutor's malevolent flame; she plans the evening's work. Garibaldi's pitiful mewing as he winds himself round her ankles. Stuck in here for at least another week. Hannah sprawled in front of the television, spooning chocolate mousse into her mouth. And Isabella has a sudden image of Aidan; his big, bearded face grinning at her from beneath the baseball cap.

She is absurdly excited about seeing him tomorrow. In London it would not occur to her to go out with someone like him. Like him? She cannot know what he is *like*. But the owner of a tinpot garage in the middle of nowhere? A man with a thick Cornish accent. Wonders what she has let herself in for, going to hear him play in some pub. Envisages a roomful of beer-swilling yokels, and him barely able to sing or play the guitar. Is embarrassed in advance. Then she immediately chides herself for being superficial, too image-conscious, and for intellectual snobbery – all of which have no place in her life now. She wonders how old he is. Probably at least her age. And that will make a change. She only hopes they will have a chance for some time alone together. And now she worries that he might not be attracted to her at all, that he only asked her out of kindness, because she mentioned about the She-Wolves.

Isabella is like a teenager about to embark on a first date; tingling at the prospect of seeing Aidan. And tomorrow will be the eighth day, but exactly a week since she abducted – I did not abduct her, she was sent to me – the child.

'I tired,' Hannah says. Goes over to her bed by herself and clambers on to it. Curls up like a mollusc.

6

Remembers: her mother battling to keep the restaurant going. But the customers had liked her father. The authentic Italian. Trade slumped. Her mother's cancer thrived. The defiant red lipstick in a shrunken monkey face.

The third place. They were both schoolteachers; serious-minded, decent people with their own three children: one daughter at university, a shy, studious son a couple of years younger than herself and another, much younger daughter. They were a pleasant family, not affectionate or demonstrative – she cannot recall any of them kissing or hugging – but encouraging, open-minded and respectful of other opinions. They had a poodle – he was bald in patches – who tried to fornicate with her ankles. She would go red and keep thrusting it away until eventually he would give up. For want of anything better he would resort to the cushions.

'He's been at it again,' the mother would say calmly, picking up another slime-streaked cushion.

She was closest to the young daughter. Read to her. Played the guitar to her, which she had recently taken up. Plaited her long, mousy hair. I like you, the girl said, looking straight ahead of her. And Isabella can remember the glow within her that this gave her. For a second she paused in weaving the hair, and then she resumed it as though nothing had been spoken.

It was a contented six months. But the area was rough, and the father was beaten up one evening when he tried to prevent some youths from stealing his car. He died in hospital a week later.

This time they advertised her. She saw it in the local paper. Like she was a dog or cat: 'Isabella is an intelligent, attractive, well-adjusted girl of nearly sixteen . . .' Shopping for a family. She felt so humiliated seeing that advertisement. Perhaps more than anything it brought home to her her true situation. Impermanence. She was important to no one. I love you, a boy at school said. So she lost her virginity to him. He didn't speak to her the next day and later she gathered he was going around boasting and laughing about it. And the bruises on her back, from pressing against the wall, still sore. The dread she might be pregnant. Her misplaced trust in a single word.

I matter. She covered an entire page of her Latin exercise book with it. And in French, another page: *Je suis importante*. And Italian: *Sono importante*. And on the fourth page she quoted from first Walt Whitman, then Browning: 'I celebrate myself, and sing myself.' 'My care is for myself; myself am whole and sole reality.' And then her own words: 'I shall not be erased. I.I.I.I.'

Sophia is a small shrew of a girl with sleek olive skin. A ring through her left nostril emphasises her long razor nose, and is incongruous with her otherwise conventional dress. She has silky brown hair cut in a slanting bob. Isabella has never seen such silky hair, gleaming like glass.

It transpires that both her parents are Italian and that they have a restaurant in Fowey. Isabella extracts this information from her after several false starts.

'How funny. My parents had a restaurant too.'

The girl's eyes stray towards the television: a game show. Raucous laughter. 'Theirs is a fish and chip place,' she says.

The glimmer of a smile as one of the game contestants – a man wearing a luminescent fuchsia tie and with a mountainous belly – performs the tom-toms on his chest and gives a wail of despair when he hears he has just lost the car he had provisionally won a moment earlier.

'So do you speak Italian?' Isabella asks her, trying to draw her into further conversation.

'No. I was born here. The odd word. I can say the odd word, that's all.'

She tucks her hair behind one ear, and briefly meets Isabella's enquiring gaze with shy eyes that are like raisins. Her hands, Isabella notices, are tiny and delicate with pale round nails, and have a tendency to flutter upwards either to her hair and that same ear, or down, to the hollow of her throat where they rest as though feeling for a pulse.

But she is good with the child. With the child her shyness disappears and her expression becomes animated, her voice takes on a warmth. Hannah seems contented enough. Isabella hovers in the doorway.

'I'm not sure when I'll be back. It might be quite late.'

'It doesn't matter.' Kneeling on the floor now with Hannah, fitting together interlocking shapes to make a house.

'You'll be OK? She gets frightened very easily. She's very scared of sudden noises. She can scream really terrifyingly. Just pick her up and—'

'We'll be fine, won't we, Hannah?' Sophia says, touching the top of the child's head.

Sharp-toothed jealousy nipping at Isabella. She wills Hannah to resist Sophia, to run towards her and cling, shrieking, to her legs. She alone wants to be special to the child. Exclusivity.

'Well, you've got my mobile number if there's a problem.'

'Yes.'

Turning the handle. Reluctant to leave. Garibaldi's laconic stare from the pillow on her bed. She glances at her watch. Seven seventeen. She is two minutes late.

'I'd better be going.'

''Bye, then.'

'Yes, 'bye. 'Bye, cara.' Raising her voice to the child. Blowing a kiss and waving.

'By-ee' comes back to her, as the child glances up. Her happy ocean-coloured eyes. A tiny reciprocal wave of her hand, like a pansy folding and unfolding.

The By-ee, the sweet little wave, buoy her. Smiling all the way along the corridor and downstairs to the crowded bar; and at Aidan, who is looking at her as she makes her way towards him. He dwarfs everyone else around him. She feels a fanning of pleasure within her at seeing him again, combined with an unfamiliar nervousness that tweaks at her in small contractions.

'Hello,' he says.

'I'm sorry. Have you been waiting long?'

'Only a couple of minutes. But I think we should make a move.'

He is wearing a black suit and a white shirt whose top two buttons are undone. Dark hair springs up from his chest. She finds it hard not to keep looking at him; is unsure where to rest her eyes. For a woman whose calm confidence in all situations has often been commented upon, and who has mixed with all kinds of people, this is extraordinary, this sense of gaucheness with Aidan. She does not know what to say or how to behave with him. She cannot remember ever having been so physically affected by any man. Perhaps Tom. But she had been an impressionable girl then.

He opens the car door for her with old-fashioned gallantry.

'It's beautiful,' she says, tucking her knees into the Aston.

'She was a wreck when I got her. You'd never recognise her now.' Easing his bulk in beside her.

He drives off slowly. Silence is a mist between them. Her need to speak pinches her throat. She is still not sure whether or not this is a 'date', and therefore how to act accordingly. Feels disadvantaged. Perhaps he is a man who doesn't like to talk when he drives. And she doesn't know where they're going. Dull evening's light dulling further. Only just over a week ago she had sat on her patio with Peter, wearing her bikini still at eight in the evening. There's sweat in your cleavage, he said.

'You look pretty.' Aidan turning briefly to her – his teeth white in the darkness of his beard.

'Thanks.'

Nobody has ever told her that before; only her father, when she was a child. But not as a woman. Attractive, yes. Striking. Unusual. Even handsome. Occasionally, beautiful. But pretty, never. She has never thought of herself as pretty; has always considered herself to be too big, too strong-featured for the adjective to apply to her. Not delicate in any way.

'I wasn't sure what to wear,' she confesses. And now it occurs to her that the black trouser suit she settled on in the end matches what he is wearing.

He remarks on that: 'We match rather well. So, how did you get on with Sophia, then?'

'She seems a nice girl. Very quiet, like you said.'

'OK with your daughter, was she?'

'Yes. She obviously loves kids.'

'She does. To tell the truth that's why she married Luke in the first place. It was no secret. She was pregnant. Her family are strict Catholics. There was no question of . . . you know.'

'Yes. So she's got a child?'

'It died. Cot death, it was.'

'Madre, how awful. Poor girl.'

'Yeah. And now she's stuck with Luke.'

'Perhaps she loves him.'

The mechanic manifests himself: crablike, sinister. She wonders if he could have killed the baby.

'Who knows? Anyway, what about the cottage, then? You taking it?'

'Yes. From Monday.'

'How long for?'

'Six months.' She glances at him.

He nods several times, as though in satisfaction.

This topic keeps them going for about five minutes.

'You'll need some help doing it. I could help you if you like.'

Which means he intends to see her again. She sits back. Begins to relax.

'Where are we going?'

'Falmouth.'

'Oh, I thought it would be more local.'

'No. I do play at a couple of local pubs sometimes, but this is a wine bar. We're booked at ten for an hour. I'm taking you for a meal first.'

'Oh. That's nice.' A surprise, for sure.

'I wasn't sure what kind of food you'd like.' Takes his eyes off the road for a second to look at her. 'You being so, well, smart.'

'I'm not. Really I'm not.'

They park on the Moor, in the centre. A few people stop to watch as Aidan manoeuvres the old car into a space. He attaches the security device over the steering wheel and they get out.

'Don't you worry someone will vandalise it?' Isabella runs her thumb lightly along the polished metallic-grey side.

'It's a funny thing,' he says, locking both doors. 'People seem to respect her.'

(And that's something else, a woman said at the last Women's Awareness group meeting. Really it is so insulting the way men refer to machines as 'she'.)

He guides her by the elbow across the street; the few seconds' contact ricochets through her. Cool night settling. Illuminated shops, pubs. Narrow alleys. A clock striking the hour.

'It's always five minutes early,' Aidan comments.

He has a long stride. Walks slightly apart from her now; a head-up-eyes-forward walk. She is starting to be more comfortable with him, with the way he takes charge. A man with entrenched values, she guesses, who could be stubborn. But fair.

'At least it's not raining,' he says, turning to her. His eyes glint, caught in the brightness of a streetlight. His hair is blown back from his forehead in the slight breeze, and settles oddly in a centre parting.

'Left here.'

They go down some steps just past the Grapes Inn that lead to a small alleyway and thence the harbour. Between a sail-maker's and an antiquarian bookshop is tucked a restaurant guarded by a huge old ship's figurehead. Fishers, says the name painted in green on the white wall of the building.

'I don't know, you looked as though you might like fish,' he says, pushing open the door.

'I do. I love it. I hardly eat any meat.'

'It's the way a lot of people seem to be going, isn't it? Vegetarian.'

'You look as though you grew up on steak.' Alluding to his height.

The inside is decorated with marine artefacts, ship's instruments and shells; nets are slung across the ceiling. The tables are simple scrubbed pine, the floor stripped wood.

'I really wasn't sure where to bring you.'

The thought he has put into the evening touches her. As does his own obvious apprehension about it.

'Stop apologising. It's lovely.'

'That's fine, then.' Smiles at her properly for the first time.

A girl comes over and shows them to their table. Most of the others are already occupied. Theirs looks on to the harbour. The water blinking in black-and-silver crescents. Boat masts nudging each other. Momentarily she feels a surge of intense, pure happiness.

He is observing her. 'You have a very expressive face.'

'Do I?' She is taken aback. Can feel the heat rising in her neck. Bends her head to study the menu. The prices aren't too bad. She was worried it might be very expensive; that he might have brought her somewhere to impress her which would cost more than he could really afford. She chooses charcoaled brill with a lemon sauce. Melon as a starter.

'I'm not very good on wines,' he says. 'I haven't a clue really. Do you want anything in particular.'

'House wine's fine.'

'You sure?'

'Yes.'

With Peter she would have wrested the wine list from his hands and taken charge.

'White, then? I know that much. White with fish.'

'That's fine.'

Though in fact she tends to have red with everything, even with fish.

'So, is it true, what folks are saying,' he asks her, when the waitress has taken their order and returned with a bottle of Sauvignon blanc, 'that you've run off?'

His eyes are so kind. They spill honesty. And isn't it true that she has run off?

'In a way.'

'Was he bad to you, then, your husband?'

She could lie. Spin an elaborate tale that would evoke his sympathy.

'Aidan, I don't want to talk about it.' Which of course makes it sound like an affirmation.

'OK, then.'

'I didn't mean to be rude.'

'You weren't. And I wasn't meaning to be nosy. It's only I don't take out married women as a rule.'

And she has the same code. Does not go out with married men.

So now he will not want to see her again.

'But you're separated, so that's all right.'

They both take a few sips from their glasses. The wine is not bad; a bit sweet.

'What about you?' she says.

'Divorced. I've got two lads, aged fifteen and twelve. We rub along fine now, the ex and myself.'

'You wouldn't get back with her?'

'Not a chance. Anyhow, she's living with someone else. The lads seem to like him.'

The waitress appears, bearing Isabella's melon and his giant prawns. Vivaldi's *Four Seasons* playing softly in the background. She can never remember which concerto is which. They all sound so similar. Hacked to death. Peter once said that somebody should blow up every hotel, shop and restaurant that played it.

'You aren't jealous?' she asks, when they're alone once more. 'I mean, about the boys having another man about the house.'

'No, why should I be?' He sounds genuinely puzzled. 'Jealousy's so negative, isn't it? If you can't change something there's not much point getting worked up. I'm still their dad. It's up to me to show them. Be there for them. It's a question of being sensitive to their needs. We're supposed to be the grown-ups. Battling doesn't help the kids.' He snaps the leg of a prawn decisively. Squeezes lemon juice over it.

So – that is the preliminaries dealt with.

He is so reasonable; speaks with reassuring common sense in his accent that makes her think of rich soil and fertile plains. Possibly he is rather too serious, too literal; she cannot imagine him cracking jokes or having the quick repartee of the many men she has known. Tom, for instance. Others since, and most recently Peter. But theirs could be a vicious humour. Aidan would not be the sort to spear his victims and laugh at their misfortune. She has always considered this a peculiarly British trait. She often thinks the English do not really like each other.

'How did you start, with cars?'

He tugs on the blunt rim of his beard thoughtfully. 'Well, I was always keen. As a young lad motors fascinated me. I was forever tinkering when I should've been working. Old cars especially fascinated me. I did a couple of years at university then I dropped out.'

'Where? What were you studying?' She can't help being glad at this piece of information.

'Exeter. Zoology. I've always liked animals and nature. I seriously thought about training as a vet. I wish I had, now. My father was head gamekeeper and forester on a big estate Bodmin way, so I grew up with wildlife all around me. The house was always full of orphaned animals of one kind or another. Well, his boss collected classic and vintage cars, and I suppose you could say I became obsessed. So the die was cast, so to speak. Anyhow, when I was at Exeter I got hold of this old Austin Seven for next to nothing, then a Morris, in my second year, and sold them both for a fat profit after I'd done them up. Somebody asked me to restore a 1940 Alfa Romeo – and that was it. I told the old man I was leaving university. He went ape.' Laughs at the recollection. His laugh is a slow, low grumble. 'I still toyed with the idea of going to veterinary college, but cars kept rolling in. It was quite extraordinary . . .

'I did really well for quite a number of years. Buying, restoring then selling. Then, a while back, the market took a tumble and someone did the dirty on me – I shan't say more than that, but it was all very awkward as he was a contact of my brother-in-law's. So, anyway, now I've got the garage. It does OK. It's steady: it doesn't thrill me, but I'm my own boss. It pays the bills. And I've got time for other things.'

What other things? she wonders.

They have scarcely touched their food. The waitress peers over towards their table, at their plates, and flits past. She has a provocative walk, a microskirt, big, china-blue eyes; but his gaze does not stray.

'I'm sorry, I've been talking too much,' he says, cracking open prawn shells in quick succession and munching. 'These are ever so good. Almost sweet. Want to try one?'

She nods and he feeds her one with his fingers, smiling at her as she takes it between her lips. A desirous warmth rippling slowly up her inner thighs. And what is he feeling?

They finish their first course, during which he has requested more bread and is almost through the second lot. She marvels at the amount he can eat.

'It must cost a fortune feeding yourself.'

'Well, I do always seem to be hungry,' he says, wiping up the butter round his side plate with a chunk of poppy-seeded roll. 'And I'm not the biggest. My older brother's six eight.'

'What are you?'

'A smidgen under six seven.'

'How do you get clothes to fit?'

'With difficulty. Shoes are the worst. Ruddy great platters I've got. Size thirteen.'

'Madre.'

'Tell me about yourself. I've been banging on.'

'No you haven't.'

'Well, anyway.'

The next course arrives and they wait awkwardly while the girl sets their plates before them and lays fresh cutlery. Black pepper? Yes, thank you. Focusing on the pepper mill as she turns it. Her hands are a child's. Her skin is flawless. Enough? Yes, fine. Off she goes.

'Well?' he says.

Well.

His expression is interested, patient. He is not handsome – his face is too broad, his upper lip too thin, his grey eyes rather small and nondescript; but their directness is compelling. It is a good face, a face to trust, a face that says: this is how things are. No secrets. A face of character, with a few lines; and strength. It occurs to her that she hasn't been in this situation for years. Her boyfriends have invariably been much younger and she has played a role: sometimes the femme fatale, sometimes the mother. Always in control. And in between the longer relationships have been the shorter flings and the one-night stands. Since Tom there has been nobody with whom she has come close to falling in love. Never has she known what it is like to lean on a man or depend on him in any way, or reveal any vulnerability.

She prods at her food with her fork.

'My job, you mean?' she says.

'Well, it's a start.'

'I'm a translator and interpreter.' She takes a bite out of the fish. The brill is succulent, tangy-fresh.

'That's interesting. Now that's *really* interesting.' He leans forward across the table towards her, elbows resting either side of his plate. When he smiles she notices he has a dimple in his left cheek, just above the beginning of his beard. 'I knew you'd do something a bit different.'

'How? How did you know?' Tilting her chin; flirtatious for a moment.

'Everything. The way you dress. Your manner. Your eyes
– the way they look out at things . . . I can't put my finger
on it. It's just a way with you. So what do you have to do,
in your work?'

She explains it to him, tells him about the book contract;
the journals, the brochures and company reports, magazine
features.

'Anything, really,' she says. 'You name it. Anything
that needs translating. Interpreting's when you have to
accompany someone. Be there on the spot. It could be a
diplomat or a company director.'

'It fits in well with your daughter, then, your job.'

'Yes.'

'What's her name? I'm sorry, I've forgotten her name.'

'Hannah.'

And for the last hour or so she has not thought of her
once. Reproaches herself. Would a real mother have done
the same?

'Aidan, maybe I should check she's all right.'

'You said Sophia's got your mobile number.'

'Yes, but even so.'

'You do that, then, if you're worried.' His unruly eyebrows are constantly on the move, and sink now in an
indulgent line over his eyes.

She makes the call from the ladies' in between the main
course and the dessert.

'She's been ever so good,' says Sophia, sounding breath-
less, after Dick has had to fetch her downstairs. Background sounds from the bar: laughter, raised voices, glasses
clinking. Lizzie's 'Who ordered beef provençal?'

'Sometimes she's difficult to settle.'

'She settled really well. I said prayers with her. She
seemed to like that.'

Isabella tries to keep the surprise from her tone. 'Did she
understand?'

'Well, she got quite excited when I said "God".'
'She would do. That's what she calls dogs – "gods".'
'Oh.' A series of giggles down the line.

They say goodbye. She presses the little red phone painted on a button to end the call. Can't help a tinge of resentment.

Aidan's eyes are pinned on her as she makes her way back to the table, past other diners, several of whom glance up at her. She feels self-conscious under Aidan's gaze.

She takes her seat again, pushes her chair in, then back slightly. Their desserts are on the table: sorbet for her, toffee pudding for him.

'She's fine, apparently.'

He senses her despondency.

'Then that's all due credit to you.'

'What do you mean?'

'That she's fine. She obviously feels secure. *You've* obviously made her feel secure. You should be glad.'

She had not thought of it like that. Eight days. And a half. And she has made the child feel secure. Isn't that an achievement?

'Thank you for saying that.'

'It's only the truth. So, what did you do today, you and Hannah?'

'We walked. It was wonderful. We found this beach about a mile away—'

'Tregurran beach?'

'Yes, that was it. It was empty. It was wonderful. We ran . . .'

He watches her intently as she speaks: her every facial expression, how she uses her hands.

'I felt so free,' she is saying; looking wistful.

He asks for the bill. He will not hear of her contributing. Looks either hurt or mildly offended, or both, when she offers.

'Not now or ever,' he says firmly.

Does she mind this about him? His stereotyped vision of male–female roles. He clearly regards a woman paying for a man as demeaning. Yet she does not have the impression he is chauvinistic. He seems to like and respect women. On balance she decides she doesn't mind; it is quite a novelty for her, actually. What would he do, she wonders, if he found himself penniless and had to be supported by a female partner?

The wine bar – Matisse, it is called – is in Church Street, in a basement beneath a tailor's. And on an upper floor the light is still on. Through the window she can see swatches of material in stacks. She can make out a dark head.

'Someone's working late on a Saturday,' she comments.

'Mr Korowski. He made this waistcoat for me. For all of us. The group, I mean.' He is putting it on now, as he speaks, a multicoloured brocade waistcoat under his jacket. 'Got to look the part,' he adds lightly.

'It's very dashing.'

'Now you're taking the mickey.'

'No. Well, only a bit.'

The place is decorated with Fauvist prints. It is seething, much the same as anywhere in London. She asks if he gets nervous performing.

'I will be in front of you.'

'Of *me*?'

'Yeah. It's far worse performing in front of someone you know.'

'That's true.' Remembering the first time she played in front of Tom, who had told her beforehand he would give her his 'candid opinion'.

'And worse still when you fancy them rotten and want to impress them.'

The remark coincides with the appearance of the other two members of the group, a bass guitarist and a drummer, both a lot younger than himself. She is saved from having to make a response. But he has taken her by surprise. And he uttered it in such a matter-of-fact way. Now he is acting as though he never said it.

He finds a stool for her in a shadowy corner near the front. She feels conspicuous. The group leader's woman. That's how it must appear. How funny. Herself *here*. And what was originally in her diary for this evening? Was tonight the opera? She doubts he has ever been to the opera. Does he ever go to art galleries? Does he know who Matisse was? Or the Fauvists? Does he ever read the arts pages of the Sunday papers? Does he *read* the Sunday papers? Madre, do these things matter?

'You all right there?'

'Yes. Absolutely. Don't worry about me.'

He, nervous of *her*? If only he *knew*.

They tune up. The conversation subsides. Candles flickering. The air rich with wine, beer, cigarette smoke and moussaka. Young people necking. Girls with apple-bums in satin jeans . . .

She does not dare look at Aidan.

' "I'm driving my car. I turn on the radio. I'm pulling you close," ' he sings. Bruce Springsteen's 'Fire'.

He handles the guitar competently, even sensitively; his voice is lyrical and easy to listen to. She relaxes, relieved. Glances round the room: the audience is obviously appreciative. And she sits up proudly, wanting to be noticed. Aidan's woman.

At half-time he comes over to her with a glass of beer in one hand and in the other a glass of red wine for her. Crouches by her stool.

'Thank you.' She takes the glass from him. 'You were all very good. I really enjoyed it. You've got a lovely voice.'

'That's the seal of approval, then.'

He brushes the flat of his hand across his glistening forehead.

Does his beard make him hot? What would he look like without it? She would like to comb her fingers through its denseness. Does he smoke? He hasn't smoked all evening, so she presumes not. They are so different from one another.

Meanwhile, the other two musicians are chatting up a pair of girls. Amusedly, she observes them in action: the confident way they are leaning against a couple of pillars; and the girls' simpering responses.

'The lads like to play the part,' Aidan says, following her gaze. 'In fact Paul, the drummer, is twenty-five and still lives with his parents, and Matt's been with the same girlfriend since they were both fourteen.'

The last song of the evening is Clapton's 'Wonderful Tonight'. It is a slow number, and most of those who were not already dancing now get up. Soldered together, they sway and grind. She feels like a voyeur on brazen, randy youth.

'"It's late in the evening, she's wondering what to wear",' sings Aidan. '"She puts on her make-up and brushes her long red hair. And then she asks me: Do I look all right? And I say, yes, you look wonderful tonight."'

And he catches her eye. Did anyone notice he had exchanged 'blond hair' for 'red'?

They finish at just gone eleven. Pack up. They say their goodbyes. Friendly but detached.

In the car he explains to her, 'We've got nothing in common, apart from the band. It's a business deal, that's all.'

Her right hand rests on the edge of the seat, near the handbrake, his on the bulb of the gear-stick. A couple of inches from each other. She is acutely conscious of his.

'God, it was smoky in there tonight. I've never known it so bad. It really affects me.'

So he doesn't smoke. Everything about him seems to be in moderation. His drinking also.

'Well, this has been a bit different from your usual nights out, I expect.' He switches on the windscreen wipers against the rain which has just started to spot.

'What do you mean?'

'Don't you usually go to fancy sorts of places?'

'Sometimes. More often not. I go to all kinds of places. I've got Catholic tastes.'

'But London,' he persists. 'If you're from London—' Shrugs and leaves the sentence trailing.

'Why are people who don't know it so afraid of London? You only take in bits at a time.' Quotes: '"When a man is tired of London he is tired of life."'

'Who said that? Oscar Wilde?'

'No. Back a century. Samuel Johnson.'

'Now I feel stupid.'

'No, no. Please don't. You're not.'

'I knew the quote, only not who made it,' he says.

'Look, I don't know the first thing about cars. Or about animals or nature.'

'So will you miss it? London?'

She thinks of all the things she used to do. Sometimes every night of the week was accounted for.

'It's rather soon to tell. But I don't think so. We go through phases, don't we? That phase is past now.'

'I seem to have been doing the same things for years,' he says. 'I'm probably a bit of a stick-in-the-mud.'

'What do you like to do?'

'Well, there's the band, of course. And my lads. And walking. I love going for long walks, spotting wildlife. Then there's the cars. And reading. I do like to read. And music. All kinds of music. I like – you know – quiet things. My house took nearly three years to do up. It's still got no curtains and bits and pieces. I'm not very good with that sort of stuff. Women are better at that. Would you like to see it?'

Come and see my etchings.

'I'd love to. But Sophia will be waiting.'

'Five minutes. It'll only take five minutes.'

So, no great seduction scene is about to take place.

He turns down an unmarked lane about a mile from Zerion. She worries that his home will be in atrocious taste and she will be put off him. Does not like this trait in herself.

It is a converted stable block, fenced off in its own garden from the main house to which it once belonged.

'I've planted cypresses. Another couple of years and you won't be able to see it.'

Inside the timbers and rafters have been sandblasted and left exposed. The floor downstairs is flagstoned throughout. The kitchen and living room are open-plan.

'Madre.'

'You like it, then.' He looks like a pleased boy.

'It's wonderful.' Ignoring the maroon satinated sofa and armchair, which is on teak rockers; the mass-produced print of stampeding elephants in a garish frame.

'Like I say, it needs the finishing touches. To make it feel homely. I lived in a caravan in the grounds while I was doing it. That wasn't fun, I can tell you. So cramped. And freezing in the winter.'

'You did everything yourself?'

'Bar the electrics. I wouldn't trust myself with the electrics. But I did the plumbing and heating and stuff. It was only a matter of reading up what to do.'

'Come on, you make it sound so easy. Give yourself some credit. You've done a fantastic job.'

'Well, maybe.' He pulls a self-deprecating expression. A

thoroughly modest man unused to receiving compliments. 'I enjoyed it. And it took my mind off things. You know. The divorce.'

'Yes. It must've been a difficult time.'

There is a slightly protracted pause. She wonders why he got divorced. Wishes Sophia weren't back at the inn, waiting.

'They're going to be making a film in Pengarris Cove in a few weeks. Did you know?'

'No. What kind of film?'

'A TV documentary. About the locals. The fishermen. Old Charlie's really chuffed. He's over seventy and's got a gammy leg, and he still sets off at the crack of dawn with the others. So now you've seen this place do you trust me to help you with the cottage?'

'It doesn't seem fair.'

'I'd like to. I'd enjoy it. I know what materials to use. You can pay me back for *them*.'

'Done, then.'

'Well, I suppose the five minutes is up, Cinderella.' Regret in his tone.

'I suppose it is.' And in hers.

'I could get you a drink. I don't have much. Only a wine box or beer. Or instant coffee. But—'

'No, it's late. I really ought to go.'

Facing each other in the vast kitchen area. Blackness outside the window. Not a sound, except the faint rapping of rain on the glass. She is unaccustomed to such total silence.

'I don't want to push myself at you,' he blurts out. 'I mean, maybe you don't want my help with the cottage. It was rather presumptuous, now I think about it.'

She smiles. 'You said that before. About being presumptuous.'

'Did I?' He takes a small step closer to her. 'When?'

'When you asked me out. Well, not out. When you asked me – you remember – on Thursday, to hear you play.'

'Yes, out. I was asking you out. And it did seem presumptuous, with a sophisticated woman like yourself.'

'I'm not sophisticated.'

'Come on, of course you are.'

'Not deep down.'

And what does the word mean, actually? It seems to her now to represent everything that is superficial. She is about to tell him about the Sophists in the fifth century BC, then thinks better of it.

'Anyway, you were saying – about asking me out.' She tilts her head provocatively, swivelling her body at the same time.

He seems about to take another step towards her, then to decide not to. The air crackles between them.

'I really like you,' he says with quiet intensity. 'It's crazy. I don't know you, and you've hardly said anything about yourself. But you've got such beautiful soft eyes. And I love how you use your hands as you talk . . . Look, I don't want to do anything out of place, that's all. You've obviously been through a lot.'

'Please don't worry.'

'If ever you need anyone to talk to, I'm a good listener.'

His gaze holds hers. She swallows.

And now he does move towards her, enfolding her very gently in his arms; just holds her there – she feels small and protected – before his face bears down on hers. He lays his lips almost chastely against hers, then he presses and parts them, again with that same gentleness, and his tongue seeks hers, tentatively at first. She can feel the little moan he gives running through his body in a tremor. His arms grip her more tightly, and she clutches his shirt under his jacket. Then his tongue is fully in her mouth, exploring, curling round her tongue. His beard is soft against her nose and cheeks, not coarse as she'd imagined. He clasps her chin in one hand and with the other lightly traces round her eyelids. She closes her eyes with pleasure. She can feel the bulge of his crotch and whimpers with need.

'Such beautiful hair.' He caresses the crown of her head. 'The colour of a red squirrel.'

He pulls away from her.

'I must take you back.'

'All right.'

But it is not. Her body is desperate for him. Every nerve ending is alight. She is conscious of what a mess she must look: hair awry, lipstick rubbed off, and her chin stained with it. Eye make-up in panda daubs.

'You look so pretty,' he says.

Outside the door of the inn he says, 'I hope – before – that you didn't think I was being—'

'Presumptuous?' she finishes for him.

His teeth flashing under the streetlamp.

'Well, you might've thought I was rather . . . fast.'

Fast. How that takes her back. She hasn't heard the word in that context since she was a girl – giggling with others about boys who were fast, who had WH – wandering hands – who French-kissed you and gave you love bites that you pretended to hide with a knotted scarf round the neck, but purposely leaving a bit showing. Fast? How little he knows about her. *How* little. Oh madre, she can never get involved. Not with him or anyone else. That is her penance.

'You look sad.'

He tips her jaw up with his finger, exposing the line of her throat, which he strokes. A small current shimmering through her.

'I'm not. I'm fine. It was a wonderful evening. Thank you.'

'It was for me too. So, see you Monday, at the cottage. I

can easily put in a couple of hours after I've finished at the garage.'

'That's terrific.'

He kisses her goodnight. She hears the throb of the car's engine after it is out of sight.

Sophia is asleep on her bed. The child asleep in hers, sucking her thumb, the knitted rabbit and new bear lodged under her chin. The television is on quietly. The night-light lends a soothing glow to the room. Garibaldi runs towards her with one of his little chirrups, and she picks him up. He clambers towards her neck then springs down. She touches Sophia's shoulder, and the girl wakes instantly.

'Oh, hello . . . I hope you didn't mind.' Sitting up. Her voice hoarse from sleep.

'Of course I didn't. I'm sorry if I'm late.' Speaking softly so as not to waken Hannah.

'No, it doesn't matter,' Sophia says on a yawn, getting up. 'She was so good. No trouble at all.'

'That's great. How would you feel about coming again?'

'I'd like to.'

'I'm moving to Pengarris. Would you be able to help me there also?'

'Yes.'

'What about transport?'

'I've got a Mini.' Pride in her tone.

Isabella pays her. Takes her phone number.

'*Ciao*, then, Sophia.'

'Oh I know *that* word.'

For a moment her pinched little face is almost attractive. She has a lovely smile that transforms her surprised-mouse expression and lends her cheeks a fullness.

'*Ciao*, then,' she says back.

Looks quite perky as she leaves the room. Bonded by a casual word in Italian.

Isabella does not wash or clean her teeth. She smells

and tastes Aidan. Smells and tastes *of* him. Lies between
the nylon sheets and relives the evening, things he said;
every innuendo in his voice. Conjures up his face, his
unruly eyebrows and steady eyes. Feels again his tongue
in her mouth, and the erotic pressure against her crotch.
She recalls how tender he was. As though he cared.

Madre, what now? Where do we go from now, Isabella,
cara?

7 ∫

Monday. The tenth day. And her London answerphone bears down on her with her other life. A discarded snake-skin assuming an existence of its own. Her French language student is past the infectious stage and is ready to recommence his coaching. Why hasn't she returned her call? the mother says. Why haven't you got back to me? demand several acquaintances and also her accountant. I'm afraid we shall have to charge you for your missed appointment, says the dentist's receptionist and her hairdresser. A stream of calls needing a response; there is satisfaction in ignoring them. But the mail: she can visualise it, like a slag heap by the front door; pamphlets sticking through the letterbox, alerting the world to her absence. She will have to go to London soon. Dreads it. At least she has an address now to where the mail can be redirected: 4, The Rise. The other cottages have romanticised names, but Timothy Abell's mind was less occupied with panoramic vistas and bracken-strewn hills than festering resentments.

And on this tenth day summer is back: a brilliant yellow, insect-strumming day. The sand glints where the tide is out. The light dazzles their eyes and heat seeps into their pores. The sea inhales in hisses then exhales in sighs, drawing back then building up into a ledge that curls slowly forward before breaking. Midges hang in a cloud. The crickets whirr.

'This is unbelievable,' Babs Carrick says, lying back. 'Who'd have thought?' Squeezing her eyes against the brightness. They are a pale, almost opalescent blue; her silver-streaked hair is pulled tightly back from her polished forehead.

They are picnicking on the lower slope of the eastern headland. The child pulls up daisies and places them singly into her plastic bucket. Humming. This is the latest development, the humming. No particular tune, just a contented drone.

'He was a sculptor and potter,' Babs says of her husband to Isabella beside her. 'We met when we were both in Ontario. I was staying in a friend's log cabin for the summer vacation. He was camping. He was fifteen years older than me. I quit university and returned to London with him. It was that simple. Thirteen years ago he wanted to come back to Cornwall, where he grew up, and we bought the shop. I'll show you some of his work later, if you'd like.'

'Yes, I would.'

'He fell ill four years after we'd moved.'

A sculptor and potter with multiple sclerosis. She did not try to prevent him. They discussed it together: the best method, the implications, her life afterwards, without him.

'I'd have helped him, if he'd wanted it.'

Isabella ponders such heartfelt and selfless love. She cannot conceive what it must be like. What it must be like first to possess it then to lose it. Feels envious – even of the subsequent grief.

'And you? All this gossip about running away from a violent husband.'

She takes an apple from the plastic box and crunches into it. Its juice runs down her chin. The sun's heat pricks her bare arms. The sea is a constant slapping sound against the rocks. She is aware of an unchanging stillness.

'It's not quite like that.'

'Will you go back to him?'

'There's nobody to go back *to*, Babs.'

Which could mean anything; could be taken literally, or not.

'I didn't mean to press you,' the other woman says. 'Look, if you ever *do* need anyone—'

'I know. Thank you.'

Aidan had said virtually the same.

'Do you know Aidan—?' Breaks off, realising she doesn't know his surname. 'He's got the garage in Zerion.'

'Aidan Argall. Sure. Everyone knows him. He's a nice guy.'

'He's going to help me with the cottage.'

Babs sits up and narrows her eyes shrewdly. 'Good. You can trust him. He's his own man. I wouldn't think he shocks too easy.'

She feels a glow at Babs's words, this endorsement of his character. And in just a few hours' time she will be seeing him.

Babs points out the fishing boats beyond the narrows. 'One of them will be old Charlie. He's your next-door neighbour. You can always tell Charlie from the other men as they pass on their way down the lane to the cove at six in the morning. You can hear him dragging his leg. His twin died at sea five years ago.'

'How dreadful.'

'Charlie married his sister-in-law, Joyce, a couple of years later. That set the old tongues wagging, I can tell you. They're like young newlyweds. It's real funny. Did you know a television documentary's being made here soon?'

'Aidan told me.'

'Ah, him again!' A smile breaking over her features.

'OK, OK.' Isabella raises her hands.

How long is it since her attention has strayed from the child? Seconds? Minutes? But suddenly where Hannah was there is only the toy bucket on its side.

She lets out a cry. Leaps to her feet – knocking over a plastic glass which had contained Babs's cider.

'Hannah – she's gone.'

Panic sweeping through her. For a few seconds she is rendered utterly useless; can only stare at where the child was a moment ago. Fleetingly some trick manifests Hannah like a mirage, then she vanishes.

'She can't have gone far,' Babs says. 'We'll look in different directions.'

Her calm penetrates Isabella's immobility. She calls the child's name. Clambers up the headland, round a bend, calling, frantically calling. Another bend. She hears the humming first.

The child, on her hands and knees. Her angel's smile.

'Rabbit,' she exclaims, pointing.

And a few feet from her is the rabbit she must have followed. Either old or suffering from some disease, it can only hop slowly away.

'Oh, madre.' Relief flooding her. 'Carina . . .'

She falls to her knees beside the child, and clasps her to her. Then she holds her away at arm's length.

'You mustn't run off. It's naughty. You understand, Hannah? You must stay with the grown-ups.'

It could be the reproval in her voice, or it could be that a key phrase has triggered some memory, but the child becomes corpse-stiff. Her face becomes red and she struggles to free herself. She lashes out, bellowing, raining blows against Isabella with her fists; adrenalin lending her strength as she flails her legs and contorts her body into a backward arch. Isabella is shocked. Has never seen her like this.

'Rabbit. *Rabbit* . . . Hannah *go*.'

The shrieking magnifies, ripping across the headland, so that the entire village, the fishermen out at sea, the people sitting outside the Ship Inn – everyone – must hear.

Isabella is bone-pale. 'Please, carina, please.'

She is too drained to deal with this attack. She clings on to the child as she beats Isabella's shins with her sandalled feet. Finally the hysteria wears itself out. The child burrows her drenched face in the crook of Isabella's arm. Hers come round Isabella's neck in a loop.

'Mummy. Mummy,' she whimpers.

Isabella is too enervated to move. Hangs on to her for all she is worth. It is as if they have been formed from a single mould, indistinguishable one from the other, where the limb of one begins and that of the other ends; faces concealed, hair merging.

'Cara, carina, carina . . .' 'Mumm-ee . . .'

'Wow, the terrible twos, eh?' Babs says a little later. 'It makes me glad mine are grown up. One forgets the tantrums.'

'They're normal?'

'Sure they are.'

What does she know about two-year-olds – or three-year-olds – and tantrums. What does she know about this child? She is filled with misgivings. Afraid the growing bond between them has been damaged.

'They get frustrated. They can't express themselves. You wouldn't think such a tiny individual could possess such mighty lungs, would you?'

'No.' She can barely talk. Is quite exhausted. Still shocked.

They are walking back to the shop. In her buggy the child gives small judders as she sleeps.

'Isabella, you mustn't feel bad.'

'I took my eyes off her. Anything could have happened.'

'But it didn't. It wouldn't have in those few seconds. God, my kids were always in scrapes. It's a miracle they survived. Sometimes I completely forgot about them.'

She smiles despite herself, picturing children cavorting like untamed monkeys.

'Why don't you put Hannah into playgroup?' Babs says. 'It might be good for her. There's one near Zerion. I'll dig out the number.'

They part outside the shop. Isabella thanks her.

'I feel stupid. I don't usually go to pieces.'

'You didn't. Don't be so hard on yourself.'

She pushes the child in the stroller slowly up the hill, past secret windows and sleeping cats; turns down the cutting. Failure straddles her. She stops outside Timothy Abell's front door.

'WELCOME,' Janet Abell has written on a sheet of paper which she has anchored under the door knocker.

The note jolts everything into perspective and causes an instantaneous reversal of mood. What is there, after all, to be dejected about? The child is safe, and that is what matters.

I just have to learn.

She unstraps Hannah, who wakes. Who smiles. Who staggers up drunkenly. And Isabella bends down and embraces her.

'There's this legend,' Aidan says, rollering white over the Anaglypta in the sitting room, 'claims a giant used to inhabit these parts. His legs could span the headlands and he feasted off children. If he didn't eat a child a day he would become ill. Then one day he got ill anyway, and one of the little girls he'd kidnapped to eat tended him until he recovered. But he'd grown to love this little girl and knew he could never eat a child again. So he went off to die. He dived from this headland into the stormy sea and was changed into a rock.

The boulder on its own a little way out – that's supposed to be him.'

'I've never known a place with so many legends.' Isabella, painting the door. Beside her, the child daubing with her own brush.

'But he was rather noble, I reckon, don't you?'

'Very Hardyesque.'

'*Mayor of Casterbridge?*'

'You've read it?'

'Ah, she's surprised. The Philistine reads Thomas Hardy.'

'I didn't mean—'

'Joking. I was joking.'

But he hadn't sounded as though he had been.

'I told you I liked reading,' he says on a sigh. Here—' Lays down the roller carefully in the foil tray, comes over to her and kisses her with the child between them.

'Mummy and man,' Hannah says.

'If you knew how I've been thinking about you,' he says against her lips. 'I've been—' Shakes his head and releases her slowly. 'It's not right in front of your daughter.'

'You didn't seem particularly glad to see me.' Teasing him. In fact she had anticipated how he would be and was unsurprised when he greeted her as he might a casual acquaintance.

She sits down on the dusty floor and he joins her.

'I felt awkward. I didn't know what you might be feeling. For all I knew you could've regretted . . . everything. And then I thought, why should a stylish woman like her . . . I mean, I'm out of your league. I'm just an ordinary bloke.'

'Don't be ridiculous, of course you're not. I wish you'd stop thinking that.'

'I will, then.' Slapping his own cheek lightly; grinning at her.

'Something awful happened this morning.'

She relates the incident. He listens attentively.

'The shock of her disappearing was bad enough,' she says, 'but the tantrum after – you wouldn't believe it.'

'Well, you had to tick her off, didn't you? I mean, kids have to learn the boundaries of what they can and can't do. I remember reprimanding Sam one day and him bawling so loud – we were in Truro – that everyone was gawping. Proper embarrassing it was. You mustn't get upset about it. Look at her now.'

And yes, look: as the child contentedly splodges her brush on the door, humming tunelessly all the while.

'She's just strong-willed like her mum.'

She stares at him. He takes her hand and massages the knuckles.

'I like your hands.'

'They're ugly – big and square.'

'Rubbish. Proper hands, I call them.'

She laughs. 'Well, that's for sure. Proper hands.' Holds them out in front of her and pretends to examine them.

'No—' Laughs also, and swipes at the air. 'You know what I mean. They look capable. Practical.' He becomes serious again. 'Look, it's hard being alone with your child,' he says, reverting to their earlier conversation. 'Worrying all by yourself. I understand that. I'll mend the fence for you. Make it safe for her. That'll be one less worry. We'll get a proper gate.'

He is so kind. She has never met anyone like him.

'I've never met anyone like you,' he says.

She smiles.

'What are you smiling about?'

'No, nothing . . . Just, thank you so much for everything.'

'Don't be daft.'

'I'm not . . . Aidan—'

'Yeah?'

'Listen – there are things . . . I don't want you ever to think I've misled you.'

'You mean you don't fancy me?'

'Now what makes you think I could fancy you? Madre!'
She laughs.

'So you do.'

'Of course.'

'Well, that's good, then. Look, I've told you, I'm not about
to drag confidences from you that you're not ready for.
Maybe one day when we know each other better you'll
feel you can tell me.'

When we know each other better. He said 'when' not
'if'.

She loves the soft modulations of his voice; the round,
sleepy vowels. And now he is looking at her with his
steady, unmasked gaze. She has the sense his eyes are in
her, that between them they have only one set of eyes,
seeing in and seeing out. Her body is going mad with its
need for him.

'I haven't stopped thinking about you,' she says.

'I could come and help you Wednesday evening, if you
like. You could come back to me after. Both of you. I could
fix a meal.' He raises his eyebrows quizzically. 'I'm busy
tomorrow night,' he adds.

So will Wednesday be The Night? And what is he doing
tomorrow?

He furnishes her with the information. 'I'm going to Bath
to look at an MGA. I'll be back late.'

He is without guile or games. He offers up his no-secrets
life on an unadorned platter. One day he will be so disappointed in her.

'To work,' he says, hauling her up from the floor, brushing
the dust from the seat of her jeans.

And for the next hour, as they transform the room – she
notices how exacting and painstaking he is with edges and
nooks – they scarcely exchange a word. But there is com-
panionability in their silence and in their working together.

An exquisite normality which, like a thirsting explorer's last sip of water, she savours. Playing at Happy Families. And every so often their glance will meet the other's and become a protracted communion. Whilst beyond the open window, against a red, dipping sun, the gulls return at leisure to their outposts, the rooks fly in slate-shadowed formation to their roosting places and flocks of shrilling starlings urgently make for the larches on the headlands. And indoors, the child chants in her funny, tuneless voice: 'Mummy-man, Mummy-man, Mumm-ee.'

Please let it continue.

'Bring her tomorrow,' Margaret, the playgroup leader, says on the phone. 'See how she gets on.' Adds, 'I've heard all about you.'

'Who from?'

'My goodness, who *not* from, you mean.'

She is annoyed; unused to this kind of intrusion. Is left with an impression of twitching curtains and prying eyes, eavesdropping ears and lizard tongues.

That night she scrutinises herself naked in the mirror above the basin. It stops at her waist, so she stands on the chair to inspect her hips, bottom and legs. Swivels round and back, assessing herself from all angles. What will he think of her body?

'Mummy hair,' says Hannah, pointing to her pubic region.

Tuesday, 10 September. And who could have imagined, a fortnight ago, that this particular morning would find her delivering a child to a playgroup in Polhearn Community Centre, in Cornwall?

Margaret is a mountainous, beaming woman with cascading flesh terminating in tiny feet.

'Well, good morning, Hannah,' she welcomes both of them as they enter hesitantly, and stoops with difficulty to the child's level. Grins into her face like an ugly gargoyle. Hannah stares warily back at her, until her attention is diverted by other children arriving with their mothers – or, in one case, their father. Her hand tightens in Isabella's.

'Hannah go. I go.'

'It's all right, cara . . . She's shy, I'm afraid.'

'They all are in the beginning. Now just look at them.' Margaret gesticulates towards the children filling the room, at small girls and boys forming into groups or running to the two helpers, or heading for the piano, or for the playhouse in the corner.

'You're welcome to stay here until she settles.'

'Would you mind?'

'No. It's usual. And I tell you something. It's worse for the mothers than the children, leaving them for the first time.'

They stand pressed close together, outsiders both; both observing: the one the children, the other the mothers. And from the surreptitious glances in her direction, Isabella guesses she is known to several of them. What rumours have been circulating? She is reminded of the game of Chinese whispers played at parties when she was a girl, and quells her irritation. Adheres a smile to her lips. And meanwhile the child's expression is one of puzzlement. A boy swaggers up to her and pokes his tongue out.

'Bugger off, thug,' Isabella mutters to him, without relinquishing her smile.

'Come on, everyone,' calls Margaret, clapping her hands. 'Get ready for our singsong.'

She organises everyone into a wide circle.

On Hannah's other side is a small girl who announces herself as Becky. She takes Hannah's hand firmly and swings it up and down a few times. She is as talkative as Hannah is taciturn.

'A-one, a-two, a-three,' cries Margaret. 'Ring a ring of roses, a pocket full of posies . . .'

They all join in. The piano rings out tinnily. The same nursery rhymes with their gruesome words sung by successive generations of children in unthinking refrain. Who knows that 'Ring a ring of roses' depicted the plague, she wonders.

Afterwards the children are paired. Becky has commandeered Hannah. It is extraordinary for Isabella to witness her opening out, copying the other child, becoming bolder by the second.

'No, not in there,' Becky is saying adamantly as Hannah places a plastic farm horse in a pigsty. She points to the stable. 'Horses go in stables.'

'In there?' asks Hannah, moving the horse.

So sweet, all the little, happy faces and the piping voices. Unformed beings only waiting to be fed into, to be made or destroyed, for experience and knowledge to knead the mind for better or worse.

When she leaves on her own she feels strange. Oddly redundant. Oddly sad. No longer needed. She recalls a pathetic tale she heard of an elderly woman caught shoplifting men's socks in Asda. They were for her husband, she claimed. He was ill. There was no money. But neither was there a husband. It turned out she was a spinster living in a one-roomed flat.

In her car she automatically reaches over to check the child seat strap. Her fingers come into contact with the rabbit and the bear. When she switches on the radio for the news, the cassette comes on instead: 'If you go down to the woods today you're due for a big surprise . . .'

She drives off in the direction of Pengarris, singing along with the tape. Suddenly she can clearly remember her own nursery school: the piano by the window, with curly candlesticks attached to brackets. The teachers seemed inaccessibly old. They were all nuns. One of them, with the pink-rimmed eyes of an albino rabbit, had an amputated finger. She played the piano in prayers. Isabella remembers the crunching discords as they sang 'All Things Bright And Beautiful'. Afterwards they painted, wearing blue overalls, and made potato men, and learned the alphabet. Twenty assorted kids kept in strict disciplinary order. Can she really remember that far back, or is she confusing her schools? She can remember her friend Melanie, because they remained close for several years, until the family moved away. Heavenly-looking Melanie who used to pinch her, and stole her pencils. And Isabella let her because Melanie told her she was a secret princess.

And then it is several schools later. Isabella is in her teens, and loutish boys with cracking yodlers' voices take bets as to the size of her breasts and who will be the first to touch them. Jealous girls. Always alone. Always observing. Thinking, thinking.

I matter.

And years later, in preparation for university, she would sit in a café, anonymous behind dark glasses, conducting a private field study of how life was led. Creating Isabella.

Half a mile or so from Zerion there comes a grinding-metal sound as she applies her brakes down the hill. Determinedly she carries on through the village and towards Pengarris.

'Hang on in there,' she says to the car.

Another Indian summer day. The sun is a glaring spotlight through the archways of branches. Insects rain down on to her dusty windscreen. And the grating noise becomes constant. When she goes to apply the brakes on a steep descent her foot seems to be pumping nothing.

'*Madre mia.*'

Her hands are clammy on the steering wheel, as it seems that her ancient nightmare is about to be enacted and the car will be propelled down the hill. She changes into first gear – there is a protesting whine from the engine – and applies the handbrake, and in this lip-biting way makes it to the bottom of the hill. There she pulls over, half on the verge, half in the lane. For a moment she just sits there, cradling her head in her hands. She is parked by a field with horses grazing in it. The roof and window of her car are open and she can hear the nearest horse tugging at grass – a soothing sound. It stretches its neck over the fence and pokes its head towards her, and she reaches through the window to stroke its nose. She ponders what to do: she could call the AA on her mobile, walk either to Pengarris or back to Zerion for help, or risk driving to Aidan's garage. It is either all uphill or level the other way. She settles on this course and turns the car round. Prays there won't be any oncoming vehicles where she will have to stop on an incline. Slowly, the MG clunks its way along the lanes. She draws up outside the forecourt and climbs out.

From behind the half-pulled doors she can hear revving, and peers inside. A figure with a torch is bending over the open bonnet of a Ford Escort. Every time he yanks a wire the engine revs. She knows it is Luke, and she experiences that same unaccountable apprehension again. She approaches him purposefully.

'Hello,' she shouts over the bent back in the navy overalls; over the squeals from the Escort.

He straightens slowly and turns round. He says nothing. His eyes are almost lacteal pale in the grime of his face. They penetrate the hollows of her skull.

'My car brakes have packed up.' Keeps her voice brisk. 'I think it's the discs.'

He rubs his hands down the flanks of his overalls – his arms are extraordinarily long and simian – and still with no word, walks over to her car, with his curious sideways gait.

'Key,' he states, when he sees it is not in the ignition. Just 'key', in a nasal-harsh tone. His teeth are like a rabbit's the way they protrude over his lower lip. She gives him the key and stands aside; and he brushes past her – apparently deliberately – climbs into her car and starts it up. He depresses the brake pedal a few times before driving into the garage and on to a ramp.

She has followed him inside, and now suppresses mingled anger and nervousness, watching as he unscrews and removes the front wheels. His ears are very small, she notices, pinned to the bullet of his close-cropped head. She can sense a latent violence in the set of his neck, in the power of his shoulders and long arms, at odds with the slightness of the rest of his body. Can imagine him working out in a gym, his eyes bulging and muscles quivering as he defies pain.

'I'm sorry Sophia was so late the other evening,' she says, in an attempt to break the tension.

He grunts and goes into the office, where she can see him making a phone call. Can hear the mumble of his voice but not what he is saying. Fury brews within her. And she is angry with herself, for allowing herself to be intimidated by him.

He reappears.

'Do you always dump your customers to make a phone call?'

'I've just phoned for the parts.'

'Oh.' And now she feels stupid. 'So when—?'

'This afternoon.'

And he turns his back on her. Starts working on the Escort again, and the revving begins once more.

Her contract for the book has arrived, and back in her room she starts to read through it. Suddenly she remembers an article she once read. It was by a psychologist on the subject of passive aggression. Until then she had not heard the term. The author explained it could be more disquieting than expressed aggression because the victim of it could not gauge the perpetrator's emotions or intentions and therefore could not respond appropriately. It is clear to her now, recollecting this article, why she feels so menaced by the mechanic.

Lizzie from the pub gives her a lift to the playgroup to fetch the child.

'So, what's this I hear about you going out with Aidan?'

'I—' She is stunned by the forthrightness of the question. The impertinence. Lizzie goes out of her way to be friendly to her but is, she knows, suspicious of her: this London woman come to ensnare the local men.

She resists a sharp retort. 'He's helping me with the cottage, that's all.'

Lizzie's profile looks disbelieving.

Hannah and her new friend are waiting together, dangling soggy paintings.

''Bye,' says Becky, and kisses Hannah on the cheek.

''Bye,' Hannah says. Runs over to Isabella. 'I painting, I painting,' she chants, waving round the splodges of colour.

'She was good as gold,' Margaret says.

'No crying or tantrums?'

'Not a tear, was there, Hannah?'

'Diff'n' car,' the child observes when Isabella lifts her into the back of the Volvo.

'By the way,' says Lizzie, as she drives, 'you had a letter. Did you see it? I put it in your room. Something formal and brown. It looked like it might be a legal document.'

'Yes. It was a book contract from my agent. Thank you.'

'Oh.'

From that 'oh' it is obvious to Isabella she had assumed it

to be connected with her 'divorce', and had been anticipating a meaty discussion which she could relay.

At the garage that afternoon, she writes out a cheque. Can feel the mechanic's breath on her neck.

She stands up and edges towards the glass door of the office.

'The suspension's next,' she says, still trying.

He ignores her as though she has not spoken.

She assists the child into the car. Is strapping her in when the mechanic mutters something that stops her in her tracks. She is mistaken; surely she is mistaken. Her face is burning as she climbs into the driver's seat. She is conscious of his eyes following her every move; of the line of her thighs as she swings her legs in.

She had thought he said, I want to fuck you.

8 ∫

'*My interests/hobbies:*' wrote Isabella when she was sixteen and a half and living with a childless couple· in their early sixties, a retired physicist and his botanist wife – who knew Linnaeus's *Systema Naturae* by heart. 'Animals, all types of music, dancing, the guitar and singing with it, cinema, current affairs, swimming, going to exhibitions, reading, fashion.' She wore skimpy tops and tiny skirts. Bum-grazers, they were known as at school.

'*My favourite book ever*: Le Petit Prince.

'*Worst book*: Jane Eyre.

'*Favourite food*: Cheese fondu, cannelloni, soft-whip ice cream with flake.

'*Worst food*: Steak – it looks so *live*. Raw onions – they make me gag. Pineapple – it makes the bits of my tongue go on end.

'*Best person:*' She wavered here, trying to think of a single person who really meant something to her. Anyone. Left a blank.

'*Worst person:*' Now she had no hesitation. Wrote down the name of the sighing social worker who made her feel like a no-hoper lost cause.

'*Like:*' Her likes were what nourished her. They prickled her flesh, sweetened the air for her, imbued her with hope and yearning and gladness, transported her to other planes, stirred her to sing or to dance in the privacy of her room, made her eyes opaque with dreams and her heart surge: 'Yellow, blue and green,' she wrote. 'They equal the sun, the sea and sky; and trees and plants and grass. Butterflies and gulls and robins. The roar of aeroplanes – where are they going? I imagine I am on one, heading for a land of palms. I like the sun on my neck – it makes me warm yet shivery. Eating sandwiches on park benches. Feeding ducks and the way they waddle and their funny webbed feet. The smell of puppies, the sound of a cat purring. The smell of horses, the sound of their hooves on packed sand. The smell of coffee. Advertisement hoardings and streetlights. The noise of pouring tea and its orange trickle from the spout. Unwrapping a present really slowly. Buses. Power stations – they *look* immensely powerful, exciting. Yellow dangly catkins from branches in spring. Swigging Coke from the bottle. Pigeons – they are so plump, like tea cosies, and the brr-brr noise they make in their throats is soothing. Streams that if you put your ear to them chuckle, and you can see the stones clearly beneath the surface. Hills. Red-brown newly turned soil. Pavement art. Accordions. Sand. Platform-heeled shoes. Indian scarves tied round hips. Street markets. Richard Burton's voice. Steve McQueen's entirety (!). Being barefoot. My newly pierced ears. Jiving. Spike' (her cactus) . . .

Her list of 'likes' covers a whole page and could go on further. It surprises her. She had not thought there were so many things.

'*Dislikes*: Getting up in the morning. Grey sky. School. Foster homes. Narrow-mindedness. Meanness. Snobbery. Prejudice. Crocodiles. Cruelty. Purple and maroon – they make me think of dying. Wars. Long fingernails. Snow. Wire fences. People yelling at each other. The way my fingers go yellow and numb when I'm cold. Fog – it's so disorientating, you feel you're not there. The idea of dying and emptiness. The sound of wool being plucked from a jumper. Nightmares. Lightning – you know that thunder follows. The stink of the sewage place down the road. Geography. Religious studies: religion has caused more wars than anything else. People who stare and make you feel they're laughing or sneering at you. Beer. The Underground – the way you're jammed against a total stranger – it's so intrusive. Yappy dogs that keep you awake all night. Drunken men. Boys who jeer and won't let you pass. Boys thinking it's fine to shove their tongues down your throat when you don't even like them. Wasps; I come up like a balloon when I'm stung—'

And here she adds 'balloons' to her list of 'likes'.

'*My appearance – best points:*' For this she had to inspect herself in the mirror screwed to the door of her room. It elongated her slightly; she knew that, as she always looked fatter in shops. She had asked the woman for the mirror – hesitant to make this request.

'I can't see how things look on me,' she explained.

'But of course, my dear, you have to tell us what you need.'

Both she and her husband were completely out of touch with young people and with today's world, with anything that was light-hearted or scandalous. They seemed bemused by modernity, were entrenched in the narrow field of their academia, which was more real than anything outside. And the loud ticking of the mantel clock in the living room where they all sat together in the evening, noses in books (there was no television), drove her insane: louder and louder, filling her head so that it was all she could hear. But they tried so hard. The botanist would make clumsy attempts at affection; but these self-conscious demonstrations from an elderly woman with dingy skin, a centre parting and short socks and brogues filled her with repugnance. Nevertheless she was grateful for their efforts and for the two years of stability provided by this, her last port of call. And there were things she learned from them. Knowledge was everything; and hers was continually expanding.

'I like my hair,' she wrote. 'My eyes. Eyebrows – they're dark, whereas you'd expect them to be the same as my hair. My mouth's quite a nice shape, but the lips are a bit pale, so that they merge rather with my skin. My skin's OK. It's rather fair and goes red easily, but I've not got freckles. I like my breasts and shoulders and being tall.

'*Worst points*: I don't like my nose – it's sort of craggy. And my chin's too big. My face is too large – a bit blobby. I wish I had a tiny, delicate face with lots of bones and angles and shadows. My bottom and thighs and hips are too big. Even when I diet so that the hip bones stick out, I'm still big there.

'*My aims/ambitions*: To escape from the "system". To go to university. Travel. Have lots of friends. Have a good career and have all the things I never did; money, for a start. I'm not sure if I'll get married. I never want children. I don't think children are very nice really. I like animals better. I'll have a cat. And I'll live in my own flat or house with lots of plants and beautiful things. People won't laugh at me or leave me out. I'll wear lovely clothes and have a sports car. I'll learn to ride a horse and go to the opera and theatre, and I'll be able to afford to hear Eric Clapton at the Albert Hall. I won't ever rely on anyone else. I'll make it all happen. I shall.'

Word has got around that Isabella is going out with Aidan. The proprietor of the Zerion post office stores is smileless when Isabella goes in for the paper. She is, after all, a married woman. She might have – so it is generally believed – left a violent husband, but she cannot escape her status.

*   *   *

There is an air of tension this evening between Isabella and Aidan, but it is of a very different kind from two days ago. This evening it is the almost unbearable tension of expectation. The atmosphere twangs with it. The smallest touch of his hand against her, his fingers briefly caressing the crown of her head, a chaste lip-to-lip kiss, a laden glance – all send shock currents darting through her.

'I got the car,' he says in the kitchen – he seems to occupy the entire area, even on bent knees as he fixes the cat flap.

'Is for Grabla,' says the watching child, whose speech in the last couple of days has put on a spurt that astounds and excites Isabella. She wonders if the child knew how to speak before but had been too traumatised to do so, or whether this is a new development. Either way she regards it as a victory.

'She's really not in bad nick,' Aidan says. 'She'll be lovely done up. She's that traditional cherry red. And the leather upholstery's very fair. I could sell her on easily.'

She smiles at his enthusiasm. 'It,' she corrects him, stopping in her painting of the kitchen shelves to inspect them. 'A car should be "it".'

'Well, that's as maybe. But I think originally the usage would have come about because of ships. Seamen cherished their ships like a woman.'

'More, probably,' she says cynically.

He pauses then, in his fitting of the plastic flap into its frame. 'I cherished my wife,' he says reflectively. 'I've always thought it important a man does things like that. She didn't want it.'

'That's such a shame.'

'Yeah, it was.'

She wants, craves, all at once, what his wife flung back at him. Is full of anger at this wasteful woman. She turns to look at him – he is stretching one leg from its cramped position and jigging it about; their eyes meet and hold.

'Sometimes you get this expression,' he says. 'It completely belies how you come across. It's so vulnerable, so soft and dark and warm and sad, it'd melt an iron foundry. I had this fox cub when I was a lad. Ever such a spiky little creature it was, but it loved its tummy being rubbed and it'd get an expression in its eyes just like yours.'

'Submission?' she teases him.

'No. I'm not a macho freak,' he says, ever serious.

'For the record, I love having my tummy rubbed.'

'For the record, I love doing it. All over, in fact.'

His burning eyes. Her burning crotch.

'Madre.' She is so pent up.

'Yeah, I know.' Shakes his head and grins ruefully.

He stands up – his head almost brushes the ceiling – and she goes over to him and kisses him. He parts her lips and for a second his tongue coils round hers; he touches her breasts through her T-shirt – then stands back. 'This won't do. We're supposed to be working. And your daughter – I'm funny like that.'

He is a man of strong principles and strong self-discipline. She respects him for these traits.

'You're funny about lots of things . . . I haven't told you about my car,' she says, when he is about to cut in. She recounts yesterday's incident.

'You shouldn't've driven it a yard like that. Bloody mad, that was. You could've got yourself killed, or badly injured. So, anyway, Luke got it fixed OK?'

'Yes.'

'I'll get it completely overhauled for you. It'll take a couple of days, but we'll do everything. The suspension. The lot.'

'That sounds expensive.'

'No. I'll only charge you for parts at cost. No labour charges.'

'I couldn't. I couldn't not pay. It's your livelihood.'

'And you're my—' He breaks off and gives a small laugh followed by a little shrug. 'Well, we're friends. And I'm not having you muck about with your safety. Really. I hate to think of your driving something unroadworthy.'

Emotion swells within her. She rubs at a white paint stain on the inside of her wrist.

'You're so kind to me.'

She knows a woman who despises kindness in men, who regards it as weakness and is bored by the lack of challenge. Isabella finds Aidan's kindness one of the most seductive things about him. She has the sense of taking refuge.

'Maybe I've a vested interest,' he says.

But she is afraid of Luke doing the work on her car. Imagines him tampering with the engine.

'Would you be doing it, or would Luke?'

'I don't know.'

When she makes no comment he raises his eyebrows enquiringly.

'Is there a problem?'

'Not really. I just . . . I've got this feeling about Luke. I can't explain it.'

'Try.'

'Well, frankly I find him weird.'

'He *is* weird.'

'He gives me the creeps. There's something malevolent about him. The way he just stares and says nothing. It's . . . unnerving.'

'I didn't realise he was that bad. Do you want me to have a word with him?'

'No. That would be quite wrong.'

'You don't have to have anything to do with him.'

'I know, but I want to use Sophia sometimes. And I'll need to phone her to arrange it.'

'He never answers the phone. She always does. Look,

he's harmless, I'm sure. It's just his way. He's shy, more'n like. You probably terrify the wits out of him.' He laughs.

'All right.'

I want to fuck you.

'I mean, someone like you, well . . . Listen, put him out of your mind. As for your car, I'll see to it myself.'

'You don't have time.'

'I'll make time.'

'Madre – Hannah, no!'

The child has the paint tin poised at her lips, about to drink from it. Her face crumples in readiness as Isabella rushes over.

She plucks Hannah up and cuddles her before she has the chance to start screaming.

'The paint will give you a pain in your tummy, carina. It'll make your tummy hurt.'

'Hannah bad?'

The small face scrutinising her own; tears standing out in her eyes.

'No, cara. You're very good. But the paint will hurt your tummy.'

The child's features settling once more.

'Paint hurts tummy?'

'Yes, cara.'

'Paint hurts tummy,' Hannah states, nodding wisely; and slithers down, repeating it to herself, patting her little belly protruding in dungarees.

'She's bright,' Aidan remarks.

'Yes, I know.'

She is inwardly jubilant: *that* is how to tackle the problem of reprimanding her. Now that she knows the child has a reasonable level of comprehension, she only has to explain to her.

'You're good with her. Patient . . . I want to make love to you,' he says softly. 'Ever so slowly. Tantalising. To me the most important thing in making love is to give the woman pleasure. It's the most arousing thing for a man.'

She goes up to him and rubs her face against his arm. She closes her eyes. The child runs over also; and here they are in Timothy Abell's kitchen which smells of paint, the three of them, enfolded together. The moment is so utterly beautiful in its sweetness that she can hardly breathe.

Beyond the window the tide is high. A few boats are still out. She recognises the red hull of Charlie's, the furthest away. She met him and his wife for the first time yesterday evening. They were blatantly besotted with one another – this sprightly woman with her silver perm, and the grizzle-haired, lame man with his salt-worn skin and dreamer's blue eyes. He explained about the tides to her, in his verbose way, how they were related to the gravitational pull of the moon. She poured out elderflower wine into the best glasses.

'He knows so many things, Charlie does,' she said, passing cheese-flavoured biscuits on a green plate patterned with pink roses. 'I could listen to him all day.'

'That's 'cause yer've only one half-decent ear,' he teased.

Seeing them together, Isabella wondered if they had always been in love; if Charlie had been jealous of his brother beforehand and Joyce had felt she had married the wrong brother.

'It's going to be full moon tonight,' she says now to Aidan. Widens her eyes and pretends to growl. He grabs at her to tickle her, and she breaks away from him, laughing. He follows her and they tear through the cottage, the child hanging on to Isabella, laughing and squealing.

He can cook. Really cook. He eschews a garlic crusher for a sharp knife and proceeds expertly to chop then crush the clove together with salt with the flat of the blade. Brushes the chicken quarters with virgin olive oil before rubbing in the garlic mixture and then squeezing fresh lemon on top. Suspended from the rafter are bundles of herbs and he takes down the rosemary and pulls off needles from the branch, which he massages into the chicken skin. He is efficient, graceful as he works. She remember's Tom's jerky, restless movements, whatever he was doing. On the wooden working block are tomatoes still with their stalks and leaves attached, and a lettuce from his garden. Small potatoes she has just scrubbed in the colander. And a punnet of strawberries that she is lazily hulling. *The Archers* is playing on the radio, and so they don't talk.

From her position near the sink she can see his vegetable plot outside. In the rapidly fading light she can make out the neat square, punctuated with green lines and cordoned off with bailer twine, to which, at measured intervals, are attached strips of silver foil to deter birds and rabbits.

A thorough man.

It is a scene, in which she finds herself a participant, of such total and unusual domesticity that she cannot keep the smile from flickering on her lips. He is wearing a purple track-suit top over his jeans that is beyond belief in its awfulness, both in colour and style, and hideous reddy-brown shoes that remind her of swedes (and how she hated swedes and turnips as a child, she recalls suddenly). In the back pocket of his jeans is the small hardback notebook he always carries. He told her that over the years it has conformed to the shape of his buttocks. Oddly, his lack of sartorial concern also makes her smile, rather than cringe. In the past she would immediately have been overtaken with the urge to whisk off a lover without dress sense to Armani. She doubts Aidan has heard of Armani. There is so much he would dislike of her old life. He would be as out of place as a baobab tree in Antarctica. She imagines his defensive disdain. He is in his element here, pottering at his own pace, doing the things, as he said to her, he has always done.

Not a man to strike out, or take risks.

He puts the chicken under the grill. *The Archers* comes to an end, and the familiar signature tune is severed as he switches off the radio.

'Sorry about that. I'm addicted.'

'You and several million others,' she says.

He is a good animal artist. Coyly he shows her ink drawings and pastels of dogs and horses he has done, and of a badger from a photograph he took at night by flashlight.

'They're wonderful.'

'I get commissions,' he says, zipping up the portfolio. 'I don't do it for the money, though.'

'You're so lucky. I wish I could paint. Landscapes. The sky. Street scenes,' she says. 'Not people. I've no interest in doing people.'

'Have you tried drawing or painting?'

'Not since school.'

'Then how do you know you can't?'

'Well, you just know, don't you? Anyway, I was hopeless. Not just bad. Hopeless.'

However, she would like to write. Sometimes, translating the works of others, she knows she could do better herself. Sometimes the desire to write is so strong as to be almost overpowering. She might scrawl a sentence, a paragraph, even a page or two. Or she might type out a sudden idea on her computer, inspired perhaps by a newspaper article or something she has seen on television; and these snippets will be put away in a drawer of her desk and never be exhumed. The drawer is almost overflowing. She is prevented from properly pursuing her literary aspirations by the wedge of fear that intercedes between her and the page. Whenever she writes more than a few hundred words it seems that she is delving too far into her own psyche, that every route takes her back to herself.

'I'd like to write,' she says.

'A book? A novel, you mean?'

'Yes. But so does everyone.'

'It doesn't matter. You should do it.'

'I can't.'

'Why?'

He catches the pursued look in her eyes.

'Isabella? What's wrong?'

The past is what is wrong. She had thought she was long over it. But in leaving London and the accoutrements of her self-styled success, she has left behind the identity she created for herself. She is having to confront herself anew; a formless embryo starting out again, ready for reinvention.

'I'm going to check Hannah,' she says, dodging his arm, his concerned, honest eyes.

The door to the spare room is ajar to allow the landing light to filter through. The child is asleep in a sausage-hump beneath the duvet. The window is open and the curtains closed. They stir in the breeze, first sucked flat, then plumping out, in time to the child's muted breathing. From the surrounding fields comes the occasional gargling bleating of sheep, and reciprocal baleful lowing of cows. The countryside is tranquil, and its tranquillity imparts itself to her. And this is what he has chosen for himself, in the same way she selected her life. She has no right to disrupt his.

He appears in the doorway, blocking out the light.

'Is she OK?'

'Fine.'

'And you?'

'Also.'

'I thought ... well, I thought you might have gone off me.'

'Hardly.'

He holds out one arm towards her then, motioning to her. She gets up and goes to him, into the enclave he has made for her.

'I've turned off the grill,' he whispers.

'Oh? And why would that be?' Smiling into the hollow between his chin and neck, feeling his beard tickling her nostrils.

'I don't want to do . . . to be—'

'Presumptuous?'

She can feel his arms relax. The gentle laughter vibrating through his body.

'Well, yes.'

'I'd rather like you to be. If *you* would.'

He gazes at her thoughtfully for a few seconds then leads her across the short gallery of the landing to a closed door. Opens it. His expression is faintly self-conscious as he closes it once more behind them. The room is fairly large; white-walled and with a brown, worn carpet that has obviously been taken from some other dwelling. Brown-and-blue open-weave curtains droop from the window, and the only furniture, apart from the bed, is an ugly oak wardrobe and a modern pine chest of drawers. The bed has a garish purple-and-yellow duvet cover over it and matching pillowcases.

'I'm not much of a one for interior design,' he says, apparently seeing the room for the first time, as though through her eyes. 'What goes with what, and suchlike, I mean.' Shrugs and looks so awkward that she feels protective of him.

'Not many men are,' she consoles him. 'It's perfectly all right.'

'It's not. It's all wrong. But I can't quite say why.' His arms hang by his side. His face is pulled down, dejected. 'I mean, before I had no reason to be fussed. The women I know – have known – well . . .' He leaves the sentence trailing.

She knows his nervousness is not only about the room.

'Aidan, I mean it, it's fine. It's absolutely irrelevant anyway.'

'You're so stylish. Even in jeans and trainers you somehow manage to look it. And your accent. Well, the Queen's English and all that. I feel a right bumpkin.' He sounds quite anguished.

'Shush.' Slaps his thigh. He captures her hand. 'As for my accent – my mother was Scottish and my father was Italian.'

Was Italian? He is probably still alive. Maybe remarried. Maybe she has half bro—. *Was* Italian. He is dead for her.

'I cultivated my accent,' she says.

Her eyes alight on the simple wooden cross above the bed. She tries not to show her surprise.

'Are you religious?'

'I'm a committed Christian. Does that bother you?' His defensive tone. His hand slipping away from hers.

'No.' But curiously, it does disturb her; she is so antireligion herself.

'I'm not heavy with it. I just believe in trying to be a decent human being. Fair, you know. I like to examine things from different perspectives. I don't go to church much. But I do believe in God. Call it gut instinct, if you like. It hasn't all happened for no reason. At least I hope not. I believe Christ was a representative of it all. Not a son, as such. One can't take things too literally.'

So here they are in his room, discussing style and accents and religion, and the scent is rapidly growing cold. They seem to be becoming snarled in knots, whereas a few minutes ago there was only a single thought in their minds. It is as though they cannot clamber back through the haze of misunderstanding to that point.

'Kiss me?' she says, tilting up her face.

'Oh God, Isabella.'

He stumbles towards her, and steadies her as she almost loses her balance, holding her upright again, his mouth fierce on hers. They don't speak again. She undoes the laces of her trainers, while he hauls off his shoes and socks and throws them across the room. His large fingers fumble with the small buckle of her belt before he manages to unfasten it, then he untucks her tight black T-shirt and hitches it over her head. She shakes her hair free. He hesitates then, gazing at her in her black lacy bra and, impatient, she undoes it herself and lets it slip to the ground. Stands before him: broad-shouldered and slender-waisted. Her breasts are heavy but firm, quite widely spaced; the coral-tinged nipples protrude from their pale aureolae like tiny stalks.

'Oh God, oh God.'

He bends his head and submerges his face in the smooth-skinned hollow between her breasts, then cups each one in turn, sucking at them, nibbling and tugging gently with his teeth so that her nipples extend further and a succession of ripples shoots up between her legs. The sensation of his beard on her flesh further increases her pleasure. She bends her head backwards, arching her throat with a sudden spasm, then she pushes him away from her and tries to pull off his track-suit top. He helps her by wriggling his arms free of the sleeves; finishes by doing it himself. They undress themselves hurriedly after that, yanking off their jeans and pants, almost tripping in their urgency as their feet become caught in the jeans' legs.

He has a fine body, carrying more weight than she expected round the waist and stomach, but not flabby. The hair is thick on his chest, tapering to a badger-stripe over his belly then splaying out in dark profusion round his penis. His erection is massive. He has the hugely muscular thighs and calves of a football player; his buttocks are taut and indented. When she stands back to look at him he rummages his hair and wears a slightly shamefaced smile as though embarrassed by her scrutiny of his nudity and his aroused state. She runs her fingers over his body.

'No.' He sinks slowly to his knees, stroking and caressing her all the way down, rubbing first his chest, then his penis against her. She can feel its secretion on her, and can smell fresh soap. He kisses her navel, lets his tongue travel over the sweep of her tummy, and stops just above her line of hair.

'Red hair down there,' he murmurs. 'I've never seen that. Like a flame. And so dense. Such dense, tight curls.'

And very tenderly parts her and places his tongue within the parting. She shudders. Cradles his head.

'I've not washed since this morning.' Conscious that he has done; worried that she might taste too strong.

He glances up at her from his crouching position. 'You're beautiful. You taste beautiful. Sweet as a nut.'

Goes back to what he was doing. Her whole body is electric and keening. She is groaning with pleasure; can feel that she is saturated as he inserts his fingers.

'I want to do it to you.' Forces him away from her and pulls him to his feet. His mouth is shining with her moisture. It sparkles on his beard. She slides down and he watches as she takes him in her mouth.

'That's fantastic,' he says as she snakes her tongue along, and then round and round the tip. Her hands gather him underneath, fondling his warm fullness. She moves her lips there.

'Isabella, I have to be inside you. Now. I don't want to come this way. That's not what it's about. I want it all to go on for ages.'

She finds herself lifted up, and he lowers her slowly on to the bed.

He gently prods with his penis on the edge of her clitoris, massages her with the tip for some minutes, then enters her with a sudden lunge so that she cries out with surprise and pleasure. After that he stirs in her very slowly, exercising all his control, his upper body raised away slightly from hers, hands gripping her waist, eyes staring into hers all the while. He is so deep, so swollen. She doesn't think she has ever known anything like this; so that she doesn't wish to move any part of her except for her muscles. Her ecstasy is almost excruciating.

'I've never known anything like this,' he says. 'You hold me so beautifully. Your muscles seem to be sucking me into you. Milking me.'

And she clasps him even tighter, squeezing, clenching her pelvic muscles, feeling him quivering. Colours flash before her as he makes little stabs within her, pausing between each; and then he begins to thrust harder, rhythmically. Their lips like leeches on each other. Tongues winding and probing. The wetness of their saliva. Their rapid breathing, locked eyes, her clenched fists, legs now gripping round his waist, feet resting on his bottom.

'I can feel your cervix. I feel so deep . . . Dear Isabella, dear Isabella . . .'

His hypnotic voice. His endearments as well as his passion . . . And the light diffusing behind her eyelids. Mystical surreal images. Forgotten names. Dimly aware of herself writhing and of her own animal cries. He has touched her G-spot, and she is flooding out from deep inside herself, shrieking, scratching his back . . . And still he does not let up, so that a tidal wave of release of another kind follows, engulfing her in a single paroxysm that becomes a series of small pulsations and finally dies away. He is stroking her hair, kissing her forehead. Her legs fall away from his. Her body feels totally exhausted.

'Please,' she says. 'A second . . . I need to breathe.'

He holds himself away from her, poised inside her, not moving, letting her recover. Her face is raging hot, her eyes burning and her mouth dry. When he hears her breathing quieten he rolls her over gently so that they are each on their sides; places her leg over his and begins again. As she becomes aroused this time he does not hold back. Faster and harder he thrusts, until it seems he is reaching into her navel. His body hair is sticky against her skin. She can smell his perspiration and her own odour of orgasm. His eyes are staring into hers, his mouth parted. She cups his testicles with one hand and with the other supports his flung-back head.

'Je-ee-sus.' Sharply gasped in her ear. His teeth clamped. And for a moment he arches completely away from her. She feels the warmth flushing through her and then he falls back against her.

They lie curled towards each other, limbs round limbs. Her mouth is parched and tastes sour; when he kisses her, his is also. The aftermath of lovemaking. The clamminess of the thighs, the matted pubic hair and the bodily oozing. The hot, silent, nothing-moving room.

'It was amazing,' she says into his beard.

He tells her, 'My whole life just seemed to flood out of my penis. It was so . . . protracted. I've never experienced anything like it.'

She nestles into him, catlike, and he traces her form with his fingertips – his hands are rough-textured, but coupled with his sensitive touch, the effect is sensuous.

'Tracing the topography of your body,' he murmurs. 'I feel very close to you, you know. It's funny . . .' He leaves the sentence unfinished.

The sweet sheen of contentment within her. And just at this moment something very akin to love.

'Me too,' she says. She suddenly thinks of the child. 'Madre, I hope Hannah didn't hear anything.'

'The door's really thick,' he says.

'She does usually sleep soundly.' To reassure herself.

'Borrow my dressing gown and go and check her if you like.'

She gets up slowly, reluctant to leave him, and to leave the warm humid cave of the bed. She can sense him watching her as she pads over to the door where his towelling robe is hanging. It is enormous.

'You look sweet in it. Lost.' He props himself up on his elbows and smiles at her.

The child is fast asleep on her tummy, her face half turned, one shoulder poking out. When Isabella touches the back of her head lightly she does not stir. Her breathing is the heavy, rhythmical breathing of tiredness and of satisfaction. This morning she went again to the playgroup. Becky hugged her hello. How important, friendship, Isabella muses. The wonderful thing about making love with Aidan was that it was making love with a friend. Sex with him had the excitement of newness, yet there was also a feeling of familiarity. It occurs to her that, with the possible exception of Tom – and that was so long ago she can scarcely remember – she has usually been the dominant one in bed, intent on impressing her partner with her skills. With Aidan she wanted only to revel and bask in all the different sensations he aroused in her, and in the awareness of an intimacy and closeness than went beyond these.

She returns to him. He is getting dressed.

'I thought we should eat,' he says, coming up to her to kiss her. One arm still out of its sleeve.

She helps him on with the dreadful track-suit top.

'She's sound asleep,' she says, of the child.

'That's good . . . You could spend the night. Will you?'

'I'd love to. I'll have to leave early to feed poor Garibaldi.'

Imagines sneaking back in, in the morning. Lizzie's reaction. Dick's eyes glossy with out-of-reach longing.

It is night now. She goes over to the window, naked.

There is a figure by the cypress trees, lit by the moon. She ducks.

'Aidan, there's someone outside, by the trees.'

He comes over immediately and looks out.

'There's no one as I can see,' he says, after several seconds.

She stares out again. There are only the dark trees swishing balletically.

'I swear there was someone.'

'I'll go down and check with the torch.'

He leaves her. She feels suddenly discomposed. Her sense of being safely cocooned is ruptured.

In the bathroom – it has a turquoise suite she would rip out, peach lavatory paper, yellow towelling curtains – she washes between her legs; the soap stings her and blends with their odours. She dries herself with an orange-and-purple towel. Picks up and puts down his toiletries: shower gel in a tube, a disposable razor, curved nail scissors, pump toothpaste, a black plastic comb, Old Spice aftershave with no lid. A man's bathroom.

In the bedroom she pulls on her jeans and top – she doesn't bother with shoes – and goes downstairs. He is bent over the cooker, and she puts her arms round him.

'Boo.'

The smell of the chicken grilling, the cheerful sound of vegetables boiling, and Domingo – she is certain it is him – singing from *Tosca*.

'You like opera?'

'Ah, she sounds surprised again!'

'No, I didn't mean . . . I only—' Conscious of how condescending she must seem, and blushing.

'It's OK . . . My mum was an opera fanatic. She was a music teacher. Yes, I like it.'

'Oh.' This makes her almost unreasonably happy. He likes opera.

'And you do, I gather,' he says dryly.

She doesn't answer; sucks in her lower lip, like a scolded child, and he laughs.

'It's the learning curve. We're on a learning curve with each other,' he says. 'By the way, there was no sign of anyone. Maybe it was someone looking for the main house, came here by mistake. It happens quite a bit.'

He dishes out the food. Huge portions on their plates. She lights a candle in an old beer bottle. They sit down opposite each other and raise their glasses in a toast. His hair is standing on end and she reaches over to smooth it down.

And how will it change things, their having made love? Aidan is not a frivolous sort of man whose emotions can be toyed with. He has no veneer. Eventually he will expect her to offer some explanation for why she is here. As for herself, she is both elated and anxious – as she envisages all the complications that must inevitably arise. She cannot separate her burgeoning mental attachment for this man from the act of making love with him.

He says, 'I want you to know I'm not like some men who . . . well, let's face it, a lot of men will do it just for the sake of it. Look, I don't just go with any woman. It has to mean something. Tonight – it was over a year since I last went to bed with a woman.'

'You're kidding.' Herself barely a fortnight. She is ashamed.

'I suppose I'm a romantic. An idealist.'

And she is afraid she will be the saboteur of this idealism.

It feels so right sitting across the table from him, in his lovely house with its appalling taste. She has become used to him over the last days: his ways, different nuances, his stubborn old-fashionedness, his dependability and kindness. And for her he has come to epitomise this region – this immense, sensitive man in touch with nature and at ease with himself.

'Won't you tell me about your childhood? I know next to nothing,' he says. 'I want to know what's made you you.'

He instantly notices the panic, followed by the guarded clouding over, in her eyes, and seeks to reassure her.

'I'm not trying to drag things out of you. Just something. Your parents, for instance. You said your mother was Scottish and your father was Italian. That's some combination.'

She cuts up a piece of chicken, eats it, and lays down her knife and fork on the plate. Takes a long sip of red wine. She looks at him in a measured way that he cannot quite fathom.

'My childhood,' she says, as though reciting the title of a book.

And proceeds to tell him what she has told no man – not Tom, who said only the present mattered; no other lover, because every one of them was inconsequential. She misses out nothing. Her father has just entered her bedroom and she is woken by his hands; now he has gone for ever; her mother has died. And there she is: young girl free to good home . . .

Aidan's eyes spilling compassion. The total silence around them. The flickering candle. She talks for two hours. He refills their glasses several times. He grips her left hand across the table, and sometimes his grip tightens at a particular revelation. He lets her smoke. He asks not a single question.

She stops speaking when she has reached the age of eighteen and is about to meet Tom.

9

'Mouse,' says the child.

They have settled into Timothy Abell's cottage, along with dozens of rodents that Garibaldi has, in the last fortnight, been rapidly decimating. Sometimes he catches one then loses it, and sits for hours apparently watching the television she has rented. Isabella shuts him out of the room, rescues the mouse huddled behind the television, and lets the cat back in – and he immediately returns to his vigil.

Several times she has caught him in the act of bringing a mouse from outside indoors. There he will be, halfway through the cat flap with the pitifully squeaking victim clamped in his jaws and hanging out either side like a *Viva Zapata* moustache. He always stops uncertainly when he sees her, pegs his ears flat to his striped skull and widens his green eyes in challenging contact, as she bars his entry. Then slowly he reverses out again and the flap swings softly shut.

They are everywhere: running down the tea towel, appearing from behind curtains, tucked in her wellington – as she discovered when she slid her bare foot inside. Sometimes there is just an organ or a part of the body, and she will tread on a liver or head or tail.

Every day she goes for a walk. The two headlands each have their own identity: the western one is rugged and barren with its gorse and bracken; the eastern verdant and cultivated. On one walk she saw a red squirrel. Aidan had told her they were virtually extinct everywhere in Britain except Scotland. She stopped still, astonished and entranced. It stared at her, nose quivering, from the tangle of brambles where she had surprised it. The beads of its eyes were cream-rimmed. A tiny animal – far smaller than the grey squirrels to which she was accustomed – and with a wispy tail that was like a question mark. It sat up suddenly on its hind legs, making a rubbing motion with its human-like hands, then fell back on all fours, darting its head away and then back towards her. For several minutes they remained like that, no more than six feet apart, herself not daring to move, when, with a swift, jerky movement, it turned and fled into the undergrowth.

Aidan said it must have escaped from somewhere. In bed he calls her 'My squirrel'.

He has taught her to distinguish between the various gulls and she is learning to recognise them for herself. She still confuses the common gull and the kittiwake, but she can tell the difference between the others – the black-headed gull, the herring gull and the lesser and great black-backed gulls. She will sit high up at a particular vantage point near the lighthouse where every inlet, projection, every crevice in the rock-face of the other promontory, can be clearly identified through Aidan's binoculars – a spare pair he had that he has lent her. The boulder is as comfortable as a padded cushion with its covering of grass like green hair. She could remain there all day watching the gulls and the movement of the sea. Sometimes the peacefulness and her thoughts might be shattered by a low-flying air force plane rending the silence with terrifying suddenness. The first time it happened she gave a cry of shock, so unexpected was it. All around birds squawked and flapped up into the sky.

At low tide she might take the precipitous steps leading to the cove and cross over to the other headland, following the path to the spot where she and Babs picnicked and the child disappeared after the rabbit; then she will take the fork that winds away from the sea until the heathland peters out and she comes to a stile. This leads across several fields of sheep and cows and inquisitive bullocks to a hamlet. One of the cottages there has a sign outside that always makes her smile. 'Worms for sale (lugworms),' it says. 'One pound per pail.' Along the lane from there she has discovered a potter's. The woman glanced up from her wheel and saw Isabella and the child peeping through the window, motioned them inside, and they watched her working. She has bought a couple of mugs and a jug that she appreciates for their simple form and natural glaze.

Over the last few days the wind has been strong, shrilling around the headlands, and the rain heavy on occasions, but she never fails to go for her walk, sometimes with the child, sometimes alone when she is at playgroup. Being fair-skinned she has never been partial to extreme heat and the weather suits her complexion. The bracing air has coloured her cheeks. The salt and the wind have lightened her hair a shade and caused it to curl slightly. She has given up wearing any make-up; feels fitter, is leaner than she has been for years and has more energy. She is cautiously happy. And the sand infiltrates her trainers; it clings to her clothes, to her skin and hair, and when she returns from her walks it transfers to the rugs and the bath and the bed. She pretends to complain, but in reality she likes it. The intrusive sand symbolises everything she never had.

On a shorter walk they came across a hollow oak in a spinney. There was just sufficient room for the child to climb inside. Hannah's Tree, they have named it.

'Let's go Hannah's Tree,' she begs, tugging Isabella's arm.

She marvels at the child's progress in just over a month. She is hardly recognisable. As for Isabella herself, she has entirely adjusted to her life here. Looks upon her previous incarnation, as she calls it, quite disparagingly. It was an existence she had pursued because it had been the one lodged in her mind since the age of sixteen. Here, with Aidan, with the child, it is as though all her senses have been awakened. She feels strangely exposed without the veneer she had assumed for years; her emotions are closer to the surface. But in another way she feels liberated. It is perhaps the nearest she has come to being her real self; and she has yet to become acquainted with this woman.

And her work is going well. She gets up early in the morning, inspired with enthusiasm. Translating the book is both challenging and exhausting; she finds she can only do a one-and-a-half-hour stretch at a go, but in that time she knows she covers more than most people would, and that she is more efficient, her usage of language richer.

Aidan has remarked on the change in her. He knows more about her than any man. He knows about her views and her values. He has encouraged this other woman tentatively emerging. He only buys red wine now. Knows her sexually in the minutest detail. He knows her every gesture and expression. He also knows her not at all.

She loves the changes in the weather as autumn sets in – once she would scarcely have noticed: a briskness in the air, the altering colours of the headland, the way the clouds sweep in and out, the metallic sea and the white spines of the waves. She loves the longer evenings and the wind's eerie whistling through the gaps round the windows. And sometimes she pictures Timothy Abell in his brown vinyl chair which his daughter burned, rocking away and scowling.

Loves the view at night of the staggered lights glittering from the village, like a lit birthday cake (and in a few weeks she will be forty. *Forty*. Madre. A couple of days ago she was astonished to notice a single grey hair in her left eyebrow, egregious amongst the dark). And at high tide the lights will be thrown on to the black sheltered water in the cove in crinkled yellow banners that illuminate the boats moored in their stream. Outside the narrows Charlie and his mates might still be out; she will see their navigational lights attached to the davit – red on the port side, he informed her, green on the starboard – bobbing up and down.

And she has become used to watching the lighthouse's rhythmical signals – two long, three short – winking on-off, on-off, like irregular heartbeats through the bedroom window; used to the dense sea mist that can enshroud all visibility early in the morning and which so filled her with panic the first time, when she awoke and could see nothing outside; not a shape, not an outline – nothing at all. It was as if the window had been painted opaque grey, or had been boarded up. And the mournful foghorn repeating its lament every twelve seconds.

'I hate it. It's as though everything is dead, as though nothing exists,' she said to Aidan, cuddling close in bed.

'It'll lift later.'

And sure enough it did. Slowly rolling back like paper wrapping being peeled away, to reveal the landscape bit by bit. She wanted to sing with gladness.

Used to the smell of a fresh catch on the beach; to hearing the front door of Charlie's cottage shut behind him as he limps off at ten to six in the morning, and his whistling dies away behind him; to the cockerel's rousing proclamations. And later in the morning, Joyce will be pegging out her husband's dungarees on the washing line where they flap in the breeze.

She takes the King Harry ferry nowadays as a matter of course, arriving there only minutes beforehand so there is no hanging about; shops at the big Sainsbury's on the outskirts of Truro, then might pop into the centre afterwards. She has become familiar with the daily pattern of life in Pengarris: the dustmen on Monday, mobile baker's Tuesday and Thursday, mobile library Wednesday. In the fortnight they have been here she has established a routine and as each day goes by she can breathe more easily.

Everybody in the village knows or recognises her by sight, and generally their curiosity has abated. There have been offers of help, words of advice. She has been touched by people's kindness.

Charlie presented her with a squid and Joyce gave her a bouquet of dried heather for luck the day she moved in. They came for supper that evening; Aidan cooked the squid as she couldn't bear to touch it and had no idea what to do with the thing. Over dinner, as the evening wore on and one wine bottle was replaced by another, Charlie became more and more loquacious; went into long explanations about on- and offshore winds and their effect on the sea, then began to ventilate his outrage about the commercial fishing industry, about European rights and about the government.

'I'll be telling all this to them television people,' he said. 'We don't want no politics brought into our livelihood.'

'You'll show them, if anyone will, Charlie,' his loyal wife said. A little tipsy.

And under the table Aidan's foot sought hers, and his eyes shone secret smiles; and the child slept sprawled across her lap.

When she was walking on Tregurran beach with Hannah a few days ago a spaniel came bounding across to them and leaped up at the child, bowling her over so that she toppled backwards on to the sand. The dog began to lick her face and to yap.

Isabella went to pull the child from under the dog. She thought she was crying; then she realised she was in fits of giggles.

A woman came running over. 'I'm so sorry, I'm most awfully sorry.' Yanking the spaniel off. 'He's just young.' And continued with her apologies. She was attractive, in a manicured way, middle-aged; a surgeon's wife, she told Isabella.

'We're having a small drinks do on Sunday morning,' she said. 'Do come.'

She has accepted, but she is wary. Recognises a type. Who does voluntary work and wears gold jewellery to walk the dog, has drinks do's. And lives in 'Rhododendron Drive'.

Also on Tregurran beach she met the woman on the cob. They were splashing about in the sea, the water up to the horse's hocks. It was plainly enjoying itself, its ears pricked and neck arched, wet tail swishing and sending spray flying as it ploughed up and down the surf parallel to the beach. She noticed Isabella and rode over.

'He adores it,' she said.

'It looks wonderful. I do envy you.'

'You ride?' She was ruddy-faced; a tough complexion and gunmetal eyes; gunmetal hair in a long plait hanging beneath a headscarf.

'When I get the chance.'

'This old boy's getting on for twenty-seven. I bred him myself. We're inseparable. When he goes I'll put a gun to my own head. The longest standing man in my life is Nabokov.'

She introduced herself as Mary Anne Evans.

'As in George Eliot,' Isabella commented.

'Precisely.' The woman looked at her keenly. She was also a writer, she said. Of pornography.

Isabella thought she was joking and grinned.

'I thought you were serious for a minute.'

'But I was.'

'Madre!' Gives a burst of laughter. 'What fun. I suppose you must be used to people's reactions.'

'I am. Mostly the blustering kind.'

'Well, you did rather throw it into the conversation in a kind of "I bake cakes" voice.'

'Talking of which, please come round this afternoon for

tea.' It was almost an order. 'I think I like you, which is rare,' she added.

So later Isabella drove to her home: a prefab bungalow on the road to St Austell, full of antiques, with a field for Nabokov at the rear and a sculpture of a nude man cupping an erection amongst the roses in her front garden.

'Man got stick,' said the child.

'That was my second husband,' said Mary Anne.

Then there is Aidan whom she has seen most days since she has been here. Once she went to another of his gigs; Sophia baby-sat. He performed a song he had composed for her:

'Secret woman, flame of the night, sprite by day, merging with the sand . . .'

Squirming in her chair. Her body hot with embarrassment. She was only grateful nobody realised it was her.

'Sprite?' she said derisively when he came to sit with her afterwards. 'I'm far too big to be a sprite.'

'Don't spoil it,' he pleaded.

'I'm sorry,' she said, contrite. Recovering from her embarrassment, she saw that he was hurt, and was immensely touched. 'It was a lovely thing to do.'

Last night they played the guitar and sang together. She sat curled at his feet, while the child lay on the rug, reaching up to twang at the strings and chuckling at the discords, joining in their singing in her odd, flat tone.

'I feel so comfortable with you,' he told her in bed, rippling his finger down the cleft of her ribcage. 'Does that sound boring?'

'No. I take it as a compliment.'

'Most women aren't good with silence. Have to fill the gaps. You – well you're not one for small talk, are you?'

'No, I suppose not.' Realised that she grew up without anyone with whom to indulge in it. That she actually did not know how to instigate it.

'There's an art to it,' she said. 'I don't have that ability.'

'Well, I like that about you. I think small talk's trite.'

Stroking her buttocks.

'And I like that.'

'Such soft skin. Such delicious, melting, welcoming folds . . . I feel very strongly for you. You know that, don't you?'

'Yes.'

'Is that—?'

'Presumptuous?'

She could feel him grinning in the dark.

'No. For once, no. I was going to say, premature.'

Oh, madre. She so longed to reciprocate, to say the same back, or more.

'It's not that it's premature. Not that. It's that there are . . . complications in my life. Real complications that can't be brushed aside.'

But he was not deterred. 'So then you do like me.'

'Very, very much.'

'Well, that's the main thing.'

And he rolled over towards her again, and they started to lose themselves once more; mouth on mouth, nipple to nipple, belly on belly – every conceivable part of them having contact. And finally he was in her again.

'I don't care what it is,' he said, taking her face between his great hands, loving her with his entire body. 'Not when there's this. Whatever it is, it doesn't matter.'

And now, at seven forty-five on this rainy morning, Wednesday, October the second, she is about to set off for London. Watches from the child's bedroom window for Sophia to arrive. A van pulls up instead of the expected Mini. She recognises it. Two people get out. Luke is with her and they are both coming to the door. She doesn't want him in her house; experiences that tightening sensation in her chest which she has whenever she sees him or even hears mention of him.

The bell rings and she walks downstairs slowly.

Sophia looks embarrassed. Blurts out, without saying hello: 'My car's clutch has gone so Luke's brought me. He's thirsty. Could he have a glass of water?'

And can't he ask for himself?

But: 'Hi. Yes. Come in,' she says with her usual air of calm, motioning them both indoors.

Sophia, nippy like a nervous bird. Her husband sauntering leisurely through the cottage, appraising the little sitting room. His insolent gaze sweeping over her computer on the table, the plants, the heavy cream curtains, the simple wooden chairs; and he runs his hand casually along the back of the green-and-white cushions of the futon-sofa.

Her eyes follow the action and she fights down anger.

In the scullery she pours him a glass of water, and he takes it from her without a word. She fiddles around at the sink to pretend to busy herself, but inadvertently catches his eyes over the rim of his glass. They are reptilian. And she is suddenly struck by a resemblance between him and a newspaper photo she once saw of Timothy McVeigh, the Oklahoma bomber. She has the impression he is deliberately playing some sort of game with her, understood only by himself. But she will not play mouse to his cat. She stares back at him. His eyes narrow and an evil expression that chills her comes into them. She tries not to flinch, held in this eye-lock, and it is he who drops his gaze first; yet she senses she has antagonised him. And meanwhile his wife glances anxiously from one to the other, as he gulps down the remainder of the water.

When he finally leaves and the van rattles off, it is as though a spring has been released in Sophia. Her relief is palpable; she becomes quite garrulous.

'You've done more to the cottage since I last came. New shelves. Plants. The futon. Everything looks really nice. I didn't tell you, but I remember it before. I came here a few times with Luke – that's why he was staring. It's so different.' Trying to excuse him. 'He used to work for Mr Abell.'

She supposes this could conceivably explain the mechanic's behaviour. But she cannot forget the malevolence in his expression.

She asks the girl about Timothy Abell.

'I was sorry for him. I thought he was lonely. People didn't like him. But I think he cared under it all . . . I told my parents you were half Italian. They think it's nice. That I'm childminding for you.'

'You really don't mind staying overnight? Sleeping on the futon?'

'No. Luke only ever watches videos. You know, horror videos and such. He loves those . . . I could clean for you as well, if ever you wanted.'

Isabella pictures the mechanic in front of the television, engrossed in a violent scene. Now he is leaning forward in his chair, to watch a knife being twisted in a woman's chest . . .

'It's just the other evening you said you've got masses of work and you didn't know how you'd do it, and the sand got everywhere, so I—'

Isabella focuses on her. 'I'm sorry. Yes, that could be an excellent idea.'

'Maybe I shouldn't've said. It's like I was asking you. It's put you in a spot.'

'No it hasn't.'

And although a moment ago she had been thinking she would not use Sophia again because of her husband, she now hears herself saying that she will need her twice a week and they must discuss a suitable wage.

The girl's face sparkles. 'I've brought Hannah some jelly babies. I hope she likes them.'

She delves into the holdall of belongings she has brought with her and rips open the packet with her teeth. Gives it to the child, who is sitting on the floor playing. 'There you are, darlin'.'

Hannah thanks her, as Isabella has taught her. She says 'fank' instead of 'thank'.

'Dear little thing – how she's come on, hasn't she?'

Sophia bends to kiss her. Jealousy nudges at Isabella.

'I've been really looking forward to this. You know – staying the night.' She says it shyly, confidingly, her eyelashes sweeping downwards over her thin cheeks.

'You will remember to keep the gate shut *all* the time.'

'You can trust me. Really. I'll be really careful.'

And what of the baby that died of cot death? *Was* it cot death? How long ago did it happen?

She finds it so hard to leave. Picks up Hannah – who wraps her legs round her – and kisses her several times.

'That's for today and tomorrow morning, carina.' Tweaks her little nose. Hannah's laugh rings out.

'I don't like leaving her.'

'We'll be fine,' Sophia says.

And on an impulse Isabella hugs her.

The girl looks surprised, then her face breaks into a smile and Isabella again notices how it entirely changes her appearance so that the meagre features are lifted from their plainness.

For the last two weeks she has found every excuse to defer going to London. Now, as the miles are eroded and the windscreen wipers dance to rain and autumn, and the motorway flings up spray from lorry wheels, so her tension grows. It does not feel as though she is going home but as though she is leaving it and is heading somewhere that is dragging her back against her will to entrap her. She fears her own weakness: that she will be lured by those things that lured her before; that after all it is her London life as a carefree single woman which most suits her. The eczema on the inside of her elbow has flared up and she can feel it becoming more irritated by the second; is always amazed at the speed with which it can flare and abate. She rubs it against the side of her body. And with every mile that is covered, and as one motorway is exchanged for another, and the road signs indicate London a hundred miles, then fifty, twenty-five – so the recent weeks recede into the past.

Now she is swinging on to the North Circular, into lunch-time blocks of wheezing traffic. And across the other carriage-way she once imagined she saw a child. Worn women push their baskets on wheels along dirty pavements into the Spar; men with ash-tipped cigarettes drooping from their mouths slink into the bookie's, checking their pockets at the same time; and the machines in the launderette whirl. And outside the newsagent's is another pushchair with another child.

Hampstead High Street is bustling in the rain. Irritable faces beneath a ceiling of umbrellas. Dodging feet. Music spilling out from shops whose lights reflect into the day's greyness. The owner of the fruit stall sheltering under his striped canopy. The dark outlines of people browsing in Waterstone's. Crowded cafés. Cars cruising, vainly searching for a parking space . . . So familiar. All so familiar. And once the very encapsulation of everything she had fought to achieve. And here is the dry cleaner's where the assistant lovingly strokes the clothes in their polythene wrapping before parting with them; here is the chemist's where the pharmacist told her to try putting yoghurt on her eczema rather than buying expensive ointments; here the Asian newsagent's where she always buys – bought – her papers; here, Café Rouge . . . And perhaps she will go in there later and sit in her old corner. And behind the façade of shops are small lanes that lead to the acres of heath where she and Peter would go for walks together; and latterly he would try to goad her, exercising his supremacy and venting his swelling male ego. Cosmopolitan, arty Hampstead with its affluent left-wing, liberal-thinking clientele, its intelligentsia, its cliques, its own kind of prejudices and élitism. And now she wants to be able to view it with disdain so that she can whole-heartedly turn her back on it a second time.

And here she is, pulling up in the nearest vacant spot to her flat . . . and she is getting out of the car, walking towards the building, past the dripping maples, treading polished leaves. And manic fingers hammer the keyboard of her chest as she descends the steps to her own front door.

Gloom and unloved darkness greet her. As she expected, the mat is heaped with mail and there is more stuffed through the mouth of the letterbox, but there is nothing out of the ordinary. Isabella tiptoeing about with a burglar's stealth. Her flat reproaches her. There is a curious deadness about it, removed of all personality. The windows are misted over, dust shimmers on the surfaces of tables and shelves, soot has blown down the chimney on to the rug, her plants are either completely dead or brown-edged and wilting in the last stages of expiry. She goes from room to room, opening cupboards and drawers, putting on lights, trying to feel a sense of homecoming. The place is untidy with evidence of her hasty departure, clothes on the back of a chair, balls of tissue paper and carrier bags scattered about, the child's toys that could not be squeezed into the car.

In the kitchen she makes a black coffee – the water erupts from the tap. While the kettle is boiling she switches on the radio in an attempt to impart a sense of normality to the atmosphere, but the male broadcaster is relating the horrors of Albania and she turns it off. When she opens the fridge she is almost buffeted backwards by the rank stench of food that has decayed. Coffee in hand, she plays the messages on her answerphone – writes down new ones. Wipes clean the tape. Starts to go through all the correspondence, getting rid of the junk mail first. One particular item catches her attention. It is a photograph, sent by an animal welfare charity, of a Chinese black bear in a capsule no bigger than itself. There it will remain imprisoned until the end of its days, while an attached catheter drains a bodily fluid purported to be beneficial to the health of human beings. The picture horrifies her and she immediately writes out a cheque for twenty-five pounds. Nevertheless she cannot banish the picture from her mind: the bear's muzzle jammed against the end of the cage, the despair in its eyes. She is not a sentimentalist, but she has never been so moved by an animal's plight.

She has the need to free herself of the image – gets up from the kitchen table and systematically sets about cleaning the house. An hour later it looks as it always has done: her own flat which she always regarded as her refuge, every object and piece of furniture chosen with the utmost care to reflect the different aspects of Isabella herself. But – she feels only an affectionate detachment towards it. Rather like returning to a lover only to tell him she is leaving him for good.

Upstairs in her room she sorts out more things to take back with her. Most of her clothes fill her with distaste. Chic dresses; power suits. Others – impulse buys – she has hardly worn and is unlikely to do so; and she has the idea of giving them to Sophia. Into the suitcase go more books and sheet music, jewellery, CDs, the correspondence she cannot deal with now, a few personal items.

Towards four thirty she is suddenly hungry and realises she has not eaten. Decides to go to Café Rouge for one of their delicious *croques au saumon fumé* with fries. Locks up the flat and walks to the High Street – losing herself in the anonymity of rush hour. Frayed-tempered drivers. Queues at the bus stops. The Tube vibrating beneath her legs. And into the newsagent's.

'We haven't seen you for ages,' the little man beneath the huge turban says. His cheeks are like Italian grapes, and he has the most beautiful white teeth, the most perfect lips she has ever seen.

'I've been away.' And then a thought occurs to her. 'Mr Shastri, your wife, she wouldn't . . .'

His wife comes downstairs from the flat above the shop, a wiry woman in an emerald sari, and it is arranged that she will come in once a week to dust over Isabella's apartment and generally keep an eye on it. Isabella pays her in advance and gives her her phone number and forwarding address. Arranges to return in the morning with the spare key.

'You've no idea what a load off my mind it is.'

'But what are you doing in Cornwall?' Mrs Shastri asks.

'Finding myself,' she says.

'Everybody seems to be running off to find themselves these days,' Mr Shastri observes, pinching his jowls and looking perplexed. 'I don't understand. What is there to find by running that cannot be found by staying?'

At the post office she fills in a form to have her post redirected. 'With immediate effect,' she writes.

Café Rouge is full. She has to wait. The gay waiter, with whom she used to discuss Peter Greenaway films, chats to her meanwhile. Finally she sits at her usual table by the window, with her *croque* and fries and a cigarette and a cappuccino, reading her magazine and watching the Hampstead types scurrying by. Is amused as she spots one or two people she knows.

Later she calls Sophia. The phone rings about fifteen times before it is picked up. Her armpits become damp with anxiety.

'I was bathing her,' the girl says. 'I couldn't get to the phone.'

'It doesn't matter.' Relief flowing through her. 'How are you both?'

'Great. We had a lovely day.' She sounds animated as she relates it to Isabella, who lies on her cool silk bedspread, lazily tripping her fingers up and down her body.

'I can't wait to get back,' she says.

She does not sleep well that night. Picks out every sound in her flat and finds it alienating rather than soothing. She cannot embrace it and make it hers again. Within her is a feeling of disonance, a sense of being neither one person nor another, a ghost passing through her old existence. She misses the child, the sound of the sea and the wind. Aidan. Physically aches for him, for his voice – the curved, soft vowels. Pictures him in his bed with the purple-and-yellow duvet half flung off him. And in her bed at the cottage. His clear eyes inside hers, the silkiness of his body hair, the concrete-hard muscles of his thighs, his lips between her legs and his beard rubbing back and forth there . . . And after making love their feet cross over and curl round one another's and they will sleep that way. And when he snores faintly she is reassured by his presence.

She piles up the car and sets off early the following morning. Deposits the key with Mr Shastri, who comes down in his dressing gown to answer the door.

'Well, it's better weather today at least,' he says, glancing up at the teal sky which the pale sun is trying to penetrate. 'You look cheerful for so early in the morning.'

And she is. Impatient in her eagerness to get away. And, driving out of London against the clogged-up traffic and fumes, she uses landmarks to make the journey seem shorter; and it is as though a band of pressure is being lifted from her.

When she comes to Bodmin Moor she calls Aidan on his mobile phone from hers. He answers, and she feels an almost dizzying rush of pleasure when she hears his voice.

'Hi, you,' she says.

'Oh, hello there.'

She gathers immediately from the formality in his tone that he is with someone.

'You're not alone.'

'No. I'm in the workshop with Luke. Hang on.'

She can hear his steps echoing as he walks from there to

his office. But the mere mention of the mechanic's name has discomposed her.

'Right—' The banging of the door. 'I'm alone now.'

'I only rang to say hi.'

'Well, it's good to hear from you.' Warm-toned now. 'Where are you?'

'Driving past Bodmin. Madre, it's so bleak. I'd hate to break down here.'

'I'd rescue you. So how's you? How did you get on?'

'Fine. I got everything done that I needed to.' Hesitates. 'I missed you.'

'I did too. I couldn't put you in any kind of place. You were just kind of floating.'

'I pictured you in your bed. Do you want to come over later?'

The phone crackles and his reply is lost. She shouts down the line a few times, disproportionately upset; is about to press the red button to end the call and try redialling when suddenly he is there again.

Joy.

'Did you catch any of that?' he asks.

'No.'

'Just as well. It was pretty filthy.'

Smiling down the line now. 'So are you coming over?'

'I could be persuaded.'

She can tell that he is smiling also. Madre, I love him.

Halfway down the main street of Pengarris something is going on. A Toyota Land Cruiser is parked, and alongside it, blocking her passage, is a red Alfa Romeo with its hazard lights blinking. The rear of the Land Cruiser is open to reveal technical equipment inside. Three men are standing round the vehicle, in discussion. She realises it must be the television team. Quite a gathering of locals are also hanging around, gawping. No doubt this will provide them with conversations and reminiscences for the next five years. Pengarris Cove put on the map. Fame comes its way. Babs is amongst them and waves to her; then the man who is double-parked darts into the road to move his car. Gestures apologetically towards her. She only catches a glimpse of him but she recognises him instantly. Twenty years later. Grey-haired now, but unmistakable. The same compact physique, the same neat, quick movements as he scrambles into the driving seat and revs up the Alfa. He had not even learned to drive a car when she knew him. Only a motorbike.

Tom.

Back at the cottage the child runs up to her and flings her arms round her. It is her most effusive action to date. Sophia looks relaxed. There is a smell of tomato soup and toast from the kitchen. Toys strewn about the sitting room.

There should be such pleasure in being back.

'I gather there were no problems, then?'

'None at all. She was ever so good. You look all in.'

'I am a bit.'

'The telly people are here. We walked into the village.'

'Yes, I know. I saw.'

Sophia helps her unload the car.

'My rocking horse,' the child exclaims when Isabella carries it indoors, and immediately clambers on to it.

'I love you, carina.' Isabella puts her lips to Hannah's.

Hannah reaches up and touches her eyelids. 'I love Mummy.'

Isabella is astounded. She cannot believe what she has heard. Hugs the child tightly.

Hannah continues rocking on the horse as if nothing momentous has occurred.

Has it? Does she understand what it means? Does anyone?

'I've got some things for you,' she says to Sophia. 'I don't know if they'll be any good.'

She lifts out the top layer of clothes from the case; also a bag she has no further use for and into which she has put various pieces of costume jewellery. Is almost dismissive in the way she gives them to the girl; covering up her awkwardness. She has never done anything like this before.

Sophia holds her hands to her face in disbelief, half weeping; exclaiming over each item as she picks it up. She is so overwhelmed that Isabella feels guilty. These are her rejects, bought in too much of a hurry, some hardly worn, or with which she has grown bored. Possibly five hundred pounds' worth of clothes that she is heaping on this simple girl, who will wear them to the pub or a girls' night out. If she goes on them.

'Most of them will need altering. You're much smaller than me.'

'I'm good with a needle and thread.' Her face is flushed. It is obvious that few favours have ever come her way. More than anyone, Isabella understands what this means.

'It's not charity. I don't want you to think that. I don't want to seem patronising.'

The girl doesn't reply. Shaking her head as she holds a red satin skirt against her, and laughing.

Isabella aches at her delight. And later will Sophia parade in her red satin and black chiffon for her husband? Will he picture Isabella instead?

'I'll take you back now, if you like,' she says softly.

The Land Cruiser and Alfa have gone. The narrow street is quiet again. She wonders whether she can avoid meeting him.

Next to her the child counts her fingers: 'One, two, three, one, two, one, two, three . . .'

'You go right here,' Sophia instructs her, from her cramped half-lying position at the back.

. . . I want to be happy. Don't let it be destroyed . . .

'Left at the telephone kiosk.'

She parks outside a reconstituted-stone council house, with white picket fencing bordering a colourful flowerbed.

She remarks on it as she helps the girl from the car.

'Luke's obsessive about gardening,' she says, jiggling her legs. 'Horror videos, gardening and cars. See you Monday, then. I mean, that's if you still want me to come and clean for you.'

'Definitely. I may even get you to fetch Hannah from playgroup if I'm in the middle of working. Will your clutch be fixed by then?'

'Oh, yes. He's good like that, is Luke.' She is laden with her bounty. Gestures with her elbow at all the bags. 'It's so nice of you. I don't know how to thank you. Nobody's ever—'

'Sophia, you don't need to. You've more than thanked me. Your pleasure is enough. I mean that. Now off you go.'

Watches her walk up to the front door, set down the bags as she fishes into her pocket for her key.

''Bye, then,' the girl calls as she lets herself into the home she shares with her mechanic husband.

Isabella toots the hooter and drives off.

Would this fit you, dear? she recalls the botanist asking her, holding up a peach nylon blouse with pearl buttons. Cast-offs.

Seeing Tom has completely unsettled her.

Aidan has bought her flowers. He kisses her passionately then grabs the child and swings her into the air, hoists her on to the yoke of his shoulders.

'Who's as high as a mountain, then? Who's as high as a mountain?'

'Me. Me. Me.'

It has become a ritualistic game. And she loves to watch the two of them, the giant of a man and the tiny child. His presence has become so dear to her. They have become like a normal couple. And he talks of the future: 'We'll celebrate your birthday in style. I want to take you out properly.' Or: 'I'll make sure your roof's properly insulated for winter.' Or: 'We must remember to put antifreeze in your car.' Or: 'I'd like to take you both to the seal sanctuary at Gweek.' He assumes that nothing will change, except for the good. And his bits and pieces are all round the cottage: a comb, his toothbrush, a motoring magazine, his drill . . . She teases him about it. Marking your territory, she says.

And she had not thought it possible, but sex with him improves and improves. And this night, as he moves his pelvis against hers and rubs the helmet of his penis gently around her swollen labia, so that every nerve ending is titillated and her fingertips and toes burn, and her body arcs with longing for him, he tells her that she must have gathered by now that he is in love with her. That he could never make love like this otherwise.

All under threat.

'Are you crying? Oh, my sweetheart, don't fret,' he says in his tender, rolling voice that has come to mean the landscape itself to her. 'We'll sort things out, whatever they are.'

10 ∫

'. . . So, cara,' Isabella writes to Sally in the first of her explanatory letters, 'I suppose we all get to a stage where we question ourselves – our needs, our directions; apparently it was my turn to reach that stage.' So far, so true. 'And now for the big shock. I have adopted a child. She is from Bosnia . . .'

She wishes she had told everyone this in the first place; wishes she had never started dyeing the child's hair. All these stories floating about: her godchild, her sister's child, her own daughter. And now an orphan from Bosnia.

It is easy to lie on paper. The recipient is distant, both literally and emotionally. It is as though everybody she knew before Hannah has ceased to exist. Is she callous? Is there something lacking in her? She does not *feel* a bad person, yet she has concocted an elaborate lie to her oldest friend.

She is pensive, disappointed in herself, as she signs off from this, her first letter.

The surgeon's wife glides around with a plate of tiny whirligig sandwiches. Her daughter is fulfilling her duty with a dish of cheese croquettes spiked with cocktail sticks.

'Tomato-and-herb relish,' she says when someone asks her what the dip is.

'Absolutely marvellous food, Deirdre,' someone yells across the room.

The boy is helping his father with the drinks. 'Pimm's or Bucks fizz?' he asks people in turn, with his father's easy smile and public-school tenor. Banking, she hears him tell someone. I want to go into banking.

The daughter is about eighteen – a year or so younger than her brother, heavily built, with a moon face. Sleepy eyes like her father's prevent her being plain.

'Don't congratulate me,' her mother is saying. 'Emma did all the food. We paid her to do it, didn't we, darling?' Hand resting lightly on the girl's neck. 'Emma's at catering college, aren't you, darling?' Emma nods.

The spaniel sniffing round everyone's feet and hoovering up dropped titbits. And Isabella stifles a laugh as it cocks its leg over a handbag resting by the turquoise moiré sofa.

'. . . so I told him he could expect his knees to outlive him by ten years,' the host, an orthopaedic surgeon, is saying in a voice intended to be overheard, glancing in her direction for verification. He has already admired her leather skirt, and 'the wondrous colour of her hair'. A man who has affairs, and his poor wife probably knows it. Isabella is surprised the woman took the risk of inviting her.

Everything about the party, about the house, about the guests, is as she predicted.

'So you've just moved here, have you?' the man with whom she has been talking for the last few minutes asks.

'Yes. About a month ago. Well, a couple of weeks in Pengarris itself.'

'Hear you've taken the ramshackle place on the headland. The man who had the garage. What was his—'

'Timothy Abell.'

'Yes, that's it. Some scandal with his—'

'Would you like a salmon roll?' Emma passing with a tray.

'Thanks. Yes.' She takes two. Nervousness giving her an appetite. Emma gives her a floral-patterned napkin and a shy smile. Poor girl, Isabella thinks, though she is not quite sure why.

She is planning her escape from this man; has to her relief seen Mary Anne arriving, draped dramatically in a dark green cape.

'Rather odd your picking somewhere like this to live, isn't it?' Eyeing her out-of-place skirt and tight black top some perversity made her put on.

And him, too, she had predicted. He is bald, not silver-haired; otherwise his military bearing, severe gaze, the navy blazer are exactly as manifested in her thoughts when she had first set eyes on Rhododendron Drive.

And:

'What do you do?' she asked him politely a few moments ago.

And word for word he replied: 'I'm retired now. But I'm a magistrate . . .'

'It's a good place to bring up a child,' she says in response to his comment. Excuses herself then, as he is about to question her further – and catches his disapproving frown when she waves to Mary Anne before making her way across the room to her.

'Thank God, a human face,' she says.

'Dear girl, how delightful. What a splendid outfit.'

Mary Anne kisses her and immediately regales her with biographical details of everybody in the room: 'The man you were talking to – dreadful, parsimonious type. He's probably into flagellation underneath all that smugness. A widower. I'm sure he drove her to her death. She became an alcoholic. He's a magistrate – but no doubt he told you that. He'd have us all behind bars if he could . . . That man over there by that incredibly shiny rubber plant – now he was an SAS officer, a death squad man. But he's seen the light' – she makes inverted comma signs with her fingers – 'and given it all up; gone into the Church. And the man with the ginger tufts in his ears like a lynx, next to the woman with the black bee-swarming hair – he *was* a priest, but he's seen the light and discovered sex and *left* the Church . . .'

Isabella screeching with laughter so that several other guests turn to look at her. The eyes of one or two men remain riveted. One youngish blond woman clasps her husband's head and swivels it back to face her. Wags her finger reprovingly and winks at Isabella.

'Now she's nice,' Mary Anne says. 'A psychotherapist, or whatever they call them . . . And that rather beautiful woman in a tragic kind of way, the one by the door, is lesbian and has just nicked the Amazon with her from *her* husband with whom she was originally having an affair . . . My dear, our host thrives on the local scandals. He laps them up. Makes him feel modern. His wife has to go along with it. But look at that rictus of a smile. The rail tracks round her mouth. That is not a happy woman.'

'Madre, Mary Anne, you take my breath away. So have you shoved them all in a book?'

'Singly, dear girl. Not *en masse*.'

'I shouldn't think anyone feels safe with you.'

'Well, some of them do steer clear, but I think they would do anyway. One of the pleasures of being a writer is you can model a character on someone and that person will rarely recognise themselves. Very few people are aware of their idiosyncrasies or habits. Now you, for instance—'

Isabella strikes a challenging pose.

'I've noticed you have an unusual and very abrupt way of completely cloaking yourself.'

She is intrigued. 'What do you mean?'

'Well, you have the most expressive features – your eyes are too marvellous and one eyebrow lifts independently of the other. You have that Latin way of flinging your hands about, sort of turning your body and thrusting forward a shoulder at the same time. But then you will be like a marble sculpture. Your face is inscrutable. It's as though you are two women.'

'I'm off,' Isabella jokes, making as if to go. 'I don't like this.'

'And perfume,' Mary Anne persists. 'Now perfume can make you think of so many things. Gives off different messages. Some women douse themselves in far too much, which of course means they don't like their own smell. You're wearing something ferny and subtle. And by now, you see, I'm building a picture. Creating a character. But *you* wouldn't know it was you. Give you different hair, another name, and we're all set.'

'And yourself. Do you put yourself in?'

'Well, a lot of the sex is first-hand. But the last time was rather a long while ago now, so there isn't quite the same spark when I write about it. Sometimes I plagiarise my own books without realising.'

'Aren't there only just so many ways of writing about the same thing?'

Mary Anne presses her fingers to her cheeks, aghast. 'My dear, what a thing to say! And I didn't expect it from you of all people. There are hundreds of ways of having sex, making love, call it whatever coy term you will. We have arguably the richest language in the world – the permutations are endless.'

'Now you've made me feel stupid.'

'No, my dear. And in fairness to yourself, I've read more badly written sex scenes than good. It's either like reading a biology textbook, or everything's referred to metaphorically so that you could be forgiven for thinking it was a jungle expedition . . . or the whole thing's so ridiculous as to be completely risible. I'll give you one of mine, see what you think.'

A couple of hours later, and she is about to leave. The surgeon corners her in the front porch. Leans his arm over her, resting his hand against the fibreglass pillar so that she is blocked.

'So nice to have such a delightful newcomer to these parts. Do give us a shout if we can do anything. That's what neighbours are for. I sometimes go jogging your way. I might drop by.' A meaningful look in his eyes which she wouldn't trust peering at her femur, and he draws back his arm.

She mumbles a reply that is both polite and deterring. Something about her work. Scorn filling her. The arrogance, the . . . presumptuousness (a fleeting smile, as she thinks of Aidan). The sheer male conceit. She makes her getaway, and steps out into the misty cold; the sweet damp-heather air.

She can hear laughter and chatter through the open window of Charlie and Joyce's cottage. The melting odours of roast beef drift outside. One of Joyce's records is playing. Dean Martin? Joyce is passionate about the old crooners. Charlie is tolerant. Well, I can't be jealous. They're all dead, aren't they? he says.

There is no bell, and when nobody hears her knock she lets herself into the lobby. Charlie's wellingtons are propped against the wall, a pair of heavy woollen grey socks draped over them. Through the glazed door she can see Hannah sprawled on the living-room floor playing with some cookery utensils. Charlie, Joyce, and a man whose face is averted are sitting close together, poring over what looks like a photo album. But she knows who it is; and her heart is thwacking against her sternum as she turns the handle.

They all glance up as she enters.

'Hello, dear, did you have a good time?' Joyce.

'Well, I bet you knocked them for six, in that get-up.' Charlie.

'Mummy!' Hannah bounding up.
'G-o-o-d G-o-d,' Tom iterates slowly.

'We were friends at Bristol, when I was at university,' she
says. Shoots him a warning look. She can see he is enjoying
the situation. His eyes, navy and thick-lashed and slightly
compressed between loose skin now – which doesn't detract
from his attractiveness – glint with relish. And even after all
these years that well-remembered expression has the same
effect on her, irritating her on the one hand so that she
wants to wipe it from his face, and on the other drawing
her, so that she finds herself wanting to appeal to him.
It was always a battle of supremacy with them. Edging
forward, hammering home, retreating, then starting again.
He was utterly unsentimental in a relationship. A charmer
who needed people but who had no close friends and, she
suspected, was something of a misogynist.

She is shocked that all this time later and despite Aidan he
still has that power over her. His greying hair is cut in the
same style as it was then. It grows forward and he wears it
very short, close around his flat ears (she used to stroke and
nibble them, fascinated by their small neatness). His face is
fleshier but his jaw is still firm with the defined cleft that he
used to say was the mark of a good lover. And yes, he was
good. But silent. She never knew what he was thinking, and
sometimes he made her feel as though he were a voyeur on
the act, spying on her pleasure, and she became inhibited
under his tireless, detached gaze.

'You're like an automaton,' she accused him when her
orgasm wouldn't happen because of her self-consciousness,
not long before he went to Vietnam. He had pulled out of
her immediately and without comment, and gone to sleep
directly. She had hated him then, had wanted to hit him
repeatedly; a feeling very akin to that which she'd had as a
small girl tearing out her doll's hair while her parents rowed

in the kitchen below the flat. Remembers getting out of bed
and putting on all the lights in order to disturb him as much
as possible; spending the night reading under the ceiling
provided by the built-in bed in which he slept soundly, with
his clear conscience.

He is wearing a safari jacket over an Arran pullover.
Jeans. Heavy lace-up shoes. He looks what he is – somebody
connected with the media. So bizarre and disconcerting,
sitting a few feet from him. He must feel discomposed
also, although if so he is masking it well. After that initial
incredulous exclamation he has shown no sign of anything
except amusement. And what is his impression of her? Does
he see a middle-aged woman? Madre, such kids they were.
She was. Extraordinary to think they were married. He is
drinking water, she notices. Earlier he refused Charlie's
offer of whisky. 'Just a tot,' Charlie tried to persuade him,
holding out a precious bottle. 'By way of celebration.' It was
returned, untouched, to the cupboard.

Charlie is beaming with the repleteness of Sunday bon-
homie: church, communion wine, beer, beef, his wife fussing
around him, and the pleasure of another pair of ears to listen
to his yarns and to his grumbles. His bad leg resting up on a
footstool.

'He's OK, this friend of yours,' he tells Isabella. 'Agrees with
me about things, y'know.'

'*Most* things, Charlie.' Tom leans forward to rest his elbows
on the low table in front of him. Smoking. 'Isabella will tell
you I'm always objective.' Wrinkles his forehead quizzically
at her.

'I wouldn't know,' she says. Stroking Hannah's hair. The
child lying on her tummy, scribbling on some paper.

'Oh, come on, Bella.'

His voice is still the same. Still exaggeratedly refined.
It seems even more so when contrasted with Charlie's
lubricious accent.

This proprietorial use of the old nickname disturbs her.

'I wouldn't agree you were always objective.' Thinking of his irrational behaviour when he returned from Vietnam. How nothing satisfied him.

He turns to Charlie. 'You see, Charlie? Never appeal to a woman's better nature. They don't have one.'

Joyce observes them shrewdly, her eyes going from one to the other.

'Well, anyway, like I was saying' – Charlie doggedly refuses to be deflected – 'if the Spanish didn't keep pinching our waters . . .'

His wife raises and drops her shoulders in mock exasperation; but at the same time she puts another wedge of fruit cake on his plate, and he breaks off to utter 'Ta, love' and to give her hand a squeeze.

Tom glances across at Isabella. She knows he is angling to be alone with her, and when she stands up to leave he does also. Annoyance pricks her: that he automatically assumes he can come back with her. And later Aidan is coming. She wonders what Joyce is making of it all. Charlie is too impressed by Tom, too excited about his role in the documentary; but she has a woman's perception. She is not small-minded like many of the local women. Confided to Isabella that she herself was a target of gossip when she married Charlie. And she has had her own disappointments: a drug-addict son who busks in London, and a zealously Christian daughter who lives in a commune in Sussex with two children she seldom sees.

'Keep your eyes open,' she whispers to Isabella as they leave.

'Yes, I know.'

The two men shaking hands. Charlie clapping Tom on the back in a good-humoured haze.

She unlocks the door to the cottage and he follows her inside. He has a jaunty, rather swaggering way of walking, hands in pockets, so that the jacket is pulled tight over his bottom. He is narrow-hipped and small-buttocked. From the back, in his jeans, he could be a boy except for his grey hair. And now for the first time he seems unsure of himself; ill at ease as he pads about jerkily, making small noises in his throat that she takes for approval. He throws himself on to the futon-sofa then immediately springs up and goes and sits in the cane armchair, where he leans back and makes fists in the air. Madre, she had forgotten what an unrelaxing man he was.

'I'd love a coffee,' he says meekly when it is clear she isn't going to help him out with conversation. 'This is quite a surprise, Bella.'

'Would you rather have something else? Wine?'

It only takes a little humility on his part to soften her.

'I don't drink any more. I've been dry for nine years.'

'Oh.' Resists a biting comment. 'Good for you.'

'It's all right. I haven't become boring.'

'Isn't that for others to judge?' Hears the primness in her own tone, and quickly addresses the child before he can retort.

'Hannah, carina, leave Garibaldi alone. He doesn't want to play.'

'He does.'

She is on her hands and knees, cornering the cat by the table. The cat's tail swishes and his ears are flattened.

'No, cara. When he puts his ears back like that and wags his tail it means he's cross.'

'Grabla cross wimme?'

'Yes, carina.'

'Why?'

'Oh God,' Tom drawls. 'Spare me.' Rolling his eyes.

She ignores him.

'Because he's in a bad mood. He's horrid when he's in a bad mood, cara. It's best to leave him alone. Do you want to come and help me make coffee?'

The child accompanies her into the kitchen. Tom has lit a cigarette and is scouring about for an ashtray.

'There aren't any ashtrays in this place.'

'That's because nobody here smokes,' she says, skirting round him to get milk from the fridge.

He hops out of her way.

'You used to.'

'Hannah hates it.'

'So I suppose you want me to put this out.'

'It's up to you.'

'Well, I will.' He runs it under the tap. 'So you make the rules here, do you?' he says to Hannah. Who takes no notice of him. Occupied with arranging shortbread fingers on a plate.

'You look in bloody good nick for your age, I must say,' Tom tells Isabella. 'Dammit, for any age, I mean.'

'Thanks.' Her back is turned. He cannot see her blushing. His comment has confused her. He is making her confused, anyway.

'You're married, then?'

'That would be telling.'

She carries the tray into the sitting room. He does not offer to carry it for her. As Aidan would. She remembers she was always picking up things after him.

After trying out various chairs again he finally selects the sofa, perhaps in the hope she will sit beside him. She takes the cane armchair he was in earlier. Hannah empties a box of fuzzy felts on to the floor. Isabella watches with a wry smile as one by one Tom eats all the biscuits.

In between mouthfuls he talks about the film.

'It'll take two or three weeks, depending on the weather. It could take up to four. But I've got another project that's cropped up, so I'd like to try and complete it in that time.'

He explains that besides filming the men fishing, he wants to show their daily lives. 'You know, getting up in the mornings, putting on their gear, mealtimes, getting ready for church, going to church. That kind of thing. I want anecdotes. Recollections. Drinking in the pub . . . All the background. I want it to be a complete portrayal of a fishing community.'

'It sounds wonderful. How many of you are there?'

'Three of us. Myself, my cameraman, and an assistant. We've worked together for years. We each know how the other thinks. Tony, the assistant, doubles as a spark, which is useful.'

'Spark?'

'Electrician. We use a battery lighting set comprising three quartz lights. We'll clip those on to the masts when we shoot at night. Nick – the cameraman – doubles as a recordist. I write, produce, direct and edit.'

She is fascinated. 'It must be so interesting. There's so much entailed. I never really considered that aspect. You know – you just switch on the box, watch something, without thinking . . . How many films do you make a year?'

'Usually three. There's a lot of preparation before and after. And you have to sell the thing too, don't forget. Though nowadays I'm fairly well known and that's not a problem.'

He says this without conceit.

'I saw something you did a month or so back – about a guy who had cerebral palsy. It was very moving. Uplifting, even.'

'So you liked it. Good.' His eyes shine. He seems genuinely pleased at her approval. That he takes his work very seriously is evident. 'It was all credit to Peter himself – the young man. He was an inspiration to everyone. He had no self-pity. A tremendous sense of humour. I tell you, it was bloody chastening talking to him.'

Are his eyes becoming suspiciously pink? Surely not.

But: 'God, I get emotional nowadays,' he says.

She is astonished. This is a new side to him, and she can feel herself warming to him.

'You know he was doing a law degree—'

'Yes. His carer—'

'Trevor.'

'Trevor rigged up a kind of lectern to the wheelchair for his books. Madre, he devoted his entire life to Peter.'

'I had a letter from them both the other day. Peter's passed his finals. And Trevor's getting married. They're moving into a larger house so that he can continue to look after Peter . . .'

And here they are having a normal conversation. So very strange, this turn of events. She cannot get over the fact that this is Tom here with her. And is *he* remarried?

'How long are you renting this place for?'

'A few months.'

He considers her for several seconds, obviously wondering what she is doing here. But doesn't ask.

'Well, well. I expect it brings back the odd memory or two.'

'I suppose.'

She is reluctant to share reminiscences with him. Alternates between wanting to be friendly and shying away warily.

'Shit, we burnt up a few lanes on the bike, didn't we,' he says.

'Too many.'

'You were terrified.'

'Well, you were *mad*,' she accuses him.

'Yes, I was, rather. I remember I slowed down when you told me I might run over a cat, though. Anyway, I've changed.'

'Is that a fact?'

'I believe so. When you give up booze you go through a fair bit of crap. You have to undergo therapy. And I attend AA meetings once a week still. Yes, sure it changes you.'

'So now you hate your parents.'

'No. What makes you say that?'

'Well, isn't that what therapy does? Makes you blame your parents?'

And what of her own father?

'No, mine are tremendous, as you know. Were, in my father's case. He died ten years ago. That was the turning point, actually. And no doubt you'd say that was significant. Angry bad boy turns over new leaf when Daddy dies.'

'I'm no expert. I steer clear of anything to do with therapy. I'm sorry about your father. He was a lovely man. What about your mother?'

'She's superb. Lecturing all over the place still. And she's founded a Russian literature society. I interviewed her for a documentary a year or so back. I called it *Septuagenarian Sirens*.'

'I wish I'd seen it . . . So, what made you switch from reporting?'

'I . . . how best to put it? I was booted from the Beeb. I rather disgraced myself on a particular job. Then my drinking got slightly out of hand.'

Slightly? she wonders.

'Was that when you were reporting from the Falklands? I saw that. Madre, that was brilliant!' Claps her hands at the recollection of Tom expounding his political beliefs, and the mike being wrested from him.

He grins sideways at her. 'I'd forgotten about your "madres". I'm so pleased you haven't lost them . . . Yes, well, anyway, I received a fair number of supportive letters about that incident. And for a while I switched to the radio. But then, what with the drinking, and personal stuff' – he waves his hand vaguely and she takes it to mean something to do with a woman – 'my career took a nosedive. Then a chum asked me to do the script for a documentary, and I thought, I like this. It was a great feeling, actually: recognising you've found your vocation. He and I worked together on a few projects. Then he met an Australian girl, and went over there, so I started on my own. Quite simply, it's the most important thing in my life. The people I meet, the places I get to, the experiences I've had . . . I've seen such heartening courage, such unexpected kindness in the most unlikely places, besides cruelty and injustice. It makes you love and loathe your fellow human beings. You see little bits of life that could be humdrum but aren't, because the individuals concerned rise above the mundane.'

She is struck by his fervency as he talks. But then he always had that passionate intensity of feeling which could also change into obsession and destructiveness. He used to find her equanimity annoying. 'I wish you'd shout occasionally,' he said to her once. 'You're so bloody boring. Always the same.'

For him that was the gravest of sins: to be boring.

He loved – *loved?* – was most infatuated with her when she first confided she had been fostered. In his eyes this lifted her from the realms of the conventional. But because it was all still too close to her, because his curiosity smacked of prurience, and because the previous day he'd said that only the bourgeois were concerned with their past, she had refused to elucidate, and his interest was only briefly sustained.

Has therapy evened out his extremes of mood? Battened down the dark side of his character?

'Isabella, I don't want to worry you, but there's a rather overweight mouse preening itself on the lower shelf of books.'

She looks in the direction in which he is pointing. The mouse nonchalantly grooming itself is sleek and fat.

'We were infested,' she tells him. 'Garibaldi's seen to most of them. He thought he'd died and gone to heaven. I haven't bought a tin of cat food since I moved here. Poor little things. He's so cruel to them. It's such a protracted way to go.'

'Well, he hasn't spotted this one.' Stroking Garibaldi, who has just sprung on to his lap. 'Could I have a drink of water? I'd fetch it myself, only I can't move.'

'I'll get you one.' Smiling at the sight of him with the cat – now rotating on his chest so that Tom is presented with its backside and quivering tail. She can feel laughter bubbling up inside her. All so strange, all so strange, she thinks again. Longs for a glass of wine.

'Do you mind if I drink wine in front of you? I won't if it's a problem.'

'No, go ahead. I'm fine about it. There's always booze at my place for guests.' The way he says *my* suggests to her that he is single.

'You're never tempted?'

'Never. So far. But there's no guarantee for the future. Once you're an alcoholic, you remain an alcoholic.'

He says this without a trace of embarrassment. There is no doubt he has been through a lot during the last few years. There is no doubt he is a clever man, a creative man, a fascinating man, a difficult and mercurial man, an attractive man. There is no doubt he is a man to whom it is almost impossible not to be drawn. And even as one is, one is resisting it. She is.

She pours some Rioja into a glass and quaffs it.

'What are you making?' she hears him asking Hannah in the sitting room.

'I make cat like Grabla.'

She tops up the glass.

There is a long pause. 'Do you like cats?' Tom says.

She giggles into her wine. He sounds so unnatural; it is obvious he has no children. This time Hannah does not bother to reply. She is very selective about whom she talks to.

A scattering of flashbacks come to her, as she finishes off this second glass of wine: Tom reading poetry to her; Tom combing her hair – and also her pubic hair; Tom taking her to a black-tie dance; Tom and her playing Scrabble. And once, when she complained that she had seven vowels, he suggested: 'You could do Ee-i-ee-i-o.' She laughs out loud – then has a sudden pang of nostalgia for that period of her life. University. The rock group. It was the first time she had experienced a sense of belonging. She can remember the pleasure of being part of a crowd.

'What were you laughing at?' he asks when she rejoins him.

She hands him the water; puts her own refilled glass on the table.

'I was thinking of a game of Scrabble we had—'

'Which I, of course, won.'

It was true, he nearly always won, and was petulant when he didn't.

'That wasn't the point.' And she reminds him of the time.

He laughs also. Between them is a semblance of ease. Tied youth. An entire chapter of their life. He lives in Ealing, he tells her, but is thinking of going to Chile for a year. Restless as ever, she teases. Not restless, he says. He just has a questing nature. That's surely not a bad thing? She cannot contradict this. For a moment his eyes hold hers. He seems to be assessing her. She looks away. 'Fate?' she hears him murmur under his breath. She feels flustered. Has the sense that her head is dissolving. She is a little drunk.

His eyes linger on her for a few seconds, then he gives one of his abrupt ferret-like movements and motions towards her guitar. 'You still play?'

'Yes.'

'Play something.'

'Oh, no. Not now. Really, I'm not in the mood.' Swinging her arms around herself.

'Don't be so bloody coy. Isabella. Bella. P-l-e-a-s-e.'

'Mummy play g'tar.' Hannah jumps up and down.

'There you go. Two against one.'

'Madre.' She feigns an exasperated sigh and holds up her hands in defeat. Fetches the guitar.

Self-consciously she plucks the strings, twiddles the tuning knobs. Plucks the strings again and sharpens the G. Her throat feels swollen. She strums a chord and begins:

' "Have you seen the old man in the closed-down market, kicking at the papers with his worn-out shoes? . . ." '

The first song that came into her mind. And too late she remembers she used to sing it when they were going out. Or subconsciously was this why she chose it? He lies back on the sofa, eyes shut, lips parted, head going from side to side in time to the song. Garibaldi purring on his thighs, his ears occasionally twitching. Hannah on her tummy on the rug, humming.

And into this small, intimate scene enters Aidan, bearing the last rose from his garden and a soil-encrusted marrow.

She sets down the guitar immediately. She can feel the colour rushing into her cheeks. And she goes over to him, framed in the doorway, looking hurt and startled. She feels caught out – yet she has done nothing. Covers her awkwardness with a flurry of words.

'You're half an hour early – this is Tom – we met when I was at university – and now he's making the documentary here – isn't it odd?'

Babbles on that the pair of them would have so much to talk about – knowing they would have absolutely nothing in common; conscious of his silence, his immobility, and of Tom homing in on the marrow and grinning incredulously. She dislikes him just then; is so sorry for Aidan. Wishes she could embrace him there, proudly, passionately, in front of Tom. But she can't. The truth is she is torn between them. And annoyed at Aidan for turning up early, and for embarrassing her; for wearing his purple track-suit and for just standing in the doorway like a yokel, so dumbstruck, with the rose in one hand and the blessed marrow in the other; while Tom quips: ' "Busk ye, busk ye, my bonny bonny bride, Busk ye my winsome marrow." That's by William Hamilton, from "The Braes of Yarrow",' he explains into the hiatus.

11

So he did not stay the night. They did not make love. They did not kiss or even touch. After Tom left they sat apart either in strained silence or struggling with a stilted conversation that was an endurance for both and saddened her. She longed to be able to talk to him as a friend, which she had thought he was; for him to put his arms round her and draw her close, and to say: I'm here, whatever. To be able to say to him: I'm muddled. Her anger towards him gone now they were alone. But his expression – simultaneously wounded and aloof – deterred her. He sat where Tom had sat, hardly once meeting her eyes and mostly playing with Hannah, fitting shapes together to make a house.

After scarcely an hour he got up to leave. His face looked set and hardened, hers was pale. She stood up also. She felt defenceless; so afraid that this was it, that she would not see him again. She had behaved badly.

'Aren't you going to stay and have a meal? I bought some salmon steaks.'

'Thanks. But no. I think you've got a bit of sorting out to do.' Dignified. He was so dignified. And his jaw came forward obstinately. She knew that proud look. She wanted to tell him she loved him; but the word was not one to utter lightly so far as he was concerned. Love and reliability were linked.

'No. I don't have. Really. He's someone from my past,

that's all.' She was starting to feel desperate. She reached out for his hand. It lay in hers like a frozen fish, and she released it.

'He's your type,' Aidan said flatly. 'Clever, witty. Good-looking. I can see that. You've known each other for years. I'm just an ordinary bloke. I do up cars. I don't make films. I'm happy with how I am, don't get me wrong. But – I don't want to get in the way. I've more pride than that.'

'You're not in the way.'

'Even so.'

And he left. And now it is exactly a week since she has seen or spoken to him; yet she realises it would be wrong for a multitude of reasons to contact him. Tom's re-entry into her life has introduced one complication too many. And meanwhile she is being wooed and waltzed along by her ex-husband. He won't leave her alone. Phones her between takes from his mobile, takes her out to dinner, calls round uninvited with champagne for her and pralines; while he drinks apple juice. Regales her with anecdotes about filming and with the day's events; discusses topical affairs and opera and issues where she is obliged to think quickly – and can admit to herself that, yes, her mind has become lazy; and, yes, their conversations are stimulating. He has introduced her to his colleagues as a 'bird I had a bit of a fling with'. And is this how he regards it now? A three-week fling? But he is romantic towards her in a way he was not when they were young. And she has not been to bed with him. She reviews her relationship with Aidan soberly and tells herself that it would not have stood a chance anyway. It has only finished sooner rather than later.

'I'm phoning from Charlie's boat,' Tom yelled over the crackling line one afternoon. 'Can you hear me? I just called because I'm happy.' And rang off.

Mad. He is self-centred and perpetually hyperactive, but he makes her laugh.

Sophia, wearing one of Isabella's dresses to baby-sit, remarked after she had met him: 'He looks like that actor – I saw him in an old film – what was his name?'

'Steve McQueen?'

'Yes, that's him. Gosh, it must be nice going out with someone who makes films, like. Really exciting.'

She isn't 'going out' with him, is she? He has tried to get her into bed, but on the whole has been respectful when she has refused. He was never much of a man for kissing. For him it had tended to be a preliminary to sex. If Isabella were to analyse her feelings towards him she would say that now that she is used to him again, they are more sisterly than anything. Sometimes there are moments when the old physical spark is present or nostalgia might lure her. But wariness enables her to see him objectively. She can think: Yes, you are charming and attractive. But I know you and remember you. And you aren't irresistible to me.

Hannah does not like him. She stares at him with mutinous eyes. Tom stares back, pulling idiotic faces, wiggling his fingers, growling in his throat, in a vain attempt to draw a smile from her.

'Your daughter doesn't like me,' he says this evening, sounding quite affronted.

'She's very particular about whom she likes,' Isabella says.

'What do I do wrong?'

'You try too hard. You're not natural with her. She picks up on that.'

'Oh my *Gad*.' Flinging himself back on the sofa. 'It's all too much effort. Thank heaven I never had kids.'

He has asked her nothing further about her 'marriage', knows no more than he did a week ago, and seems unbothered. Likewise, she has asked him nothing. He has not mentioned Aidan to her, and it is obvious he assumes she can no longer be seeing him, since he has visited her every day or asked her to meet him at the Ship Inn, where he is staying. She adds arrogance to his list of failings.

Can remember him saying, years ago, when she dared question his fidelity: 'I can't stand possessiveness.'

'For "possessiveness" read "commitment",' she countered.

But he has shown her video extracts of their filming, and she is impressed by the insightful cameos. She has to admire him. He has a knack of drawing out his interviewees in a way that is not intrusive.

'The viewer feels part of their lives,' she told him.

'That's exactly the effect I try to achieve,' he said. 'Of course, it'll all be edited. There's an art to knowing what to leave in and what to take out. It takes ages, going through each frame.'

Oddly, about his work he is not in the least conceited. He is modest, loves approval, and takes a boyish delight in what he is doing that she finds rather sweet.

He has filmed Charlie bringing Joyce tea in bed at five in the morning; Charlie pouring himself cornflakes in the kitchen, Charlie shaving and simultaneously cracking jokes; putting on his thick socks by the front door. A camera close-up of his withered leg. Another close-up of him kissing his wife full on the lips – and their puckered mouths, the old, loose skin of their faces and closed, loving eyes . . . Follows him down the lane where he meets up with another fisherman, Rickie, and his son. And at this hour in the morning the light is grey on the greyness of their faces as they prepare the boats on the hard-standing. There is one that is owned by four of them, with a cuddy and a couple of bunks for longer jaunts. But these boats are smaller, and Charlie's has an outboard motor.

'Nick's a great cameraman,' Tom said, as the video showed Charlie leading the line out from the pully attached to the davit. Later the lens focused on struggling mackerel as they were hauled aboard, then on Charlie putting them swiftly

out of their misery with a blow to the head. And now here
was the lighthouse, and the waves were lashing the rocks;
the rain began to drive down, and the rivulets streaked down
the creases of Charlie's cheeks as he steered the boat . . .

'We had to stop filming then, and pack up the equipment
to stop it getting wet,' Tom told her.

Other rushes: of the men in the Sun, recounting the day,
airing their opinions, relating tales of their grandfathers;
Charlie and Joyce playing bowls at the British Legion club
in Zerion; one of the young fishermen – Charlie's cousin's
son – snogging with a girlfriend under a lamppost – and later
this same young man complaining of the winters, and of no
money, and of wanting a change.

'I can't see it continuing,' Tom said. 'Younger generations
won't want it. He's typical, I'm afraid.'

'It's sad. A whole way of life,' she remarked.

'Yes, it is. Very sad.'

Sometimes, when he is in a reflective mood, when he is
not nervy or trying constantly to be amusing, or to indulge in
quick repartee, she is almost on the brink of allowing herself
to feel something deeper for him – and then with a gesture
or word or action the moment will be severed.

She keeps hoping Aidan will ring. Or is he waiting for her
to do so? She can't. There is too much to explain. Imagines
what he must be thinking of her. Bitter, no doubt. And that
grieves her.

She has kept the marrow; cannot face eating it. It is in the
bottom of the small fridge, taking up too much space and
serving as a constant reminder. The rose died after three days.
She has put the petals in an envelope. Isabella, who has never
behaved in a sentimental way before. Missing Aidan.

But this evening Tom is with her.

'A boring little fart,' he is saying. 'A white blob on a white
wall. But he's fucking good at his job. Gets murderers and
rapists to talk.'

They are having supper on trays in front of the television, watching a documentary made by someone Tom knows.

'Thousands of children and young people go missing every year,' his acquaintance says. 'What happens to them? Where do they go? How is it possible for them to apparently disappear into thin air?'

'Split infinitive,' mutters Tom, holding a chicken drumstick with his fingers and gnawing on it. 'Hey, Bella, don't get up. I want you to see this.'

'It's late. I've got too much work to do.' Avoiding his outstretched hand.

'You won't be able to do it with the box on.'

'I will. It's just straightforward, boring translating.'

'You were keeping me warm. It's fucking cold in here. At least find Garibaldi for me.'

She ignores him. Goes over to her computer and opens *Rural France through the Ages* at page ninety-three. Tries to block out the tormented voice of a mother:

'She were just three year old. One minute she were with her friends in the park. Next she were gone. You'd think the police would've found some clue, wouldn't you? A [bleep] nightmare this whole thing's been. And folks've been spreading rumours it's us. That we've murdered her and done sommat with body. My *baby*, for God's sake. How dare they? Two years of [bleep] hell it's been. And now the police don't want to know any more, do they? I mean, she's just another [bleep] statistic, far as they're concerned, isn't she? What do they care? But I tell you sommat, there's people out there who are wicked. You read about it. Well, what they do to tots . . .'

Against her will Isabella watches the woman blowing her nose into a handkerchief she pulls from her cardigan sleeve, and her own eyes start to water. The camera switches to another room, and three paedophiles with convictions, their faces blanked out, are interviewed next.

'. . . The English influence in the fourteenth century is much in evidence in the bastide towns of Aquitaine, as a result of the occupation by Edward, Prince of Wales, otherwise known as the Black Prince,' Isabella keys on to the screen.

'Bella,' Tom calls across. 'Do you remember that night in the B & B when we were here together, and we were bonking away in our room and you were making a hell of a racket, and the landlady was giving a dinner party just below us, and suddenly we realised they'd all stopped talking?'

'I thought you were watching the programme.'

'I am. That doesn't prevent the train of thought.'

She could hardly forget. And the next morning she could not bring herself to glance at the landlady.

Does not wish to think about sex with Tom.

'I don't want to discuss it.'

'Dear oh dear. Has the lovely Isabella become a prude in the autumn of her years? Or perhaps it is a case of: And so she pined, and so she died forlorn, imploring for her pot of yokel clotted cream to the last . . . With apologies to Kea—'

Isabella striding furiously over to the television. Switching it off and yanking out the plug.

'Out,' she articulates with quiet precision.

He looks amazed, then pretends to shrink back in fear, throwing his hands up. When she doesn't smile, he says, 'Christ, Bella, don't take things so seriously.'

And that is his trouble. Except for his work, he takes nothing seriously.

Her shoulders drop. She makes a tutting sound, and returns to her computer. She can sense Tom looking at her but refuses to turn round. And a minute or so later the television comes on again, and a father metaphorically beats his chest over his ten-year-old son's disappearance after a family quarrel.

For half an hour, until the programme finishes, they don't

speak. Then from his reclined position on the sofa, Tom says, over a commercial for cornflakes: 'Contrary to what you might believe, I have been doing a fair bit of thinking. And yes, I did behave pretty badly towards you. I acknowledge that. But meeting you again like this – shit, you must agree it's extraordinary. I don't know what your situation is now, or even what you're doing here, but you know I'm not the conventional sort who's going to start sermonising about—'

She gets up then and goes over to him. Gives him a quick hug across the sofa. He gets up also, misinterpreting her action, and tries to pull her into his arms.

She resists. 'Go now,' she says gently.

'Can't I stay?'

'No.'

'Some time?'

'I don't know.'

'"Give her time," advises Agony Aunt Maud,' he jokes.

Kisses her on the lips. Briefly his tongue is in her mouth. His jaw is rough with the day's stubble. No beard. She responds to the kiss from curiosity; thinking, Was this how he used to kiss? Unmoved. He smiles. His blue eyes, on a level with hers, are like a boy's. A glint of – what? Smugness? Victory? – in them. He taps her chin and nose with his forefinger and he is gone. She watches his jaunty outline disappearing past the dark clumps of bushes along the cutting and locks the front door.

She clears up the sitting room and turns off the lights, and is poised on the stairs when what sounds like the creaking of the outside gate stops her in her tracks. She runs up the remaining stairs to her room and presses her face up to the window, squinting to see. But it is too dark. The reflection of the landing light outside the bedroom makes it harder.

It is Tom. It is bound to be him, chancing his luck a second time. Smiling at the cheek of it, she opens the window and calls his name. There is no response, and she shuts the window once more. Uneasy.

She is persuading herself that she was mistaken about the gate when there comes another noise. A dull crash this time, which she recognises as one of the flowerpots falling over; they regularly topple on to their sides in the wind. But there is no wind tonight. Therefore somebody must have collided with it. She is suddenly afraid. And now another sound, thin and metallic, comes from downstairs: the letterbox flap opening and closing. She becomes motionless. Fear crawls up her arms like scarabs. Her heart limps a march. A slow thud, stop, thud, stop, thud. She unplugs the bedside lamp and armed with this creeps downstairs. She can hear the unmistakable creak of the gate again, and the latch falling. Nothing more. Several minutes pass – she barely breathes in the darkened room, her hand raised with the small lamp in it, in readiness – when the night silence is broken by the whine of a car starting and driving off down the lane. She switches on the light and immediately sees the envelope poking through the letterbox.

It is a plain brown envelope, and written on it with a black marker pen is a single word: SLUT.

She stares, horrified – then realises it is bulging with something inside. Very slowly, dreading what she will find, she opens it. Drops it again with a gasped intake of breath. A used condom falls out, oozing milky semen. She claps her hand to her open mouth, and fights down the urge to scream; can't control the little shuddering noises that escape between her fingers. For a couple of minutes she remains like that, nauseous with repulsion; too shaken to think what to do.

Her first instinct is to dial 999, and she goes over to the telephone. Is poised to dial, when through her abstractedness it occurs to her that this could be unwise. Trembling, she dials Tom on his mobile instead. Come round now, she will say. Aunt Maud worked quickly, he'll say.

'It has not been possible to connect your call. Please try again later,' recites the computerised voice.

She could look up the number of the Ship Inn and ring him there. But the impulse has gone. She would end up having sex with him, when she only wants to be held close.

Aidan, Aidan. Lifts the receiver again and transfers it from hand to hand. I'm frightened. I need you. I'm sorry. And then a terrible thought causes her to replace it. Suppose it were him? Suppose there were a side to him she had not suspected? Suppose this were his revenge? Not Aidan. Oh madre, no. She inspects the single word again. The writing slopes backward whilst his slopes forward. There again, he would have disguised it.

I *know* him.

But this moment, too, is lost. She prevaricates about whether to phone Babs. But she is reluctant to involve her; it is late and there is nothing she could do. Isabella is not used to running to anyone with her problems. At this moment, though, she feels utterly alone. Resolutely, she takes the envelope and uses it to pick up the condom, and, with her features compressed in disgust, goes outside to flush it down the loo. Wishes that the toilet were indoors. And even though she is fairly certain that the car driving off belonged to the trespasser, she is nonetheless jumpy with nervousness. The sky is thick with cloud. The other cottages are in darkness. The light streaming from hers shines on the shrubs, and on the pot lying broken on its side; illuminates the open gate. The sea swishes rhythmically.

In the cottage the phone is ringing and she dashes inside, then stops as she reaches it; her heart commences its thudding march again. The answering machine cuts in with her recorded message followed by the hum. There is a pause of a few seconds, then:

'Slut,' whispers a voice.

And the person hangs up.

She dials 1471 and is informed: 'You were called today at 11.07 hours. We do not have the caller's number to return the call.' Bangs down the receiver. And immediately lifts it again. She will leave it off the hook. For a minute or so the computerised voice orders her to replace the handset; this is followed by a long gap, before a mechanical wailing starts up. This, too, ceases after a few minutes. The room feels eerily quiet. There is nothing in the least comforting about it. The taste of threat lacquers her tongue.

In her small room with its sloping ceiling Hannah sleeps with one arm flung outside the duvet, her rabbit and bear pushed against her turned cheek. The glow from the night-light delineates her small humped form. Isabella touches one of her springy curls (her hair is newly dyed), and lays her cheek against the child's.

Is filled with a lonely sense of desolation and imper-manence.

On the way back from the playgroup in the morning she slows when she comes to Aidan's garage. The mechanic is just visible in the shadows of the open doors. She drives past a few yards, changes her mind, reverses and parks. She will not, she resolves – getting out of the car and walking towards the workshop – be intimidated.

At the sound of her footsteps he turns, and briefly an expression of surprise flits across his face. In one blackened hand is a crumpled piece of sandpaper; in the other a half-eaten sandwich. She can smell sardines on his breath. Break-fast? His rabbit teeth form an irregular fringe over his lower lip. And now he angles his head back and slants his eyes in a leer at her.

She faces him squarely, says with a cold clarity she does not feel: 'I'd like to speak to Aidan, please.'

He seems to be deciding whether or not to respond. Then he crouches down so the curve of his back is presented to her,

and busies himself sanding the filler above the wheel arches
of a Land Rover.

She is aware of her right temple ticking. Cannot remember
ever having felt so intimidated by a person. His rudeness, his
contempt, are so blatant. She tries to muster authority into
her tone.

'I just asked you something.'

'He's not here,' he says at last. 'He's in Bristol.'

His grating voice seems to be emitted through the padded
rings of flesh at the back of his neck. He continues rubbing
away with the sandpaper. There is a steady viciousness in
the action. She notices that his nails are bitten almost to the
cuticle, buried in the spatulas of his fingers.

'The car's suspension needs doing. I want to book it in.'

Remembers Aidan's offer to check over the entire car
himself. She cannot expect him to do that now.

Perhaps the mechanic has decided he could be in trouble
for rejecting business, as he stands up reluctantly, disappears
into the office and reappears with the diary.

'Thursday of this week.'

'I'll drop it off first thing, then. It's Sophia's morning with
me. She could give me a lift back.'

He frowns at the mention of the connection with his wife.

He doesn't say anything; goes back to work on the Land
Rover.

'You'll tell Aidan, then?' she persists.

He gives one of his grunts. She lingers, torn, trying to
decide whether or not to leave a note for Aidan. The need
to see him right now is almost overwhelming.

'Do you have an envelope?'

'In the office.'

She goes in there. On the desk is a framed photograph
of Aidan's two sons leaning against one another, laughing,
crew-cut heads touching. None of the usual pin-up calendars
or posters, thank God. She tears a sheet from a notepad and

scrawls on it: 'I miss you.' Hesitates, and adds: 'I love you.'
Stares at what she has written – those three small words of
such magnitude; finds an envelope in the drawer and puts
the note inside. She marks it for his attention and puts it by
the photo.

Driving back, she sees Lizzie outside the pub, watering the
flower tubs, and stops to say hello.

'I hear you and Aidan have finished,' Lizzie says, after they
have exchanged a few sentences.

'What?' Isabella is taken aback.

'I heard you're going out with the dishy producer who's
making—'

'We're old friends, Lizzie. That's all. That's really all.
Madre, I do wish people wouldn't . . . oh, forget it. Sorry.'

Winds up the window again and drives off. Deeply upset.
What has he been saying? What has everyone been saying?
Has she lost him irrevocably? And there is the letter propped
against his laughing sons . . .

Sophia is at the cottage, having let herself in with her
own key. Isabella does not mention having just seen her
husband.

'Hi. Coffee?' she asks, without looking up.

'Love one.'

Sophia goes into the kitchen, and Isabella sifts through the
post on the table in the sitting room.

'Even the junk mail is forwarded,' she calls through the
open door. 'You'd think they'd be a bit discerning . . . I'm
just binning a total of about two million pounds, a car and
the Spanish villa I've always dreamt of. Oh, and here's an
interesting one: I've been chosen for some final grand draw
and stand to win a time-share of a château in the Loire.'
Recognises Sally's handwriting on one of the letters and
reserves it to read with her coffee.

Sophia brings it to her, with a couple of biscuits on a plate.
She is particularly quiet. Lately she has lost her shyness and

usually chatters away freely. Isabella glances at her. The girl's eyes are puffed and red.

Isabella pats the chair beside her. 'Come and sit down.'

Sophia does, and sits there gnawing on her lip. Isabella puts her arm round her narrow shoulders. She has a hollow chest, emphasised by the beige skinny-ribbed pullover she is wearing.

'Hey, what's up?'

'Don't. You'll start me off again,' Sophia says.

'It doesn't matter. Let yourself cry.'

'It's nothing.'

'Of course it isn't nothing.'

'You're so good to me,' the girl blurts out. 'I love coming here. I don't know what I'd do if I didn't have this job. I really like you. I love little Hannah.'

'Ssh, it's fine. You're not planning on leaving, are you?'

She shakes her head, sniffing. Her eyes and nose are running and she wipes her face on her jumper's sleeve.

'Well, I'm not about to give you the push, I can assure you. You're a godsend as far as I'm concerned. So what's the real problem? Can you tell me?'

'Oh, I don't know . . . Look, I shouldn't say anything . . .' She sighs several times and presses her wrists against her bent head. 'It's Luke,' she says. 'He's so strange sometimes, that's all. And after Grace died—'

'Your baby?'

'Yes. After she died . . . well, you know, I . . . well, you know, didn't feel like . . . well, in bed. Doing it, like.'

'Of course. I can understand that.'

'Only I couldn't say all the things in my head. And he's always angry with me. And he goes out at night sometimes, and I don't know where he's off to. And whenever I talk about my job and how happy I am working with you, his face goes all black and his eyes become all strange. He wasn't always as bad as this. He's got worse. Been getting worse . . .

Sometimes I think he's crazy . . . I don't know . . . And I miss
my Gracie something terrible.'

Her skinny body is hunched taut with the effort of not
crying. And all Isabella can do is murmur banalities.

But she knows the identity of last night's visitor.

'Did Luke go out last night?' she asks casually, when the
girl is calmer.

'Yes. About ten it was. He suddenly got up and drove off.
I ran after the car, yelling. My neighbour saw and I felt so
stupid . . . Well, I was upset. I don't know where he goes.'

Here.

She wonders whether to tell her. What? Your husband's
stalking me? *Is* that what he is doing? She can see no purpose
in upsetting Sophia further. She is only amazed at herself for
not having realised immediately. And now she recollects the
mechanic's surprised expression when she strolled into the
garage. Had he assumed, therefore, that she would guess it
was him, that she would not dare come near him? Did he
want her to guess? What is the psychology behind this man's
warped thinking? And on Thursday she will be seeing him
again, when she takes the car in.

'Perhaps he just drives around,' she says to Sophia. 'Clearing his head. Thinking.'

'Maybe.' She sounds unconvinced.

'Did you have a good relationship before?'

Sophia puckers her lips contemplatively. 'Fair. I mean, he
was always very silent. But courteous. I like that. And when
he said anything nice, you thought, well, he must mean it
as he never spoke much. And I liked how he was good with
his hands. And nobody had ever really looked at me before
Luke. I didn't think I'd ever meet anybody. So . . . And then
I got pregnant. And we married.'

A tale like thousands of others, she thinks.

'You don't have to stay with your husband if he makes you
unhappy, Sophia.'

She looks shocked. 'Oh, but I'm Catholic,' she states in a tone that staunches all further comment.

When Isabella is alone she reads Sally's letter:

Darling Issi,

This is the first second I've had to put pen to paper since I received your bombshell of a letter. You think you know someone and then they do something that utterly confounds you! I want to speak to you. Why the hell didn't you put your address or phone number on your letter? Anyway, I'll just have to assume this will be forwarded to you. You're amazing! What a truly wonderful thing to go and do. I don't know how you kept it so quiet. I'm longing to see you and to meet Hannah. Perhaps I could dump the brats and come and stay. Although I don't know when. I have to tell you things are pretty atrocious here. Geoff was getting frightful headaches and has been diagnosed with a brain tumour. He is going into hospital tomorrow to be operated on, and frankly I'm bloody terrified. We're both clinging on to each other with that awful fear that there's no time left. I can't believe it, and neither can he. It seems utterly unreal. If it's malignant the chances aren't good because not only is the tumour large, but the cancer could spread further as a result of disturbance from the op. The worst of it is trying to appear positive with the kids, and having to go about doing things as normal, when in you is this awful ache that feels like a tumour itself. As you know I've just started my three-year psychotherapy course at Gloucester, but now I'm not sure I can take that aboard. We'll see. Fingers crossed.

For God's sake, phone. Actually I'm rather hurt you haven't, but no doubt you've got your reasons and all will be revealed. I'm sorry this letter is so depressing, and so short, but I've a million things to organise, as you can imagine.

Much love to you, Issi, and to your Hannah. Pray for Geoff, even though I know you don't believe in anything. Cross your fingers too.

Sally XX.

*   *   *

Isabella lays the letter down on the table. She has been unforgivably selfish. Reproaches herself for thrusting aside Sally of all people. And the letter was written four days ago. By now Geoff will have had the operation.

As she dials the familiar number she is apprehensive. Childishly, her fingers *are* crossed. Let him be all right, let him be all right – as the phone rings and rings, and she fears the worst.

And when Sally finally does answer, she knows from her quavering voice that it is bad news.

'Cara, it's me.'

'Oh God, Issi.'

She listens helplessly to the storm of sobbing at the other end, saying nothing, filled with bleakness; waits for the sobbing to abate.

'Are you still there?' asks the tremulous voice.

'Of course, cara.'

'Geoff died. He had a massive brain haemorrhage under surgery. He was on a life support machine. They . . . switched it off yesterday. I had to give permission. I can't bear it. Issi, I just can't bear it—' Breaks off, in sobs again.

Shocked tears streaming down Isabella's face. Geoff? *Geoff?* It is not possible. Gentle, overweight, balding, amiable Geoff. And weren't he and Sally a brilliant couple together? Humour rebounding from one to the other. Her oldest, most loved friends.

'Cara, I'm so desperately, desperately sorry.' She can scarcely speak, unable to hide the fact that she is crying also.

'I know. And the kids are in a terrible state. The whole thing's a nightmare. I keep hearing him laughing. You know, that gunshot blast of a laugh. I want to snuggle up to him. That great hairy belly of his. I can't believe I'll never snuggle up to him again. Oh—' A long, heartbroken sigh that breaks Isabella's heart.

'Is your mother with you?'

'Yes. She's been staying since . . . oh goodness, I've lost all sense of time. What's today?'

'Monday. It's Monday.'

'I think she came Friday. Two days before he . . . they turned it off.'

She sounds as though she scarcely knows what she is saying; beside herself with her grief.

'When's the funeral?'

'I'm not sure. Friday maybe. Oh God, that's something else to organise. I'll phone you. Oh shit, I don't have your number even. And I haven't asked anything about you. I'm so—'

'Don't be stupid. Don't worry about me. I'm fine.'

But she is not. She wants to rush upstairs and howl. Has an overwhelming need to see Sally and Geoff together and relive the scores of times spent in their company over the years.

She gives Sally her telephone number, makes her repeat it, and says goodbye.

And sits on, slumped by the phone.

Tregurran beach is deserted. She takes her shoes off and carries them. The tide is out, and beneath her bare feet the sand, swept into peaks and scoops by the wind, is cool. It swirls into her eyes and makes her blink as she walks towards the sea. The salt air bites into her cheeks. Pools have formed between boulders, and in one a seagull – no, a kittiwake, she corrects herself, feeling a stabbing pang for Aidan – is bathing, dipping its head and slapping its wings in the water, then shaking the drops from itself. She smiles sadly, watching it. It flies up with a startled cry as she approaches. The sea is rough: moss swathes rolling over each other, crashing on the shore and sluicing over rocks. And she stands at the edge, the current tugging her feet, sucking the sand from beneath them so they are implanted in shifting troughs which massage the balls of her heels. The roar of the sea is a colossal sound that fills her head. A sand crab scuttles past her, stops, scuttles back, and then away again. What motivates it, she wonders. She walks about aimlessly; comes upon a stick lying where the sand is more compact, and with it draws the outline of a woman. Hopeless. She is hopeless at drawing. A child could do better. And she is reminded of the conversation she'd had that evening with Aidan, the first time they made love, when he showed her his paintings.

Pain wrapping round her.

She sits with her knees huddled to her chin, thinking and staring out to sea. Something tickles her foot, and she brushes away a huge ant. Things leap separately in and out of focus: pieces of driftwood, sculpted by the tide; small tussocks where the beach peters out; the slimy dark mounds of sea-weed; the trails of a bird's claws in the sand, and paw marks; stones which, when one examines them closely, are like mar-ble – rose-coloured and shot through with white veins. She picks one up to feel its texture. It is cool and satisfying in her palm. She closes her eyes. Imagining what it must be like to be blind. And remembers an incident with Tom when they were newly married. They were at a restaurant and an old man with papery skin was playing the violin there. Sarasate.

'Once he was our age and had aspirations to be a virtuoso player,' Tom said.

'I wonder what happened,' she replied, taking in the Art Deco room and the diners intent on their food, or talking over the musician's heartbroken sawing.

'The war, probably.'

Perhaps she should give Tom a chance. Perhaps they are not so wrong for each other. The things that used to bother her no longer affect her in the same way. He could come and go as he pleased. If he were to learn about Hannah, he would most likely approve of what she had done.

Remembering – how she had always thought of herself as the colour green. She wanted to be surrounded by green, merge with it, drown in green. Sometimes she imagined herself as a tree.

'But you're so obviously red,' he contradicted her when she told him, early on in their relationship. 'Red hair, red-blooded. Your perception of yourself is entirely wrong. You'll always stand out wherever you go.'

'But it's how I feel inside me,' she argued.

And now he latched on to this. 'Red on green . . . That's interesting,' he mused. 'The two opposite colours. You are two completely different women.'

The conversation comes back now. Truer than he would have envisaged.

What colour would he be? Silver. Quicksilver. And Aidan? The colour of Tuscan soil.

Some way out are a couple of fishing craft, rising and disappearing with the swell of the waves. Tom and his colleagues were going out with a driver today to get some shots of Charlie in his boat from a distance. It is definitely them, as when she lifts her binoculars she can see that one of the vessels is much larger than the other, and can make out Charlie's red hull.

Aidan's binoculars. She still has his binoculars. They will provide an excuse to see him. How will he react to her note?

She lies back, covering herself with her waterproof jacket. Tom, Aidan. Aidan, Tom. Hannah, Hannah. She half dozes; motes floating in the air are distorted through the cracks of her eyes and become images that merge in a contrapuntal stream: her father stroking the blade of his nose as he worked on the restaurant's accounts; her mother's old-fashioned underwear drying on the kitchen radiator; her grandmother's hammock-hung breasts beneath her flowered pinafore; Geoff's teasing grin as he served the ping-pong ball and tried to trick her with false starts; the stabbed schoolmaster bleeding in the checked floored hallway and the bald poodle licking the blood. Aidan's steady grey gaze scorching her. And she can feel his hands beneath her buttocks, supporting them . . . And now the sand sieving through her fingers, the buffeting sea and clamouring gulls and whining wind, are absorbed along with her images and thoughts into her subconscious.

She is on the point of sleep when the air is split by what sounds like an explosion. She sits up with a jolt of fright. Peering out to sea, she can just decipher what seems to be a spiral of smoke. She looks through the binoculars. And now, clearly, she can see a thick plume sweeping into the clouds, and flames beneath it engulfing the smaller of the two boats as it lifts on the waves. She can make out figures moving around in the other.

And she bounds up and starts to run; sprints back to the car to use her mobile phone. Knows with certainty that she has just witnessed a terrible disaster.

Monday, 14 October.

'Everything is chance,' Isabella writes in her report book, which has become more of a diary. 'For the most part our lives are governed by events beyond our control. Psychiatrists talk of being in control of our own lives, but I am beginning to realise that virtually everything is circumstantial; a sequence of cause and effect. What choice did Hannah have when her mother left her or when I took her? What choice did I have when my father came to me that night and left the next morning; when my mother died; when I was sent from place to place? Even marrying Tom was a reaction to all that had gone before. And what about the inner self? The inner self that exerts its power is as unpredictable as any external influence. Therefore, do we have no responsibility? Does our responsibility begin and end with behaving honourably towards one another? Do we have a choice in loving?'

A lapsed moment of concentration killed Charlie.

Tom is devastated.

'We couldn't see what was happening from our position,' he tells her that evening, drinking coffee after coffee and smoking cigarette after cigarette in her sitting room. 'It was very rough and the boat was pitching about. I was just thinking, There'll be some great shots. Charlie's boat was disappearing and lifting then plunging, and he was busy lining . . . Nick was closing in on him with the zoom. And then I heard him say, "Christ, Charlie's engine's on fire." We yelled out to him, but he couldn't hear a thing over the wind and the sea. Rickie was driving our boat, and he turned at right angles to cut across Charlie, who was still lining and didn't notice a thing. But before we could make it there was this massive explosion as the fuel tank caught.'

Tom pauses, looking anguished as he relives the incident.

The cliché 'he wouldn't have known a thing' springs to Isabella's mind. But who knows that he wouldn't? Perhaps a second could become an hour, distorted by searing agony. How long would it take, she wonders, for every main organ in the body to be singed through so it ceased to work? Would unconsciousness have rescued him first?

'We couldn't get close,' he continues. 'You felt so power-less, just watching the flames engulfing Charlie and the boat. I tell you, Bella, I tell you . . .'

Doesn't finish the sentence. His mouth twisted, cheek muscles drawn in. She cradles his head against her and strokes his hair as she would Hannah's.

'I've been all round the world. I've lost count of the people I've met, and who've died in war zones were I've been reporting. I've stayed in people's homes in villages which no longer exist. I've seen suffering and human injustice, and you're never inured against it. But this little patch seemed hallowed somehow. It's affected me as much as anything I've seen. I grew to like and respect Charlie. These people, the old way of life – it's all vanishing. And now Charlie's gone.'

She continues stroking his hair. She feels no need to comment. Her own sense of emotion is, at this point, almost overwhelming.

'Joyce is remarkable. It's like she was expecting it. Apparently he used to keep an old oil rag in the boat. She reckons that caused the fire. He had a habit of keeping it near the engine, and it could have caught fire when the engine was hot. She said he'd become forgetful recently. She took it so calmly when we told her, but you could see what she was really feeling.'

'She's been through it before.'

'You think that helps?' he says sharply, edging away from her.

'I didn't say that. Only I imagine it might make you more on your guard. You realise nobody's inviolable.'

'I don't believe in being that clinical.' He stands up and paces about. 'I don't think emotion can be rationalised. But you've always been one for rationalising, haven't you?'

'Look, I know you saw it all. I'm not trying to deni-grate—'

'I marvel at you, I really do. Sometimes I don't think you've got any feelings. Nothing ruffles you, does it?'

What does he know?

Something snaps in her. His back is to her, and she stands up and grabs his sleeve, so that he turns in surprise. Her eyes are alight with lividness.

'When did you ever trouble to find out what my feelings are? You're completely selfish,' she shouts, gripping his arm and shaking it in fury. 'You don't know the first thing about me. You're obsessed with the grand-scale things, with stran-gers' dramas, but you never bother with the people you know. You just play with them, like a child picking up toys then chucking them. Well, I'm fed up with you. You crawl back out of the woodwork, thinking you can take up where you left off, thinking you're this wonderful, reformed, irresistible man and nobody else thinks as profoundly as you . . . I could, I could—'

Piercing shrieks come from Hannah's room. Isabella's tirade is cut off, and she releases her hold on Tom, who is looking astounded, and dashes upstairs. Hannah is jumping up and down on the bed, tugging at her hair, her mouth a giant 'O' as she lets rip scream after scream. It is terrible to hear them, to see her like this. What half-buried experiences have just been resurrected? Madre, how this takes her back to her own childhood.

'Oh, carina, I'm sorry. Cara, sweet Hannah, shush, it's all right.'

She hoists the child into her arms and gathers her close, murmuring soothingly and stroking her forehead until she is calmed. She is filled with self-reproach.

'Mummy cross,' sobs Hannah, wrapping her legs round Isabella's waist like a frog; and her body gives tiny involuntary convulsions.

'Yes. But not with you, carina. I wasn't cross with Hannah. And I'm better now. I promise I won't be cross like that ever again. I promise, promise.'

Tucks her back into bed, reads to her, sings to her. The child's features become peaceful once more. The mottling of her skin fades. Her elfin face peeps sleepily over the dalmatian-patterned duvet. And Isabella goes downstairs – avoids looking at Tom – and into the kitchen.

What does he know? What does he know?

Bitter with injustice.

Pours herself a glass of wine, which she gulps down, and refills it twice more. Its oaky warmth caresses the sorrow in her throat. Too much has happened. Everything seems to be collapsing.

'You think that'll help?' Tom regarding her from the doorway.

'Leave me alone. Anyway, you can talk.'

'I've learnt my lesson.'

'*Do* me a favour.' Downing this glass also. The bottle three-quarters empty.

'You're punishing yourself. Nobody else. Not me.'

'Madre, you're smug. You've learnt all this at AA, have you? I *want* to get drunk, Tom. I *want* to obliterate everything.'

'Fair enough. But the trouble is you only obliterate it for a limited period. You wake up to it again the next morning, plus you feel fuck-awful.' Coming towards her and trying to prise the bottle from her. She resists him and it crashes to the ground, where it splinters into fragments and the remainder of the wine snakes along the floor in a vermilion slick.

They both stare at it. Abruptly, the light of her rage shrivels. In deference to Charlie, in deference to Geoff, in deference to a small child upstairs who has undergone her own traumas, they must not quarrel. Her anger cedes to a mind-sapping tiredness.

This time when Tom requests to stay the night, with a simple 'I need you, Bella', she does not reject him. There is no reason. She is slightly drunk, but not enough to prevent her from being aware of what she is doing.

First, she goes about the evening's routine in the usual way. She uses the loo outside, washes and cleans her teeth, switches off the lights, locks the front door, checks Hannah; and finally goes into her bedroom. Tom is almost undressed. He is more than seven years older than herself, and his body is good for a man of his age; though she likes chest hair and he has virtually none, and he is rather on the thin side.

Used to Aidan's body.

'Don't pull the curtains,' he says as she is about to. 'I love it with the moon coming through. Faintly pagan.'

He still has his pants on, small navy briefs. Aidan wears boxer shorts. She gets undressed; he makes no move to help her and she feels, as she used to with him, self-conscious. A sense of detachment comes over her, so that even as she stands there naked, even as he stoops to fondle her breasts, with a murmured 'How could I have forgotten these?', and puts his mouth to her nipple; even as she looks down at his bent head and can feel her nipple hardening as a natural response despite her not being aroused, it is as though this were happening to someone else. She notices the protrusion of his pants. And she wants only to get on with the business of fucking. This is the word Isabella uses to herself. She wants to vent her pent-up feelings which are fermenting within the confines of her body. Then she wants to sleep.

She pulls away and climbs on to the bed. Draws the duvet over her. He hauls it off.

'What's all this, then? Can't I look at you?'

She is compliant, but that is all. Doesn't he sense her passiveness? Perhaps this excites his 'male hunter' instincts. When he goes down on her it seems almost incestuous, and she can hardly bring herself to do the same to him, although she feels obliged to do so. His penis is so different from Aidan's. Circumcised, for a start. She feels like a prostitute, going through the motions.

He surfaces and immediately enters her. He is as silent as he ever was. As intent on expertise as she remembers. She is glad of his silence now, and she orgasms quickly, in a wave of release, as silent as he. When her vaginal muscles stop quivering and her thighs slacken their grip, he turns her on to her stomach and takes her from behind, coming that way almost straight away.

The rain battering Timothy Abell's windows. Once he had lain in his monk's bed which had been in the same position. Such activity the last month has seen in Timothy Abell's bedroom.

'It was nothing like that twenty years ago, was it?' Tom says, lying on his back, his arm loosely around her neck. So: he enjoyed it. And was it good for you, dear? Slightly hysterical giggling repressed in her head. Over in six minutes. With Aidan they went on for an hour or more, stopping to touch or caress or lick or change position. She would fall asleep to the accompaniment of his fingers and lips and beard playing on her back.

'I don't remember,' she says.

She wonders when she can decently get up.

'You were much noisier in those days.'

'I didn't have a child to wake up.'

'That's true. So – you accused me of being disinterested earlier. What's happened to the man, then?'

For a second she thinks he means Aidan, then she realises he is referring to Hannah's father.

'I don't know.'

'Sounds careless.'

She smiles in the dark.

'Well, at least I asked,' he says.

Silence between them. The rain biting into it. The shadows on the walls and filigrees of moonlight. Tom making shapes of rabbits' heads and running dogs with his hand.

'You remember my best friend Sally?' And she tells him about Geoff.

'That's awful. Why didn't you mention it earlier?'

'I only heard this morning. And Charlie rather eclipsed everything.'

The day seems to have gone on for ever.

'Charlie,' Tom says heavily. 'I have to admit I'm in a bit of a quandary, I mean, I shouldn't really be thinking about it now – it seems disrespectful – but I don't know what to do about filming. I'll have to come to a decision pretty soon. The awful thing is it would give a whole different dimension to the film. It could be amazing. Really poignant. But that sounds as though I'm exploiting his death, which is the last thing I'd want to do. Maybe I shouldn't go on with it.'

'Ask Joyce.'

'Yes, of course. That's what I must do. I'll ask her first thing tomorrow.'

His voice is muzzy, and she slips out of bed, puts on her dressing gown and goes downstairs to do some work. Wide awake now, her mind leaping about with thoughts, whereas a short while ago she had longed for sleep and to put the day behind her. First, she needs to pee. All the wine has gone straight to her bladder.

She unlocks the door and steps outside, straight into a prism of light. Briefly she is dazzled by the torch flashing up in her eyes, then it drops away and there is a scurrying of feet from behind the bushes, down the cutting and towards the lane.

He has been skulking about again.

Oddly, now she knows who it is, she is less afraid. Know thine enemy? And on Thursday, when she takes the car in, she will tackle him about it. I don't know what you're talking about, he'll say.

The next morning. And Tom, a skimpy towel fastened round his waist, is in the bathroom, shaving. The buzzing of his electric razor is like a bumble-bee trapped in a glass.

Aidan used to shave round the neat outline of his beard with a hand razor. It was a feat of geometry.

Hannah watching Tom, mesmerised.

'Boo,' he says, turning suddenly. But she doesn't react.

'She looks at me quite disdainfully sometimes,' he says to Isabella ten minutes later, over his breakfast of coffee and cigarettes.

'She doesn't like the smell of cigarettes.'

'Tough.' Then he adds hurriedly, noting Isabella's warning expression, 'Anyway, I'm going. The atmosphere's getting dangerous.'

Springs up from the chair, pulls an ogre's face and wiggles his fingers at Hannah, grabs his leather jacket from the back of the chair and saunters out of the cottage – to Joyce's, next door.

She is glad to see him gone. He exhausts her. It was probably a mistake to have sex with him; on the other hand it hasn't really changed anything. It is as if it didn't happen. A short, emotionless coupling. She feels neither closer to him nor more distant. The same. A kind of friendly exasperation.

Upstairs, when she is kneeling to dress Hannah, zipping up her jeans and doing up the belt round her pale little middle with its protruding belly-button, Hannah traces an outline with her finger round Isabella's lips.

'Mummy smile,' she says.

Isabella clasps her tightly. 'Oh madre, you're special. Have I ever told you you're the most special little girl in the world?' She draws back slightly from her. 'Do you want to make me smile, then?'

Hannah nods solemnly, her malachite eyes burrowing into Isabella's.

'OK, then. Look, I'm going to smile. You can help me.' And taking Hannah's fingers of both hands in her own, she raises them to the corners of her mouth and smiles hugely.

Hannah giggles, chanting, 'You're smiling, you're smiling.'

But there is little to smile about. The whole village is in mourning. And when Isabella goes to see Joyce later that day, she is wearing brown.

'I don't have anything black,' she explains. 'I wore this for Phil's funeral too. I don't suppose Charlie would mind.' Gives a small half-laugh which ends up as an extended sigh. 'I told Tom he should do the film. "Make it," I said to him, when he came to see me this morning. He was so proud of being in it. Well, it'd be like a tribute to him in a way, wouldn't it?'

Stoic, this second time. But her eyes are bemused, and she is stooped-shouldered. Always small, she now seems diminutive.

'I thought we'd have more than three years,' she says. 'He was a character, wasn't he? Though of course you didn't know him long.'

Confides then that she was always in love with him secretly, that his brother, her first husband, was a drinker, a bit of a hothead. They weren't identical twins, she said.

'Charlie could be rather long-winded, bless him. He'd

take for ever to get to the point' – smiling wistfully at the already-past – 'but it was always interesting. Always worth listening to. He had his strong opinions, as you saw, but he was a true gentleman. And a gentle man, moreover. My daughter's coming tomorrow. But she never approved. Still blames me for marrying him. Well, for a long time it was against the Church, wasn't it? And she's got religion bad. No doubt she'll say this is God's punishment. And I'll have to listen to it all. He and I might have been old, dear, but there's no rules about age, when it comes to love. I'm going to miss him. You tell your friend Tom to make that film the best thing he's ever done.'

When Tom phones she gives him Joyce's message.

And: 'I want to be on my own tonight,' she says.

'That's good. So do I,' he replies tersely.

And she remembers how childish he can be when he is peeved; how everything has to be on his terms or not at all. Once, when she was critical of him, he accused her of being schoolmarmish. An all-or-nothing man, depending on his mood at the time and his level of interest. So at the moment he is newly infatuated, but Tom's enthusiasms are in the place where he happens to be; and then he moves on.

Missing Aidan is like an ulcer that keeps flaring up.

There is a small incident that afternoon. The cottage is cold and she lights a fire, before remembering she needs to go to Babs's shop for one or two things. She lets the fire die down first, and puts the guard in front of it. Or is almost certain she has. She walks to the village with Hannah, buys the things she needs and chats to Babs for ten minutes. When she returns the fireguard is pushed to one side. She is mystified. Her first thought is that someone has been here. But the cottage was locked and the windows shut, and there is no sign of forced entry. Her next thought is that Garibaldi might have knocked into it; but she discounts this, as the guard would have fallen over. Her final thought on the matter is that in her present mental state it is probable she did not put the guard in front of the fire at all.

Thursday morning. To her surprise Aidan is at the garage alone. When she sees him she feels almost weak. Her eyes start to water. Heat spreads up through her neck. They say hello awkwardly. Politely he asks how she is. She lies that she is fine, as he holds himself so aloof and untouchable, haughty, in his oil-streaked overalls.

'I saw your car was booked in. I told you I'd do it myself.'

'There was no need. I wouldn't have held you to that. I couldn't have expected—'

'I keep my word,' he says. Implying? She feels as though she is being strangled; all her emotion stifled within her. I'm so unhappy, she wants to tell him. His curtness, in contrast to the warm tone she is used to, makes her shrivel.

'Could I have it back this evening? I've got to leave for Gloucestershire early in the morning.'

He lifts his eyebrows slightly, and she blunders on, wanting his sympathy: 'My best friend – the one I had the rock group with – her husband's just died. The funeral's tomorrow afternoon.'

'I'm sorry.' A gentler note creeping into his voice.

'It's awful.' She is close to tears.

He looks down at her, and a gamut of expressions flits across his face as he clearly does battle with himself.

'Come into the office for a bit,' he says, after deliberation. 'Do you want a coffee?'

'If you've time.' Remembers: 'Oh, and Sophia will be here soon to pick me up.'

She sits on one of the leatherette chairs and watches him spooning instant coffee into stained mugs and adding the water. Stirs powdered milk and one sugar into his own, and hands her the black coffee. A brief, rueful smile as though to say, I remember, see?

Yes.

'So there's Charlie's funeral too, next week. Monday, I gather.'

'Yes. It's ghastly.'

Tells him how she heard and saw the explosion from the beach.

'I realised who it was. They were filming.'

Wishes she had not raised that particular subject. The air is taut with significance. He rubs at a grease mark above his watch. She stares round the office. The photograph on the desk reminds her suddenly: he has not mentioned her note.

At the risk of being humiliated, she asks, 'You got my note?'

'What note?'

'I left you a note when I came here on Monday morning. By the photo of your sons.'

He frowns. 'I didn't know you came here. I thought you rang and booked in. I didn't get a note.'

So Luke took it. Did he read it? Should she tell Aidan about him?

Ask me what I wrote in it.

He is busily searching for it, first behind the photograph, then beneath the desk.

'I don't know what could have happened to it.'

The puzzle over its fate absolves him from having to ask about its contents.

She finds it almost impossible to drink her coffee. Cannot swallow. Cannot bear his indifference towards her.

'Aidan, I'm very sorry about what's happened.'

Her hand is close to his on the desk. It would only be a matter of edging it a couple of inches and—

'Forget it. You never made any promises.' Moves his hand. 'You were fair all along. It's my fault for getting involved.'

'But it wasn't like that. I felt the same.'

As he glances at her sharply, Sophia's voice calls out, 'Anyone around?' And his features cloud over once more.

'I'll drop your car off later. Luke will follow me and bring me back to the garage.'

A surge of determination seizes her suddenly.

'No, I *won't* let it go just like that.'

Stands up abruptly and, taking his face between her hands, kisses him with great tenderness. She moves away as he begins to respond.

'I meant what I said. I still do. If you'd read my note you'd have realised. You're too bloody proud, that's your trouble.'

And has the pleasure of seeing him look completely confounded.

She leaves the little office. Doesn't need to turn round to know that he is standing there, with his shoulders forward, flummoxed, rubbing his beard. And she still has his binoculars.

She is one of the first to arrive at the Cotswold church, and waits outside. When she sees her, Sally breaks down. Incoherent words studded with sobs.

'There's been so much to do. I keep wanting to turn to Geoff to help me.'

'He's laughing up there, hearing you say that,' Isabella tells her, squeezing her hand.

'Crap. You don't believe in an "up there".' Sally's quavering smile through her tears.

'For Geoff I do.'

'Yes. He was a *good* man. Was. Oh God. *Was.* Oh, Issi, I'm in *agony*.' And the torrent starts again.

People arriving, hanging around outside in the drizzle. Subdued. Funeral etiquette. Faces she hasn't seen for years, others encountered more recently. One or two people come up to her and enquire about the Bosnian orphan they have heard she has adopted. And then she spots someone she recognises slightly and tries to place. He comes over to her.

'Hello. I didn't know you knew Geoff.'

The pinky-fresh complexion and large ears; kindly, downward eyes. Where—?

'You don't remember, do you? Out riding. We met riding. I rang you.'

'Madre, of course, I'm sorry.' The banker. No, solicitor. Neil something.

'I've phoned a couple of times, but I got your machine and didn't bother to leave a message.'

'I'm staying in Cornwall for a while longer.'

She is actually quite pleased to see him. Remembers from riding that he was self-effacing with a good sense of humour. Not in the least pompous.

'London's loss,' he says.

The predictable exchange follows: How do – did – you know . . . ? Geoff was a client of his, but they had become friends, he explains. And as he says it his droopy dark eyes become moist, as do hers. He touches her upper arm in a way that has no hidden motive.

'Shitty, isn't it?' he remarks, shaking his head, his slightly jowled cheeks quivering, so that fleetingly she resists a smile.

'I remember you like opera,' he says. 'We talked about ideal settings for it. And you were waiting to do a deal on a book.'

'You've got a good memory.'

He claps his hands to his head. 'Now what the heck was I going to say next?'

Looks like a pleased schoolboy when she laughs.

'So how long is the "while" for in Cornwall?' he asks. 'You said you were staying there a while longer.'

'Yes . . . A few months.' Waving her hand vaguely.

'I don't suppose you'd want a boring old solicitor turning up one day, would you?'

'Which one would you have in mind?'

'Well, actually I could list a few. Of the boring kind. With respect, and without prejudice, of course. No, seriously – I love Cornwall. It brings back childhood memories. Doesn't it for everyone? I could stay in a bed and breakfast, or whatever.'

She hesitates. She does not want to mislead him. 'I *am* involved with someone,' she says. Even if this is no longer the case, she could not be attracted to Neil.

'I wouldn't have expected otherwise. And if you weren't, I'm not the sort to impose myself. I'd be glad to see you as a friend. My wife died sixteen and a half months ago of breast cancer. I happen to be that rare man who *likes* women.'

The 'sixteen and a half months' touches her. He counts every day. She likes him. A man as a friend? She has never had a man as a friend.

She writes down her number for him. 'I've got an answerphone there also. Leave a message this time.'

He gives a jocular military salute. A man of about her age, with three young children, unwillingly flung into the den of divorced lechers and confirmed bachelors. Perhaps in time he and Sally . . .

Right now Sally is wending her way with her daughters into the church, to the ghostly traces of the organ. Her fair hair is lank and flat. Her head seems as though it is too heavy for her to support. The two girls are like wilted tulips. They form a single clinging, weeping nucleus, surrounded by close family: Sally's mother and sister, Geoff's parents, his brother. Around them pack in the rest of the congregation. Assorted sniffing and blowing of noses, whispering, shuffling feet and escaped sobs echo and reverberate, dying away a little with the appearance of the vicar.

'Today is, for everyone here, a day of terrible sadness,' he commences . . .

I hate churches. I hate death.

The image springs up before her, realistic and horrific, of her own decaying skeleton.

Neil is sitting beside her, and she reaches for his arm instinctively.

'It's the first funeral I've been to since my wife. I hate churches,' he whispers.

And they hold hands to comfort one another.

She had thought she would stay at Sally's, but realises there is no room, with various branches of the family there. Pretends she has booked into a hotel, and kisses her friend goodbye; promises to speak soon, visit soon, bring Hannah with her. It is six thirty, and she heads back to Cornwall, anxious to see Hannah. Wake her up and see her smile, feel her little arms around her neck. Disseminate the weight of her soul.

The owl from the churchyard skims low in front of her headlights through an arch of trees as she drives through sleeping Zerion.

And in his converted stable, is he asleep? I love you, Aidan.

One funeral down, one to go.

Past midnight. Weary from driving. Glad to be back. But Sophia is not on the futon in the sitting room. Isabella frowns, disturbed. Can hear sounds from overhead in her own room, and listens for a minute. Then, with foreboding, she tiptoes upstairs.

They are having sex on her bed. Sophia and Luke. He has her pinioned beneath him. She stares, aghast, leaning against the doorway for support. Sophia notices her and lets out a shrill cry. Luke doesn't move.

'Get off me,' the girl begs, struggling, as Isabella just stands there, dizzy and speechless.

Luke doesn't budge, leering across at Isabella, his slight, muscular body poised over his wife's, his hands tight over her wrists. Then, still with his eyes fixed on Isabella, he gives a final thrust, and throws his head back silently. She watches him withdraw, penis still engorged, dripping on to her duvet cover. And he rolls away from the girl.

Sophia, weeping, rushes up from the bed and grabs her clothes.

'He insisted – it was his idea – he made me – I didn't want to.'

Luke getting dressed laconically.

Isabella trembling to such an extent her teeth are chattering.

'Get out of my home.'

It is all she says. She can only wait for them to leave – Sophia, hysterical, dishevelled, is already downstairs. Luke deliberately takes his time.

'See you,' he says softly, as he sidles out of the cottage, prodding his wife in the back.

For half an hour Isabella sits on the rug downstairs, hugging her knees. Garibaldi appears from the direction of the kitchen, with leaves and twigs attached to him, and winds himself round her a few times before settling, purring noisily, on her lap. She strokes him for a while, then lifts him from her. His claws have jammed into the wool of her black dress, and she has to unhook them before she can detach him. She goes upstairs with the tread of an old woman. Into Hannah's room. The night-light glow of innocence. Her thumb between the oblivious, parted lips. The fluff of hair. The rabbit and bear on the pillow. She has a slight cold, and the tiniest clicking sound is emitted from her mouth.

Isabella lies down carefully beside her. Her skin is neroli-scented. Her breath is tinged with marzipan. She stirs. Eyes like half-parted pods.

Murmurs, 'Mummy back.'

'Yes, carina. Mummy's back.'

And so, the prosecutor says in her head, the worm turned for Isabella Mercogliano, and everything started to close in on her.

13 ∫

Dear Isabella,

I'm so sorry about what happened. Luke came round in the evening and refused to leave and said he would do all kinds of things if I didn't do what he wanted. So anyway like I said I'm really sorry although it wasn't my fault. I've taken your advice and this morning I've left him for good. Thank you for everything you've done for me. I'll really miss working for you. I feel terribly upset about everything and I'm really depressed to tell you the truth. I don't know what I'm going to do and I'll miss Hannah awfully as I really love her. She became like a daughter to me.

Lots of love,
Sophia

The letter, in neat, rounded writing on lined airmail paper, is hand-delivered two days later while she is out. Sophia has enclosed the key, and some jelly babies for Hannah. There is no contact number for Isabella to reply to. Which, despite Isabella's sympathy for her, is probably as well.

She is preoccupied and constantly anxious; finds it hard to sleep, hard to concentrate on her work, and drags herself about lethargically, plagued with uncertainties and fears. Perhaps she should return to London now that her friends know of Hannah's existence and sufficient time has elapsed for her to be confident there is no police search. What reason is there to remain here? There are several for not doing so: a warped stalker, a shattered love affair and constant reminders all around, the invidious gossip, and a spirit of gloom that has settled over the village since Charlie's death. Yet this village, the whole area, has won her over: she has grown to love the landscape, the pace of life, the harshness and the gentleness, and to feel that this is where she belongs. Also, having only recently begun to discover aspects of her character long suppressed, she is unwilling to revert to her old lifestyle and the other Isabella. Granted, she had been content for many years as she was, but the listlessness she had latterly started to experience in numerous small ways demonstrated that her inner self was finally protesting and seeking to be vented. Most of all, she would miss the sea.

Hannah is happy here.

But she has fallen out with her friend. Becky spent an afternoon with them and Isabella took them for a walk to Hannah's Tree. Two of them could not squeeze into its hollow and the other child monopolised it. Tears were the outcome, and the adult-devised treaty between the two is frail. At playgroup the pair studiously avoid one another.

'Don't like Becky,' Hannah stated the other day, pouting.

Hannah's love affair, it seems, like her own, is over.

Sometimes, lying in bed, reflecting on everything, she contemplates emigrating to Italy. She has retained her dual nationality. But the problem of a passport for Hannah seems insoluble. She goes over and over this in her mind; worrying about the future, the prospect of having to show a birth certificate or adoption papers – depending on whether she claimed Hannah to be her own natural daughter or not; plays with the idea of somehow having the forms forged. Madre, what obstacles loom ahead, which she cannot envisage ever circumnavigating, and which she can only see increasing. Her thoughts hop from one thing to another at night. Her own mortality obsesses her. The ghoulish image of her disintegrating corpse keeps recurring. And there is plenty of time to brood, lying by herself in bed – with its turned mattress and laundered linen; dispirited that Aidan has not contacted her after their meeting; listening to autumn rattling Timothy Abell's windows; falling asleep, apprehensive. Fuck me, her father says in the mechanic's voice, pulling the sheet back from her adolescent body in its flannel nightdress.

And meanwhile the wild young men of the village are subdued after Charlie's death; have called a truce in their rivalry over a couple of girls who weren't worth it anyway. His death has numbed everyone. There was nobody who didn't respect him; and the younger generation are re-examining their future – sobered into a sense of duty, albeit transitorily. Charlie had been a part of their lives for as long as they could remember. He had been the patriarchal figure who had taught them what they knew. He had been the spokesman, the one to smooth over disputes. And he had been the link between them. In one way or another they are all related, however distantly: first cousin, third cousin, third cousin once removed . . .

Early this Monday morning she walks with Hannah to the cove where, from the boathouse, they watch three young men unchaining the boats from the mooring blocks and pushing them down the ramp. Inside are strings of lobster pots tied together. 'Joyce', as Charlie had painted on his boat's hull above the registration number, is conspicuous by its absence. It used to be in the cradle on the concrete apron.

'Be back in good time, lads,' she hears one of the brothers, the elder of the two, call.

For later today it will be these three young men who will bear Charlie's coffin.

They watch the men climb into their boats and row a little way out – the oars make a clacking sound – before starting the engines. Checking, no doubt, that no oil rag lies carelessly close.

The morning is clear, with an almost pellucid light, but cold. Isabella warms Hannah's hand in hers as they follow the track that winds up the slopes of the eastern headland. Higher, on the upper meadows, a pair of tractors, glittering in the tablet of sunlight, drone on a constant note as their ploughs trail up and down the length of the fields; and strip by strip the blond stubble is replaced by brown soil, which alters the entire aspect of the countryside.

'You'll have to come with me to church this afternoon,' Isabella tells Hannah, speaking to her as she would to an adult; helps her over a network of tree roots, then lifts her over a stile. Hannah in her little red wellingtons.

'Wi' you?' Her latest habit is to repeat everything.

'Yes, cara. Sophia's not coming any more.'

'S'phia no' coming?'

'No, carina.'

Hannah's expression is thoughtful, as though she is trying to comprehend and digest this.

And that is another thing: she will have to find someone to replace Sophia.

'That must be Joyce's daughter next to her,' she whispers to Babs, who is sitting beside her in Zerion church, and indicates a fair-haired, square-jawed woman with a bulldog stance next to Joyce. 'She looks very formidable. I wouldn't want to cross her.'

'I think you could hold your own,' Babs whispers back.

Isabella swivels her head; spots Janet Abell a couple of rows behind them, and mouths hello. Janet's bland face appears to respond.

'That's another odd one,' Babs mutters, turning also. 'The place is full of them.'

'Too much inbreeding,' says Isabella.

'You're not kidding. Tales of incest abound.'

'Truly?'

'You ask Mary Anne.'

Who has just entered, stately in a black cape. And behind her, Lizzie and Dick. The whole of Pengarris and half of Zerion crowding into the Methodist church, come to pay their respects. Tom arriving with Nick and Tony, and, simultaneously, Aidan. The two men end up sitting beside one another in the corresponding pew to Isabella, on the other side of the aisle. Tom winks at her. Aidan opens the prayer book in front of him, inclines his head forward, and closes his eyes.

The vicar begins his address, his voice resonating off the whitewashed stone walls. He is elderly, with a face that has receded like a turkey. 'Who, here, did not love Charlie Minear—?' How funny: she'd not known his and Joyce's surname. 'Who, here, didn't enjoy his hospitality or wasn't treated to an anecdote that took for ever to reach its conclusion?' Ripples of quiet laughter from the congregation. 'Who, here, was not enriched in some way by him? I know I was. Charlie Minear was a personal friend of mine – we grew up together – as well as a valued member of the Church, so it is with true sadness in my heart that I speak to you now . . .'

Hannah's hand biting into Isabella's. She can feel the child's body tensing against hers.

'Do you want to sit on my lap, carina?'

'I 'fraid. I 'fraid.' Her voice piping out. Reproving heads turning in their direction.

'I know. Here, come on to my lap and you'll be fine.'
Lifting her over.

A few seconds later: 'Man's cross,' Hannah says loudly;
her fingers claw at Isabella's skirt.

More heads swivelling. And a woman near her mutters,
'Fancy bringing a young child.' Isabella flashes a falsely
simpering smile at her, then glares. Tom is looking gleeful.
Tut, tut, tut, he is going with his finger to his lips. Aidan's
profile is as though carved from rock.

Finally, after several more interruptions, when she senses
Hannah is about to start bawling, they leave. Make their
way down the aisle, with everyone's eyes on them. And
tomorrow they will all be discussing her, the disruption
of Charlie's funeral service, how the vicar had to halt his
address. She will apologise to Joyce. But she, more than
anyone, will understand.

She sits on the bench outside, Hannah half lying across
her. Can hear them singing 'For those in peril on the sea'.
The leaves all round are dropping, with the barest popping
sound. The ducks fly up from the pond suddenly, with a
loud quacking, their wings making a distinct creak as they
disappear.

'I don' like church,' says Hannah. She pronounces it
'jush'. Her eyes are fixed on the disappearing ducks.

Isabella soothes her forehead. Such a pretty, high forehead, she thinks.

'I don't either.'

She waits for everyone to come out. First, the brothers,
and Ricky's son, as pall-bearers. The congregation follows,
filing out slowly, blinking in the daylight. Tom comes over
to them.

'Well, you provided a bit of light relief.'

'It was rather embarrassing.'

'Couldn't you have left her with Sophia?'

'She was busy.'

'Oh well, I shouldn't worry. Give everyone something to talk about when they've got the weather out of the way. Actually, it was a very moving service . . . You've been avoiding me.'

'It was getting out of hand,' she says.

'I don't agree that it was. Can I come over later?'

'Madre, you don't give up.'

'I'm going back to London tomorrow anyway. We've finished the job.'

She receives this news with a mix of emotion: a sense of loss, of an ally departing, and relief, like an amphibian coming up for air.

'I'm not going to bed with you, Tom.'

'You're behaving like a virgin queen, for fuck's sake. Once, twice, what's the difference?'

'It shouldn't have happened once.'

'Correct me if I'm wrong, but unless you were faking it the other night you seemed to quite enjoy it.'

'That's not the point. I know how it is when you love someone.'

'How very sweetly old-fashioned.'

His flippancy infuriates her. 'Shut up.'

'Not potted yokel?'

She doesn't answer.

'You stagger me. Talking of whom—' Waving to Aidan as he passes. Aidan, looking severely ahead of him, wearing the same black suit he wears for performances.

'*Don't*,' she says fiercely, capturing his arm. 'Why did you do that? You're so childish.'

Recollects reading somewhere that everyone possesses the components of adult, parent and child. In Tom the child is strongest, then adult; no parent at all. Whereas in herself the adult and parent are uppermost. Recently the child in her has been struggling to emerge more. This strikes her suddenly, now; and explains her increased sense of vulnerability.

'Calm down,' Tom says. 'You'll have all the time in the world to sort out your love life when I've left.'

So he returns with her. They play Scrabble and he crows every time his score is higher than hers. She makes omelettes. They talk, gossip, bicker. He fondles her neck. Like an isthmus, he observes. Her neck is like an isthmus. She is slightly afraid of his leaving.

'Bella, contrary to what you may think, I do care about you. I'd like to stay in touch.'

'I would too.'

'The only thing is, I live with someone. So be careful about phoning. She gets a bit narky.'

'Bastard. Typical.'

Madre, thank God she didn't get involved with him.

The rain pelting down as Isabella drives back from taking Hannah to playgroup, the trees leaning in the wind, leaves cascading; and ahead she sees the Aston nosing slowly out of the lane where he lives. Accelerates to catch him up. Hoots. Flashes. Is he deliberately not slowing? Finally he brakes and stops. She gets out and runs up to the car, head bent against the rain. Jazz blaring out. At least he would genuinely not have heard her hooting. He switches it off. He is wearing his suit, she notices when he opens the door, the same one, but with a bright tie and a carnation in the lapel.

'I was following for ages,' she says. 'You look smart.'

'I'm going to my cousin's wedding in Exeter.' His gaze meets hers briefly then is averted to the dashboard, where he toys with one of the knobs.

'Aidan, Aidan, Aidan.' She shakes her head and sighs. Looks at him despairingly.

'What?'

'I need to talk to you.'

'There's nothing to say.' Turning off the engine, nonetheless.

'Yes there is. I've got your binoculars, for a start.'

'You can keep them.'

'Please, Aidan.' Her hair plastered to her head, to her face; the rain penetrating her pullover and trickling down the polo neck.

'You're getting wet . . .' He knocks his fist against his thigh several times, his lips ground together determinedly. 'Let's just leave it, eh? I'm not just going to come running now your friend's gone. That's not me. And I'm getting late,' he adds more brusquely, as though he has done enough prevaricating and has reached a decision. Turns on the ignition, revs the engine.

She cannot bear to watch him drive off. Lays a preventive hand on the steering wheel, and says quietly: 'He's not a "friend", he's my ex-husband.'

His jaw is slack with astonishment. He turns off the ignition once more.

'Jee-ee-ze.' He makes his clicking-of-tongue noises and rubs his beard. All the familiar reactions. Which makes her smile.

'He wants you to go back to him, I suppose.'

'No. We divorced years ago.'

'But I thought—'

'Please come round this evening? After the wedding?'

'Yeah. Yeah, I'll do that.' His features relax. Perplexity in his eyes, but warmth too. 'I'll be late, mind. Ten, maybe eleven.'

'It doesn't matter.'

Ludicrously happy suddenly. Outlandishly, wildly happy. Her whole face is brimming with it.

'God, you're beautiful,' he says.

He climbs out of the car and embraces her. His huge hands form a 'Y' around her chin, and he kisses her, rubbing the rain from her cheeks with his beard; loving her with his lips and tongue. He tastes of the mouthwash he uses, which reminds her of Pernod. His shirt smells newly ironed, his hair of almond shampoo. His skin of Aidan. She loves the smell of his skin: clean, sweetish – reminiscent of beetroot, salty.

'Pheromones,' he said, when she commented on it once. 'They're what draw animals to one another.'

'Your poor suit,' she observes, when they move apart.

'It'll dry.' He glances unconcernedly down at himself.

'It'll be all rumpled. And the carnation's had it.' Brushing down his jacket, fluffing out the crushed petals of the carnation.

'I don't care. Not about anything.' He grins his open grin that she remembers.

He gets back in the car and holds her hand through the open window.

'I don't want to leave you. But I'll see you later. I'll bring you back some cake.'

'Drive carefully. Promise you will, won't you? The conditions are awful.'

Madre, if anything were to happen to him now. Comforts herself that at least the car is solid enough to see him out of most kinds of trouble.

She drives off. Already planning the evening: the champagne, the music, her perfume, her underwear, what she will tell him. What she will not tell him.

And Tom is probably setting off about now also. Perhaps they will pass on the motorway. And Aidan might brandish a victor's wave as he overtakes, and Tom will think, Who the fuck was that waving in the old Aston? It looked like . . . No, it couldn't be. Heading back to Ealing, to some long-suffering woman whose life depends on his whims and to which part of the world they will take him.

*   *   *

It is a few minutes after nine thirty. Schumann's Piano Concerto is softly playing. The fire is gently smouldering. The champagne is in the fridge.

'After the annual harvesting the fields would, for a limited time, become common property,' Isabella types on her computer. 'All the villagers would gather the remains of cereals which had not been harvested. Animals could graze freely . . .'

She can't work any more. Grasshopper-on-edge as she waits for Aidan. She gets up and goes for a walk around outside. The lights from the other cottages in the row glimmer out. The night is damp, slightly foggy. She uses the lavatory, then returns indoors.

Her computer has stopped working.

She presses the relevant keys, but to no avail. And then she realises: the CD has also stopped playing. She bends down to check the plug and sees that it has been pulled out.

And the fireguard has been removed from in front of the fire.

She straightens up slowly. Her body is rigid. It is as though ice cubes are being rubbed along her arm, leaving a wake of tiny hairs on end.

The mechanic is here.

She makes for the door – just a couple of strides – but he is there first, appearing from the kitchen. He captures her hand with his. In the other is a flick-knife, blade open.

She opens her mouth to cry out, but he presses against her, his jaw thrust up to hers. She can feel the knife blade against her throat, and he lightly plies it back and forth there, sadistically teasing.

'Don't yell. You might wake the child,' he says.

Her heart commencing its slow march, then accelerating; faster, faster, louder, louder. It seems to be taking her over; she is nothing but a beating heart.

He stinks. Onions. Beer. Lust.

'What do you want?' She can hardly form the words between her clenched teeth. She feels almost paralysed with her fear. Never could she have imagined such a paralysing fear.

'Now that's a daft question.'

He moves away a little, lowering the knife, and she puts her fingers to her neck and leans against the door for support. He studies her assessingly. His eyes gleam with his sense of power; watching her for her reaction. And now he is trailing the knife towards her stomach and with its tip is lifting the fabric of her jumper. Smiling as he notices her suck in her breath, and she whimpers.

'Kneel,' he orders, in his hoarse rasp.

She slides down on to her knees.

'Now crawl round the room. Go on, *move*.'

Kicking her when she doesn't instantly respond.

She can feel her stockings laddering. Her knees hurt, and she tries to adjust her position.

'Stay down,' he commands, as though to a dog.

She scrubs round the room like an amputee, and he follows, prodding her with his foot, kicking her back. She makes no attempt to disobey or argue or plead; knows that the first two would incite and the last excite. She would not, anyway, be able to speak coherently. Round and round the room she grovels.

This isn't happening, this isn't happening, this . . .

He hauls her to her feet. 'Get undressed.'

She is shaking. Cannot stop shaking; her body is like a pneumatic drill.

'I've . . . got my period . . . I'm . . . bleeding.'

Her teeth are chattering, and the words emerge disjointedly.

'Get on with it.'

'I've got a Tampax in.'

'Pull it out, then.'

There is no Tampax. She stands there, head bent, hair flopping forward. Utterly, utterly helpless.

'You're lying. Slut.' And he hits her forcefully across the face.

The impact sends her reeling. Pain shooting through her jaw. She bites down a sharp cry.

'Don't try and pull one over me. Undress. Top part first.'

She has on a black silk-knit tunic over her leather skirt, and lifts it slowly over her head, sobbing dryly. Her hair crackles with electricity. She caves her shoulders forward, trying to shield her breasts, acutely conscious of her womanliness, of her body being private to her, and of the black half-cup bra she'd put on for Aidan.

He is riveted to her breasts, like a famished reptile. Spittle forms in one corner of his lips. He jiggles the knife about, taunting her. She can scarcely breathe. Her mouth is sucked dry. Her face is throbbing, and she can feel numbness setting in on one side.

'Bend over. I want to see your tits when you bend over. Put your hands on your knees and stick your arse up.'

Humiliated, she complies, and he leers over her for a few moments, then lunges at her breasts, squeezing them with his blackened, nailless fingers, scraping her soft flesh with their rough texture.

'Get that thing off.' Gesturing to her bra.

She puts her hands up to herself protectively.

'Aidan will be here soon.'

Praying: Be here. Please be here . . . The faint hope he will arrive in time.

'Fucking liar. Whole village knows it's finished. You've been whoring around.'

'No, really—'

His face looms over hers; the flashing row of his teeth.

The flashing line of his knife. And she shrieks out as a scorching sensation zips down her right arm to the elbow. A strip of blood forming. She staggers slightly and clutches the table leg.

'I'm not playing games.' Unbuckling his belt with one hand and gripping her wrist with the other. 'Now get your bra off.'

Her arm is dripping. It is too sore to raise to unfasten the hooks at the back. She struggles with her left hand but is trembling so much she can't locate them. He watches her efforts with curled lips, then grows impatient and wrenches her head back by the hair – a clump comes away – and tugs the bra off her.

And all the while, through her pain, through her fear that he is going to rape her, mutilate her, while he abuses and debases her, is the deeper terror that he will actually kill her.

He undoes his jeans and drags them off, over his trainers. He is not wearing pants. His erection is like a glistening pole, purple and veined.

'Rub your tits against my cock. Go on. Get down on your knees and do it.'

The knife so close to her left nipple he could slice it off.

Weeping, she crouches and rubs her Chanel-perfumed flesh against his rancid, oozing penis.

'Cup them round it tightly.'

He grasps her breasts again, crushing and bruising them.

'Now suck it.'

'I—'

'*Suck it,*' he repeats. 'You do it to everyone else.'

He forces back her head and pushes his penis into her mouth. She gags as he jerks it down her throat. Thinks she will choke. Her injured jaw prevents her from opening her mouth wider, and his thighs grip her battered face like pincers. She tries not to swallow, not to taste his sourness.

Suddenly he pulls out of her mouth, and she immediately retches. Vomits there, in front of him. He stares in disgust.

'Clean it up. I can't have that near me.'

Propels her into the scullery, knife to the small of her back. From under the sink she takes a wad of paper roll, a cloth, and a bottle of disinfectant. She scarcely knows what she is doing.

In the sitting room he watches as she scrubs. Relishing her degradation, as she rubs at the carpet on all fours, in her leather skirt and laddered black stockings, and with her bare breasts swinging like a cow's udders. His erection has died and he is angered because of it.

She does not screw the disinfectant lid back on. A vague idea forming in her mind.

'Get the rest of your clothes off,' he orders, when she has finished. And starts massaging his penis to make it hard again.

She undresses under his gaze. Steps out of the skirt, peels down her hold-up stockings, and finally her G-string briefs. Shivering and ashamed and defenceless. Her mouth tastes vilely of vomit.

'Watch me,' he commands, as he masturbates.

And when she averts her eyes he hauls her by her bad arm and makes her lie down, while he crouches over her and goes on doing it. She suppresses the cry of pain. A subtle change is occurring within her: a sense of defiance lending her fortitude. She is conscious of it: so slight, but managing to infiltrate her fear, nonetheless.

He is shorter than her, but his ape-like arms have enormous power in them. She can imagine him cracking her bones with their grip. He stops masturbating, and moves to one side of her. Lifts her buttocks over him. His T-shirt has ridden up over his navel, and her thighs rest against his flat, tattooed stomach.

'Piss on me.'

'*What?*'

'You heard.'

She tries to twist away from him, 'I can't.'

'I want you to piss on me, slut.' He lifts the knife to her pubic hair.

Once again she begins shaking uncontrollably. Sweat pours from her armpits down her sides.

'I went earlier. I can't help it. It's the truth.'

He grunts. Apparently convinced. Pushes her off him with his foot.

'Lie on your front, then.'

And she realises he has every intention of buggering her.

For a second they are face to face, and she knows her opportunity is now or not at all. With a burst of resolve she reaches out for the bottle of disinfectant and flings the contents in his eyes.

He lets out a bellow and presses his knuckles to his face, rocking in agony. He has dropped the knife and she snatches it up and stabs him hard in the shoulder with it, barely aware of what she is doing. Again and again.

'Bastard, bastard, *bastard* . . .'

Screaming insanely, regardless of Hannah upstairs. Savage in her released rage and retaliation. Kicking out and clawing at him as, half blinded and bleeding heavily, he tries to lock her in a hold and they grapple towards the table. On it she catches sight of Aidan's binoculars, and she grabs them just as his hands encircle her throat. Brings them down, with every fragment of her strength, on the stubbled bullet of his head.

He falls back, partially across her, and she drags herself from under him.

'Mummy, Mumm-ee.' Hannah shrieks upstairs.

And outside: the growl of the Aston.

Isabella, collapsed on the floor by the sofa, just a couple of yards from Luke, whom she may or may not have killed. Too weak, too shocked, too much in pain, too invaded, to move.

And Aidan opens the front door and steps inside.

14 ∫

Aidan calls her my darling, my little love, my squirrel . . .
He nurses and cossets her, cooks for her, lies beside her in
bed, caresses her without having sex; wakes her when she
is writhing about in the midst of a nightmare. For a week
he scarcely lets her out of his sight; has organised a friend
to take charge of the garage. He shops for her, helps with
the housework, hangs out the washing, shepherds Hannah
to and from playgroup.

'I'm not an invalid,' she protests.

'But you are. That's exactly what you are.'

Her arm is stiff but healing; her jaw sore, but the swelling
subsiding. The mental wounds are slower to heal.

At Truro hospital, where he drove her that night, they
told the weary-eyed registrar she had stumbled over a
ceramic plant-pot in the dark, gashing her arm on a broken
piece as she fell face down on the concrete.

'Nasty,' he commented, having worked a sixteen-hour
shift. Looked sceptical. Had heard it all before.

They have told people in the village the same. She is
touched and surprised by their concern.

She has no energy, cannot concentrate for any length
of time, frets about falling behind with her work, can't be
bothered even to read the papers.

He reads extracts to her, picks out amusing stories in an

attempt to elicit a smile from her: how two keen 'twitchers' in a leafy suburb had been hooting to each other from their gardens for the past year, each believing the other was an owl responding; how an elderly naturist professor gardened and cooked whilst stark naked, and expected his au pair to do the ironing and housework in a similar state of undress – she had accepted the job, Aidan explained, understanding him to be a naturalist; how a modern-day druid had his sword, Excalibur, confiscated from him as an offensive weapon and appeared in court dressed in his druid's robes.

'Two humans masquerading as owls, a naked professor, and a druid. No wonder foreigners all think the British are eccentric,' he said.

And she might begin to laugh, but then her laughter alters, and the tears are trickling down her cheeks. Often she does not realise she is weeping. She will be sitting at her computer or in front of the television, staring ahead and silently crying. It is impossible to exorcise the ordeal from her mind. The images constantly are replayed.

But Luke has removed himself temporarily from the village.

'She won't dare do nothing,' he jeered weakly, when Aidan threatened him with the police and elbowed him, bleeding and half undressed, out into the night. Left his trail all the way to the van in the lane.

He is right. She does not dare.

The horror of reliving every detail in the witness box. Her private life, inconsequential though it should be, dredged up.

. . . Ms Mercogliano, I understand that since you have been living in this area you have acquired something of a reputation where men are concerned.

Objection!

She has never understood how barristers can defend

clients they know to be guilty. To her it is entirely wrong.
A kind of prostitution. Outlandish that an already traumatised victim should have to be subjected to interrogation
and intimate minutiae exposed in order to trivialise the
defendant's crime.

'But if there's a chance the defendant's innocent, doesn't
he have a right to be represented?' Aidan says mildly when
she voices her opinion.

But she is not in the mood for objectivity and becomes
angry with him, accusing him of being insensitive.

'Anyway, I'm not having my personal life laid out like
a scarf.'

'It wouldn't be like that. Your name wouldn't be revealed.'

'People would know. They'd put two and two together.'

'Suppose he pleaded guilty?'

'Please. Don't go on at me.'

Squeezes her eyes closed, with a tortured expression.

'OK, I won't.' Soothing her forehead with his fingers.

. . . And, says the smirking barrister, there are other
factors which have come to light, that His Lordship might
be interested to learn . . .

Nevertheless, she is afraid that by not taking action she
is leaving the door open for the mechanic; that when he
returns to the village he will seek her out. Unfinished
business.

Aidan tries to reassure her this is unlikely. She remains
unconvinced.

'His resentment will have built up in him,' she says.
'Eating into him. He'll want revenge. He's not balanced.
Not normal.'

'Then report him. For your sake. For other women's
sake.'

'I can't. Stop making me feel guilty.'

And round they go again.

Fear, specific and unspecific, is with her the whole time.

She has got into the habit of glancing nervously about her; whips round at every unexpected noise; is suspicious of every creak and rattle in the cottage or outside; jumps at the sound of the letterbox; blanches when the telephone rings. Normal things that once went unremarked now give rise to panic in her. And she is concerned that Luke has a copy of her key, recollecting the afternoon she returned from Babs's shop to find the fireguard in a different position.

Aidan changes the lock and fixes a safety chain; attaches locks to the windows also.

He blames himself for what happened.

'You told me you mistrusted him. And I was dismissive. I just thought he was peculiar. I should have *seen*.'

He reproaches her, too, for not confiding in him.

'But it came to a head when we'd had our . . . rift,' she says.

He castigates himself over this also: for not trusting her, for being jealous. He, of all people, who has always viewed jealousy as so negative.

'Although, if you'd been more open in the first place, there'd have been no need for any jealousy. I'm a man as likes to know where he stands. That's all I ask.'

They have still not discussed Tom. She has not raised the matter, and neither has he, although she senses he is longing to. She does not have the energy for explanations or to deal with the inevitable questions that would arise.

Wishes she could feel strong again. And her body is repellent to her. It feels desecrated, as though it will never be clean again. She is forever washing, or cleaning her teeth or rinsing out her mouth. Cannot bear to look at herself naked. Despises her feminine shape and dresses hurriedly in loose jumpers and jeans.

She has told Hannah she is not well.

'Mummy not well,' Hannah says sorrowfully. 'I make better.' Puts her arms round Isabella and kisses her.

Loving Hannah. Trying to behave normally for her sake.

And will Aidan grow impatient with her? She is not used to being feeble or to being pampered. Has always been so self-sufficient.

'How can you think that?' he says. 'I *want* to look after you. You've got to give yourself time to recover. You expect too much of yourself.'

'I'm angry with myself,' she tells him today, on their first walk since it happened. 'I didn't react the way I'd always imagined I would in a situation like that. Everything just went from me. I disintegrated. I just gave in. I was a complete wreck. I just let myself be humiliated. I'm so angry.' Kicks at a stone, which arcs in the air before landing a few yards away.

'But you didn't just give in. You mustn't say that. It's not true. Look what you did in the end. You were so brave. *You* humiliated him. *You* punished *him.*'

'But before that . . . I didn't even try.'

'Your life was at stake, for goodness sake. He had a knife jammed to you. You're brave, little love. You're brave.' Enfolding her in his arms as she breaks down.

Hannah rushing over to them from the spot where she was filling her pail with sand; clasping their legs, demanding, 'I want hug. I want hug.'

Laughing through tears. Aidan stooping to hoist Hannah on to his shoulders for a piggyback.

'One, two, three . . .'

The fishermen go about their day as usual. No Charlie whistling, dragging his foot and outpacing them.

The village without him is gradually slipping back to normal. The wild lads are getting drunk and quarrelling again, and moaning about the dark mornings. The Sun

Inn resounds once more to darts matches and beer-drinking competitions and karaoke nights. The landlord has posted up details of the football teams.

A fox is on the prowl, having dispatched Joyce's bantams, and a couple of other people's chickens, besides the surgeon's wife's pet ducks.

'A vixen with young ones more'n like,' Aidan comments.

A local farmer is keeping vigil with a shotgun and people are taking bets: whether he'll catch it, and how soon. The money is going into a memorial fund, in honour of Charlie, for fishermen's widows and dependants.

Isabella is torn: glad, on the one hand, that Joyce will benefit, perturbed on the other by the bloodlust, and sorry for the fox. Sentiments she wouldn't voice publicly. No room for sentimentality in the country. But she has a Londoner's attitude. She is used to London foxes, encouraged by urban households who put out food and milk for them. A clattering in the night of an upturned dustbin, the sharp cry of a vixen on heat, are the total of the disturbance to city dwellers, who will swap notes excitedly about a fox sighted in a garden or on the shed roof. Here, however, they are vermin; a scourge – as the locals pit their wits against one wily creature and gamble their pennies. There again, she is sorry for the fate of the chickens and ducks.

For Joyce it has been one thing too much. This catastrophe, so minor compared to the other she has just been through, has defeated her.

'I don't know as I'll bother replacing them,' she tells Isabella. 'All that work for nothing. And without Charlie I don't need all those eggs. I can get them from Babs.'

'They were so pretty. And I'll miss their clucking,' Isabella says.

'So'll I. And the old rooster. I'm amazed the fox got

Buster. He'd have put up a fight, I can tell you. It's like the end of an era,' she adds wistfully.

Days passing. Storms lashing the headlands. The sea mountainous; and the men go out regardless, in challenging spirit, in their yellow oilskins. She falls asleep with the blinking of the lighthouse and wakes to the lament of the foghorn. Tregurran beach is brown with tossed wet sand, dead bracken blown from the cliffs, and banks of seaweed. Occasionally she meets the surgeon's wife and her dog. Once the surgeon himself. The long threads of his hair on end in the wind. And he flattens them over his bald patch as he comes over to speak to her. Lips forming into a smile. Preparing himself for chat-up mode, she thinks.

Mary Anne is in bed with flu. Telephones Isabella: 'Would you like to ride Nabokov? You'll have to tack him up yourself. I can't move.'

She leaves Hannah with Joyce. She has not saddled up a horse on her own before, but has watched the girls at the Hampstead stables doing it countless times, so in theory she knows what to do. Nabokov stands obligingly still, tied loosely to the ring attached to his timber shelter, as she fumbles with the bit. She need not have worried. He opens his mouth as soon as the steel bar makes contact with his muzzle, and it slips in easily. She slots his big, hairy ears through the headpiece (they make her think of Bottom, and of youthful productions of *A Midsummer Night's Dream*); pulls his coarse mane carefully from where it was caught beneath the browband.

'Good boy, good boy.' Undoing the throat-lash strap she has accidentally buckled to the noseband, and realigning it.

Doing up the saddle's girth is less complex but more of a problem: he has puffed himself out and the two ends won't meet. She can see him holding his breath – his legs are planted firmly, his barrel sides solid. She leads him forward a couple of paces; he breathes and deflates, and before he can repeat the sequence she quickly fastens the girth. And then they are plodding down the lane, through Zerion, at a leisurely rate. He doesn't flinch as they squeeze past a tractor with a clattering trailer behind it. People stop and chat to her, friendly, smiling, patting the cob's neck: 'Nice to see you about again . . . I didn't know you rode . . . How's your little girl? . . . Are you better after that nasty fall?' The sight of a horse bringing out their geniality.

It is the first time it hasn't rained for four or five days. The lanes are slippery. Branches and leaves are strewn about. Nabokov picks his way with a cautious rhythmical clop. His body is like a kitchen table beneath her. His ears are constantly pricked forward, except when they seesaw in response to her leg movements. It is the slowest two miles she has ever accomplished. When they come to Tregurran beach he puts on a spurt, and with a swish of the tail and the tiniest of bucks he canters towards the ragged hem of the sea. He slows a little and she slackens the reins and lets him trot of his own accord into the waves. Back and forth they trot, the horse striking out his legs in front of him. The surf sprays up around them and waves break against her calves, drenching her. Needles of salt scour her cheeks. The wind tears at her hair. She laughs in pure exhilaration; pure, obliterating, transient happiness.

In the evening Aidan drives her to Falmouth to see a production of *Lady Windermere's Fan*. They leave during the first act – driven away by an old man on Isabella's other side who takes up half her seat besides his own with the spread of his belly and thighs, his walking stick, and a stinking bag of fish that becomes more overpowering by the second. The pair of them depart like naughty children, smothering giggles and navigating agitated laps, as Lord

Windermere appeases his wife: 'Margaret, none of us men may be good enough for the women we marry . . .'

'I must try that on the Tube sometimes,' she says, once they are in the street. 'Carry a bag-load of fish with me. Yuk, it's still up my nostrils. And he was wheezing against me.'

'Poor old guy,' Aidan reflects. 'There's something very pathetic and lonely about it, if you think, isn't there? A man of seventy or eighty at the theatre alone. Bad chest, bad hip more'n like, and a bag of fish he'll cook for himself.'

'Madre, that's made me feel shitty. I shan't be able to get him out of my mind now. You're so much nicer than me.'

They walk to a nearby Italian restaurant, converted wine vaults reached via steeply angled steps. They cause her to remember when she took Hannah back to her flat.

'Today something extraordinary happened . . . At approximately 10.00 o'clock this morning, Saturday, 31 August . . .'

Is that all it is – only just over two months ago? It seems incredible.

A beggar is huddled in the shadows a few yards along, and to alleviate her conscience about the fish man, she gives him a pound. He reeks of booze.

'I shouldn't have encouraged him, I suppose,' she says to Aidan.

The restaurant is fairly busy this Friday night. She recognises a couple from the surgeon's wife's party: the nice-looking blond therapist and her husband. They recognise her also; smile hello. The woman gives Aidan a friendly little wave.

'I do her car,' he says, as the waiter shows them to a table in a secluded corner. 'I took her out a couple of times before she was married.'

A pang of jealousy snatching at her.

'Did you sleep with her?'

'I don't go to bed with every woman I take out, you know.'

During the meal she becomes aware that his fingers are drumming on the table, then wandering up to his beard, then his hair. Grabs his hand as it moves towards the candle, about to tackle the dripped wax. Smacks his wrist lightly.

'So, what's up?'

He tilts his head from side to side and studies her contemplatively. 'All right,' he says finally. 'The other evening, well, *that* evening, you were going to tell me about Tom . . . I haven't mentioned it as I didn't want to upset you. But it's bothering me. I need to know, Isabella.'

'Yes.'

Over the murmur of the other diners she isolates the music in the background: the cavatina from *Cavalleria Rusticana*. The flowers on the table are silk – why can't they have real ones, for the sake of fifty pence? The woman near them has a squawking laugh. How can her partner stand it? Aidan's right hand is tanned, with pale threads of ancient scars traversing it. What were the incidents that caused them?

'We were married when I was at university. We had our honeymoon in this area – what a ridiculous word that is; we spent a few days away. He was a journalist then. Anyway, after about a year he went out to the Republic of Vietnam as a reporter. By the time he returned I'd graduated. He was impossible to live with. He hated being married. So we divorced. That's all there is to it. When he turned up here it was the first time I'd seen him since we split up.'

He nods slowly, plainly not satisfied.

'But you said you'd run away from your husband.'

'No I didn't. Others said it. *I* didn't. They just surmised. It was simpler to go along with it.'

'You're not married, then?'

'No.'

'Then Hannah's father—?'

She doesn't answer.

'Why won't you tell me? I'm an open book. You know everything about me. You're not being fair.'

He raises his voice in frustration, and she leans forward and lays her finger against his lip.

'I adopted her.' It isn't entirely a lie. 'I can't tell you any more.'

'Please look at me,' he says. And his eyes penetrate hers. 'When you arrived here you seemed to be running from someone.'

'It wasn't someone. It was some*thing*. A situation.'

'But you won't tell me what it is.' His voice is flat with hurt. 'You're so secretive. It's insulting, you know that? I thought we trusted each other. And after all that we've been through these last ten days . . . I don't know, sometimes I—' Shrugs. Doubt written across his face.

She feels a quickening of panic. She is so afraid of driving him away a second time. She cannot conceive of their not being together. Has come to value him more than anyone she has ever known.

'Please, caro, don't be hurt. I know it's easy for me to say that . . . Look, I just . . . I did something.'

'What kind of "something"? Was it so awful?'

'I don't think so. Others might.'

'I'm not others,' he says in that proud, wounded tone of his.

'I know that.'

'I suppose I've got no right, really.'

'Yes you have. Of course you have . . . I'd hate to lose you, caro.'

Her eyes are black with tenderness, and he gazes into them.

'I love it when you call me that.' Sighing.

Neither of them speaks for a moment. He swirls his sautéed potatoes round in the tomato sauce. Pushes the plate away from him.

'You'll tell me one day, when you're ready?'

'Yes.'

God knows how. The postponement of playing her own executioner.

'I suppose that'll have to do, then. Just a couple of things. Are the police involved?'

She doesn't answer.

'Isabella?' he presses her.

She can't meet his eyes, and bends her head to hide the colour in her cheeks.

'No. But they might be one day.'

And now he really will tell her he's had enough, that under those circumstances he must finish with her. Who could blame him?

She feels him touch her face, his hand gently lifting her chin so that she is forced to look at him.

'You haven't hurt anyone, I mean physically? It's a terrible thing to ask, but—'

'No. Never in my life.'

'And you haven't taken any money, nothing like that?'

'Madre, no.'

'Well, that's something.'

A child. But no money.

'I trust you.'

And in two days' time it will be her birthday. Her fortieth. And Hannah's third. She has decided they shall share a birthday. Has bought her a swing that Aidan will put up in the garden, on the patch where Timothy Abell used to dig his potatoes. And what if it were her birthday? Would her mother be remembering when she gave birth? Wondering? Remorseful?

'Do you want me to tell you the best birthday present of your life?' Aidan says on the phone, from the garage.

'Keep it as a surprise.'

'Are you sure? Are you sure you don't want me to tell you that new people have moved into Luke's place? That he's left the area for good?'

For a few seconds she experiences a sense of relief. But it is quickly replaced by an odd deadness. In her head he has not gone for good. His quiet, brutal voice is in her ears. His face leers over hers. She is consumed by images. Keeps seeing the knife – and it is magnified, filling her vision. Now his chewed fingers are aiming it at her nipples, now he is stroking her vagina with its tip and she can feel it piercing and carving and slitting. Sometimes she feels like Munch's painting, and she is hurtling through a tunnel, her scream a gaping wound in her face. And there, blocking her exit at the end of the tunnel, is an immense, veined phallus.

Amongst her birthday cards is a letter from Neil:

Dear Isabella,

It was splendid to see you a couple of weeks ago, albeit at such a tragic occasion, and I just wanted to scrawl an impulsive note. As this means not resorting to the computer and my writing is less legible than a spider's, it could be something of an ordeal for you.

Long day, today. Had to represent a client in court. A bit of a yawn case, but I mustn't complain. It pays the bills. Well, some. If ever you need a good lawyer . . . Joke. You seem like a woman whose life is thoroughly in order.

London is a heaving, dismal, damp place at this time of year, and for a strapped-for-cash lawyer living in the wrong part of Islington it is even more dismal. So a (young) man's fancies turn to . . . As I mentioned to you, I have no wish to impose on you, and should hate you to feel obliged in any way, but it would be lovely to escape from London for a few days and have the bonus of seeing you again, as a no-strings 'chum'. I could take you – or you and your friend, since I recall you said you were involved – out for a meal; the rest of the time

I would simply do my 'own thing' (ghastly expression, that, to be ranked alongside 'chill out'). I wonder if I could trouble you to give me the name of somewhere local to stay for two or three nights. Ideally the middle or end of this month would suit me, as December tends to get silly with work. But you must tell me when it would be convenient for you. Or maybe it wouldn't. I have no desire to embarrass you, or to put you out.

That's it for now. My youngest is yelling for her fish fingers.
All best wishes,
Neil.

She is surprisingly glad to hear from him, and writes back immediately with some provisional dates and the telephone number of the Ship Inn.

Aidan has bought her a gold-link bracelet for her birthday.

'I asked the girl in the shop. She said I couldn't go wrong with it,' he says, looking worried as she opens the box.

'She was right.'

Tears in her eyes. He fastens it round her wrist, and she stares down at it, settled neatly there; rubs her thumb around it.

'It's beautiful. I shan't ever take it off.'

'You might need to sometimes.' He grins down at her.

'No,' she says emphatically.

'And for Hannah . . . For Hannah,' he teases gently, holding the untidily wrapped parcel aloft before giving it to her.

'P'esn't for me, p'esn't for me,' she squeals, dancing around with Becky, who is reinstated as her best friend.

It is a cloth doll with yellow tresses and ribbons. 'My name is Hannah,' it says on the pink box.

Her nem is hana.

'I thought it was appropriate,' says Aidan, watching them playing with the doll.

'It is. Thank you so much.'

They are at his house. Balloons hang in the hallway. HAPPY BIRTHDAYS, he has painted on them. The paint has dripped.

In the garden, in the deepening dusk, the girls chase about, in and out of the cypresses, waving sparklers and exhaling huff. Newly enraptured with each other.

'There's smoke coming out of my mouth. I'm a dragon,' cries Becky.

Hannah copies her: 'I'm a dragon, I'm a dragon.'

They wait for Becky's mother to come; Aidan shields them from the cold, one either side of him, within the cave of his jacket. They are tiny beside his hugeness, snuggling against him.

She settles Hannah in the spare room for the night. Goes downstairs, into the open-plan kitchen, where he is preparing dinner for the two of them.

I don't deserve him.

The ticking of the kitchen clock. Classic FM on quietly. He is grating nutmeg into fettucine, then blending in an egg yolk. Dipping his finger into the creamy mixture to taste. Plenitude seeping into her. And she creeps up on him and covers his eyes with her hands, startling him so that he drops the wooden spoon into the sauce.

'Guess who loves you.'

'Can't.'

'Try.'

He prises her hands from his eyes and grips them; turns round to her, his expression serious.

'No. I want to hear you say it.'

His gaze flows into hers. She is drowning.

'I love you.'

'And I love you.'

It solves nothing. Probably complicates it. But, madre,

the relief, the joy, of saying it. The relief, the joy, of hearing it.

And after dinner, after the champagne, the cake, the single red rose, the Cointreau, she goes to bed with him and lets their love wash her body clean.

15 {

She has two weeks. Perhaps one day she will review them as the happiest she knew. Two weeks. Thirteen days to be precise. Remarkable for being unremarkable, for the fact little happens.

She will look back and remember Guy Fawkes Night, and the whole village gathered round the leaping bonfire on the eastern headland. Hannah's anxious little hand slotted into hers. Aidan's arm round her neck. The air alive with the zinging and crackling of fireworks that lit the sky before tumbling like iridescent ash into the sea. The muffled tattoo of the waves. Children silenced by wonderment, warming numbed fingers over the roasting chestnuts. Harry from the Sun ladling mulled wine.

Will look back on the dinner party she gave, when Babs flirted with the vicar, who entertained them with card tricks, and Mary Anne and Joyce discussed sex in old age.

And on long walks; and on a visit to the seal sanctuary in Gweek. Will recall the glow of pleasure she felt when she was asked to give a talk about her work at a WI meeting. And on winning the karaoke competition at the Sun – the teasing, and laughter around her, and buying everyone a round of drinks; and when they toasted her she knew she was finally welcomed into the community. 'I hope you're planning to stay permanently,' someone said.

Will remember the comparative serenity, the peace of mind she felt during that period. Time on 'hold'.

Loving Aidan. Loving Hannah.

Hannah's first fleeting glimpse of snow.

'Luk. F'ost,' she said, having just learnt the word.

'No, carina, this is snow,' Isabella corrected her. Then could not explain the difference.

'Frost: a state of freezing . . . Frozen dew,' her dictionary informed her. 'Snow: atmospheric vapour frozen in crystalline form.'

'Snow comes from the sky, carina,' she said.

'Li' mag'c?'

'Yes. In a way.'

Will remember reading to Hannah in bed from *Wind in the Willows* and her rapt expression from the pillow. The rabbit and bear either side of her.

Hannah's funny tuneless hum as she played with her toys. Hannah's shadowed eyes and pointed chin and rounded tummy and spindly, mottled legs. Hannah's developing inquisitiveness and obstinacy as she was on the verge of acquiring her own identity. Hannah's affectionate nature and her consideration.

'Mummy wukking,' she would say when Isabella was at the computer. 'I be quiet. Ssh.' Finger to her lips, finger to her doll's lips.

Pushing Hannah on her swing.

'I want higher. *Higher.*'

Her sweet, tiny, cold, carefree face. The sunburst smile. And it is this image Isabella will always hold of her.

And then it is Saturday. Thirteen days since her birthday. Eleven weeks since that other Saturday. And like that other one it unfolds. Saturday, 16 November. Isabella will have reason to remember the date. She goes about her usual routine; puts the kettle on, grinds the coffee beans, opens the curtains to bright sun . . . and silver grass. Fusses over

Garibaldi. Feeds him. Gets herself ready. Wakes up Hannah. Dresses her – she has learnt to fasten the buckles of her own shoes. Makes them both breakfast. Clears it away. Hannah carries her mug, bowl and spoon carefully to the sink. Ten o'clock; and they go outside. She pushes Hannah on the swing.

'Higher.'

The phone is ringing. She lifts Hannah down from the swing and runs indoors to answer it.

It is Neil, finalising arrangements for his visit. They chat for a bit – Lovely to hear from you – See you soon – and ring off.

She has been five minutes at most. Returns outside.

The world is frozen. She will look back and remember that also: the brilliant sky and monotone, shimmering landscape. And the swing with Hannah's bear on it.

Hannah is not about. Where is she?

The gate is open, and Isabella feels a twinge of alarm. But she suppresses it; reminds herself of that other occasion on their picnic: her needless panic.

'Hannah,' she calls from the garden. 'Cara.'

No response comes, and apprehension plucks at her. She makes a quick tour round the back of the cottage – perhaps Hannah is hiding. Lately she has begun to be mischievous. 'Boo!' she will exclaim from behind a corner.

She is not round the back.

And now Isabella's fear is clutching at her, and she runs to the gate and peers left along the cutting towards the lighthouse and right towards the lane. There is no sign of the child.

'*Hannah!*'

Straining to hear a reply; listening out for her humming.

Her panic taking a serrated hold of her. And she runs

down the cutting towards the lane. Not a soul about, this frost-hung Saturday morning. A cat lying on the wall observes her frantic sprint through laconic slits.

At the bend she stops, breathing fast, her lungs burning. From here there is an unhampered view to the village, and she can see that, apart from an elderly couple hanging on to each other and pushing a shopping basket on wheels, two neighbours chatting, a woman beating a rug outside her door, and a pair of mating dogs, the little street is deserted.

Up the hill she runs, her breathing catching in her chest, her arms waving about in an uncoordinated way; past the car park, past the surgeon's house, in the direction of Tregurran beach.

'Have you seen my little girl?' she shouts to a gardener hoeing the edge of the driveway. No, he is afraid he hasn't.

Of course, she would not have ventured this far. Would have had no reason to take this route. And Isabella is almost demented with terror for the child. She turns and tears back in the direction from which she has just come.

'Hannah! Hannah!'

Back down the cutting, past the same cat and, hope upon hope, maybe she has returned home by herself. Runs inside.

'*Hannah!*'

And out again, making for the steps that lead to the cove. Gruesome images of the child's body on the rocks below filling her head.

It is high tide; only the two uppermost steps are exposed. Dear God. Madre. Dear God, dear God . . . Isabella muttering to a deity she has never believed in. Feeling an ineffable dread as she scans the rocks for a flash of colour against their greyness. Or perhaps Hannah has been borne away on the waves, like a dummy.

'Isabella, what's happened?' Joyce's rollered grey head out of her open window.

Doesn't hear her. Running about distractedly. Stumbling up the embankment that leads to the chapel, pushing the door, then tugging it, in case the child has gone in there; but it is locked fast. It always is. Continues climbing – falling and slipping on the frozen bracken, grazing her hands, scraping her knees, catching her jumper on gorse branches. Impervious.

Just ahead of her is the hollow oak, and for an instant optimism surges sweetly through her again: it is such an obvious place. Isabella bounds forward. No child is concealed in its trunk. And she clings to the tree, squeezing closed her eyes against this final dashing of hope.

For another half-hour she searches. By now it is approaching eleven. There are people about. They see her running directionlessly, crazed and dishevelled. Someone – who? – asks her what is wrong. Someone takes her elbow as she sobs that she has lost Hannah, that Hannah has gone, Hannah has gone . . . And starts to babble wildly. And whoever it is leads her back to the cottage. They try to make her sit down; but she dashes upstairs into the child's room.

The animal mobile is bobbing slightly from the vibration of her footsteps. She lies on the child's bed, smells her vanilla skin and sweet hair on the pillow and duvet. Stares up as the lion and zebra, giraffe and monkey, hippo and gazelle gently dance in unlikely amity above her head.

Resigned.

Knows she will never again see the child. That she dreamed her. That everything around her is an illusion.

Aidan drives her to Truro police station. Two of them interview her. One is a woman. They are sensitive in their questioning, soft-voiced. A cup of tea arrives, and they encourage her to drink. Are patient when she can hardly whisper. Aidan's concerned eyes next to her, his hand almost crushing hers.

How tall is she?

She has never measured her. Tiny. So tiny. Hardly reaching her hip.

Hair colour?

Red.

Your beautiful hair.

But fluffy. Like a dandelion in seed.

Your dark eyes?

No. Grey-green. Shadowed eyes, like the sea. Serious, watchful eyes. And skin so fine, so translucent you could see the veins.

Her face is haggard. She huddles doubled up in the chair in the clinical white room, nursing her stomach, while they quiz her, taking her painfully step by step through the morning, which has already assumed a distant, unreal quality.

'Try not to worry,' the woman officer says.

'Five minutes,' Isabella says. 'I wasn't even five minutes.'

'You mustn't blame yourself.' Glancing at her male colleague.

'Is there anyone she knows that she might've gone to?' he asks.

She shakes her head.

'You look after her yourself?'

And through her anguish she realises that, however subtly masked the question might be, he is trying to ascertain whether she herself might have harmed the child.

'Yes. I had someone for a few weeks who helped out. But she left.'

'Why?'

She gives a small, involuntary moan as she thinks of the circumstances.

'She moved from the area.'

'Do you have a contact number?' the woman – hardly more than a girl really – asks her.

Again she shakes her head.

They address Aidan. She doesn't hear what they ask him, or his replies. Fixated by a fly traversing the ceiling. They must have tiny sucker pads on their legs, she thinks, to enable them to grip. Imagines the ceiling crashing down, crushing the fly; all of them. Slabs of plaster, like the shattered commandments, on the floor, and pieces of her statement – a word here, a word there – in the WPC's handwriting, floating on the pink clouds of dust.

She knows the child is dead. One day a fisherman will find her. Will spot the red dungarees. And did her real mother feel like Isabella, as she gave up her child? The drip-drip of haemorrhaging longing? Maybe she watched from a window to see who took her. Left it to fate. And if after several hours the child had still been there, outside the newsagent's, she would have reclaimed her.

Isabella has failed the test of motherhood. She could not guard the child from harm. And maybe, after all, God exists, and this is his punishment; he has meted out his own brand of irony.

'We'll keep you closely informed,' the WPC assures her.

'I want to die,' she says, as Aidan helps her up from the chair. Isabella, who is petrified of death.

News of this kind circulates fast. Over the next few days she is besieged by visitors. Everyone rallying round, trying to keep her mind occupied, attempting to console her, bringing her cakes and jars of honey, chutney, or posies of flowers.

She wants to be left alone.

And all around are reminders of the child. But there is no sign of the knitted rabbit. Gone with her.

The days drag and pass.

'"Distraught mother fears worst,"' runs the headline in the *West Briton*. Four lines in the *Independent*, and maybe other papers, for all she knows. How does the national press hear about these things?

'It's their job,' Aidan tells her.

'I hate them,' she says.

He tries to persuade her to eat: 'You can't just give up. Please, squirrel.' Holding his own fork to her.

'I can't. I'll be sick.' Pushing it away.

She is wan and thin. Her black irises are matt. Like a beautiful spectre, he says.

'We're not giving up,' the police say.

And she is shocked to learn they have interviewed a couple of local men with a record of sex offences with children. Would never have dreamed that people like them could be living in this hallowed little area.

From the shore she watches a boat set off with police and rubber-clad divers. Overhead a helicopter lumbers in slow, monotonous circles between the headlands and hovers round the narrows, sending the gulls squealing. A sea mist like a chiffon dress on a dancer, lifting, falling. She tortures herself. Expecting at any minute to hear the cry from the ground: They've found something. The sinister droning of the chopper, the rumbling of the boat engine becoming more distant, the crackling police radios . . . And small groups of villagers watching the theatre. Babs and Joyce flanking her, supporting her. And she sees the child swimming amongst the fish, weaving between the vegetation beneath the sea. A water baby.

She lies awake night after night, with Aidan's back curved against her, plagued with ghastly, vivid imagery. Found on a Saturday. Gone on a Saturday. Saturday's child. Nowhere child. On loan for eleven weeks. She herself was born on a Saturday.

And now it is Friday; the afternoon. She sits on the swing

in the drizzle, absently levering herself back and forth. Hears a car turning into the cutting from the lane and watches with bleak presentiment as it draws up outside the cottage. She swings faster, trying to focus on the rhythmical movement.

They get out of the car: the woman sergeant accompanied by a man she has not seen before. He is not in uniform. The twin thuds of the car doors shutting. Of her heart. She does not stand up as they approach via the open gate – no need to bother about it now – and come towards her, grim-faced. Isabella continuing to swing desperately, lips clamped against the finality of the bad news.

'We've found her, Isabella. She's fine,' the WPC says.

She stops swinging. Stares at them both with disbelief; a smile spreading across her face, becoming laughter. Laughing and crying. Slumped on the swing, sobbing into her hands.

In her emotion she does not register their sombre expressions.

The woman's hand, soothing on her head. Isabella leaning against the serge of her uniform.

'Your childminder took her, Sophia Gundry.'

'Sophia? *Sophia* took her? Not Sophia, surely.'

'Yes, that's correct.' The man speaks for the first time.

The woman officer looks from him to Isabella. Compassion puckering her forehead.

There is something wrong. Something they are not yet telling her. They are too serious. And why haven't they brought the child with them?

'Where's Hannah? What's happened? Why isn't she with you?' Her voiced raised and high-pitched with her sudden anxiety. Her mood undergoes an abrupt reversal from the euphoria of a moment ago.

The man steps forward. He is tall and stout. Prominent-eyed. She immediately notices his lashless, prominent eyes;

and his huge, dilated nostrils. They are like funnels. And they loom close to her as he introduces himself as Detective Sergeant . . . She doesn't catch the name.

'I'm afraid Mrs Gundry has made some serious allegations against you,' he says.

The blood pumping back and forth in her ears, like the sea. Dark, amoeba-like patches swimming in front of her eyes. She holds on to the chain of the swing.

'What kind of allegations?' Hears her own voice from over the horizon.

'That in fact you are not the child's mother. Apparently she read some diary you'd been keeping. Miss Mercogliano' – he sneers over her name – 'I have to inform you I am arresting you on suspicion of abduction.'

'Ms,' she says faintly. 'Not Miss. Ms.'

He grabs her roughly by the arm.

So. It is over.

16

The WPC leads her down a linoleum-floored corridor – it reminds her of the hospital where her mother died – to the charge area, in Custody. It is a large room with a computer on the table. The young woman motions for Isabella to sit down. She seems uncomfortable, having switched from her role of consoler to that of arresting officer. Isabella stares down at her ugly knuckles which Aidan loves because they are serviceable.

The detective sergeant enters with a short, rotund man. He is introduced to her as the custody sergeant, and he positions himself in front of the computer, shifts about in his seat, then presses various keys on the computer. He sits back and gives a small nod to his colleague, who flares his cavernous nostrils and begins speaking in a monotone:

'This person has been arrested at 16.57 hours this day, Friday, 22 November.'

Was arrested, she notes. He doesn't know his tenses.

'To summarise: for the past three months she was caring for a young child on the pretext of being its mother, when this child subsequently went missing. The child was duly found at 11.07 today – as already recorded – having been abducted by a Mrs Sophia Gundry, who for a short while was employed as a childminder and cleaner by Miss Mercogliano.'

'Ms,' she murmurs, polishing the Formica of the table with her fingers.

'What did you say?' The custody officer glances at her over his computer, and pauses in his tapping.

'Ms. I like to be addressed as "Ms", not "Miss".'

'For God's sake.' The detective sergeant rolls his eyes heavenwards. 'I was saying – Mrs Gundry was taken in for questioning during which it emerged that *Miss* Mercogliano—'

Woman-hater.

'—is not the mother, but in fact she herself abducted the child.'

'How did this fact come to light?'

'Mrs Gundry claimed to have seen a diary that Miss Mercogliano kept.'

The G in her name is silent, but he pronounces it heavily. He makes it sound as though he is gargling. It is a beautiful name with a musical lilt, pronounced correctly, but his tongue falls clumsily over the syllables, and she cringes every time he says it.

'It was the detail Mrs Gundry went into that convinced us she was telling the truth. It seems Miss Mercogliano took the child concerned from outside a London newsagent's, then ran away here, to Cornwall. She dyed the child's hair the same as her own so it would appear it was her child. All very calculated.

'After hearing Mrs Gundry's statement I drove with WPC Harries to Miss Mercogliano's rented home at Pengarris Cove and arrested Miss Mercogliano for the abduction of a child against its volition.'

'Did the suspect put up any resistance?'

'No. None.'

The custody sergeant stops printing and turns to Isabella. 'Ms Mercogliano,' he says, acknowledging her preferred prefix, 'you have just heard the arresting officer's account. Do you wish to add anything?'

'No – yes, I do. I did it for the child's good. I did not take her against her own volition. She had been abandoned.'

And where is she now? What will the future hold for that child from now on?

She despairs at the thought.

The custody officer forms his lips into a moue and scrutinises her.

'Ms Mercogliano, the allegation against you is extremely serious. I am authorising your detention here for twelve hours, pending enquiries. If necessary we will seek permission for this to be extended, in order that the officers can continue their enquiries. Because of the weekend interlude, you will not be heard in the magistrates' court until Monday.'

He exchanges a few words with his colleagues, nods curtly to her and leaves the room.

She immediately turns to the other two: 'Hannah – who's looking after her? Where is she?'

They are not at liberty to say, the detective sergeant tells her.

'Please. I have to know.'

And the WPC says that she is in care. Safely in care. Until the mother can be traced.

Her ears are pounding. 'What do you mean, "in care"?' she demands. 'What does that mean?'

The child she was nurturing so carefully, so instinctively. The child screaming, confused, wetting herself, calling for Mumm-ee. For 'Grabla'.

'Is she in some institution? You have to tell me.' She bangs her fists down on the table. A pencil lying there rolls and bounces with the vibration.

The WPC takes pity on her. Tells her that a local social worker, a conscientious family woman, has taken her into her own home until suitable alternative arrangements can be made.

'Look, you must remember she's alive. She's safe, at least,' she says. 'Yesterday you thought—'

The detective sergeant glowers. 'I think you've covered the matter now, Constable.' He presses his hands together, making a steeple with his fingertips pointed. 'Miss Mercogliano, I am informing you of your rights. They are as follows. You are entitled to consult the Code of Rights book if you wish. You may also make two telephone calls – one to tell someone your whereabouts and another to a lawyer.'

And she suddenly remembers – it had completely slipped her mind – Neil is arriving this very evening. Perhaps he is already here. She starts to laugh, then cannot stop. Tears flowing from her eyes. Gasping. Her cheeks itching and burning. Her neck feels as though it is swelling. She cannot get her breath.

The WPC rushes over to her. Makes her put her head between her knees.

'Breathe deeply, breathe slowly,' she says, resting both her hands on her shoulders and pressing down firmly. 'There. Good. That's good . . .'

Isabella is dimly aware of her voice, of her asking the detective sergeant to fetch a glass of water, of the blood pumping through her ears and behind her temples. Her head feels as though it is swimming on her neck.

'Let yourself exhale for as long as you can . . . Now inhale . . .'

Gradually her breathing pattern is regulated. She drinks the tumbler of water that the WPC is holding out for her.

'Better?'

'Yes. Thank you. I'm sorry.'

She sits back, recovering for a few moments, ignoring the detective sergeant, who is shifting about impatiently in the chair opposite her.

'I just need to make one call,' she says, when she is composed.

He pushes the phone across the table towards her. Mutters, 'Nine for an outside line.'

The demolishing of the only relationship that has ever mattered to her.

She dials Aidan's number. He answers. His ripe bass; tender with gladness at hearing from her:

'Where *are* you? I've been trying to ring you. I drove to the cottage. I was worried.' His voice echoes slightly in his large kitchen. She can picture him there.

Matter-of-factly she explains what has happened and the reason for her arrest. Self-conscious with the other two present. A withering inside her as she listens to the change in his tone – flabbergasted shock, then an edge of strain. Already distancing himself.

'I'll drive there now.'

'No,' she says forcefully. And asks him to contact Neil on her behalf at the Ship Inn.

His, 'Well, 'bye, then' is bemused, as though she is unfamiliar to him, and she replaces the receiver with a sense of painful inevitability, clamping her teeth together to prevent herself from betraying her emotion in front of the detective sergeant.

Out of the corner of her eye she sees him getting up, going to the door. He tells her the WPC will search her; appraises her with contempt when she looks horrified, before making his exit.

'It's standard procedure. I'm sorry, Isabella,' the WPC says. And her expression is genuinely so.

Her eyes smarting with humiliation as she strips under the apologetic gaze of the other woman.

Afterwards she is led up a flight of stairs and along a corridor, then halfway down another, where they stop outside a heavy metal door. Suddenly she feels weak; her bowels feel loose.

'There's a toilet in there,' the young policeman with them says, motioning to the cell when she requests the ladies'.

Isabella turns to the WPC.

'I'll accompany her,' she says. And they continue along the corridor, past a door labelled 'storeroom' and another labelled 'lockers'.

The WPC unlocks the door to the ladies' with one of the keys that hang from a chain round her waist, and waits outside. Isabella catches sight of herself in the mirror above the basin as she washes her hands: gaunt and anaemic-looking in the harsh fluorescent glare.

Her cell is about nine foot by twelve, the walls adorned with graffiti, and with a wooden bench which she is told also serves as a bed. Behind a brick partition is an aluminium toilet whose wooden seat has been stuck down. The reek of shame.

She will be fetched in an hour or so to be interviewed and to give a statement, the WPC explains. Later she will be brought a meal. Does she have a lawyer coming?

She hopes so. Sincerely hopes so.

'I'll get you a couple of magazines,' the young woman says. 'And some tea. It's pretty disgusting. How do you take it?'

'Milk. No sugar. Thank you.' Manages a wan smile.

'I'm afraid I have to take your belt and bag.'

The door clunks behind her. Alone with her sense of unreality. Unbelievable that she should find herself in here. A few months ago, as she went about her normal, chic, ordered existence, who could have imagined this? And her mother's bones jumping about in outrage.

She sits on the bench and, for something to do, reads the graffiti: 'Fuz are batastds.' 'Harf a spliff is beter van nun.' 'Pig-shit shit.' 'I love Tracy.' 'Well I dont but shes a good scrue.' One particular piece of graffiti makes her gasp, so shocking is it. In red is written, 'If you want to be fukt good fone my dad. He fuk me evry nite and Im forteen.'

The tragedy of an entire underclass represented on the wall.

The WPC appears with a paper cup of tea and *Woman and Home* and *Good Housekeeping*.

'That's so sad,' Isabella says, pointing at the red writing.

'Awful, isn't it? Of course, it may not be true.'

Her father's fumbling fingers pressing into her smooth slit – before retreating in alarm at his own actions.

'What was she like? Why was she in, a girl of fourteen?'

'For stabbing and practically killing another girl. Nice, eh?'

Madre, there is so much sadness everywhere. And she had wanted better for the child.

An hour or so passes. She reads how to make bramble jelly, and how to disguise a pear-shaped body. In her opinion the woman in the photograph looks better before her makeover. Muted voices outside the door. The sound of a key in the lock.

'Well, I always fancied being locked in with a beautiful woman,' jokes Neil, coming up to her and kissing her on both cheeks.

She guesses he rehearsed that. Is only glad he has arrived.

'So why did you do it?' he asks her.

'I did it because . . . Do you know the French word *éclat*?'

'I'm not sure. I'm not much of a linguist.'

'*Éclat de: éclat de soleil*. A burst of sun. That's what her face did. And inside me I . . . it singed me. I can't explain it. It wasn't something I can just explain.'

'But it was out of character.'

'I suppose so. Until then I'd never done anything out of the norm. My life was very structured.'

But leading up to it were pointers, had she chosen to tweeze them from her subconscious and examine them. A random collection of influencing factors accumulated over the years, which a psychologist would have latched on to with a satisfied snap of the fingers.

'And you regret it.' Spoken with the rhetoric of assurance.

She wraps her arms around herself. Looks tiredly up at him. At her peeling nails. At the window with no view and her silver reflection in it.

'Isabella? Surely—'

She turns back to him, and he is struck anew by how her face can switch from plain to beautiful with a flicker of expression in her eyes; she shakes her head as she thrusts out her palm in a typically eloquent gesture: 'What can I say? How can I possibly regret it?'

'It's ridiculous you're being held over like this,' he says when she has recounted the circumstances to him. 'I'm going to kick up a fuss. After you've given your statement we'll try and get you out of here.'

His hair has been cut very short, so that his big florid face, his large ears, are exposed. Fleetingly she smiles.

'It's such a relief to see you. I'm sorry – I forgot everything. I should have phoned to cancel—'

'Don't be daft. It's fortuitous you didn't. At least I can be of use.'

'It was supposed to be a break for you. Will you represent me? As my lawyer, I mean.'

'Of course, if you want me to.'

'I'm so sorry,' she says again, close to tears.

'Hey, it's OK. You're going to be OK. We'll get you out of this mess.'

His baggy brown eyes emanate reassurance. She wants to put all her trust in him, but she is too much of a realist.

'I've just remembered – I'll have to borrow a suit from somewhere,' he says, glancing down at the jeans he is wearing. 'I can hardly turn up at the magistrates' court in these.'

The interview room is on the ground floor. It is the same room where six days ago she was questioned gently and comforted, and Aidan sat beside her gripping her hand all the while.

'You do not have to say anything. But it may harm your defence if you do not mention, when questioned, something you later rely on in court . . .' the detective sergeant cautions her.

She recalls as faithfully as she can the sequence of events of that Saturday morning three months ago. He refuses to believe she had intended to hand the child over.

'When you took her you didn't know she'd been abused,' he says.

'Yes, but as I've explained, she'd obviously been abandoned.'

'You should have taken her directly to the police, without going home.'

'Don't say anything,' Neil advises her. 'My client has no further comment to make,' he says.

The interview is terminated, the time noted, the tape recorder switched off.

'Oh, and by the way,' he tells the detective sergeant, 'I find your manner most offensive.'

He does not succeed in having her released from custody.

'Town planners, that's what they are,' he says back in the cell, where somebody has put a mattress, pillow and blanket on the bench.

'Town planners?'

'That's my term for anyone with a tiny mind. Not an original thought in their heads.' Utters this at the top of his voice, in order to be overheard.

'The detective sergeant's a misogynist.' She raises her voice also.

'He's too stupid to know what that means.'

For a second they grin at each other conspiratorially.

'The thing is,' he says in a normal tone, 'they *know* you're not a threat. They realise you're not likely to go around grabbing other children. They probably even believe your story. But the problem is it doesn't fit in anywhere, doesn't relate to a case history they can look up. Abduction against volition – and on paper, that's what it is – is deemed to be an SAO and as far as the police are concerned, that's all that's relevant.'

'What does SAO mean?'

'Serious arrestable offence.'

'Madre, the things I'm learning.'

'Isabella, this will be a crown court job. You must expect that. And you must be prepared for a lot of publicity. It's an unusual case, to say the least: an abandoned, abused child abducted, and then abducted again.'

His eyes stray round the room then rest on her. 'I hate the thought of you stuck in this dump . . . Listen, as soon as I leave here I'm going to get on the phone. Find out who the best local barrister is.'

'It's all going to cost a fortune.'

'Not for my part, it won't. But a good barrister doesn't come cheap.'

'Oh, madre.' She slumps back on the bench; unfolds one part of the grey blanket. Rough as hessian.

'You mustn't brood and despair. I know it's easy for me to say that. But . . . I'll come and see you tomorrow. On Monday we'll go for bail. Two days. That's all. Be strong. You *are* strong.'

She used to think she was. Now she is just so weary.

'I landed myself in this. I can't be self-pitying.'

'Tell me, did you really think you'd get away with it? What about the future? How could you have kept up the deception?'

'I don't know. I don't know what I thought,' she answers truthfully. 'I only knew that I wanted Hannah's welfare.'

He takes her hand. His is neatly manicured; broad and

short-fingered. He still wears his wedding ring, she notices
for the first time; finds that very poignant.

'You're so kind. Thank you for everything.'

'We're chums, aren't we?' he says, getting up.

At the prospect of his leaving she is suddenly afraid.

'Joyce, my next-door neighbour, has a spare key to the
cottage. My report's on the bookshelf between Delia Smith
and Webster's dictionary. The photos and the mother's letter
are inside.'

'It'll be my bedtime reading tonight. I'll go directly to the
cottage now. What do you want me to tell Joyce?'

'The truth. She'll hear soon enough anyway. Everybody
will. And could you ask her to feed Garibaldi, my cat? Poor
little Garibaldi. Poor Hannah. Oh madre, Neil, I'm so *scared*.'

The same policeman as before enters bearing supper on a
tray: a bowl of tomato soup, three triangles of white bread,
sparsely buttered, jelly, and a plastic cup of water. He sets it
down on the bench and goes out. A moment later the key
jangles in the lock again. This time it is the WPC.

'I've brought you your belt and bag back,' she says. 'There
was no need to hold them. We had to confiscate the lighter
and cigs, though.'

'What about the nail file?' Isabella asks.

'We didn't find—'

'Joke. I was joking.'

'Oh, right. Anyway, I've got hold of some toothpaste and
soap for you. And here's a letter. It's a copy. The original had
to be kept as possible evidence . . .'

Night has fallen. She reads the letter whilst having her soup
(she is surprisingly hungry):

'Dear Isabella,' Sophia begins.

You have no idea how sorry I am about everything – taking
Hannah and then telling on you but everything got out of hand

and after that awful night when you found me and Luke I was really miserable. I stayed with my parents for a bit but we weren't getting on so I left there and my dad paid for me to rent a flat except that it was just a room really. Every day I used to drive from St Austell back to Pengarris trying to get the nerve to speak to you. I hid near the chapel and watched you and Hannah together playing. I missed Hannah so much and it sort of got tangled up in my head so that she became Grace and I longed to talk to you but didn't dare. I knew she wasn't your real daughter because the time before the last that I worked for you I found your report as it fell out when I went to get the Delia Smith. First of all I was really shocked that you'd nicked her and then when I saw the photos of darling little Hannah all bruised I knew you'd rescued her really and it was a good thing to do so I never said anything when I next saw you and you were always so kind and generous to me. Well last Saturday I hid in my usual place and I hadn't any thoughts in my head about taking her or anything but suddenly you went into the house and there was Hannah all alone and I went over to speak to her and she was so pleased to see me it just happened.

I want you to know she missed you. I looked after her really well but she kept asking for mummy and Grabla—

'Oh no.' The words escape her in a small moan. So clearly can she picture the child; that final image of her on the swing. Her blissful face. Higher. High-er, Mumm-ee . . .

I was going to give her back I promise. I was planning how I'd just drop her off when you were inside the cottage. It got impossible keeping her in the flat and my landlady was suspicious and I couldn't think what I was going to do and so I really was going to bring her back. But it turned out that Janet Abell lives near me and saw me with Hannah and phoned the police and so they came and found me. I had to tell them about you not being the mother because I didn't want to go to prison but I felt so mean as you are so nice and good and now you will never forgive me what with that other time and everything. I have to go to court about taking Hannah but they are not keeping me here. I was here for nearly eight hours and now I'm waiting for my Dad to get me. He's going to be livid. The nice policewoman says she'll give you this letter. I feel really awful about getting you into trouble. I hope they let you go too.

Love
Sophia

She takes off her shoes, but other than that she does not undress for the night. She cannot think she will sleep, on this plank of a bed, with the pungent smell from the toilet permeating the cell, with her mind churning and every thought and uncertainty leading to an entire new set. Loose threads flying. Yet she is mentally and physically exhausted. Her neck and shoulders ache. She rolls over on to her tummy. A finger of light penetrates through the eyelet in the door. It seems to penetrate her mind, almost to hypnotise her. She is floating, suspended somewhere. Facts that a few seconds ago were substantial drift into the abstract. In this most unlikely of bedchambers she sleeps properly for the first time in a week.

She awakens at just gone seven, almost drugged; fuzzy-mouthed, having slept for nine hours. Uses the loo. Washes herself in the tiny basin and dresses. Breakfast is brought in by a policeman who has obviously been on night shift. He is pallid, except for the fierce acne on one cheek.

'Ah, breakfast in bed,' she quips as he puts the tray on the bench: one sausage, one egg, one concrete piece of toast, a dollop of baked beans.

His reply is a kind of strangulated grunt. He looks as though he loathes his job, at this hour, in this depressing place.

She lives for the rattling of keys. And what must it be like day after day, year in, year out? She might yet discover for herself.

And now it is later on in the morning and this particular rattling of keys heralds Aidan. She springs up as he comes in. He kisses her awkwardly, briefly, his lips landing on the corner of her mouth. He is a Brobdingnagian in the Lilliputian confines of her cell. His complexion is jaundiced, as though he has spent a sleepless night.

'I recognise that wrestling-with-yourself look.' She attempts to be light-hearted. But it falls flat in these sordid circumstances. And the reek from the toilet is awful. She wishes he had not come.

He denies it. He says he is sorry to see her in here, that's all. He tells her he met Neil the previous evening, after he had visited her.

'So you got the full story.'

'Yeah . . . He showed me the photos of Hannah. They were dreadful. I don't know how anyone could have done that.'

'Quite. That was my reaction also.'

Pause. Waiting for him to comment. 'So?' she pushes him.

'Well, it's just I believe there's a proper way of going about things.' Avoids looking at her as he says it.

'I'm not expecting you to stick by me.'

When he makes no reply to this she feels suddenly cold.

He goes over to the small barred window, where his hulk blocks out most of the scant light.

Belatedly he says, 'Of course I will. I mean, when you took her you were probably mixed up.'

'When I took her initially, maybe. But when I decided to keep her rather than hand her to the police I was utterly clear about what I was doing.'

She knows it is not what he wishes to hear.

'Look, I can't make the truth palatable for you,' she says to his back. 'I've got my own worrying to do. Frankly, all I care about is what is going to happen to Hannah.'

But this isn't so. She cares desperately about him also.

At this moment all she craves is for him to hold her, to feel his arms solid and proprietorial round her, to hear his voice ring with conviction instead of doubt. It is too much to expect. She is more trouble than it is worth to him. In the comparatively short time she has known him she has been nothing but trouble; and this seems to be the conclusion he is coming to.

'Is someone feeding Garibaldi?' he asks suddenly, turning round. His face is ravaged.

'I told Neil to ask Joyce to.'

'I could—'

'You don't need to concern yourself.' Which comes out far more harshly than she intends, so that she immediately apologises. 'I'm sorry. I didn't mean it like that.'

She leans against the wall, her back against it, elongating her neck to release the tense muscles.

They are diagonally opposite each other, just a couple of strides away, facing one another like uncertain soldiers come face to face across a trench.

'What are you doing this weekend?' she asks, trying to make normal conversation.

'There's a gig I'm playing at tonight.'

'Oh yes, of course. I forgot.' A gig. Ordinary life. His reality.

'I can't say as I'm in the mood,' he adds. 'And my lads are coming tomorrow. They'll spend the night. But I can get away to see you, if you're still here.'

'There's not much point. Is there?' A dry thickness in her throat like a bone trapped horizontally. She gives a small cough.

'Yes. I want to see you,' he says, his voice cracking.

'It'll be all round the village soon. After the hearing on Monday.'

He pulls a grimace. He has evidently thought of that. It disturbs him, as an intensely private and, above all, honest man. Sucked into the vortex of her scandal. Judged because of her. The whispering: 'He must have known.' 'If he didn't, he does now so why is he still hanging round her?' Guilty by association. And he has two school-aged sons: Your dad's girlfriend's a child-snatcher.

Understands his predicament.

He kisses her goodbye. For a few beautiful seconds his kiss holds her. His grey eyes, slightly bloodshot this morning, search hers unhappily. He tuts. He sighs. He shakes his head. He stumbles out. A man whose conscience will not be able to provide easy answers.

She settles down to read one of the magazines but is too sad to concentrate.

The next lot of key-rattling is lunch. Shreds of chicken floating in a sauce the colour of London pavements. But she has gone from having no appetite to being constantly hungry. Would not mind what she was given. Besides – eating provides a diversion. Ten minutes of the day accounted for.

Neil visits in the afternoon.

'You look surprisingly rested,' he remarks, kissing her on both cheeks. She notices a food stain down his Aran jumper.

'I've had a lot of time to do just that,' she answers wryly. 'Resting and thinking.'

'Positive thinking, I hope.'

She throws her hands out non-committally.

'Well, I've also been doing some thinking.' Sitting down next to her on the bench. 'I tell you, your report was an eye-opener. I've taken charge of it, along with the photos and the mother's letter, for safe-keeping. My God, those photos . . . I don't mind admitting to you I shed the odd tear or two.' Blinks hard as he says this.

'There's good news and bad news,' he goes on. And her spirits lift and slide accordingly. 'Actually the bad news isn't anything we didn't already anticipate. They've successfully applied for an extension to the twelve hours. You're being detained until the hearing on Monday morning. The police are trying to trace the mother.'

He notices her crestfallen expression and touches her arm.

'Please don't be disheartened. Really, it has no bearing on anything.'

'But how will they find her?'

'There's no guarantee they will. But the DSS is the obvious starting point. Now look, the good news is what we have to focus on.' He claps his hands with deliberate heartiness. 'I did quite a lot of ringing around various contacts yesterday evening and I got the name of an excellent-sounding barrister with a formidable reputation.'

'Does he charge formidable rates?'

'She. Well, as I mentioned yesterday, good barristers don't come cheap, but she charges less than her equivalent in London. Anyhow, I took the liberty of phoning her at her home last night and summarised the case. She was fascinated by it and is keen to take it on. She agrees with me that as an indictable offence the matter will be beyond the jurisdiction of the magistrates' court, therefore you won't be putting forward a plea. The thing to focus on is getting you bail. I'll be talking to prosecution before the case is heard, so he knows the full circumstances. Now, you mustn't worry.'

'No.'

'And the other bit of good news is that I've managed to borrow a suit,' he says, intent on trying to jolly her.

'Where from?'

'The landlord of the inn. He and I are roughly the same size.'

'Could you bring me a change of clothes? I need a change of clothes.' Flicking her hand disgustedly over her leggings and long, shapeless jumper.

'With pleasure. I'll have to check it's permitted, though.'

The key in the door. Four o'clock, and a woman officer she hasn't seen before brings her a paper cup of tea and a couple of digestive biscuits.

'Could my . . . lawyer have some tea also?' She turns to him and smiles, and he is struck anew by her unconventional beauty.

'I think we might manage it.' The woman goes out and returns a few minutes later. She is big, unfeminine, with a heavy black fringe.

'I warn you, it bears no resemblance to the real thing,' Isabella tells him.

'Think yourself lucky,' the officer says, giving a small grunt as she locks the door behind her.

'It's hot, anyhow,' Neil says.

For a short while they don't speak. She takes a biscuit and blows on the steam rising from her cup.

'You wrote something in your letter a few weeks ago,' she remembers. 'It was quite ironic.'

'What was that?'

'You wrote that I seemed like a woman whose life was thoroughly in order.'

'Well, you did. That's how you came across.'

'I once believed it myself. And when I got your letter I was just recovering from a trauma. You must've read about it in my report. Or diary. Whatever you prefer to call it.'

'I didn't know whether to raise that subject or not. Since you have . . . You should have reported him, Isabella.'

'I couldn't, for the reasons I wrote.'

'Maybe you'll decide to when all this is over.'

'When all this is over,' she repeats. 'What a lovely thought.'

Another, longer silence.

'You know I met Aidan last night?' Neil says. 'He came to the Ship.'

'Yes. He visited this morning. He told me you showed him the photos and letter.'

'That's right. I thought it might help, when he realised . . . Anyway, so how's he taking everything?'

'Badly. No, not badly. He's confused.'

'Sure. I can understand that.'

The bone of pain is in her throat again.

'I love him, but he can't deal with what I've done. Do you know, Neil, before this I can't remember ever having told a lie. Oh, maybe a fib to save someone's feelings, but never a proper lie. And I tell you something. I'm glad that part is over. The lying.

'Will you do me a favour? Will you tell Aidan not to come tomorrow? I can't face seeing him in here again.'

17

Ten o'clock this Monday, 25 November. Hers is the first case to be heard in courtroom number one.

'The whole thing will be over within ten minutes,' Neil says, observing her frozen expression. 'I've spoken to the prosecutor. He's amenable to bail . . . I expect the magistrates will be the usual bunch of old farts.' Trying to humour her as the WPC opens the side door leading directly to the Dock.

Her pent-up nervousness is released in a spasm of laughter she conceals with a cough. Neil gives her elbow an encouraging squeeze as she is about to walk in.

She feels everybody's eyes on her. Cannot, for several seconds, bring herself to do anything but stare at the ground. Dimly aware of movement and muted voices. Hesitantly she raises her eyes to look around.

Her impression is of a large, modern room, about thirty feet in length. From the main doors there are three rows of tip-up chairs where a few members of the public – there for free theatre, she presumes – are already seated. In front of these, and at right angles to herself, are the tables and benches for the lawyers, now only occupied by Neil, nearest her, and the prosecutor. Along the opposite wall are another couple of rows of seats with tables for the journalists. There are four of them this morning, scribbling away, in between looking across at her, no doubt interpreting the revelations of her body language, noting her apprehension, her auburn hair and her sallowness. She feels a wave of pre-emptive antagonism towards them. Runs her tongue over her dry lips. And maybe they note this also. Now her glance wanders to the Clerk of the Court at his raised desk, in front of the lawyers, and finally towards the Bench, on a dais a few feet across from her. One woman and two men. The woman has the stereotyped appearance of anyone's grandmother (but not her own maternal grandmother, that self-centred, denunciating crow). In the middle, on a larger chair than the other two, presides the chairman. He is balding, and sits pole-upright. Lances her with glacial eyes. She feels a jolt in her ribs – has recognised him instantly. The man from the surgeon's wife's party.

Mary Anne's gleeful remark comes back to her: He'd have us all behind bars if he could.

On his other side is a man in a grey suit who could be a retired schoolteacher.

'Next case is the Crown versus Miss Isabella Mercogliano, Your Worship.' The Clerk of the Court stumbles over her name and she represses a hysterical giggle.

The prosecutor stands: small, with receding hair and a non-existent mouth. He hands some papers to the Clerk, who in turn presents them to the senior magistrate; she gathers they comprise her statement. The lawyer then explains the charges to the Bench.

'This is a matter which can only be heard by the crown court,' he says, 'hence no plea is being offered.' He proceeds to outline the case.

The journalists' hands flying across their notepads. And what will they conclude from his résumé? What will they conclude from observing her? Who can guess at her thoughts as she fixes her gaze blankly ahead of her?

'. . . Abandoned child . . . Drove home with . . . Abused

... Decided to ... Rented a cottage ... Pretended ... Reported missing ... Arrested ...'

She catches only snatches of what he says. She is conscious of the chairman peering at her in between writing, over his bifocals which he he has just put on.

I am not ashamed. I am not ashamed. Repeating it over and over; as, when she was a young girl, she had covered pages with the words: I matter – in three languages.

'I invite you to commit the defendant to the crown court without hearing any of the evidence,' the prosecutor concludes.

The Clerk turns to Neil. 'Do you agree there is a prima facie case?' he asks.

Neil stands up. 'Yes, I agree.' And sits down again immediately.

The chairman looks across at Isabella. 'We commit you to crown court to stand trial.' He says this in a slow, ringing tone, as though condemning her to be executed.

He's probably into flagellation, Mary Anne said. And she fights down a fit of laughter; feels her face becoming red.

Neil gets to his feet again and addresses him: 'Your Worship, I would ask you to grant bail for my client. I've discussed this with my friend' – turns briefly to the other lawyer – 'who is in agreement.'

He sits down once more and the other man stands. 'Your Worship, there doesn't appear to be any great risk of the accused absconding, and in those circumstances I'm instructed that the prosecution will agree to bail on the accused's own recognisances.'

The archaic language, the pomposity, the whole show steeped in the arcane, strike her as ridiculous. And how the old git wallows in it all, she thinks. The Your Worships. He is whispering now with the Clerk of the Court, conferring over her fate. And will he exercise his punitive powers?

'Very well,' he says. 'We grant the accused conditional

bail.' He looks at her severely. 'You will be heard at the crown court, on Tuesday, the seventh of January. Your passport must be lodged with this court by two p.m. this afternoon. You must present yourself to the same police station of your choice each Monday, and under no circumstances are you to have contact with the child. If you do not comply with these conditions you could be liable to arrest.'

But – for the moment she is *free*.

She goes with Neil to the WRVS-run canteen. And there, at a table with an older man she presumes to be the father, is Sophia. Shock registers in the girl's face as they enter.

'Would you rather leave?' Neil asks, when she whispers to him who it is.

'No.'

She feels no animosity. Sophia has been caught up in her own web of circumstances. She goes up to the table.

'Hello, Sophia.'

The girl seems to shrivel into the chair. She can't meet Isabella's eyes.

'Isabella, I'm . . .' It is obvious she does not know what to do or say. The man beside her has a jaw like a flowerpot; and he juts it out further and folds his arms.

Isabella touches the girl's cheek – thin, drained of colour. 'It's all right. There's no need to say anything.'

Tears come into Sophia's eyes.

''Bye,' murmurs Isabella. 'Good luck.'

They have their coffee by the window.

'So now we get moving,' Neil says. 'I'm taking Eileen – the barrister – your report, et cetera, this afternoon, and the copy of Sophia's letter. And she's been kind enough to squeeze us in for an appointment tomorrow afternoon, before I go home.'

'Madre, you're going back tomorrow? Some holiday this has been. Can't you take an extra day?'

'I'm afraid not. And there are the girls.'

'Yes, of course. Neil – I couldn't have managed without you.'

'You'd have got hold of another lawyer.'

'No. It's everything. Not just that. You've given me such moral support. You've been a real friend.'

'I'm glad. We aim to please.' Pulling a mock-serious expression.

'Your wife must've loved you very much,' she says softly. Takes his hand as he sucks in his lips and momentarily his features buckle.

Outside the building photographers are waiting with their cameras. Caught by surprise, she has no time to avert her face. Neil grasps her elbow, and hustles her down the street.

'I'm afraid that's just the start,' he says.

And now it is sodden evening and Timothy Abell's cottage is his, not hers. The cold outside needles through the gaps round the windows and door, whilst inside the night storage heaters do little to relieve the draught. She lights a fire, opens a bottle of wine, then picks up Garibaldi and cuddles him. But he is used to her again. After his initial enthusiastic greeting, then his subsequent sulk period, followed by more enthusiasm, he is back to his normal self – only deigning to be fussed when he is inclined. The computer has a film of dust on the screen. And tomorrow she must recommence work. And there is a pile of letters to wade through. Messages on her answerphone. Also on her London one, when she accesses it. She is listless. Does not know what to tackle. And wherever she turns there is the child.

Waiting tensely for Aidan to arrive. A knock at the door – and here he is, in his purple track-suit. The barest glimmer of a smile, followed by the lightest brush of his lips against hers. He takes the glass of wine she gives him and only comes to sit beside her when she pats the cushion. His hands are balls of tension. She notices a gash on his left knuckle and puts her finger gently on it.

'That looks sore. How did you do it?'

He glances down dismissively. 'I caught it in the jack. It's nothing.'

'It doesn't look nothing.'

'It is. Really.'

Neither knows what to talk to the other about. Every subject seems barbed. She curls up against him, lonelier than when she is without him. She *is* without him. His arm is around her head, but it is weightless.

Yes, the gig went well, he tells her. Yes, the boys are fine. He took them to the sports field. Oh, and he's had an offer on the XK. That's great, she says. Her tongue feels swollen with pain.

But eventually he can no longer avoid the topic.

'So, when's the crown court hearing?'

'The seventh of January. I was surprised they actually gave a date, but apparently that's how the system here operates.'

'Well, at least you know how you stand.'

'I suppose so.'

Silence. She, squeezing her eyes shut, her face hidden by her hair. The soft fabric of his sleeve against her cheek. Her folded legs pressed into his solid thighs.

'How . . . I mean, how do you feel about it?'

'Fatalistic. I've just got to try and get on with things.'

The problem with them, she realises, is that they are both naturally poor communicators, reticent about their true feelings. And he is a man who does not veer from the straight and narrow.

'Let me explain just one thing to you, without trying to justify myself,' she says; and hoists herself up into a sitting position. 'I didn't want her to go through what I went through.'

'Well, now she is anyway.'

The implicit disapproval in his remark makes her defensive.

'You're a little intransigent, don't you think?'

'That's as maybe.'

She longs to hear warmth in his tone. Tries to keep her voice even as she asks:

'Do you still love me?'

He turns to her. His expression is tormented.

'That's the problem. I do.'

'And you regard loving me as a problem.'

'I didn't say that. I—'

'Yes you did. Exactly that. Not that I'm blaming you.'

'I don't *know* you.'

'No,' she agrees. 'But nobody ever can know anyone completely. You know various aspects of me, better than anyone else has ever done. They haven't changed. And I never lied to you.'

'No.' On a sigh. 'To be fair, you didn't. You warned me. I shouldn't have—'

'What? Got involved? Of course not. Neither of us should.'

'Oh, I don't know, I don't know . . . I want you so bad still. I want everything back the way it was.'

'So do I. But it was spurious.'

He relaxes a little. Their talking seems to have helped. He lies back, the upper half of his body reclined on the sofa-futon. He strokes her hair and her cheeks with a feather touch.

'I hated seeing you in that place. It was terrible. To see you degraded like that.'

'I've committed a crime.'

Feels his body stiffen when she says that.

He stays the night. They make love. But it is like a requiem and it resolves nothing. And afterwards each of them lies awake for much of the night; and each is aware of the other's wakeful state but does not reach out.

Isabella has a recurring image of the graffiti on the cell wall, the red-ink revelations of the fourteen-year-old who almost killed another girl. Oh madre, how easy it is to lose one's balance when the path is already pitted. And the child: what are the odds of her being another casualty?

They get up early the following morning. She piles on clothes to keep warm. He does not have breakfast with her.

'I need to get my head round this,' he says. 'I have to straighten out what's right and what's wrong in my head, in my own time. Reach my own conclusions.'

'I realise that.'

'Look, I'm not saying this is it, or it's over. I just . . . I can only give you my support if I work things out a bit. It's not that I'm accusing you. I don't know what to think. If I'm to be honest to you, I have to be honest to myself first.'

'Well, that makes sense.' Tries to smile. Her mouth doesn't comply.

'I'm sorry,' he says.

They kiss goodbye. Lovingly. She knows it is over.

And now to face the world.

Babs says calmly, 'Seems you're a page-three girl.'

She has made page three of the *Telegraph* and the *Daily Mail*. 'Toddler in abduction drama,' 'Abandoned child abducted not once, but twice,' run the respective headlines. And there she is in the photographs, caught unawares, her hair swinging across her jaw as she tries to avert her face, her eyes huge and alarmed.

'Oh, madre.'

'I know you better than to make snap judgments,' Babs says. 'There's more to this.'

They chat until a customer comes in. She ignores Isabella. And it is to be a foretaste, she realises as the day progresses.

But Joyce tells her: 'Your solicitor showed me the photos of the little mite. Seeing those, who could blame you? 'Course, there'll be those as'll say what you did was wrong. Maybe in the eyes of the law it *was* wrong. But I saw how you were with her. You made that little girl happy. I saw her blossom.'

The people who matter, she thinks.

But not Aidan.

Eileen, the barrister, is in her fifties, with a brisk manner and a high, domed forehead like Elizabeth I. A huge cheese plant takes up one corner of her room. Her desk is a mass of papers. Amongst them Isabella notices her report and the photographs, also the various newspaper articles. Eileen waves her hand – bony and freckled – for them to take chairs, and buzzes for a secretary to bring coffee; after a few polite preliminaries she comes directly to the point.

'Having read your statement and report and seen the evidence I think it likely that if the case proceeds you may well be found guilty of the charges,' she says, drawing deeply on a small cigar. She holds up a preventive finger as Isabella is about to interrupt. 'However, it seems to me that there are very strong mitigating circumstances in your favour, and I would hope that I could persuade the prosecution to do a deal with us. If you plead guilty they will take this into consideration and also you won't have to give evidence or be cross-examined. Of course, it is not for me to tell you what to decide.'

She extinguishes the cigar and lights another.

Neil says, 'We'll have to consider it.'

'The mother's letter is of immense value to our case,' Eileen adds. 'Possibly more than the photographs.'

'Is it likely I'd go to prison?' Isabella asks. Takes a long sip of coffee and studies the cup.

'I would say the most probable outcome would be a non-custodial sentence.'

'What does that mean?'

'A suspended sentence. Possibly eighteen months. Something like that.'

The meeting is over within twenty minutes.

'What was your opinion of her?' Neil asks, outside chambers.

'Daunting. Efficient.'

'That's exactly what we want.'

'What do you think we should do?'

'Follow her suggestion. You?'

'Yes. I suppose so.' She huddles into her coat. Drizzle. Winter. She longs for summer. Italy. When this is over . . .

'Not sure?'

People skirting by them in the narrow, cobbled street. The afternoon light already fading. Shop windows gaudy with Christmas decorations. Another year about to expire. Why is she so afraid of death? What is so great about life?

'No, it's all right. I *am* sure. But – I'll have a criminal record, won't I?'

'The risks attached to pleading not guilty are very high,' he says gently.

'It's all right,' she says again. 'I've made up my mind.'

They walk back to their cars. He is driving directly back to London. Over the last few days they have become close. She knows she will miss him. They come to his Rover first.

'It's so strange here now,' she says, as he beeps open the car door. 'There's nothing. Without Hannah . . . And Aidan . . .'

'I'm on the other end of the phone. I'll be thinking of you.'

'I don't know where I'm at, any more. *Who* I am,' she confides forlornly.

He hugs her. A bear-enveloping hug.

Her agent rings. She manages, finally, to calm him. Sally phones. 'It's my turn to listen,' she says. But, generally, she does not bother to take the calls. Stands by the answering machine. In case. Never Aidan.

Do they expect her to shut herself away? Never to go out? The locals react in various ways. Some cut her dead; others are ill at ease and behave unnaturally. She has her small team of backers: Babs, Joyce, Mary Anne, Janet Abell and, curiously, Deirdre, the surgeon's wife, and also Margaret from the playgroup. Lizzie turned the other way when she saw her in the street, and when Dick made a move to greet her she nudged him angrily and pulled him on. When she ventured into the Sun on her own one evening everybody stopped speaking. It was excruciating. Then conversation started up again, artificially loudly, and she departed without saying a word.

'London divorcee and local girl in child kidnapping scandal,' shrieks the *West Briton* on Thursday.

And she knows she cannot remain here. She applies for a court hearing so that she can return to London.

The first week of December. Her last walk on Tregurran beach.

F'ost, said the child. No, carina, this is snow.

It wafts spasmodically to the ground, merging with the sand. A pregnant, cement-toned sky in which the sea's horizon dissolves. The gulls' spiked cries rising over the foghorn's lament. And the occasional electronic bleat of a metal detector, as a lone enthusiast seeks to cheer himself this dismal morning. They are alone, these two figures, with no interest in each other. He intent on his fortune, she remembering so much that was nearly good. Briefly was good. She wishes the day were fine, that she could have her final, proper glimpse of the sea. Later on the fog will lift, but she will be gone. Madre, how sad she is, but has no right to be, since there is nothing she has not instigated.

And would you do it again, Ms Mercogliano? Certainly I would.

The car is packed up. As many of the child's toys as will fit are squeezed into corners. Everything that she bought for the cottage, including all the furniture, she leaves. 'Keep it for yourself or sell it,' she wrote to Janet Abell, enclosing the key in the envelope. 'Thank you for your kindness.'

She posts her note to Aidan: 'Caro, the Isabella you knew and the one you didn't loves you. Remember that.'

Off she drives, away from what she had come to regard as her sanctuary, through the village, past neat gardens with gnomes and Christmas wreaths, cottages with cobalt-blue shutters; and Babs's post office; and clucking chickens. Not a single goodbye. She has gone, they will realise later – left without a word. Aggrieved; their hospitality abused. The brown-and-white countryside opens out around her, and here are the ruins of the old monastery, here the circular cottages where the Devil never dared show his face. And Aidan's garage – quickly past there, with her hankering heart; and the Fox's Retreat and the church. Out of Zerion, through other villages, past other landmarks; no child in the seat beside her. What has happened to the knitted rabbit? Does she still have it? Has she become watchful and withdrawn again? Have the fits of hysteria recommenced? Where is she? Tears blurring her vision so that she has to swerve to avoid an oncoming livestock carrier. It hoots long and loud as it judders by with its bleating contents. The snow drives down.

*   *   *

Mrs Shastri gives her back the key.

'So you won't be needing me to come in any more,' she says, without a trace of condemnation in her lilting voice. She is serene in her turquoise sari and reading glasses on a gold chain. Yet every newspaper on her shelves carries a story about Isabella.

She unpacks. Reacquaints herself with her flat. Garibaldi pads about tentatively, shying and leaping back from objects, then races around like a rat. Mrs Shastri has kept the place in immaculate order. And now her computer is in its old position, the guitar is in the corner where it always stood. One could be fooled into believing she had never left. There was no interlude. There are new invitations to prop on the mantelpiece: exhibitions, fashion shows, openings, conferences. There is only herself and Garibaldi. It is as though nothing has happened.

Christmas approaches. She sends no cards. Stacks the ones she has received in a pile on a table, then, in a mood of defiance, strings them up round the fireplace and under the window sill. No card from *him*. Outside: the gleaming pavements and frantic feet and the sky that never quite relinquishes night. The Salvation Army playing carols. She spends the days working, catching up on the book; goes for walks on the heath; riding with Neil. Whatever she does, wherever she goes, a sense of pointlessness accompanies her.

Neil telephones.

'They've found her.'

'Who? What are you talking about?'

'The mother. She's a druggie, apparently, with a five-year-old son in care, and has a past conviction for child abuse.' He sounds jubilant.

'How did they find her?'

'Social workers were worried as it seems they'd been keeping an eye on her for some time, and suddenly the child was gone. They became suspicious. And she was still drawing benefits.'

'How old is she?'

'How old? What's that got to do with anything? She's twenty-two, I gather. Anyway, the *other* bit of excellent news is I've just heard from Eileen. The prosecution have agreed to the lesser charges in return for the guilty plea. The judge is sure to accept his recommendation. It's almost certain to be a non-custodial sentence . . .'

As she replaces the receiver she tries to register some feeling. She feels nothing.

It is on the nine o'clock news: 'The mother of a young girl recently at the centre of a most unusual and complex case has finally been traced. The twenty-two-year-old woman, who is not yet being named, already has a son in care and has past convictions for child abuse and possession of drugs.

'The plight of three-year-old Hannah, abandoned nearly four months ago outside a newagent's in North London, has touched the hearts of the nation. Meanwhile, Ms Isabella Mercogliano, who found the child in an abused state and is accused of abducting her, before, in a bizarre twist, the child was abducted from *her*, is regarded by many as being something of an avenging angel . . .'

Tom phones her at nearly midnight, when she is about to go to bed.

'I can't believe it. I just got back from Chile, and I switched on the news,' he says, without bothering about a hello. Without apologising for the time. 'What a hat trick.'

Predictable. He is so predictable.

He has to see her. Soon, he demands, sounding urgent.

'You're great. I love you, Bella. And we must get you lots of publicity.'

Who is 'we'? Ignores the declaration. Tells him that during the last couple of weeks she has had a lifetime's publicity, that she is not a product to be marketed. That the child's predicament does not warrant exploitation. That it is late.

He accuses her of being pious, says he will call again, rings off. Not one question did he ask about her.

She lies in her bed with its silk cover – where sex was always on her terms, where love never happened, and which no mad mechanic ever sullied. She knows she cannot revert to the person she was, but nor does she need to dismiss her entirely. She realises her total rejection of her old life was extreme. Equally, her infatuation with Cornwall was extreme. How much of it was to do with the child and with Aidan? She cannot separate the place and the personae. Perhaps now she can become more objective. She does not have to eschew one lifestyle for the other. Does not have to scorn one place in order to appreciate the other. One day she will go back there. People become used to things: Janet Abell running off and getting pregnant by a married man; Joyce marrying her husband's brother; the priest who discovered sex; the married woman who took a lover then ran off with his wife; Mary Anne scribbling pornography and gazing out from her study at her husband's bronze erection. And the wild young lads – they will, in the future, doubtless commit their own peccadillos. Let them recover. And she will saunter into the Sun, and they will all turn round in astonishment, but gradually the conversation will resume normally again; she might buy a round of drinks . . .

She thinks of the twenty-two-year-old mother. Twenty-*two*, madre. The no-hoper girl who is destined to sink ever deeper. Of her own mother and her implacable determination that the wheel of repetition be broken. Of her father and how he has influenced her life and her attitude to men. Of the child, adrift in a limbo in which she cannot picture her; captured for ever in a bubble, as a blurred, blissful face above a swing.

'All sorts of people can become foster carers and adopters,' she reads the following morning in the *Ham and High*. 'Children in this area need local people to offer them a home. We can help you explore whether fostering or adoption is right for you. We will provide training, individual support, finance. To request an information pack telephone . . .'

It commences as a tiny dot within her, then it grows, fans out, infusing her with heat.

All sorts of people? Even someone with a criminal record? Surely she is advantaged because of her unique relationship with the child?

All at once she is invigorated with purpose. If it takes every penny she has, if it means harassing every authority, if it entails going through all the courts, she will not give up until she has explored every avenue to achieve her aim. She will grasp this hope.

That is the first thing that happens, this Saturday, 21 December.

The second thing occurs later in the day. It is the afternoon, and she is working at her computer; Garibaldi on her lap; Roberto Alagna singing Puccini. And she gets up to answer a single, short ring of the doorbell. A young woman stands there.

'I'm sorry to trouble you. You don't know me – but was your father's name Filipo?' she asks.

Dark. Thick, coarse hair. Raptor nose. The eyes. There is no mistaking the eyes. Her own.

They stare at one another.

'Come in.'

Isabella shows her inside. Makes tea.

'What a lovely flat,' the visitor says, sitting on the cream sofa, stroking Garibaldi, looking round her and lingering over the framed, enlarged photo on the glass table of the child on Tregurran beach. And beside that, Aidan, resembling a South American explorer.

She found Isabella through all the publicity, she says. It took her a while to pluck up courage. She is a secretary, she answers, in response to Isabella's question. Nothing high-powered. Staring at Isabella with open curiosity. Isabella continues to question her politely. Within herself she is trembling. All sense of time has become distorted. The cubby-hole of her childhood is exposed.

'He was a wonderful father,' the young woman says of the man they both knew differently.

So he is dead.

'He loved opera,' she reflects, as Alagna sings of his love for Tosca. 'We always made him turn it down. He played it so loudly.'

'Did he ever . . . touch you – molest you? Sexually, I mean.'

'Mol*est* me? Papa mol*est* me? What are you saying? How dare you? You're mad. I should've realised, with what you did.' Putting down her cup and saucer and standing up. A stocky figure in a too-tight miniskirt.

They part stiffly. Will not see each other again. Their own truths exchanged to gnaw at them. Why me, not her? *Did* he with me? Did I imagine it? *Did* he with her and she has forgotten? Or maybe she was lying to herself. Why was she so quick to tell me that he was a wonderful father?

He is dead. Let them each cling to what she wants to believe. To what Isabella needs to believe in order not to have wasted twenty-seven years. The past in his coffin.

The third thing.

She puts on her coat and opens the front door to go for

a walk. As she does she sees someone getting out of a car a few yards up the road.

He sees her simultaneously. Is walking towards her slowly, in his purple track-suit top, with his long, swinging stride. His shining eyes flowing into hers as he approaches; while she remains where she is, disbelieving, incapable of moving a limb. Trying to smile. Not to break down.

It is the uncertainties which enable one to continue hoping.